GENOMIC DATA

A Mystery Novel By

NATASHA BAJEMA

NUCLEAR SPIN CYCLE
PUBLISHING

For John and Maria

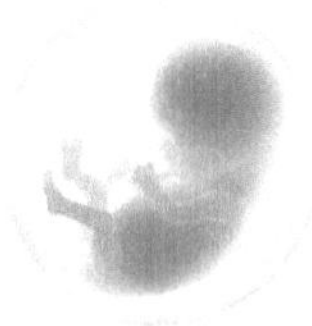

Prologue

The future is closer than you think. In 2012, scientists proved the utility of the gene editing technique CRISPR for modifying the genome of any living organism. CRISPR is significantly cheaper, easier, and quicker to use than previous techniques and has vast potential for accelerating the treatment of disease and development of new products to improve human life. In November 2018, Chinese biophysicist He Jiankui announced the birth of twin girls whose embryos he modified using CRISPR to improve genetic resistance to HIV, creating the first genetically modified humans.

But the true potential of CRISPR depends on genomic data—i.e., digitized gene sequences and genomes of living organisms. Scientists have not yet sequenced all living organisms, and have only made partial connections between certain gene sequences and functions as expressed in organisms. Gene sequencing involves the conversion of DNA sequences into digital information that can be read and analyzed by computers.

When a human genome is sequenced, it can be stored in an online database or sent by email. From there, the genome can be downloaded, synthesized back into DNA, inserted into an egg cell, and theoretically be brought back to life as a human clone.

ONE

The Wedding

—————————————

New Delhi, India
25 September 2028

LARA KINGSLEY SUPPRESSED the urge to sprint toward the nearest emergency exit. She swayed slightly, stomach churning. Despite her discomfort, Lara couldn't help but gawk at the extravagant wedding décor. An overabundance of turquoise, blue, and white floral garlands smothered every inch of the expansive venue. Her nose tickled in anxious anticipation as she imagined a thick cloud of pollen descending upon her. Her chest tightening, she inhaled short, shallow breaths and remained as still as possible.

Clutching her hands, she focused on Vik Abhay and his groomsmen as they formed a tight circle on the dance floor. The speakers blared as the Indian music took on a staccato rhythm, but the usual thumping of the bass in her chest was absent.

The disco ball sparkled and spun slowly overhead, sending harsh rays of light around the reception hall. A bright flash pierced her eyes, causing her to wince. She longed to knead away the sharp pain and splash water on her face, but that wasn't possible. Her legs became as heavy and sluggish as her eyelids.

Am I supposed to feel this way?

Finn had warned her about the confusing transitions between the digital and physical worlds. But, of course, she didn't believe him and had to learn firsthand. She glanced at his avatar to tell him he was right, but he was too busy speaking to the mother of the bride to notice. A drone hovered above his avatar, projecting his image into the room. Finn seemed perfectly fine, while she still wasn't used to the sensation of being at Vik's wedding but not really *being* there.

Shouldn't this be more like playing a video game?

It wasn't. At all.

In an attempt to get her bearings, Lara adjusted the setting on her headset, releasing some pressure on her temples, and straightened her goggles. She couldn't decipher between a normal level of virtual reality dizziness and the background noise of her more familiar malaise. She'd been feeling off for several weeks, going so far as a doctor's visit after experiencing sudden and unexplained bouts of fatigue. Her doctor suggested she get some rest and monitor her symptoms. It was probably just a bug weakening her immune system.

Maybe it's allergies? A stab of fear shot through her body as she thought of Loki, her Doberman puppy. She'd gotten him several months ago, and it was a plausible explanation. *Hopefully not.*

Closing her eyes, she prepared to sneeze. But then, the tickle was gone again. She inhaled deeply, and the rubbery odor of her goggles filled her nose. Lara laughed out loud at the powerful illusion. Her flower allergies wouldn't be bothering her this time.

It's easy to forget what's real and what's not. She exhaled sharply in relief. *Maybe coming to the wedding as an avatar is a blessing in disguise.*

Relaxing her stance, her body wobbled as if her legs were Jell-O, making her wish she had something solid to lean against.

Every detail of the wedding decorations, the attire, and the refreshments screamed over-the-top. The same nausea and revulsion assaulted her at every wedding she'd attended. The pomp and circumstance, her rejection of wedding traditions, and her own failed romances were all excuses she might have used to explain the feeling away if someone were to ask her about it.

Come to think of it, I'm not a fan of any type of celebration—birthdays, Thanksgiving, Christmas. She tilted her head, contemplating the connection. *Spending time with family. That's what they all have in common.*

Her parents died when she was eight years old. And her best friend, Sully, the closest thing she had to family since then, died almost a year ago. The anniversary of his death loomed over her like a dark cloud.

The crowd hushed in anticipation of the performance. The spotlight moved across the floor and centered on Vik. He wore a cream jacquard tunic that fell to his shins, satiny cobalt-blue pants, a matching blue and gold sash, and a turquoise turban. The bold colors of his lavish attire accentuated his bronze skin and dark brown eyes.

He looks so handsome.

When Vik caught a glimpse of Lara's avatar standing in the audience, he beamed at her. From the spot next to him, her ex-boyfriend, Rob Martin, met her eyes and grinned mischievously.

Where'd he come from?

Her eyes widened with surprise, and he returned a playful wink. She'd been so distracted by the bold colors and shimmering lights, she hadn't noticed him standing on the dance floor dressed in a cream-colored tunic, cream pants, and a turquoise sash.

Lara glanced nervously at her current boyfriend, Finn Stewart, to see if he'd noticed the exchange. His avatar displayed a stony expression. He wasn't talking anymore, but rather staring directly at the dance floor as if he was piqued by something.

"Did you know Rob could do the Punjabi dance?" Finn asked

in a pinched tone, grabbing Lara's sweaty hand. Her skin tingled at his touch, sending a quiver up her spine.

Oh, he noticed all right.

Lara shrugged her shoulders nonchalantly. "Not really. But he's been in New Delhi for the last two weeks. Maybe he had time to practice? The groomsmen have been together since the private ceremony three days ago." As she said the words, a wave of disappointment washed over her.

I should have been there, too.

Finn didn't respond, but he did infringe even further into her personal space in the simulator.

Lara would've preferred to celebrate with Vik and Shanaya in person—to enjoy the special moment with all five of her senses. Her inability to travel to India for Vik's wedding was yet another consequence of her fallout with her National Guard battalion commander.

Despite imposing several disciplinary measures, Lieutenant Colonel Earhart refused to forget the crimes she'd committed in the name of protecting U.S. national security. Earhart insisted she attend drill weekend two days before Vik's wedding despite her giving advanced notice of the travel dates. She was pretty sure it was intentional and considered filing a complaint. But with the written reprimand in her personnel file and mandated therapy sessions, Lara wasn't about to test his patience any further.

Experiencing the sights and sounds of the reception was more than she could've hoped for when she first got the bad news. Lara stole another glance at the bountiful flower arrangements and decided it was for the best.

This will have to do.

When Indian pop music boomed from the speaker system, she snapped out of her momentary discomfort caused by Finn crowding her. The wedding guests clapped to the rhythm, and the DJ raised his hands toward the roof to stir up the audience. Without thinking, she pulled her hand away from Finn's and joined in the fun, gently moving her body to the rhythm of the beats.

Okay, this isn't so bad.

After a few moments, Vik and his groomsmen began flicking their hands and feet in tight unison and dancing a rehearsed routine in a circle. Rob's overgrown brown curls bounced to and fro as he seemed to fully embrace the dance. After several minutes, the music came to a stop, and the crowd whooped with approval. The groomsmen followed Vik off the floor.

As she clapped, Lara looked to her left for Finn, but his avatar was gone.

Where did he go?

Pressing her lips tightly, she turned slowly to scan the entire room for the drone projecting his image. Finn was nowhere to be seen. Frowning, she returned her attention to the dance floor.

A sudden calm descended as the bride took center stage with her troupe of bridesmaids, bedazzling the room with their beauty. Shanaya's dark brown hair was pulled back from her face, curled locks tumbling out from underneath a sheer turquoise veil. An intricately bejeweled gold maang tikka hung on her forehead, matching the thick choker around her neck. Over a floor-length gold jacquard skirt, she wore a gold embroidered blue top, revealing her bronze-skinned midriff. A turquoise sash hung loosely around her slender body.

Simply breathtaking.

Her bridesmaids wore blue and turquoise saris embroidered with gold. Their hands were painted with henna, and their bare arms stacked with gold bangles.

Shanaya's parents spared no expense.

The music started again, this time with a ballad sung a cappella by a famous female Indian pop star. After a few moments, the tune morphed into a fast-paced, punchy Bollywood song.

Shanaya and her bridesmaids began waving their arms around in swift, wide circles, kicking up their long skirts. Their ornate hand gestures, flat flexed feet, and neck movements were flawlessly synchronized to the music. It was mesmerizing. When the song returned to a slow ballad, they moved their hips in fluid circles, elongating their torsos like belly dancers.

The music finally stopped, and the crowd cheered briefly as Vik and the groomsmen joined Shanaya and the bridal party on the dance floor. The lights dimmed, and the DJ revved up a new round of pop music from around the world.

Lara sensed a presence beside her. She turned her head to the left, expecting to see Finn's avatar beaming down from the drone. Instead, Rob was standing next to her, grinning from ear to ear. He held out his hand.

"May I have this dance?" Rob asked, bowing slightly.

She slapped at his hand, but her own hand passed right through his. Caught off guard by a strange vibrating sensation, she stumbled, lost her balance, and nearly fell to the floor. Recovering her footing, she desperately fought the urge to throw up as rising bile left a bitter taste.

So that's what haptic feedback from the simulator feels like.

Rob gave her a strange look.

Lara swallowed hard, regained her balance, and laughed it off. "Apparently, I'm just as klutzy in digital." Her stomach roiled again, threatening to empty itself. She pasted on a fake smile to hide her discomfort.

"Guess so." Rob chuckled.

Vik peeked through the crowd and waved eagerly for them to come over.

"C'mon, let's go break it down on the dance floor," Rob said, flashing her an irresistible grin. "It'll be like old times." He paused, looking her avatar up and down as if he was checking her out. "You think you can manage to dance in that contraption you're wearing?"

"Uh… yeah. I should be able to move about," she said. "The refresh rate on the Pentagon's augmented virtual reality system is amazing. The field of view reaches nearly two hundred degrees. It's like I'm really here." She moved her head around. Her voice sounding uncertain, she said, "See, I can swing my head around with almost zero blurring…" She stopped herself cold as another bout of dizziness came over her. *Okay, maybe not.* "That is, if I stand completely still."

Finn had also warned her about trying to move across the floor on her first time in the simulator. Moving through virtual space was not recommended for first-timers. Lara checked the room for any sign of his avatar.

Did he leave the simulator?

Rubbing his chin, Rob glanced up at the drone hovering above her avatar. Lara followed his gaze and gulped, resisting the urge to duck and cover. She'd already had to push away flashbacks of her experiences with drone improvised explosive devices in Afghanistan.

At least I'm not really under it.

"It's mind-boggling what we can do with mixed reality systems these days," Rob said, staring up in awe at the small projector drone that projected her image into the reception hall. "I can't believe Shanaya's uncle was able to get these things and make it link up with the Pentagon's system. It's like you're actually here." He motioned for her to join him and turned toward the dance floor.

She trod carefully, following Rob toward the center of the crowd, trying to avoid any unnecessary collisions.

See, moving about is not such a big deal.

Before entering the augmented virtual reality simulator, Finn told her about motion sickness and haptic feedback. He advised her to refrain from passing through real objects. Such an experience was known to trigger intense visual and sensory feedback, which could be disorienting for the brain and cause physiological effects. Especially for a first-timer like her. "Locomotion enhances the sensation of virtual immersion, making a person easily forget his or her lack of physicality," he explained firmly.

I'm not gonna miss having fun at Vik's wedding because I'm scared of a little nausea.

Every time she took a step, the drone projector moved with her, casting a visible image of her avatar as she navigated the crowd. Unexpectedly, a sharp tremor traveled through her body, causing her to hold her breath. Her eyes instinctively darted to her right side, where a man's hand had grazed the edge of her avatar, producing more vibrations. After she exhaled, the bitter taste returned at the back of her throat. Then she moved her body carefully around people to avoid further contact and keep her world from spinning.

Rob turned back to make sure she was still coming. She took another few steps. *Easy does it.*

When she finally reached the middle of the commotion, Vik and Shanaya were grooving to the music with broad smiles. Rob created a wide berth around them to give Lara space to move about without interference.

"Congratulations! I'm so happy for you both," Lara shouted to Vik and Shanaya over the music.

They smiled warmly at her and continued to bounce around the floor. Rob pointed at something behind her. She turned slowly, and the muscles in her forehead constricted. From across the room, Finn's avatar glared at her. As much as virtual images could glare.

Uh oh. What's his problem?

Finn waved urgently. She hesitated to move toward him at first, but then took a few strides in his direction.

Without warning, a man accidentally walked through her avatar from behind, distorting her vision and sending a strange rippling sensation through her body. Lara's body tensed and an unexpected surge of dizziness came over her. She became acutely aware of the bulky backpack clinging to her body.

She staggered backward, gasping for air. Her arms flailing, she attempted to grab someone to catch herself. But her hand slipped through the person's body, causing another cascade of vibrations. Tumbling to the floor, the impact sent a shock wave through her system. Her body heaved, and she turned to the side and retched. Then darkness enveloped her.

TWO

The AVR Room

Lara rolled onto her back, struggling to remove her goggles and headset. Her head throbbed from the fall, and she recoiled at the sour tomato taste in her mouth. When she finally yanked the equipment off and thrust her eyes open, Finn was staring down at her, his eyebrows drawn together. He still wore the black simulator bodysuit, a sharp contrast to his light blond buzz cut and gray-blue eyes.

Next to him stood a woman, her copper-red hair pulled tightly into a bun. Her skin was drawn taught over her cheekbones, and her right eye twitched slightly. A putrid odor wafted through the air, causing Lara to wrinkle her nose. When she caught sight of the vomit, Lara groaned. Her cheeks burned with embarrassment.

"Are you okay? What happened to you?" Finn asked, his forehead creased with worry.

Lara tried to lift her head, but an intense swell of dizziness returned. "Not sure. I bumped into a few people on the dance floor and got disoriented. Before I knew it, the nausea overtook me, I ended up on the floor, and apparently threw up."

"Sounds like simulator sickness to me," Kaitlyn said in a

pinched tone, folding her arms across her chest. Even with her nose wrinkled, the light dusting of freckles across her cheeks and her wide, ocean blue eyes made her disgust seem almost adorable. "There's a reason you were told about haptic feedback."

Lara's face flushed pink. *So much for my good first impression.*

She'd met Kaitlyn Costello for the first time shortly before going into the simulator and had not intended to show this woman any sign of weakness. Kaitlyn was a close childhood friend of Finn's. Her father, a senior military officer, just happened to work at the Pentagon for Finn's father, a two-star Army general assigned to the Joint Staff. She worked as a speechwriter for the Chief of Naval Operations after coming off her last tour as a top-ranked Navy helicopter pilot.

Over the past ten years she'd known Finn, Lara had heard plenty about Kaitlyn. Sometimes Finn would joke she was the one who got away—that is, before he met, married, and divorced his high school sweetheart.

Lately, Finn and Kaitlyn had been spending more and more time together at work. It was one of several sore spots in Lara's new relationship with him.

Smart, trained to kill, successful, well-connected, and drop dead gorgeous even while wearing her tan Navy service uniform. It's hard not to resent her. Lara sighed. *But I guess I have to try to like her.*

After all, Kaitlyn had helped Finn make the arrangements for them to use the Pentagon's Augmented Virtual Reality (AVR) room to attend Vik's wedding. Lara didn't know what she would've done if she'd missed every part of Vik's special day.

But what is she doing here now? And why did she cut our time short?

"Don't worry... even the toughest operators get sick during their first immersive state," Finn said, his tone softening. "Almost everyone has symptoms, and many vomit."

"It's called the poison berry theory," Kaitlyn added pointedly.

"Poison berry what?" Lara's brow knit together as she struggled to sit up again.

Kaitlyn held out her hand as Finn positioned himself behind Lara, locking his arms under her armpits. Wanting to close her eyes and pretend none of this was happening, Lara mobilized every ounce of willpower, grabbed Kaitlyn's hand, and allowed Finn to lift her to a standing position. Lara tottered for a moment, but Finn's steady hands kept her from falling.

Her stomach did another slight flip. She bent over in anticipation of the next barfing session and remained like that for a few moments.

Kaitlyn returned to the AVR control panel. "The poison berry theory of virtual reality sickness is an evolutionary explanation for why people often throw up in the simulator." She paused to type in a few commands. "The unexpected sensory input combined with dizziness are known symptoms of poisoning. People who are poisoned have a better shot of survival if they throw up."

"My brain thought I was being poisoned, so I tossed my cookies?" Lara asked, straightening her body.

Kaitlyn nodded quickly, turned away, and rushed about to put things back in order. The rustling of papers filled the pocket of silence as Kaitlyn arranged the stack and put them in a binder, clicking it shut.

Lara surveyed the square-shaped simulator room, which looked the same as when they arrived, minus the gross pile of her spaghetti lunch. The airy space was thirty-by-thirty feet with high ceilings, allowing plenty of space for movement. The interior of the AVR room was covered with green padded walls, which appeared to glow in the dim lighting. Above her, the black-painted steel structure gave off a trendy warehouse vibe.

It's hard to imagine we're deep inside the bowels of the Pentagon.

"Guys, I have to get going," Kaitlyn said, flicking on the full lights.

Lara's eyes stung at the sudden brightness, and she shielded them for a moment as they adjusted.

Kaitlyn handed Finn a roll of paper towels, cleaner, and a plastic bag. She picked up the binder from the control panel. "Can you guys get this place cleaned up and aired out quickly?" She grimaced again at the barf on the floor. "The room needs to be ready for the admiral in less than one hour. He'll never let me use it again if it smells like this."

"Sure thing, KitKat," Finn said as she closed the door behind her.

Bye, bye, KitKat.

Lara relaxed her body and fiddled with her gear in an attempt to remove it. "Can you help me out of this thing?" she asked, pointing to the robust backpack she was wearing.

Finn moved in closer, his eyes gleaming with amusement. He set the paper towels and cleaner on the floor. Then he leaned in and lifted the backpack over her head. The smell of his earthy, sandalwood cologne wafted past her nose. He set the backpack on the floor and reached for her hands.

He ran his fingers gently up her arm, their warmth tickling her skin, causing her pulse to speed up. Even after dating for three months, he still drove her crazy whenever he touched her. It didn't help that he was the most handsome man she'd ever laid eyes on—piercing blue eyes, chiseled features, and a muscular frame.

She'd never told him about her initial crush. She'd first developed a thing for him when they met ten years ago during Q Course to qualify for the Army Special Forces. Of course, back then, he was dating his soon-to-be wife. And now he was divorced and dating Lara.

Finn kissed her on the forehead, wrapped his arms around her, and hugged her tightly.

Whispering in her ear, he said, "I'm sorry you had to cut the wedding celebration short. I know how much you wanted to party with Vik and Shanaya." He pulled away to study her face and stroked her cheek. "Kaitlyn pinged me to give me the bad news. I'm afraid we were out-ranked."

Lara raised her eyebrow. "So that's where you ran off to…"

And here I thought he got jealous about Rob again.

She relaxed her stance and gazed into his eyes.

"It sure was funny watching you from out here," Finn said, the corners of his lips turning upward.

Lara narrowed her eyes. "And why's that?"

"You had the best VR face I've seen in a while. And that's saying something. My team has been using this facility a lot lately."

"VR face?" She gave him a skeptical look, not liking the sound of it.

Finn chuckled. "Most people are slack-jawed when they wear the head-mounted display and engage with virtual reality."

Lara stuck out her tongue at him.

"Don't worry, you're beautiful... no matter what face you make," Finn said, laughing.

Lara grabbed the paper towels and cleaner, dropped to her knees, and wiped up the vomit with one hand while holding her nose with the other. Then she sprayed the floor generously with lemon anti-bacterial spray and dried the floor as best she could.

"Thank goodness it's a tile floor," she said with a pinched nose. "Not sure if we could eliminate the smell otherwise." When she finished, Lara climbed to her feet and cleaned her hands with a paper towel. The citrus scent barely overpowered the stench, but it was definitely better.

"Probably why they didn't go with carpet in here," Finn said, holding the garbage bag open for the soiled paper towels.

Lara inspected the room one more time, giving a satisfied nod. When she turned back to Finn, he had a naughty come-hither look on his face. He moved closer toward her, his eyes shining with desire.

"You know, we still have plenty of time for a dance..." He grabbed her by the hand and twirled her around.

Lara's stomach lunged, and she pulled away from him. "Uh... I don't think I'm ready to move around... still feeling pretty nauseated."

Finn's face went slack, and his body tensed.

Lara glared at him. "Babe, I just threw up. I smell like vomit. I want to go home and take a shower."

"You didn't have a problem with your nausea when you were dancing with your ex-boyfriend in the simulator." He pursed his lips into a hard, flat line.

Oh, here we go again.

Lara's eyes widened, and she took a step back. "You've got to be kidding me. I wasn't dancing with Rob. I was celebrating Vik and Shanaya's wedding."

He glowered at her.

"You're jealous about what you saw in the simulator?" Lara asked.

Finn shuffled his feet. "I saw the way he looked at you," he mumbled. "That was real. Rob is still in love with you. And now that he's working for Kingsley Investigations, you're spending so much time together. It's only a matter of time before—"

"Seriously?" Lara said, putting her hands on her hips. "If I had a thing for my ex, I wouldn't be going out with you. End of story. Either you trust me, or you don't."

He stared sullenly at the floor.

"Should I be jealous of your KitKat?" Her tone was intentionally harsh.

Finn flinched. "Kaitlyn and I grew up together as military brats and were stationed at the same post more than once. We're very good friends. She is also happily married. And she hasn't confessed her love for me. That makes it very different."

"Not to me," Lara said.

Finn crossed his arms. "You told me Alexa broke up with Rob because he's still in love with you. I remember that day when you were bathing Loki in the bathroom with Rob there. When I arrived, there was something in the air. I felt like I was caught in the middle of you two. He came to proclaim his love for you that day, didn't he?" He took a deep breath and waited for her answer.

She'd avoided talking about the bathroom incident. Lara

couldn't deny the truth that Rob still loved her. *But do I still love him?* It didn't matter. She had no intention of rekindling their relationship. Not after what he'd done. *I can't trust him again after that kind of betrayal.*

"Why can't you understand I don't like your ex-boyfriend working so closely with you?" Every muscle in Finn's body was tense. "You bend over backwards to give Rob a job at your firm, but you won't come back on active duty for me?"

Aha, that's what this is about. Lara wasn't going to take the bait. *My Army career is none of his business.*

Since they started dating, Finn had pressed her to change her mind about going on active duty. When he signed up to go back in, she wasn't sure if their three-month relationship would have a shot. It seemed like an eternity to Lara, considering her dating history. But at the same time, they hadn't been together long enough to endure extended periods apart while she stayed in D.C. and he ran into combat zones and put his life at risk. To their mutual relief, Finn began his first tour at the Pentagon, working for the Assistant Secretary of Defense for Special Operations and Low-Intensity Conflict.

But he wouldn't let the issue go. They'd already fought several times. The man was like a dog with a bone.

We have two whole years to test our relationship. Why the rush?

She turned toward him. "Yes, Rob and I have a past, but we're just good friends. He recently lost his job at the FBI. I'm not going to leave him in a lurch just because you might get jealous."

"That glance in the simulator didn't look like good friends to me," Finn growled.

"Oh, grow up." Lara threw up her hands in defeat and strode toward the door of the simulator room.

"Where are you going?" Finn asked, a slight tremor in his voice.

Lara whipped around to face him, fury in her eyes. "Home, Finn. I'm going home. To take a shower and get some rest. And if you're worried about Rob coming over to the house, don't be. He's across the world in New Delhi. Where I'd rather be right now."

She turned and left the room, tears welling in her eyes.

THREE

Sidecar Blues

———————————

September 30, 2028

LARA SAT cross-legged on the thinning grass in the fenced-in backyard behind her townhouse. She tried to ignore the faint coppery scent of blood as she held a Kleenex to her nose to stop yet another bleed. The warmth of the afternoon sun on her face, she watched her best friend Maggie Brown run around the yard, her auburn hair whipping to and fro as she played fetch with Loki.

Because Lara had promised Maggie they'd go for a run at some point, she was dressed down in gray sweats and tennis shoes which were now both smudged with paw prints.

The Doberman pup chased happily after his favorite squeaker tennis ball and returned it to Maggie. Every time he fetched the ball, an annoying squeak pierced the air once more. *The noise is a small price to pay if it keeps him out of trouble.*

When her nose stopped bleeding, Lara balled up her Kleenex and put it on the ground. She smiled to herself, leaned back on her hands, and closed her eyes, soaking in the vitamin D. It was her favorite time of year. The crisp blue skies, cooler air, the smell of wood burning in neighboring chimneys, and colorful leaves drifting slowly to the ground lifted her mood.

Then, like the crash of an ocean wave, she remembered her fight with Finn and the several days of his radio silence. Her stomach rolled, and she shivered. It was as if a giant cloud blocked all the rays of sunlight, causing the temperature to dip. She pulled her new black leather jacket around her, letting its warmth and soft texture comfort her.

After their fight, Lara had called right away to apologize for her part, but Finn didn't pick up. And he hadn't returned her calls for five days, causing her to fret about whether their brief romance had reached its inevitable end.

He was way out of line about Rob.

Hoping to distract herself, she stared down at the mess on the ground in front of her. To her right, an electronic tablet served as a paperweight for the universal mount assembly manual. The tablet screen displayed the instructional video she had paused earlier when she'd gotten stuck.

Her Harley Davidson Street 500 motorcycle stood a few feet away from her. The frame of the nearly assembled sidecar and a single tire lay on the sidewalk. A few leftover bolts, nuts, and pins lay strewn about.

Maybe this project was too ambitious.

She scrutinized the parts, praying silently they were extras and not evidence of her mistakes. She pulled the manual from underneath the tablet, the pages fluttering in the breeze, and tried for the hundredth time to make sense of the next step.

Her posture stiffening, she crinkled the edges of the paper with her fist. As she shifted her body, a few dry leaves from the mulberry tree overhead crunched underneath her weight. She glanced at the loose wiring hanging from a side panel and furrowed her brow.

It shouldn't be this hard.

More than four hours had passed since she'd started assembling the sidecar. She was stumped on how to connect the electrical wires to her bike.

"Hon, when you gonna be done with that already?" Maggie asked, tossing the ball across the yard. "We were supposed to go for a run an hour ago."

"Sorry." Lara sighed heavily. She threw up her hands in surrender. "I'm still stuck on the last step. If I were an electrical engineer, I'd have this done in a few minutes."

"That's some hard yakka, mate," Maggie said.

Yakka? Does that mean work?

"I thought you studied engineering at MIT and were good with drones," Maggie said. "Isn't that your specialty in the Army?"

Lara grunted. "I studied mechanical engineering at MIT. Being a drone expert doesn't mean I understand how to connect electrical circuits on this contraption. Also, I got a few live jolts as a kid. I'd rather not experience another one."

"Why don't you take the bike to a mechanic?" Maggie asked.

"Because I don't like paying for things I can do myself."

Maggie gave her an amused look.

Yeah, yeah, yeah.

Loki ran over to Lara, nosed her in the cheek, and then licked her ear. She set the instructions on the sidewalk, pulled him into her lap, and caressed his face with both of her hands, kissing his wet nose and stroking his velvety ears. His breath smelled like the fish treats he'd eaten earlier, but she didn't care.

This will never get old.

After a few moments of snuggling, Loki ran off again. Over the past five months, he had grown fast and gotten rather big, already weighing in at sixty pounds.

Maggie pointed to the blood-filled tissues on the ground. "You should go back to the doctor," she said, looking Lara directly in the eyes. "These bloody noses could be a sign of something. And your incident in the simulator. It's adding up."

A sore topic.

"I'm fine, okay?" she snapped, padding her nose with a new tissue. The blood had finally clotted, and the tissue came away mostly clean.

"Don't go crook on me for being clucky, luv. I'm just worried about you." Her voice took an unusually stern tone. She threw the ball again, and Loki chased after it. "Good fetch, Loki," Maggie called before turning back to Lara. "When's Vik coming home? Have you heard from him?"

Lara sighed with relief. She didn't want to talk about her nosebleeds or the simulator. "He texted me a picture yesterday of him and Shanaya at a fancy luau at their resort on Oahu. He'll be back in another week." Her mind drifted to several texts from Vik, asking about her health. She hadn't responded.

"Have ya hooked any clients lately?" Maggie asked.

Another sore topic.

Lara pressed her lips together. It had been five months since she and Sanchez solved the Westlock murder. Despite her efforts to drum up work, she had yet to land a new client or a surveillance job.

Lara wagged her head. "Nope. It's been hard to convince people I know what I'm doing. My last job made the papers because it led to three deaths at the building site where I installed the surveillance system—including my client, who was a well-known fixture in powerful circles. I'm not sure what to do at this point. Kingsley Investigations is bleeding itself dry."

Soon, I'll be dipping into Sully's inheritance to stay afloat.

"Have you thought about expanding your repertoire?" Maggie asked, lowering herself to sit on the grass across from Lara. "Maybe you could get into the crime solving business like Sully."

Sore subject number three. Maggie is on a roll.

Before she could make a snide comment, Loki galloped toward her and tumbled into her lap, causing her to giggle. "I'm still mulling over all the options," Lara said, scratching behind Loki's ear.

After his death, her best friend Sully had left her all his assets and his townhouse worth over two million dollars. In his farewell letter, Sully expressed his hope that she would carry on his mission of fighting crime and bringing the bad guys to justice. Although she'd successfully solved two murder cases, Lara remained uncertain about whether she wanted to get into crime solving. She preferred installing surveillance systems for wealthy clients.

"Didn't Mario suggest he would be willing to put you on retainer with the D.C. Metropolitan Police Department?" Maggie asked.

"That was a few months ago," Lara said. "He said he would try after Commander Jamison cooled down some... but I'm not sure five months is enough for the commander to forget all my transgressions. Maybe you could ask Detective Sanchez for me?"

Maggie went silent for a few seconds, her face flushing. "Sweets, I wish I could help you there, but I don't think he wants to hear from me right now. Especially not after yesterday."

Oh crap.

Lara's eyes widened. "What did you do?"

Maggie averted her gaze, her face paling slightly. "I finally broke up with the bloke. It was a long time coming... we just want different things." She squiggled her finger in the dirt. "Now that my parents are coming to the United States for an extended visit, it had to be done. But the timing isn't the best with his mother spending her last days in the hospital."

"How long does she have?" Lara asked.

"Mario said she could go any day now."

Lara gulped. To her surprise, a slight ache rose in her throat. Somehow, she'd grown quite fond of Sanchez—her old arch nemesis.

"So... your parents are coming to visit you?" Lara asked, changing the subject.

It would be the first parental visit since Lara and Maggie had become friends three years ago. Lara knew things weren't great between them because Maggie rarely talked about her parents. And when she did, there was usually a scowl on her pretty face.

Her parents were famous Australian scientists and had won the Nobel Prize for their work on gene splicing. Although she didn't mention many details about her mum and dad, she often talked about the pressure of filling their shoes.

Maggie grimaced. "I'm not sure I would call the trip a *family* visit. More like a tour of the genetics labs around the country to hobnob with other big-deal scientists. Anyway, I reckon they'd want to meet my boyfriend and that would have given Mario the wrong impression about my intentions. So, I ended it."

Lara suppressed a grimace. Her relationship with Sanchez had changed for the better during their last case. But the detective was notoriously moody. A breakup would make for a bad-tempered Sanchez, even in the best of circumstances.

Maggie scrutinized Lara's face. "How are things with Finn?"

Lara groaned, rolling her eyes.

"That bad?"

"Don't even get me started," Lara said. "He doesn't like Rob working for me. At least that's what he says. But I think he's frustrated I didn't jump all over his idea to go active duty together. He still wants us both to try out for Delta Force. I'm not even sure that's an option for me anymore. With the written reprimand in my personnel file, they might reject my application outright."

"Didn't you already give Finn an answer on that?" Maggie asked, raising an eyebrow.

"Kind of. I said no. Then, after some pressure, I said maybe. But I don't like the idea of being a solution to Finn's problems. He thinks his marriage didn't work out because he deployed all the time and left his wife at home. He says if we deploy together, we'll stay together. I'm not sure I agree."

Maggie frowned and tilted her head. "Have you changed your mind?"

"No, but other things have changed. I can't seem to get work anymore. And I've messed up my relationships with my team in the Guard. My commander forbade me from telling them what really happened. He claims my acts of defiance might spread across the unit like a terrible disease." She shook her fist at the sky and groaned theatrically.

"Your commander is quite the mongrel, isn't he?" Maggie said supportively.

What the hell is a mongrel? Sure, I guess it sounds bad enough.

Lara nodded. "Anyway, my whole team has read the biased news stories about the incident. They pretty much think they're stuck with a disgraced team leader. So, to answer your question, yeah, I'm thinking about it again." Lara ran her hands over the dry, prickly blades of grass. "Of course, Finn won't give me enough space to see how I feel about it."

And now he's getting jealous of Rob as a proxy.

"Well… how *do* ya feel about going back in?" Maggie asked.

"I'm not sure. I've always liked the tempo of combat missions, being in the field and running down the bad guys. I guess I'm considering it?"

"What's the minimum service term?" Maggie asked.

"Two years," Lara said, lobbing the ball across the yard.

Loki ran after it, his ears flopping behind him.

"Finn's current assignment is working counterterrorism at the Pentagon. That's supposed to last two years, but it could always be cut short if they need to call him up for a combat mission. I know he's super eager to get back into the field."

Maggie rubbed her chin. "If it's only for two years, couldn't you at least give it a try? Then you could see if things work out with Finn. If not, you've had another adventure."

Lara nodded. "That's what I've been thinking. Finn said he could pull some strings to get me a tour at the Pentagon. That way we could both be there together. What do I have to lose?"

Maggie shrugged.

Why am I so uncertain, then?

Loki romped about the yard, a tennis ball in his mouth, shaking his head and grunting like he'd just caught a squirrel. Rob had offered to take good care of him if she needed to deploy overseas.

But could I leave Loki behind?

Hot tears moistened Lara's eyes. Just then, Lara noticed flecks of torn white tissue with blood scattered about the yard. She looked down at where her used balls of Kleenex had been, but they were gone.

Loki!

She was about to scold the pup when Loki barked several times up by the townhouse. Lara turned to see a handsome man with short, curly brown hair poke his head out the back door and grin at her.

Rob's home from India.

FOUR

Kingsley Investigations

"So, this is where you've been hiding," Rob said with a broad smile. His long, unruly curls had been shorn off since the wedding, making his brown eyes look bigger. From his unkempt appearance, Lara got the sense he'd tumbled right out of bed and thrown on some clothes without giving his attire any thought. He wore dirty blue jeans, a grungy black t-shirt, and his favorite brown leather jacket—the one she'd given him for his birthday.

He always looks so handsome in that jacket. Even when his clothes don't match.

Rob strode down the stairs, walked across the grass, and paused to examine the mess in the yard. Loki came running to greet him, offering Rob his slobbery ball, which he took and tossed across the yard.

"I thought you got back late last night," Lara said, shielding her eyes from the sun. She attempted to hide her irritation under a wide smile.

Maybe I shouldn't have given him a key to the townhouse.

Now that he worked for Kingsley Investigations, she didn't really have a choice. Vik had his own key to gain access to the office. As her employee, it was only fair Rob had one too.

Of course, she'd given him the key when she was still optimistic that jobs would start rolling in. When that didn't happen, she'd started paying Rob to run errands for her to tide him over. She knew it wasn't nearly enough to make ends meet. Things would have to turn around for Kingsley Investigations before Vik got back from his honeymoon, or she might have to let both of them go.

Rob raised his eyebrows and tilted his head to the side. "You don't seem all that happy to see me. Why is that?" There was an edge to his voice.

He reads me like a book.

Lara glanced at Maggie for help, but she gave Lara a he's-your-problem-not-mine look. Lara needed to talk to him about Finn's jealousy, but the timing had to be right. Heat blazed in her cheeks.

Not ready to talk about it.

Lara didn't respond. Instead, she continued pulling blades of grass from the ground, creating a little pile beside her. An awkward silence ensued.

Maggie cleared her throat and stood. "Luv, I'm going to make me a cuppa. You want some tea or coffee?" she asked as she headed toward the door. She passed Rob, gave him a friendly nod, and then turned to give Lara a wink.

Lara shook her head. "Thanks, I'm fine. But can you feed Loki his lunch while you're at it?"

Maggie nodded and disappeared into the townhouse. Loki ran after her as if he smelled the food she was about to put in his dish.

After a few more moments of silence, Lara broke the ice. "How was your trip?" she asked, hoping to dodge his earlier question. Tension built in her chest as she waited for his reply.

Rob rubbed his eyes and suppressed a yawn. "Good, good. Got back early this morning. The jet lag is killing me."

"Then why aren't you in bed sleeping?" Lara sniffed hard as warm, thick drops of blood formed inside her nose again. She stood and brushed herself off. A lightheaded feeling came over her, and she swayed a bit before finding her balance. Rob didn't seem to notice.

"Well, I was," Rob said. "And then I got a troubling phone call from my former work buddy, Special Agent John Carter, and couldn't get back to sleep."

"Oh?" Lara furrowed her brow. "Why would he call you? I thought you were persona non grata for your old FBI buddies after you got fired."

Rob kicked at the ground, his shoe thudding softly against the earth. "Pretty much. Carter's the only one who believes I'm innocent of the allegations against me. Lucky for me, he was there when our boss, Harry Cogan, gave the order to keep running the surveillance operation on Sully. Of course, after the fact, Harry denied authorizing the operation, and there is no hard evidence to back up my claim. It's just his word against mine and Carter's. Although he's on my side, Carter finds it hard to grasp that Harry double-crossed the FBI for money. He thinks our disagreement over the surveillance op is all a big misunderstanding rather than some dark conspiracy to cover up Harry's double dealing."

It sounds like Carter can't decide whose side he's on.

"But why did he call you?" Lara asked impatiently. Rob had been dealt an unfair hand, but he tended to wallow whenever given the chance. She had no intention of enabling that; she wanted him to move forward instead of clinging to past injustices.

"Carter told me he found a tangible connection between Justyne Marsh and General MacFarlan. When the general was arrested, they recovered his burner phone and traced calls to Justyne's office at DARPA. Apparently, the new information has lit a fire under his butt to find out if there is any truth to my claims about Harry. Of course, you and I both know it was Harry's idea that I work with Justyne and MacFarlan in the first place. But Carter needs hard evidence."

"And has he found anything on Harry yet?" Lara asked.

"Nope. He's come up completely dry," Rob said, letting out a sigh. "Even though he's determined to prove my innocence, I think he's somewhat relieved about it. Carter is a good kid. He wants to find the truth and clear my name. But he still considers Harry to be a father figure."

"Yeah, Harry is up to his eyeballs in the illicit trade ring," Lara said "That's crystal clear. We just need a way to prove it."

"Carter thinks we must have missed something when we were chasing down John Fiddler and stopping him from releasing the bionic bugs. Maybe it was right in front of us the whole time." He creased his forehead and made direct eye contact. "Do you think we can go have a look at Sully's old files? Maybe there's something we missed after Justyne's arrest."

Ugh. I haven't been over there since I moved all my parents' boxes.

Lara flinched, her heart skipping a beat. "Uh... I don't think there's anything useful at the storage unit." She'd prefer to avoid the old ghosts of the storage unit if at all possible.

Rob nodded as if he understood her real reason. "Anyway, Carter needs our help. That's why he called this morning."

"What sort of help?" Lara asked.

It's not like we're doing anything else at the moment.

"Well, my old team at the FBI won't go anywhere near the situation until Carter comes up with solid evidence of Harry's corruption. They're worried they'll get heat if they help with his digging expedition. Carter won't be able to pull off an investigation without assistance from law enforcement." Rob averted his eyes and crossed his arms, his voice hesitant. "Do you think Sanchez might be willing to help us out?"

Rob doesn't want to ask anyone for help.

"I'm not sure," she said, running her finger up and down the coarse bumps of her jacket zipper. "Sanchez isn't in a good place right now. Maggie literally just broke up with him yesterday. Plus, his mother is in the hospital and doesn't have much time left."

Oh, how I love Maggie's timing.

Rob leaned forward, and his eyes widened. "Lara, I think your nose is bleeding."

She touched her nose and then inspected her finger. "No big deal," she said, sniffing hard again and tilting her head back just a bit as she pinched her nose.

"Did you get a chance to go to the doctor since your collapse at the wedding?" Rob asked, a cautious look on his face.

Lara scoffed at him. "Seriously? Not you too. Look, I went to the doctor last month. She couldn't find anything wrong with me. She thought it might be stress and took some blood."

"And?"

"Everything looked fine."

"Your doctor would want to know about your symptoms and run more tests," Rob said with a stern tone.

"I'm fine, okay?" Lara pinched her lips, signaling the end of the conversation.

Silence fell between them for a few moments.

He lowered his head. "Since Kingsley Investigations doesn't have any work at the moment, I had to ask my dad for money to cover my bills until I can get back on my feet. And you know what he said?" Rob swallowed hard as if he was holding back his emotions. "He lectured me on how to lead a successful life like my older brother."

How could family be so cruel?

Lara didn't know what to say. She wanted to hug him, but the last thing she needed was to send mixed signals to Rob.

Law enforcement wasn't the future Rob's parents wanted for their son. The Martin family ran one of the most successful publishing houses in New York. It was the first traditional publisher to abandon the old business model of print copies and brick and mortar bookstores and specialize in digital formats— ebooks, audio, interactive online worlds, and mixed reality. Rob's older brother had worked his way up from the mail room to become one of the company's senior editors.

Rob began pacing, his feet shuffling the grass. "When I got fired from the FBI, all my parents could talk about was how this reflects on them... how it might harm their reputation."

Lara let go of her nose, hoping the bleeding had stopped completely this time. "They should be ashamed."

"They're also mad at me about my breakup with Alexa. They say she's the best thing that ever happened to me."

"Ugh." Lara wrinkled her forehead. "Is that why you hooked up with Alexa in the first place? To make your family happy?" She shuddered at the memory of his infidelity, which still stung on occasion.

Rob shrugged. "Maybe."

Her stomach roiled. "Did your father agree to give you the money?" Lara asked, desperately wanting to change the subject.

"My dad said he'd float me the money…"

"There's got to be a 'but' in there somewhere," Lara said.

"Only if I finally join the family business." Rob kicked the ground hard, sending a small stone into the air. A ding rang out as it hit her bike, causing her to glare at him. He winced and gave her an apologetic look. Then he pointed to the mess on the ground next to her bike. "What are you trying to do here?"

"I'm not *trying* to do anything," Lara said indignantly.

"Well, it looks like you're stuck on something," Rob said, bending over to inspect her assembly job. "What are these nuts and bolts for?"

Lara cringed. "They must be extras."

"Let me guess," Rob said, grinning. "You couldn't connect the electrical wiring?" He lowered himself to the ground, grabbed the pliers, and started tinkering.

I didn't ask for help.

Lara watched Rob in stony silence as he effortlessly connected the wiring from the sidecar to the side panel on her bike. Rob somehow always knew when she was at her wit's end. He'd step in and help her, even when she didn't ask for it.

He probably knows I'd refuse his help.

She began pacing around the yard, thinking about Rob's round of bad luck. He was a good guy who generally wanted to do the right thing. Even if he stupidly placed trust in the wrong people, like Harry. And made stupid decisions, like cheating on her with Alexa. Lara still wanted to help him in any way she could.

After a few minutes, he finished connecting the wiring. Rob looked up at her, smiling with his eyes. "There, that was easy." A dark brown smear of grease marked his ruddy face. "You think Loki will ride around in a sidecar?"

"Yup, that's the plan," Lara said flatly, still pacing.

"Do you want me to put the tire on?" Rob asked.

Lara's stubborn will eased. "Sure, why not?"

Rob cheerfully pulled up his sleeves and climbed onto his knees. He reached for the tire and a wrench and went to work.

"What if *we* can help Agent Carter," Lara said, stopping abruptly and thinking out loud. "I've got plenty of financial resources. And we don't have anything else to do right now."

Rob looked up at her, his eyes wide with surprise. "You'd do that for me?"

Lara shoved her hands in her pockets. "Of course I would. That's what friends are for, right? Sully would be happy if we used his money to vindicate you, get your dream job back, and put the dirtbags responsible behind bars."

Rob smiled, his eyes slightly moistened.

"But I need you to do something for me in return," Lara said, seizing the moment.

"Anything," Rob said eagerly.

"I need you to stop flirting with me."

Rob's smile turned into a frown.

"Finn and I have been fighting nonstop since the wedding. Because of you."

"Maybe he needs to stop acting like a jerk," Rob said.

Lara put her hands on her hips. "You just said you'd do anything for me. Did you mean it or not?"

"Fine. I'll stop flirting with you," he muttered, returning to his work on the bike.

Lara was about to give him instructions when her smartphone buzzed with a text. She glanced at the screen. "Speak of the devil," she said.

"What devil?" Rob asked.

"Sanchez. Who else?" She stared at her screen in disbelief, reading the words over and over.

"His ears must have been burning. What does he want?"

"He actually wants me to come by to see him at a crime scene," Lara mumbled, stunned by the notion. Then she glanced at her bike and sighed heavily.

"Want to borrow my car?" Rob asked, a hopeful look on his face.

He wants me to ask Sanchez to help us.

Before she could answer, he tossed her the keys. She caught them before they landed on the ground.

"Good catch," Rob said, his brown eyes twinkling. Then his face went slack. "Sorry about the mud. I know how you hate it when I go off-roading."

What's the point of off-roading in a self-driving vehicle?

FIVE

The Crime Scene

Lara pulled up in Rob's muddy Jeep outside a large, cream-colored brick mansion situated along Rock Creek in the Kalorama neighborhood located in the heart of downtown D.C. The estate was atop a hill and built in the French provincial style; it invoked memories of her first backpacking trip across Europe with Sully.

Lara gazed up at the manor for a moment to savor the beauty of the scene before facing the shocking reality of the crime within. The mansion was breathtaking—the stately turret, steeply pitched roof, and black-trimmed French windows.

Before exiting the vehicle, she glanced one more time at the GPS to make sure it was the right address. The posh area was often called Embassy Row, known for hosting more than seventy embassies and diplomatic residences while being home to many movers and shakers in the Beltway.

Yup, this is it, all right.

She rubbed the back of her clammy neck and took a quick breath. Then she climbed out of the Jeep, slammed the door, and stepped onto the sidewalk, careful to avoid getting any mud on her jeans. A light breeze rustled the pine trees in the yard, sending the woodsy fragrance of a Christmas tree past her nose.

A few uniforms milled about in the gated courtyard out front, but they didn't seem to notice her arrival. There was no sign of Detective Sanchez.

On the street, the massive presence of the D.C. Metropolitan Police disrupted the idyllic scenery. She counted a total of eight squad cars and two FBI cruisers. She also spotted two unmarked vehicles that likely belonged to detectives. All the economy cars seemed out of place in the midst of an overabundance of luxury.

Something big must have happened here.

She was about to make her way up the stone stairs when she noticed a man sitting in a black sedan parked down the street a good twenty feet from the last patrol car. She stopped for a moment and tried to get a better view of the car without being too obvious. The man's muscular arm rested halfway out the window. From her vantage point, she couldn't get a good look at his face or a read on his license plate.

Probably just another detective, anyway.

She turned toward the house. Without warning, her pulse sped up and her head throbbed painfully. The idea of possibly walking in on a gruesome murder scene with blood spattered on the walls and dead bodies on the floor filled her with dread. If she saw something, even the slightest bit of gore, she'd never erase the images from her memory.

I don't want to know.

Despite being an operator in the Army Special Forces, she couldn't deal with the notion of brutal violence taking place in her own city. This was the reason she'd resisted getting involved in crime-fighting in the first place. She just didn't have the stomach for it, something Sully always found ironic given her experiences on the battlefield. "That was different," she'd argued with him.

It's too close to home.

The afternoon sun beat down on her like a fire-breathing dragon. She shielded her face with her hands and pressed her finger hard against her sweaty temple. Inhaling and exhaling slowly, she remained still for a moment. She forced herself to move forward, dragging her feet along with her as if they were made of lead.

Why would Sanchez call me to a crime scene?

The mystery behind his request drove her crazy, propelling her forward despite her angst. Lara trudged up the stone stairs to the entrance of the mansion, dry acorns crunching under her tennis shoes. Taking a deep breath of the fall air to calm herself, she rang the bell.

A young female police officer answered the door and blocked the view inside. "Can I help you?" she asked, her face scrunched as if she'd answered a ton of questions from nosy neighbors and wasn't in the mood for further interruptions.

"I'm Lara Kingsley. Detective Sanchez asked me to come by."

The officer's eyes widened with recognition. "Oh yes, he's expecting you. Please come in." She held the heavy door open and motioned for her to enter.

Lara stepped into a spacious, oval-shaped foyer, her shoes clacking on the polished marble floor. A wrought-iron baluster staircase wound up along the curved wall to the second floor. At the center of the space, a massive crystal chandelier hung from the ceiling, glittering in the sunlight that poured in from the second-floor windows. Lara sniffed a light lavender scent floating through the air and spotted a diffuser on a console table.

Upstairs, she glimpsed the yellow crime tape in the hallway and winced.

That's where it must have happened.

She looked away quickly, not wanting to imagine the gory details of the crime scene. The French door on her left was closed. To her right, another French door led to an elegant sitting room with a shiny, black grand piano. Evidence technicians scurried about like ants, scouring every inch of the house, dusting for prints and picking stray hairs off furniture.

"Detective Sanchez is outside in the backyard," the female officer said, pointing to the back of the house. "Just proceed all the way down the hallway. The double French doors lead out onto the terrace." Appearing to sense Lara's hesitation, she added in a reassuring tone, "You'll find him."

Lara swallowed hard, her fists clenched. *Thankfully, he's not upstairs.*

Moving toward the back of the house, she caught sight of a huge stone terrace and lush gardens peeking through the tall window panes. Lara strode toward the double French doors, opened one of them, and stepped out onto the patio, a strong breeze whipping her face.

The backyard extended several acres, and a sturdy stone wall surrounded the expanse of the property. Outside the wall, a thick forest covered the back edge of the estate. Lara assumed the solitary gate in the wall led through the woods and down to the creek. More crime tape was visible in the woods beyond the open gate, along with a few navy jackets with yellow FBI lettering.

Distracted by a familiar buzzing noise, Lara looked up and flinched. Several quadcopter drones passed overhead, presumably scanning the scene for evidence and taking video clips. Clutching her side, she shifted her gaze to the team of police officers with German Shepherds; they were searching every square inch of the property.

The sound of men talking to the right of the patio caught her attention. Detective Sanchez spoke to a younger black man with wavy black hair, a thick mustache, and a goatee. The detective used his hands to emphasize every word.

As Lara walked down the terrace steps, Sanchez looked up at her and smiled warmly. He wore a distinguished dark gray suit, a nice contrast to his salt-and-pepper hair. In his navy suit and tie, the stocky black man gave off the aura of every other detective. Except for his eyes. They were an unexpected steely gray color, which stood out against his dark skin. In the light, they almost had a blue tinge to them.

"Quite the crime scene you've got here," she said, reaching out to shake Sanchez's hand.

"Thanks for coming out last minute, Lara. I really appreciate it."

She smirked at him. "I never thought I'd see the day when you actually invited me to a crime scene instead of telling me to stay out of it. I was not going to miss this…" She paused to give him a curious look. "Wait, where are your fancy glasses?"

On their last case together, Sanchez had made repeated use of the glasses with pilot facial recognition technology and data analytics, leveraging video footage from the District's CCTV cameras.

"Uh…" Sanchez looked at his feet. "The police commissioner cancelled the pilot after only a few weeks."

"Because a certain detective grew too fond of using them?" Lara poked at him.

"Actually, I was the least of his problems. Turns out it was rather tempting to use the glasses for everyone, and most officers were crossing too many lines."

"Somehow, I'm not surprised," Lara said, not hiding her sarcasm.

"This is Detective Ben Franklin, my partner in justice," Sanchez said, smirking at his own joke.

"You must be the PI I've heard so much about," Detective Franklin said, reaching out his hand with a flourish and flashing his white teeth. His voice was unexpectedly deep.

"Mostly good, I hope?" Lara asked, giving his hand a firm shake.

"Nothing but good things," Franklin said with a hint of sarcasm. "You have definitely lived up to your reputation."

What does that mean?

After giving her a onceover, Franklin shot a look at Sanchez, who was staring down at his feet and nervously kicking an acorn. "Now I know why he's kept you all to himself." He turned back to her and winked.

What the hell does that mean? Does Sanchez think I'm hot or something?

Lara's temper flared slightly, and a flush crept into her

cheeks. "If your partner has kept me to himself, then I assure you it's because he doesn't want to share his secret weapon for closing cases." She turned to Sanchez and grimaced. "How many have I solved for you now? I just can't keep track."

Sanchez snorted and shrugged his shoulders at Franklin. "She's right. I don't know what I'd do without her."

Lara did a double-take and stared wide-eyed at the detective, but he shoved his hands in his pockets and looked away. "How's your mother doing?" she asked, wanting to change the subject.

Sanchez winced. "Not good."

Lara nodded. "I'm sorry to hear that."

He brushed it off, drew a long breath, and shuffled his feet.

"Why did you call me out here?" Lara asked.

"Well, I was hoping you could help us out on a case."

"What's the case?" Lara asked.

"Um, it's a bit… complicated," Sanchez said, his forehead wrinkling.

Detective Franklin spoke up first, appearing to sense his partner's reluctance. "An eight-year-old girl named Molly has gone missing. Someone snatched her out of her own bed right under the nose of the babysitter, who was watching TV in the living room downstairs."

"A girl is missing?" Lara shrank back, feeling her face turn ashen.

Sanchez pointed to an open window on the second floor. "The kidnapper must have smuggled her out of her bedroom and climbed down onto the lower roof. From there, the perp used a ladder to get the girl down to the ground. Since the gate was locked, they climbed over the stone wall and escaped into the woods. We think the kidnapper may have used a kayak or canoe on the creek as the getaway."

"But why do you need *my* help?" she asked, fumbling for an explanation. "Certainly, you have experts on the force who can assist you. And doesn't the FBI share jurisdiction over kidnappings?"

Sanchez cleared his throat. "Uh… yeah."

Lara furrowed her brow. "I don't have any experience with missing persons. How do you think I can help you?"

The detective kicked up some dust with his feet. "Well, the parents of the girl requested your assistance," he said. "In fact, they asked for you by name."

Lara's jaw dropped, her mind spinning. "What? I don't know anyone who lives in this neighborhood."

"You don't know Julian and Cynthia Langston?" Sanchez asked.

"I don't think so." She rubbed her chin. The name sounded familiar, but she couldn't remember why. Lara searched the recesses of her memory, but nothing jogged loose. "Did they say how they know me?" she asked.

"The Langstons said they were going to hire you last fall for a surveillance job," Sanchez said. "Now they want your help to find and bring home their missing daughter."

Her stomach fluttered. "The Langstons?" Lara paused, her eyebrows squished together as she tried to remember the exact details. "Yeah… they were going to hire me, but then they said no and went with someone else."

Sanchez grimaced. "Well, they insisted you were essential to this case."

Frowning, she touched the base of her neck. "But that doesn't make sense. Why would they want *my* help?" She looked back and forth between Sanchez and Franklin.

What about my damaged reputation?

Both of them stared back at her blankly.

After a few moments of awkward silence, Franklin held up his hand to Sanchez. "I gotta go check on the evidence team inside the house." He looked at Lara and bobbed his head. "Nice to finally meet you. I hope we get a chance to work together." He gave her a wink before turning away.

They both watched as Franklin strode across the backyard, up the terrace, and into the house.

Finally appearing to gather the nerve, Sanchez turned to Lara, making strong eye contact. "The Langstons are the kind of people who are used to getting what they want. They are personal friends of the D.C. mayor and the police commissioner. My boss insisted I call you and get you on the case."

Lara ran her fingers through her hair, her expression pinched. "I don't know about this…"

"Look, everything about this case is an exception," Sanchez said. "Normally, I don't run cases in the Second District. And I'm not known for skills in solving missing persons cases. I have this case because of you. And you can imagine how things will go for me at work if I don't solve the case, or the Langstons are unhappy for some reason."

Lara rubbed her chin and tilted her head. *What business do I have getting involved in a missing persons case?* She didn't know the first thing about finding a kidnapped girl. *What if I fail?* She didn't want the responsibility. Not to mention Rob's case would keep her busy for a while. *No, I'm not doing this.*

Lara fidgeted with her hands. Even as the thought of the little girl tugged on her conscience, she said, "I'm really sorry, detective, but I don't think I can help you on this case. It's not… I don't know the first thing about kidnappings. You're better off without me."

"C'mon, Lara. Don't make me beg." Sanchez shoved his hands in his pockets. "The Langstons are willing to pay whatever fee you want."

Any fee I want? Lara put her hand on her forehead, suddenly feeling lightheaded. Some moisture made her nose tickle, and she sniffed, a metallic taste forming at the back of her mouth. *Another bloody nose?*

"If it helps you decide, you'd be doing me a personal favor, and I won't forget it," he said, giving her a hopeful look. "The police commissioner promised me a promotion to the rank of captain if we solve this case. Plus, it could mean huge accolades from the mayor. If we find the girl, I guarantee we can put you on retainer. Then I'd be able to give you some regular work. That would be a good thing for you, right?"

He's actually begging. I could ask him for something.

Lara tapped her finger against her lips, contemplating her options for a few moments. Then she looked up at him. "If I help you on this case, would you help me clear Rob's name?"

Sanchez tilted his head. "You mean prove he didn't do what the FBI said he did?"

Lara nodded. "And find evidence on the dirty cop who turned him in."

His eyes lit up. "I'd have to ask my boss for permission. Even if he says yes, I can't use department resources for a personal investigation."

"I'm paying for the investigation from Sully's inheritance. Could you just send the bills to me?" Lara asked. A wave of dizziness came over her, and her chest tightened. *Not again…*

"Sure, that might work. Let me talk it over with the police commissioner. If he wants your help bad enough…" His voice trailing off, Sanchez raised an eyebrow. "So… you'll work the case with me?"

"Yeah, sure," Lara said, looking around, desperate to find a place to sit down.

"Great, I'll let the Langstons know. *I'll give you a call when we've wrapped up the crime scene. Then we can go over what the evidence crew found and talk to the Langstons.*"

Lara reached out her hands, swaying back and forth. She stumbled a few steps but caught herself.

His eyes widened. "Wait, are you okay?" Sanchez reached out his hand to steady her.

Lara swallowed hard. "Yeah, I think so. I've been feeling a bit off lately."

"You should see a doctor." He put his hand lightly on her shoulder and met her eyes with his own. "It could be something serious. My mother refused to see a doctor when she started having symptoms. And now she's dying of cancer." His face paled, and he lifted his hands open-palmed in an apparent effort to reassure her. "Not that you're dying of cancer or anything. But you should see somebody. Just to be certain."

Lara's eyes widened. "Thanks." *I think.*

"You can see yourself out?" Sanchez asked.

Lara nodded and turned back to the house. Just then, her smartphone buzzed, and she glanced at her wrist. It was a text from Finn. *Finally.*

WE SHOULD TALK

Lara returned his text:

MEET UP TOMORROW MORNING?
I'M TRAINING LOKI TO TRACK SCENTS
6 A.M. AT ROCK CREEK PARK

Finn replied:

SOUNDS LIKE A PLAN

Tight knots formed in her stomach. Lara knew she needed to clear the air with Finn, but suddenly the prospect of talking to him filled her with dread. The Rob thing would be easy enough to get over, but what if she was really sick? That would bring her Army career to an end.

Would that be a deal-breaker for Finn?

SIX

Puppy Training

October 1, 2028

THE RISING sun grazed the tips of the trees in Rock Creek Park, sending potent rays into Lara's face. A flock of chirping birds high up in the oak trees announced the start of a new day. Vibrant autumn colors decorated the trees in the morning light. The grass under her feet, still slick with dew, moistened her tennis shoes. She inhaled deeply, taking in the pungent earthy smell of the wet soil.

The park was a favorite spot in the District for many locals. On weekends, several streets closed, allowing bikers, runners, and dog walkers to peruse the vast grounds in peace. During the early morning hours on a weekday, the park was completely abandoned. It was the best time to visit. Surrounded by a thick forest running along a creek nestled deep within a rocky canyon, it was easy to forget the intense political rat race that took place only a few miles away.

She covered her eyes with her hand to see into the dark forest, scanning the dense undergrowth for Loki. She glanced

45

over at Finn, who was bundled up in workout clothes and a training jacket. He blew on his hands to keep them warm.

The conversation between them remained stilted and sparse. Lara did her best to avoid difficult topics—their fight about Rob, future plans for her Army career, and her growing concerns about her health situation. The landmines were everywhere, and it wasn't easy for her to navigate them. As long as Finn seemed quite content to follow her lead, Lara refused to make it any easier for him to talk about what was really going on.

I already apologized. It's his turn.

She pretended to focus on the dog training and the breathtaking scenery and waited for him to break the ice.

"You agreed to take on a missing persons case?" Finn asked, his brow furrowed.

"Do I really have a choice?" Lara asked, her breath visible in the cold air. "An eight-year-old girl's life is on the line. If her parents think I can help, I'm gonna do whatever I can to find her."

"I know Danny appreciates your help on this one," Finn said.

Lara flinched at Sanchez's nickname. It also bothered her to no end that Finn was on a nickname basis with the detective. She wanted to ask Sanchez the story behind using the name Danny over Mario but hadn't found the right time. Now, apparently Finn and the detective were talking quite regularly. About cases. About her.

"He's really hoping to get that promotion to captain, you know. He said a mix-up with you lost him the last one."

Mix-up? Is that what he's calling it these days?

Lara's nostrils flared as she recalled the detective throwing her in jail because she refused to produce tapes from the FBI's informant. That wasn't a mix-up; Sanchez and his boss had crossed the line, threatening her with jail time.

I also thought that was ancient history.

Lara attempted to contain her anger. "Well, I'm headed over to the Langstons after this to meet with Sanchez. I'll do the very best I can to make sure he advances in his career," she said snidely, suppressing an annoyed grimace and directing her gaze at the woods.

A sudden breezed whipped up a few loose leaves from the ground, filling Lara's nose with the smell of pine and wood smoke from nearby homes. She zipped up her puffy down coat a bit further to protect her neck from the cold air.

Loki bounded out of the trees and across the grassy field toward Lara, the chewed-up plush bear hanging from his mouth. When he reached her feet, he dropped it and looked up at her eagerly.

"Good boy, Loki!" she said, cupping her hands around her mouth.

Finn stood next to her, watching the demonstration with intense curiosity. "You're training Loki to be a detection dog?"

Lara nodded. "Maybe. If he catches on. For now, it's fun, and it helps us bond. Who knows, it could come in handy on the missing persons case."

"Don't you think the police have already searched the Langstons' property with K9 units?" Finn asked, still skeptical and warming his ungloved hands with his breath.

Playing detective again?

Lara clenched her jaw. "Yeah, I saw the K9 units on the grounds yesterday. Maybe Loki will find something they didn't. It can't hurt for him to try."

Before starting the exercise, she'd let Finn conceal the bear along with another toy in the forest. He'd insisted on placing them himself, claiming he didn't trust her to make the challenge hard enough. He spent more than ten minutes in the woods finding the toughest hiding spots. When he returned, he declared it impossible for Loki to find and retrieve the items.

We'll be very happy to prove him wrong.

Lara kept two small pieces of cloth with scents matching the hidden toys in her coat pocket for the training. She held a small piece of cloth to Loki's nose. He sniffed the material for a few seconds.

"Loki, find it," Lara said.

The pup obediently raced off through the long grass in the direction of the woods.

"This should take a while," Finn said, smirking. "I hid this one in an elevated spot."

"You better be playing fair," Lara said, her tone a tad too sharp. "He's a dog, you know, not a giraffe."

"Don't worry. It's within reach."

"Right." She gave him a skeptical look. Out of the corner of her eye, she spotted a man in a black sedan parked behind Finn's car, watching them.

That's strange.

The car must have arrived after them because the street was empty when they'd first gotten there. When she noticed the engine was running, Lara remembered the car at the Langstons' mansion and raised her eyebrow.

Is that the same car I saw yesterday?

Noticing the shift in her attention, Finn pointed and asked, "Do you know that guy?"

"I don't think so," Lara said, unease settling in her bones.

They both stared in silence at the car for a few moments.

Turning to her, Finn cleared his throat. "Um… about the other day…" He shuffled his feet in the dry leaves, their brittle breaking a soft undertone to his words.

Keeping one eye on the sedan, Lara crossed her arms. "Why didn't you return my call?"

He gave her a blank look, his shoulders hunched. "I'm sorry… I had to think."

"About us?" Lara asked, swallowing hard.

His posture stiffened. "Yes."

Uh oh.

Lara's throat constricted. They'd fought. She called to apologize. And he didn't return her calls. Because he had to think about things? And tell her things in person?

What things?

Her heart pounded like a drumbeat. If she didn't know any better, they were on the verge of a breakup. But she couldn't figure out what was going wrong between them. Even though Finn frustrated her at times, the notion of them breaking up terrified her.

Please, not yet.

Finn kicked the dirt with his shoe and avoided her gaze. "Danny told me you asked for his help to clear Rob's name."

Gah! It's always about Rob.

"Uh huh," Lara said tonelessly, balling her fists. She wasn't sure what annoyed her more—the constant whining about Rob's feelings or the fact that Finn was so buddy-buddy with Sanchez.

"You didn't tell me you'd taken on Rob's case," Finn said, dismay in his tone. His arms hung limply at his sides.

Lara flattened her lips and ground her teeth. "You didn't return my calls. You didn't even text me. We haven't spoken in five whole days. And now you're upset about me not telling you something?" She threw her hands in the air, unable to hide her irritation anymore. "I give up. Communication goes both ways, Finn."

Finn flinched at her harsh tone but said nothing.

Lara folded her arms across her chest. "Look, you said you didn't like Rob working for me. If we clear his name, then he'll return to the FBI. In other words, your little problem will be solved." She paused and raised her eyebrow. "Or would you prefer we keep working together indefinitely?"

"Geez, Lara. I was just asking about it." He gave her a cautious look before opening his mouth again. "I wanted to apologize for flying off the handle about Rob the other day. But apparently, I fucked that up real good."

"Yeah, you sure did." She wasn't going to let him off the hook.

As a stony silence settled between them, Lara's eyes darted back to the black sedan. The engine was still running. In the driver's seat, a gray-haired man in his fifties watched them, and he wasn't even being subtle about it. Behind his unruly, thick beard, Lara detected something familiar.

Who is he?

She opened the camera app on the smartphone attached to her wrist. She raised her hand slightly to get a picture. As Lara was about to get the right angle, Finn took a few steps closer to her and grabbed her arm.

Dammit. Missed my shot.

"Lara, I'm sorry." Finn ran his other hand over his buzzed hair. "Look, I'm just scared of getting hurt again. This is my first real relationship since my divorce. I don't even know if I can manage a healthy relationship while serving in the Army Special Forces." He shrugged helplessly. "I'm completely out of practice with this stuff."

Lara's heart softened slightly, and she made eye contact. "Well, I'm not the best at relationships either. So, we really are a hopeless pair."

He gave her a half-smile and took her hands in his. "Lara, I want to trust you. Rob's feelings for you shouldn't matter. Okay?" He looked at her, his eyes earnest. "I'll stop being such a jerk about it."

Lara gave him a skeptical look.

"Okay, okay. I'll try my best to stop being a jerk about it."

"Better," Lara said, smirking. Her stomach remained tense, and a feeling of relief eluded her. "I was wondering if you were really frustrated about something else."

"What do you mean?" Finn asked.

"I know you want me to make a decision about signing back up for active duty, but—"

"Yeah about that… I'm sorry if you feel pressured. It should be your decision. I just thought it would be fun for us, you know?"

"I know." She gulped.

Without warning, a jolt of panic raced through her body. *Where's Loki?* She shielded her eyes and looked for him. Finn noticed and turned his gaze toward the forest.

"Are you sure you put the toy within reach?" Lara asked, scanning the forest.

He's never been gone this long before.

"Yes. I promise."

"Loki, come!" she shouted. Her heart racing, she watched urgently for any signs of her pup. *Then* a wide smile crept across her face as she saw Loki racing out of the woods with the stuffed carrot in his mouth.

He found it!

She turned to Finn and grinned triumphantly. "I told you he could do it."

"Yes... yes, you did," Finn said. He grabbed her hand and pulled her close to him, his touch sending heat up her spine. He grazed her nose with his lips and then kissed her deeply. Warmth spread through her body as she returned his kiss.

At the sound of eager panting, Lara pulled away from Finn. Loki dropped the toy at her feet, looking up at her and wagging his stubby tail. Lara pressed the clicker and gave him a treat.

"Good boy, Loki," Lara said.

The sound of a car honk made Lara jump. She looked up and cringed at the sight of Rob's Jeep.

Okay, not the best timing. She'd hoped to tell Finn about it before Rob arrived. Knots tightened in her stomach when she realized the black sedan was gone. Before she had a chance to think about it, Finn touched her arm.

"What's Rob doing here?" Finn asked, his eyes narrowing.

"He's giving me a ride to the Langstons." She flashed him a toothy grin and kept it pasted on her face.

"You could have asked me for a ride, you know," Finn said, his voice strained.

Well, I wasn't sure if we were breaking up or not.

"Rob works for me now, and he wants to be helpful," Lara said flatly, avoiding eye contact. She bent down to attach the leash to Loki's collar. "He had an errand this morning, and it's on the way." She told the lie to spare Finn's feelings but also to avoid talking about the real reason for the ride. Rob insisted on chauffeuring her around until she figured out what was going on with her health—something she'd failed to tell her own boyfriend.

There's not much to tell yet.

"I can take Loki home and put him in the crate if you want," Finn said.

"Thanks," Lara said, "but Loki is coming with me. It'll be his first official outing as my right-hand pup." She grinned.

Finn smirked.

"Catch you later this week?" Lara asked. "Maybe for dinner?"

"Okay," Finn said, pressing his lips together. "How about tomorrow at my place this time?"

"Sounds good," Lara said, hurrying toward the Jeep, Loki in tow. She didn't need to see the look on Finn's face. Because she had a pretty good inkling.

Finn isn't happy about Rob as my chauffeur. Join the club.

SEVEN

Missing Persons

"You do realize I don't even have to be conscious to make it to my destination in a self-driving car," Lara said angrily.

They'd been arguing since Rob picked her up at the park. As the Jeep stopped in front of the Langstons' mansion, she grabbed the door handle, ready to escape the stale air and confined space.

"Lara, we're just worried about you," Rob said, his tone defensive.

"I passed out once," she snapped. "It was simulator sickness."

"What about your bloody noses and dizzy spells? Sanchez said—"

"You talked to Sanchez about my health?" Lara asked, heat flushing through her body to her neck.

"He called me yesterday to offer his help on my case," Rob said. "We got to talking about it… he noticed something was off with you yesterday."

She waved her hand dismissively. "If you guys worry any more about me staying alive, you might actually suffocate me to death. And then what's the point?"

Rob didn't respond. She refused to look at him but felt his

steely gaze. If she glimpsed into his brown eyes, all would be forgiven.

I'm not in a forgiving mood.

Letting him off the hook would only encourage more overprotective behavior from Maggie and Rob. She wanted her life to go back to normal—her carefree health, independence, and normal conversations with friends. Mostly, she wanted to ride her motorcycle again and enjoy the fall weather on the open road.

Sanchez caught her eye as he waited for her on the landing in front of the main entrance. *Wearing his finest for the Langstons.*

He was dressed in a navy suit, a red tie, and a starched white shirt. His badge hung on his belt, glinting in the sun. A wool coat hung loosely over his arm. Under her puffy down coat, Lara had not dressed to impress. If the Langstons were desperate to hire her, they'd be fine with her comfortable choice of black leggings and a large sweater.

Lara climbed out of the passenger seat without saying another word and slammed the door. A pang of something stirred inside her.

What if they're right? What if I'm sick?

Biting her lip, she walked around to the back of the Jeep and opened the trunk. She grabbed Loki's leash and gave it a slight tug. The pup jumped to the ground. As soon as Sanchez saw the dog, his smile disappeared.

Ha. That didn't take long.

"You think Sanchez will be able to give you a lift home?" Rob craned his neck to look at her through the back of the Jeep.

"We'll work something out," Lara said. She closed the back door and tapped the side of the Jeep. She watched as Rob drove off, twisting the leash handle in her hands. She suddenly wished she'd been nicer, maybe even thanked him before he left.

He really cares about me. I don't make it easy.

Taking a deep breath, she made her way up the stone stairs toward the house, Loki running just behind her on his leash. The detective's face tightened, and he crossed his arms.

"What?" Lara asked. She didn't feel like dealing with one of the detective's foul moods.

He pointed his finger at Loki and cleared his throat. "I'm not sure the Langstons will appreciate a strange dog running around their house."

"He's not a strange dog." Lara gave him a hard look, warning him not to push further.

He frowned deeply.

"Didn't you say the Langstons would pay me any fee I wanted? If they want me to help find their daughter, Loki and I are a package deal today. They can fire me if they don't like it."

Sanchez held up his hands in surrender, shrugged, and opened the front door. He allowed her and Loki to enter first and closed the door behind them.

As she strode into the large, oval foyer, the detective's cologne—a cinnamon and woody amber scent—wafted toward her. She inhaled the pleasant smell, her body relaxing for a brief moment. She stopped in the middle of the foyer, and Loki sat next to her.

"So, is Rob working as your personal driver now?" Sanchez asked with a smirk.

Well, here we go.

Before she could reply, the detective broke into hearty laughter, his whole body shaking.

Lara glared at him, suppressing a chuckle. "That's not funny. Rob and Maggie are not letting me drive anywhere by myself at the moment. And I think you already know why… since you've been conspiring with Rob behind my back."

Not bothered in the least by her insinuation, the detective chortled harder, slapping his knee and wiping a tear from his eye.

Lara rolled her eyes. "Great. I might be dying, and you're cracking up. I'm so glad to know you care." She let the sarcasm drip off her tongue as she strained her ears. A soft whirr from the heating vents was the only sound in the house. "Where are the Langstons?"

"They're running an errand at the moment. Julian and Cynthia wanted to give you some time to see the place for yourself before you chat with them."

"Any leads on Molly's whereabouts?" Lara asked.

"None," Sanchez said. "We've blanketed the surrounding area with more than a dozen cops and FBI agents. They've come up with nada. Zero leads on the girl's location or her kidnapper's identity. No ransom note. No sign of a struggle. Hardly any evidence left behind. The only trace evidence was a small splotch of blood on the girl's bedroom wall near the window. Unfortunately, the DNA matches Molly, so it's a dead end." He sighed and crossed his arms. "If we don't turn up some leads fast, this case will go from slightly cold to freezing." He clutched his chest and looked at her. "I'm hoping you can help us crack this one."

"You do realize I'm way out of my league on this case, right?" Lara asked, frowning deeply. "I'm not some magic wand you can wave around to solve hard cases for you."

Sanchez gave her an incredulous stare. "Don't worry, I'm fully aware of your skill set. Along with its many limitations. And that's why you're not working this one on your own." He pointed to the sitting room next to the foyer. "Let's start in here."

Lara removed the leash from Loki's collar. As soon as he was free, Loki went on the prowl, sniffing everything he came across. She followed the detective into the sitting room and took off her coat.

For the size of the house, the space was quite small. It almost had a cozy feel. That is, if it wasn't twice the size of her entire living room. The sitting room was furnished tastefully with a few ivory-colored couches, mahogany side tables, a full-sized black grand piano, and a wood-burning fireplace. Above the sculpted mantle, Lara glimpsed a row of family pictures set in polished silver frames. At the center, a picture of the Langstons posing with a young Asian girl caught her attention.

That must be her.

Molly had long, smooth raven-black hair and thick bangs

framing her oval face. Her round, dark brown eyes were complimented by a cute button nose. In the picture, she wore a light pink princess-waistline dress with a black sash and large bow at the waist.

"Tell me about Molly," she said, biting her lip. The image of the small girl's frightened face sent a quiver up and down Lara's spine. *Only eight years old. That's how old I was when my parents died.*

She shuddered as a torrent of memories flooded her mind, including images of being sent away to live with strangers. With every fiber of her being, she could relate to what Molly must be experiencing—the fear, disorientation, and unanswered questions.

But why didn't Molly resist capture? Scream? Fight?

Sanchez flipped open his notebook and turned to the first page of his case notes. "The Langstons adopted her from China when she was two months old. Her given name is Mo Chu, but they call her Molly. Julian Langston runs a multi-national corporation called GenTech Industries. It's *the* top biotechnology firm in America... worth more than a few billion by now. Cynthia is a stay-at-home mom, but heavily involved in the arts and the community."

Lara rubbed her chin. "Why aren't there demands from the kidnapper?" she asked, tilting her head. "The Langstons are a wealthy, well-connected family. Wouldn't money be *the* motivation for taking Molly?"

Sanchez rubbed his chin. "We were wondering the same thing. Doesn't seem right."

"How are the parents handling things?"

"As good as you can imagine. Cynthia is an emotional basket case about Molly's kidnapping and hard to manage at times. Julian seems more aloof; calculated one minute, and then the next he's yelling orders at anyone who crosses his path. There's quite a bit of tension between the Langstons. It could be signs of an unhappy marriage or just the stress of the situation. Who knows?"

"Do you think they're hiding something?" Lara asked, an eyebrow raised.

"Dunno. Everyone handles these things in their own way. Maybe you'll pick up something when you meet them."

Just then Loki dove behind the couch, sniffing at the fabric and along the floor. He checked every inch of the couch with unfettered energy as if he'd found something.

Sanchez pointed at Loki. "What the hell is he doing?"

"I've been teaching him to track scents."

Sanchez shook his head in disbelief. "If you say so."

Just then, Loki pulled a dusty stuffed bear from under the couch. He lifted it with his mouth and carried it over to Lara, his tail wagging.

"Oh look, he found one of Molly's old toys. Now we've solved the case," Sanchez said, not hiding his sarcasm.

"Can I see Molly's room?" Lara asked, ignoring the detective's barb.

"Okay, let's go see the upstairs." Sanchez led her back into the foyer and up the wrought-iron baluster staircase to the second floor. Loki raced after them, his ears flopping up and down with each stair.

When they reached the second floor, the yellow crime tape was gone. Lara followed the detective down a long hallway past several oak doors with antique crystal knobs and several original framed artworks. Sanchez opened the door at the far end of the hallway, and a stream of sunlight poured out.

They walked into a large, bright bedroom with light pink walls and gleaming hardwood floors. But that's not what captured Lara's eye when she entered.

The wall behind Molly's queen-sized canopy bed drew her attention immediately. It was decorated with an intricate hand-painted mural with more than twenty colorful butterflies. She stared at the wall for a moment, holding her breath—it was magnificent. As a child, she would have died and gone to heaven for such a wall.

Molly's parents clearly cherish their daughter.

"Is this exactly how things were left after the kidnapping?" Lara asked, raising her eyebrow.

"Yep," Sanchez said.

Lara went to work, studying every detail of the room. The bed was neatly made. A floppy pink bunny sat propped up against the colorful bank of pillows. Nothing was out of order. It was almost as if Molly hadn't been in the room the night of her kidnapping.

Did the kidnapper make Molly's bed?

Lara strode toward the bed, picked up the stuffed bunny, and turned it over in her hands.

"Loki, here." He ran to her and sat in front of her. She let him smell the plush toy. "Find it," she said firmly. Loki sniffed for a few seconds and then bounded away, sprinting down the hallway and thumping down the stairs to the first floor.

Sanchez gave her a skeptical look. "You think he's going to find something?"

"Maybe."

The masonry stone wall in the backyard outside attracted Lara's eyes. She peered out the large window. Just below the window sill, the roof of the sunroom sloped gently toward the ground. Squinting her eyes, she estimated the drop from the sunroom roof to the ground to be less than six feet.

"This is where Molly was taken?" Lara asked.

"Yup. Right out of her bed. The babysitter put Molly to bed and didn't see or hear anything out of the ordinary. At least, that's what she told the police," Sanchez said.

But her bed doesn't look slept in.

Lara continued staring out the window onto the roof. "The kidnapper climbed up the roof, entered the house through Molly's window, and took her from her perfectly made bed?"

"That's the current theory. To get on the property, the kidnapper climbed over the stone wall, went to the shed, got a ladder, placed it against the roof, and climbed in through the window."

"How did the kidnapper climb over the wall?" Lara asked.

"We found several fibers of professional grade climbing rope caught in a crevice."

Lara rubbed her chin. "If the kidnapper planned an escape from the roof, he or she must have known about the ladder in the shed. Otherwise, the plan would have failed. The kidnapper must have also known the exact layout of the house to enter through Molly's window." Lara furrowed her brow and stared at the detective. "Do you think the kidnapper knew the Langstons?"

Sanchez frowned. "That sounds plausible."

Um. More than plausible.

"Any prints or DNA from our suspect?"

"Nope," Sanchez said. "Everything we found points back to Molly."

"Are there any surveillance cameras?" Lara asked.

"The house and grounds are covered with hidden cameras," Sanchez said, "but the system was offline on the night of the kidnapping. I have my cyber techs going over the code to see if it was hacked. Maybe Vik could take a look at it?"

Offline? What are the chances?

"Vik and Shanaya are on their honeymoon at the moment," Lara said, wrinkling her forehead. Vik had texted her that morning, bugging her for answers about her symptoms. Apparently, Rob told Vik he was worried about her. She didn't know how to respond without causing unnecessary worry, so she didn't. "Can the system be accessed remotely?"

"Yes. The Langstons can control the system from their smartphones."

Lara's pulse quickened. "In other words, the system could have been deactivated specifically to enable the kidnapping."

"We already ran that lead down. My techs checked the code," Sanchez said, as if reading her mind. "The Langstons didn't deactivate it remotely."

But maybe someone else did.

"What about the babysitter?" Lara asked.

"In her statement to the police, Alicia claimed she didn't touch the system."

"You said there was blood?" Lara asked.

Sanchez pointed to the pink wall near the window. Lara scanned a large area next to the window at her waist level but saw nothing. She bent over and looked a bit lower. Still nothing.

"No, it's up there." Sanchez pointed at a tiny smudge of blood at the height of Lara's shoulder.

She screwed up her eyes to see it clearly. "Huh. Isn't that smudge too high? How would Molly even get it up there?"

Sanchez turned his head to the side. "Maybe when she was being carried, she touched the wall?"

Lara grunted.

"And you think the kidnapper carried Molly down the ladder, across the grounds, and escaped with her on the creek?" Lara asked, looking toward the ceiling. "At eight years old, Molly probably weighs fifty pounds. That's a lot of weight to carry down a ladder, across the yard, and over the wall."

"Maybe Molly climbed down the ladder herself?" Sanchez asked.

"Without a struggle or scream for help?" Lara asked, squeezing the bunny rabbit. "That doesn't make sense. Molly *must* have known her abductor."

"Possibly. We found the last sign of her at the riverbank. That's where we picked up traces of blood, a few strands of hair, adult-size footprints, and Molly's footprints."

"Only one kidnapper?" Lara asked.

"That's our working assumption."

Something continued to nag at her. "If Molly was taken from her bed with the babysitter watching TV downstairs, then why is the bed still made?" Lara asked.

Sanchez cocked his head. "Good question."

Loud barking came from Loki downstairs, startling them.

"Can we go have a look outside?" Lara asked.

Sanchez nodded.

They made their way downstairs, and Lara followed the

sound of Loki's whine, which was accompanied by a frantic scratching noise. He was at the back of the house, pawing at the French doors. As soon as the detective opened the door, Loki bolted into the yard and made a beeline for the woods. In response to the cold air, Lara pulled her puffy coat back on and zipped it up all the way to her neck.

A few minutes later, Lara and Sanchez traipsed through the thick woods behind the property. Appearing to have the time of his life, Loki bounded back and forth across the grounds, sniffing through piles of dead leaves, picking up sticks and dropping them. Her heart sank.

He might have forgotten the scent by now.

When they reached the river bank, Sanchez pointed to the spot in the dirt. "This is where we found the footprints, blood, and hair."

"Loki, here," Lara called out. In her hand, she still held Molly's plush rabbit.

Sanchez raised his eyebrow. "We had dogs search every inch of the woods. Plus, he doesn't seem… all that committed."

Lara raised her hand to stop him. "Isn't it worth another shot?"

Loki bounded toward her, his pink tongue hanging out the side of his mouth. She held the stuffed animal to his nose again.

"Loki, find it," she said.

Immediately, he began smelling the leaves at her feet with a heightened sense of urgency. Then he ran off toward the riverbank.

"Rob said you called to offer him your help on his case," Lara said.

"Oh yeah." Sanchez frowned. "Sadly, Commander Jamison refused to approve it."

Lara's face fell. *Crap.*

After a few moments, Sanchez's face broke into a broad grin. "But the police commissioner overruled him."

Lara punched him in the arm. "Why didn't you just say that?"

The detective chuckled. "And miss out on a chance to push your buttons? Never."

From across the woods, two sharp barks cut through the air. Sanchez gave her a curious look as they turned toward the noise.

"Loki's found something," Lara said, rushing toward the spot across the woods.

When she arrived, the Doberman was sitting at the base of a tree near the stone wall and panting. A small red paper object lay at his feet on the ground, partly covered by a pile of leaves. Lara bent over and reached for it, but Sanchez grabbed her arm to stop her. Giving her a stern look, he pulled out an evidence bag and a pair of plastic gloves, which he pulled on. Then he stooped down to pick it up and dropped it gingerly into a plastic evidence bag.

"What is this?" he asked, staring at the red paper object through the plastic.

"That's a folded paper butterfly," Lara said.

Her body tensed as forgotten childhood memories flashed through her head. An image of her dining room table at her old house took hold in her mind. She remembered sitting in the dining room and folding paper animals with her father. They looked exactly like this one.

"Is this Origami or something?" Sanchez asked tentatively.

"No, that's what paper folding is called in Japan," Lara said automatically, snapping out of her daze. "Paper was invented in China and arrived in Japan much later. In China, the tradition of folding paper is called *zhezhi*. People in medieval China didn't like to waste anything, and paper was considered precious. They would make toys for children from old scraps."

Sanchez stared at her. "How do you know this stuff?"

"Uh… my father taught me when I was a kid," Lara said, a sharp pang rising in her chest.

He gave her a strange look. "You do know some random shit, but it might mean nothing. Anyone could have dropped this here."

Lara wrinkled her nose. "That would be an odd coincidence.

Think about it. Molly has butterflies on her wall and loves them. The kidnapper climbed the wall to get in and probably got out the same way. No, this definitely belonged to Molly, and she dropped it the night of her kidnapping."

"We'll check it for prints. Probably another dead end, though."

"Excellent." Lara rolled her eyes. "With your inflexible, know-it-all attitude, we'll solve this case in a real jiffy."

Sanchez's faced darkened. Then he pointed to the terrace. Lara turned to look as Loki sprinted toward the house, barking fiercely at Julian and Cynthia Langston.

Good, they're home. I have questions for them.

EIGHT

The Interview
____

Lara savored the semi-sweet hot chocolate as she sat on a plush patio chair next to Sanchez and across from the Langstons, looking out over the stone terrace at the lush gardens in the backyard. Loki lay quietly under the wrought-iron table, attached to his leash, occasionally raising his head at the sound of birds chirping and squirrels running across the grounds.

The mid-morning sun warmed Lara's face despite the chilly fall air. Even so, she clutched the hot mug, snuggled into her coat for added warmth, and tried to ignore the throbbing in her head. Sanchez nudged her in the arm and gave her a triumphant I-was-right look. Ignoring the detective, Lara stole another glance at Julian.

Refusing to break the frosty silence, Julian sat across from her, sipping from his mug and glaring at the table. Though foul-tempered and nearing the end of his fifties, he was an attractive man. He boasted a full head of salt-and-pepper hair, thick black eyebrows, and a gray beard. Despite allegedly taking the day off, he sported a tailored pinstripe suit and a silver tie, giving the impression he wore nothing else, even during his downtime.

A dark scowl remained on Julian's face from the first moment he'd met Loki. Julian had not been very happy to learn that Loki had run free through their house. To avoid getting muddy paws everywhere, he insisted they hold the interview on the patio, even with the cold temperature.

Cynthia had strongly objected to sitting outside but eventually lost the argument with her husband. Now she huddled in her thick fur coat and glowered at Julian, her gloved fingers tapping on a file folder on the table, the soft, muted thrumming a rhythm of impatience. Beyond the signs of stress, she was a beautiful middle-aged woman—likely, a full decade younger than her husband. Her brown eyes and the worn lines on her face betrayed the anguish of a mother experiencing the harsh reality of losing her child.

Sanchez placed the red paper butterfly tucked inside the plastic evidence bag in the middle of the table. "Do you recognize this?" he asked.

A subtle ripple of tension spread across Cynthia's face, followed by confusion. After Julian's posture stiffened, he didn't move a muscle and kept his stoic face focused on the table.

"No, what is it?" Cynthia asked, a slight tremor in her voice.

Leaning forward in her chair, Lara said, "My dog found this folded paper butterfly in the woods. We believe it belonged to Molly. Are you sure you don't recognize it?"

Cynthia's lips trembled until she pressed them tightly together. Her fearful eyes met Lara's for a brief second. Then they darted toward her lap where her hands were now tightly clenched. Lara glanced down at Julian's hand gripping his wife's arm, his knuckles turning white.

He doesn't want her to talk. Why?

Behind the caked-on layers of makeup, Lara detected faint mascara smudges at the corners of her eyes. Shedding tears was a normal reaction to the terrible circumstance of having her daughter taken from her—ripped out of the safety of her own bed in the middle of the night and with no promise of return.

To have so much power, but still feel completely powerless.

Lara had done her research on the couple prior to the interview. Paying an enormous ransom or pulling powerful strings were no obstacles for the Langstons. Cynthia was a patron of the arts and spent most of her time hosting posh events at museums and galleries. A well-connected and wealthy businessman, Mr. Langston also provided generous support to several political campaigns. He'd recently spent a huge sum to ensure the current mayor's electoral victory.

That explains the mayor's investment in the case.

After a few moments, Julian released his grip on Cynthia's arm *and* folded his arms across his chest. "My daughter doesn't know how to fold paper like that."

"I see," Lara said, studying the Langstons' faces for information.

"We'll have it tested for prints to know for sure," Sanchez added. "Perhaps the butterfly is something the kidnapper gave Molly?"

Cynthia nodded as if in a trance.

Lara couldn't shake the feeling there was much more going on behind the scenes than a missing child.

There's something they're not telling us.

Flipping backward in his notebook, Sanchez cleared his throat. "You mentioned you had a babysitter on the night that Molly was taken. Do you think it's possible she had something to do with your daughter's abduction?"

Julian shook his head. "No. Alicia Novak is the daughter of our long-time gardener. We've known her family for more than twenty years. Plus, Alicia is only thirteen years old. How could she possibly be involved in a kidnapping? She was watching TV in the entertainment room when it happened."

"Do you know about what time the incident occurred?" Sanchez asked.

"It's in the police report," Julian snapped. "Alicia didn't hear anything out of the ordinary that night. We came home from a black-tie gala around one in the morning. Cindy went upstairs to check on Molly. But she wasn't in her bed, and the bedroom window was left open. That means it could have happened any time after Molly went to bed at around eight."

"But Molly's bed was still made," Lara interjected. "That suggests she didn't sleep in it."

Julian waved his hand dismissively. "Molly wears flannel pajamas, gets too hot at night, and sometimes asks to sleep without covers."

Lara and Sanchez exchanged dubious looks.

"I'll need to speak to your babysitter to get her version of the story," Lara said in an authoritative tone. She pressed her temples as her headache shifted from the occasional thud to incessant pounding.

"Alicia has already spoken to the police and gave a full statement," Julian responded. "She doesn't know anything more that can help us."

"Well, I still need to speak to her," Lara said firmly. "She's probably the one person who can be of most help in finding your daughter."

Julian stared blankly at her. "I'm sorry, but that won't be possible. She's visiting Poland with her father."

Sanchez and Lara locked eyes again.

"When will she return?" Lara asked.

"I don't know," Julian said flatly. "There was an unexpected death in the family."

Interesting timing.

Massaging her forehead, Lara glanced at her notebook. "Okay. Let's go back to the night in question. Do you think your daughter knew her abductor?"

"No, that's not possible," Julian said firmly, shaking his head and keeping his stony expression intact. Cynthia grabbed a tissue from the box in front of her and blew her nose.

"Do you have any idea who might have taken your daughter?" Sanchez asked, his pen ready. "Enemies? Disgruntled employees? Rivals?"

"The cops already asked me those questions," Julian growled. He shifted around in his seat, his steely gaze directed at the detective. "Don't you communicate with your colleagues?"

Sanchez gaped at Julian, a small vein popping in his head.

"Maybe one more time for Ms. Kingsley, since you hired her to help you… she doesn't have access to the police reports."

Glaring at the detective, Julian said, "As I said before, we don't know anyone who would want to take Molly. I don't think this has anything to do with someone seeking revenge against me. It doesn't make any sense. Don't you think they'd want a sizable chunk of my fortune? We've heard nothing from the kidnapper."

Cynthia whimpered as if she were recounting the night of the incident, her eyes filling with tears.

"What about the birth parents?" Lara asked. "Could they have come back for their daughter?"

Julian pinched his mouth. "They abandoned Molly on the side of a road to starve to death in the countryside in China," he said gruffly. "We adopted her when she was a baby. I don't think her birth family would come looking for her at this point."

"I assume you arranged for the adoption through an agency in the United States?" Lara asked.

Cynthia sniffed loudly and nodded, pushing the file folder on the table toward Lara. "The Miracle Springs Eternal Adoption Agency organized Molly's adoption for us. The whole thing from start to finish. There's a copy of the records in the folder and a recent photo of Molly."

Lara reached for the folder, flipped it open and squinted, trying to ignore the intense throbbing pain in her head. The photo was similar to the one Lara had seen on their mantle, but without the Langstons—in her pink dress, Molly posed next to the grand piano in the sitting room.

Lara's eyes quickly scanned the adoption records. "I don't see the Chinese orphanage listed here. Do you remember how your adoption agency acquired the child?"

"It's not listed on the form?" Cynthia's wet eyes widened, and she sniffed her nose again.

Lara studied the form again and shook her head. "The section for the name of the orphanage was left blank."

Cynthia furrowed her brow, a tear rolling down her cheek.

"I'm not sure we ever talked about where Molly came from. The agency assured us that everything was legitimate, and no one had any claims on her. We paid them fifty thousand dollars, so I'd sure hope not."

Fifty thousand dollars for a child?

"Is there anything else you can tell us about your daughter?" Lara asked, rubbing her forehead.

"Ms. Kingsley, do whatever you need to do…" Cynthia said, her lip trembling. "Please find my baby. Please!" Tears streamed down her cheeks, ruining the remainder of her makeup. Without warning, she jumped up from the table, ran across the terrace, and disappeared into the house.

The muscles in Julian's face tightened as he appeared to suppress his emotions. "I'm sorry for my wife. She's beside herself with worry and having trouble keeping it together. As a result, I've had to hold down the fort and make sure we're doing whatever we can to get our daughter back."

"That's quite understandable, given the circumstances," Lara said. She shared at least one thing in common with Julian—the ability to compartmentalize her emotions in a crisis. "I have a few more issues I'd like to cover if you don't mind."

Julian nodded.

"I assume you have a surveillance system to protect against intrusion?" Lara asked.

"Yes."

"And you didn't receive any remote alerts about the open window or from motion sensors outside?" Lara asked.

"We didn't." His face fell. "Our babysitter disarmed the system with her code to receive a package in the early evening. She forgot to reset the alarm."

Lara's mouth fell open, and Sanchez sat up straighter in his chair.

"But that's not what your babysitter told the police on the night of the incident," Sanchez said, his jaw hanging.

Julian put a hand through his gray hair. "Alicia was too afraid to tell the truth and lied about it. When her father and I sat her down and explained to her that she'd done nothing wrong, she told us about the alarm system."

I need to talk to Alicia and get her story.

"What sort of package did your babysitter receive?" Lara asked. The world around her spun just slightly, and Lara willed herself to focus.

"Our neighbor's daughter came over to deliver an order of Girl Scout cookies." Julian smiled. "I admit, I have an obsession. I just can't get enough of the Thin Mints."

She wanted to press Julian further about the cookie delivery when a sudden bout of dizziness took over. Instead, she gripped the arms of her chair as discreetly as possible and swallowed several times, trying to regain her bearings.

Turning to Sanchez, Julian said, "Detective, we're willing to offer one million dollars as a reward for information that leads to Molly's recovery. Could you make sure the announcement goes out on the news media?"

Sanchez nodded. "Yes, sir. We'll set up an operations center to manage the incoming tips right away. The reward will go a long way to finding Molly. Hopefully, the leads will start pouring in."

Julian rose from his chair, and the detective followed suit. "I'd better go see how my wife is doing."

Clutching the arms on the patio chair, Lara said, "One more question..." Julian shot a warning glare at her, but she ignored it. "You wanted to hire me last year for a surveillance job and then decided to go in a different direction. Now you're hiring me to find your daughter when I have zero experience with missing persons cases. Why?"

Julian wrinkled his forehead, as if he was trying to recall the details. "I don't remember seeking your assistance for a surveillance job." He turned quickly toward the house and motioned for them to follow him.

"You hired me to find your daughter without a referral?" Lara asked, grabbing Loki's leash and following Julian back into the house. "How did you even find out about my PI business in the first place?"

"Cindy noticed your advertisement on the FishBowl social media platform. We were desperate to try anything to get our daughter back. She was convinced you could help us. So, I asked the police commissioner to get in touch with you right away. And here you are."

As she stood, Lara's eyes bulged. *What advertisement is he talking about?*

Vertigo overtook her as she staggered to the right, her arms flailing out in front of her. Before she could find any way to steady herself, her knees buckled. Then her vision faded to black, and she tumbled to the ground.

"Lara, are you okay?" Sanchez asked, reaching for her. "Lara?"

His voice sounded distant and garbled. Pain shot through her body when she landed. Then silence. Blackness.

* * *

WHEN LARA finally opened her eyes, several concerned faces were staring at her from above—Sanchez, Maggie, and a young man who appeared to be an emergency medical technician. Loki eyed her anxiously and licked her face.

Lara lifted her head slightly, but the EMT told her not to move. Ignoring his order, she turned her head to the side to take in the scene. She was lying on a couch in the sitting room inside the Langstons' mansion. Her chest rose and fell in rapid movements. The heart rate monitor beeped loudly.

I must have fainted.

"Ma'am, I need you to stay calm," the EMT said.

A plastic oxygen mask covered her nose and mouth. She motioned to the EMT that she wanted to talk.

The EMT removed the oxygen mask. "Only for a few minutes. Your brain needs the oxygen."

"What happened?" Lara's voice sounded weak.

Sanchez's face was pale, his eyes bloodshot. "You got a bloody nose and then just passed out in front of us. You lost consciousness for almost an hour. We called 911, and then I called Maggie. I thought you'd want her here. The EMTs put you on oxygen and checked your vitals. We were…" He turned away, unable to speak further as if overwhelmed by emotion.

"Hon, your heartbeat was all over the place," Maggie said, her lip trembling ever so slightly. "Were you feeling any symptoms before you passed out?"

Lara rubbed her head. "Uh… I guess my heart was racing a bit and my head was throbbing." She contemplated possible causes. "Do you think this happened because of my stint in the simulator?"

Maggie shook her head. "I doubt it, luv."

"Too much time in the sun this morning?" Lara asked, searching her brain for plausible explanations.

Maggie shook her head again.

"Well, I'm feeling better now," Lara said, trying in vain to sit up. "Can I go home?"

The EMT frowned deeply. "I'd prefer to take you to the emergency department for a full diagnostic and make sure nothing is wrong."

Lara pulled up her nose. "No. No more hospitals for me. I'm fine."

"No, you're not fine," Maggie said. "This wasn't just a fainting spell. You were out for quite a long time. I'm worried there's something going on. You need to see a doctor. Right away."

"If I agree to see my own doctor, can I go home now?" Lara asked.

The EMT sighed. "Ma'am, I can't force you to seek proper medical treatment, but if you insist on going home, I will ask you to sign a waiver."

Lara gave a dismissive wave of her hand. "I'll sign whatever you want. I just want to go home."

NINE

The Double-Cross

October 2, 2028

LARA SIPPED HER COLD BEER, enjoying the bittersweet taste and the slight burn at the back of her throat. She sat in Sully's favorite cushy leather armchair, her mind lost in the conflicting details of the Langston case and overwhelmed with images of a scared little girl. Loki lay at her feet on his dog bed, busy chewing a string toy and blissfully ignorant of all the human drama around him. For a moment, she wished she could switch places with him.

The Langstons are hiding something.

Muffled voices in the background brought her back to reality, and her eyes refocused on the bookshelves in her library. Lounging on her new couch across from her, Rob and FBI Special Agent John Carter debated the facts of the case against Harry Cogan.

In the chair next to her, Sanchez sipped a glass of whiskey, his feet propped up on the leather ottoman, seemingly lost in thought. For once, the detective was dressed down, wearing a pair of jeans and a sweatshirt. But he still had his usual five o'clock shadow.

They were supposed to be focused on the quest to clear Rob's name and put his boss behind bars, but Lara couldn't get her other case out of her head. *Maybe Sanchez is thinking the same thing about the Langstons.*

Lara leaned toward Sanchez and asked in a low voice, "Any new leads on Molly's whereabouts?"

Sanchez chopped the air with one hand. "Nada. I'm working on getting an appointment with the adoption agency. You got time tomorrow afternoon?"

"Sure," Lara said. "Maybe we'll learn something useful."

"Maybe," he said, taking a drink of his whiskey, "but I'm not holding my breath." Then he gave her a serious look. "When are you going to the doctor?"

Lara sighed heavily. "Later this morning. Maggie is taking me."

He eyed her suspiciously. "Good."

"How's your mother?" Lara asked, shifting attention away from herself.

Sanchez winced. "I spent last night at her bedside in the hospital. She's deteriorating quickly." He glanced at his watch. "I should probably get back over there soon." Sanchez nodded toward Rob and Agent Carter. "When do you think they'll stop bickering about Harry and make a plan to catch this bastard?"

Maybe I should help them along.

Lara turned her attention back to the conversation on the couch. Her notebook from Sully's case rested in her lap. She sipped her beer again and listened as Rob and Agent Carter droned on and on about what they knew while sipping single malt whiskey imported from Tasmania.

After much hemming and hawing, Lara had finally decided to open Sully's precious bottle of Sullivan's Cove whiskey he'd been saving for a special occasion.

I suppose the mission to clear Rob's name is special enough.

The guys couldn't stop raving about the vanilla, caramel,

fruit, and oak flavors. *As if. They probably just read the label on the bottle.*

Rob looked tired and unkempt, wearing a dirty pair of jeans and a grungy t-shirt. He'd even forgotten to shave his uneven beard that morning. As his polar opposite, Special Agent Carter was put together from head to toe, wearing a starched button-down shirt, a red tie, navy slacks, and a navy jacket. His FBI badge hung on his belt.

Agent Carter looked much younger than she expected, possibly in his late twenties, given his boyish looks and smooth face. Although she'd heard plenty about the young upstart from Rob, she'd never met the kid in person.

Lara scratched her head. *Wasn't he dating Dr. Stevens at one point? But I thought she was in her mid-thirties.* She recalled the night she spent in the safe room watching Rob and his team remove the surveillance bugs from Sully's townhouse. Rob had told Agent Carter to cozy up to the medical examiner to get the autopsy report from Sully's death. *I wonder if they're still together.*

"I know he's made some mistakes, but Harry has been like a father to both of us," Agent Carter said, raising his voice. "There's no way he'd betray us or risk his wife and kids to make money on the black market. There's got to be another explanation."

Rob waved his hands around in frustration. "But then why would Harry lie to the FBI's Internal Investigations Division about me? He said I carried out the illegal surveillance operation against Sully on my own. You and I both know he was the one who told me to do it." He pounded his fist on the couch. "Harry was involved in the illicit trading ring and was working with Justyne and MacFarlan. It's the only explanation that makes sense."

They're getting nowhere. Just angry with each other.

Lara opened her notebook. "Guys, why don't we start from the beginning and work our way back through what we know in a systematic manner. That way, we can identify the gaps and make a list of leads to follow up on."

Sanchez gave her an encouraging smile. "That sounds like a great idea. Getting emotional won't help us nail this son of a bitch to the wall."

Rob hung his head in shame. "Yeah, you're right. Sorry about getting myself worked up."

"That's okay, Rob," Lara said gently. "That's why we're all here… to help you figure it out and get to the truth. You're still too close to the situation. I'm sure Harry's betrayal cuts deep. So, can we start from the beginning?" She waited for Rob to acknowledge before continuing.

"Okay, fine," Rob said.

Lara flipped through the first few pages of her notebook. "The first relevant entry in my notes is about my visit to DARPA, where I met Justyne for the first time. We went out for lunch afterward, and she told me she wanted to find CyberShop to get justice for her dead lover. I should have known then that something wasn't quite right. But she got emotional about losing Frank. And I got distracted." Lara pressed her palm to her forehead, her cheeks flushing warm at the memory.

"It happens to all of us," Sanchez said reassuringly. "When you get as cynical as me, you see through everyone's bullshit. But then you don't trust anyone anymore either. Trust me, you're better off as you are."

"I agree. It's better to give people the benefit of the doubt until they prove you wrong," Rob said.

Lara gave them a crisp nod. "Justyne told me she was working the case with the FBI, with you as her liaison, Rob. She claimed the NSA arranged her detail assignment at DARPA specifically to support the NSA's lead counterintelligence investigator. That's when she gave me her theory about someone at DARPA collaborating with an insider at NSA headquarters known by the pseudonym CyberShop. The DARPA person and NSA insider were selling Top Secret encryption technology on the Dark Web."

"Yeah, turns out she was talking about herself and herself," Sanchez said wryly.

"Justyne misdirected the investigation by asserting Stepanov as the number one suspect. In reality, Stepanov was Frank's boss at the NSA and suspected Justyne might be CyberShop. But he had no evidence to back up his suspicions. She succeeded in throwing me off the real scent for quite a while." Lara glanced over at Rob. "I figured Harry must have assigned you the case to work with Justyne when the NSA called the FBI for help. Do you remember if and how that happened?"

Rob nodded, wrinkling his forehead. "Several months before Sully died, Harry pulled me aside to give me information on a sensitive operation that he wanted me to lead. He told me someone from the NSA asked for our assistance. But I have no way of proving that was true since he didn't relay the information in writing. If Harry and Justyne were indeed working together, I don't think there would be any record of it."

Lara scribbled in her notebook. "Okay, we have our first to-do item. Someone needs to call the NSA and find out if they ever officially reached out to the FBI about CyberShop and requested assistance. If there's no record of it, then it was part of Harry's deception."

"I'll take that one for action," Agent Carter said, typing a note into his smartphone.

"Hold up." Sanchez raised his hand in the air. "So, you're saying Rob was working with Justyne. But she was lying about working with Rob and just using him as a cover. Rather, she was working with someone else at the FBI to sell advanced tech on the black market. And now we think that someone else is Harry."

"Yeah, that about sums it up," Rob said, avoiding eye contact.

"Good. Let's talk about Fiddler." Lara shuddered at the memory of the old man. Sometimes in her dreams at night, his sullen gray eyes still haunted her. "He might know something more about who Justyne was working with at the FBI and if that person was Harry. Fiddler paid one hundred thousand dollars as a deposit and ended up reneging on the drone purchase."

Rob's face lit up. "Oh yeah… Fiddler wanted to send the file of paperwork and evidence related to the drone show to the NSA. Said he didn't need the deposit back, but this was of the utmost importance to him."

Does the file still exist?

"Fiddler later explained he wanted to clear his daughter's name," Lara said. "Rob, do you know if the paperwork on the drone show ever got sent over to the NSA?"

Rob directed his gaze at the ceiling, a shimmer of hope in his eyes. A few moments later, the light dimmed again. "Crap. Fiddler gave the file to me and I gave it to Harry, who was supposed to give it to Justyne to deliver to the NSA. If it contained anything implicating him, Harry would have destroyed the evidence before sending it onwards. That's how he can point the finger at me with so much confidence. There's no paper trail anymore."

Lara raised an eyebrow. "Most likely, Harry sent over a scrubbed version of the folder to the NSA that contained evidence incriminating Justyne. I bet the district attorney used it to secure Justyne's conviction and missed Harry's involvement entirely. That means she might hold a grudge. Maybe she'll help us get something on Harry."

"We need to get our hands on the original folder," Rob said, wringing his hands.

I wonder if Sully had a copy of the folder in his files. Lara was pretty sure Justyne managed to steal it from the storage unit.

"When I call the NSA, I'll ask if they ever received the paperwork from the FBI." Agent Carter made another note on his smartphone. "Then we'll have a better idea about the folder's whereabouts."

"Should we try talking to Fiddler?" Lara asked. "Maybe he knows something more. What if he kept another copy as an insurance policy?"

"Good idea," Sanchez said.

Rob gazed at Lara intently, remaining quiet for a few seconds. Then he shook his head vehemently. "No. I don't want to put you through that. Fiddler wouldn't have any reason to tell us what he knows. And who knows what he'll want in exchange for helping us. Shouldn't we look through Sully's files first?"

When Rob has a bee in his bonnet... he never stops buzzing about it.

Lara glowered at him, irritated at his attempt to protect her from Fiddler. "I already have that on my list. But yes, that's a good idea." Sully's files sat untouched in the storage facility since his death and the subsequent police investigation. She'd only visited the unit a few times to store some of her things after moving into Sully's townhouse. And the last time, she'd deposited all of her parents' old things that were delivered by the son of the executor of her parents' estate. Even from a few miles away, the contents of the boxes haunted her.

They're long dead. I don't want to know about their past.

"What happened to the money Fiddler paid for the drone show?" Sanchez asked.

"Harry said we should use it to make the drone show happen and avoid all the red tape at the FBI," Rob said.

Oh Rob. Talk about hook, line, and sinker.

Rob lowered his head. "By the end of the operation, the money was all gone. We didn't keep any records for how it was spent."

A perfect slush fund without a paper trail.

"Did your boss use it to pay people off?" Sanchez asked, frowning.

"I think so," Rob said. "But Harry gave me full credit for pulling it off. Even gave me the call sign Droneman." He fidgeted with his glass and avoided eye contact.

Lara suppressed a smirk as she recalled the first time she heard Rob call himself Droneman from inside Sully's safe room.

"I always wondered how you got D.C. Council to support the drone circus in the first place," Sanchez said, shaking his head in disgust.

Lara glanced down at scribbles in her notebook. "Come to think of it... Justyne mentioned your higher-ups probably didn't know about your activities as Droneman."

Rob froze for a moment, his face losing a shade of color. "She called me Droneman?"

"Yeah. Why?" Lara asked, her pulse spiking.

"I never told her about my Dark Web pseudonym. I interacted with CyberShop using the pseudonym to acquire an encryption scatter device for the drones to make them jammer-proof. But I never told her that I was operating undercover as Droneman. Harry must have told her it was me."

Agent Carter held out his hand. "Let's not jump to conclusions. Justyne's knowledge of your pseudonym doesn't mean Harry or anyone else at the FBI told her about it. I'm not saying she didn't have an accomplice in our agency. I just want to make sure we stay objective until the facts are clear. Maybe the explanation is a simple one... What if Justyne was surveilling you and overheard the name? You did use it quite a bit back then."

Rob's face flushed, and he shifted around in his chair.

"Or maybe she just put two and two together," Sanchez said, *rubbing his chin. "It's kinda obvious, don't you think?"*

Lara cringed on Rob's behalf. *Must be like going to the dentist's office. Having everyone shine a spotlight on your mistakes.*

"Well, at least I can vouch for Rob on the surveillance operation against Sully," Agent Carter said. "I was there when Rob wanted to shut it down. Harry insisted on keeping it going even though Sully was no longer a suspect."

"Wait a minute," Lara said, tapping her finger to her lips. Her thoughts inadvertently drifted to the piece of paper Vik found in one of Sully's old books after their last case. "I found a slip of paper in Sully's handwriting with the pseudonyms CyberShop, @AngryGeneral, and BlackDragon. I can't figure out why Sully wrote them down as a list. Maybe they're connected somehow. We know that CyberShop is Justyne, and @AngryGeneral is MacFarlan. What if Harry is BlackDragon, and that's how they're connected?" Lara asked.

Rob shrank back, a look of confusion on his face, and then seemed to recall her telling him about it months ago. "Didn't you say that Hai Xu had a black dragon tattoo on his chest?" he asked. "He's a far more likely candidate for the alias, don't you think?"

"Yeah, I thought about that," Lara said. "But Hai was a member of the Chinese People's Liberation Army and was working against rather than with MacFarlan. It doesn't make any sense for him to be BlackDragon."

Does it?

Rob's eyes lit up. "If Harry was BlackDragon, maybe Sully knew about Harry's involvement in the black market. And maybe that's why Harry wanted to keep the bugs in Sully's townhouse."

"Yeah, Sully must have gotten too close to the truth." Sanchez gestured with his finger as if cutting his throat.

Lara glared at the detective for his crass gesture. "If Sully knew the truth about Harry's activities... could that be why Justyne killed him?"

A lightbulb went off, and Lara realized something. Even though she knew how Sully died and who killed him, she didn't fully understand why Sully was killed. *Maybe it's all related somehow.*

"You think Harry gave the order?" Rob asked, his hand resting on his forehead. "He certainly set up Justyne and me to take the fall for his activities. She got blamed for the murder, and I got pinned with his other activities."

Lara nodded. "Assuming Harry is the big boss of the illicit trade ring—"

"We are making a lot of assumptions again," Agent Carter interrupted.

"Harry Cogan sounds like a dirty cop to me," Sanchez said.

"Let's get back on point. At the moment, the paper trail only points to Rob," Agent Carter said. "I agree Harry is not looking completely innocent. But we do need to stay objective until we have evidence."

Geez, this kid does wear rose-colored glasses. That might get him killed someday.

Rob inhaled sharply, his face twisted with anguish. "I don't care what the paper trail says or doesn't say. Harry put the nails in the coffin of my FBI career when he told the Internal Investigations Division about my affiliation with MacFarlan. But he's the one who asked me to help MacFarlan with the black op. Then he told the investigators about my involvement, and I'm the one who got fired. It's a textbook setup." He bunched his fists. "Harry wanted me gone from the FBI for a reason." He shook his fists at the ceiling. "There. Is. No. Other logical explanation. He fucking double-crossed me."

Lara furrowed her brow. "But how far does his operation go? That's what I want to know."

Agent Carter rubbed his chin. "Well, we know someone convinced MacFarlan to acquire critical defense technologies from the Pentagon for sale on the black market scheme. Maybe that someone was Harry, maybe not." He pointed first to Rob and then Lara. "Then MacFarlan concocted a plan to use the two of you to steal the tech from Spectral."

Lara bobbed her head. "MacFarlan knew Rob's career at the FBI was in jeopardy when he threatened me at the World War Two Memorial."

"Isn't it blatantly obvious to everyone?" Rob asked in a shrill voice, throwing up his hands. "Harry was friends with General MacFarlan. Justyne and the general were in cahoots. They were all working together. When Justyne got sent to prison after Sully's death, they needed a new game plan. And they chose me as the fall guy."

Agent Carter pinched his bottom lip. "I just don't believe Harry was playing the middleman between MacFarlan and Justyne. There's no evidence he was involved like that."

Rob sighed audibly, his exasperation growing more visible.

Lara tapped her finger on her lips. "My CIA guy, Randy Hickerson, was working with the general until they had a falling out. Or at least, Hickerson stopped trusting MacFarlan. And then the spook used me to secure the general's downfall. I'm certain

Hickerson knows more than what he told me. I should give him a call." She made a note to remind herself.

"Where did MacFarlan end up?" Sanchez asked.

"He was tried by court-martial," Lara said, flipping forward a few pages in her notebook to the Project Gecko case. "He was found guilty of a long list of crimes and ended up at Fort Leavenworth. Probably for the rest of his life."

"Should we go talk to MacFarlan?" Rob asked, studying her face to gauge her reaction.

Lara grimaced. "Maybe. I'll put it on the list." If she was being honest, she never wanted to see MacFarlan again. But the general was their best chance at getting information about Harry. And with a sick daughter, he might have an incentive to help them.

Sanchez leaned forward, his dark brown eyes bright for an instant. "I can't remember if I told you… During our final search of Spectral after Hai's death, my evidence team turned up some surveillance bugs in Zhang's office. They were standard issue from the FBI."

Agent Carter's eyes widened.

"We traced the serial numbers of the bugs to the FBI headquarters," Sanchez said. "We made a few calls and discovered there was no ongoing FBI investigation into Spectral. The bugs were throwaways, scheduled for destruction and disposal."

"Find any prints?" Agent Carter asked.

"Just MacFarlan's," Sanchez said.

"That means someone at the FBI misappropriated them for an off-book surveillance operation," Agent Carter said. "Send me the serial numbers. I'll look into it and see if I can find anything."

Sanchez nodded.

"I'll bet you a hundred bucks Harry was behind that too," Rob said, scowling at his former colleague, his voice bitter.

Lara noted the item on the to-do list. "Right now, the to-do list includes searching Sully's files, calling the NSA, getting the drone show evidence, checking out the surveillance bugs found at Spectral, and talking to Hickerson, MacFarlan, Justyne, and maybe Fiddler." She paused, waiting for everyone to acknowledge. "Does everyone know what they're doing next?"

There was a loud knock at the front door. Everyone looked up and then glanced nervously at each other, still tense from the discussion. Loki raced to the door, barking frantically and running in circles.

"You expecting someone?" Rob asked.

Lara bobbed her head. "That would be Maggie. She's taking me to my doctor's appointment."

"Well, there's some good news. I thought I was going to have to handcuff you and take you there myself," Sanchez said grimly.

Handcuffs might still be necessary.

TEN

Doctor's Appointment

Resting on her hands, Lara rocked back and forth on the examination table and stared up at the huge flat screen TV on the wall, illuminated with an outline image of her body and details from her medical profile. The nurse robot had already been in the room to take her vitals, and a panel in the upper righthand corner displayed her temperature, blood pressure, height, and weight. At the bottom corner, a digital clock showed the time since her urine sample was sent to the lab for analysis.

"Are you going to tell Finn about your fainting episode?" Maggie asked, looking up from her smartphone for a brief moment.

Lara sighed. "We're supposed to have dinner tonight. I'm planning on telling him then. I'm sure it will be a super fun conversation."

Maggie nodded and went back to fiddling with her phone. Lara would have preferred to see the doctor on her own, but her friend didn't believe she'd follow through. Going against Maggie's advice, Lara had conducted extensive online research using the latest Web Doctor app powered by artificial intelligence and diagnosed herself with all sorts of deadly illnesses. This had only increased her dread about the visit to the doctor's office.

The thin paper gown brushed lightly against her skin and crackled softly with every movement. It was tied tightly behind her back, but cool air from the vents seeped between the cracks, making her hair stand on end. Goosebumps sprang up all over her arms, and Lara rubbed her hands up and down them, the bumpy texture making her want to scratch. Her legs shivered as they dangled over the edge of the table. The paper cover underneath her crinkled as she shifted. She'd already put a rip in the side of the gown and was holding it shut with her right arm.

Lara swung her legs in circles, partly to keep warm, but also to release her nervous energy. Beyond the TV screen, the room was dull and uninteresting.

At the Washington Medical Center for veterans, the evaluation rooms only contained the bare essentials—a standard examination table, a folding chair for sitting, a scale, a countertop with shelves for storage, and a stool for the doctor. A few health-related posters decorated the remaining white walls. The slate blue linoleum floor was clean, but it had seen better years. When they'd first arrived, the smell of disinfectant seemed to permeate everything, but she was beginning to get used to it.

Her eyes drifted involuntarily to the wide array of medical supplies on the counter of the shelving unit—several boxes of different-sized latex gloves, syringes, cotton balls, hand sanitizer, a jar of tongue depressors, and a reflex hammer. A disposal container for used needles with a biohazard symbol stood in the corner of the unit. A plastic tray lined with a cloth lay on the edge of the counter; it held a pair of latex gloves, a set of labeled collection tubes, several needles and syringes, and a rubber tourniquet.

Ugh. I know what that's for.

Lara shuddered at the thought of the pin prick. She dreaded every type of medical test, especially those that involved sharp objects. When she considered what she'd seen on the battlefield, her fear of doctors made no sense. Even a simple blood draw caused her a bout of heightened anxiety. Without any other explanation, Lara traced it back to the loss of her parents in a car accident. She'd spent several weeks as a young girl sitting next to her father's hospital bed, waiting for him to wake up from a coma.

Doctors always bring terrible news.

Maggie groaned and looked away from her phone.

"What?" Lara asked, eager for a distraction.

Shaking her head in disbelief, Maggie said, "This is a complete nightmare. My boss wants to meet my parents when they come for their visit. He requested that I reach out to them on his behalf."

"And I'm assuming you already asked your parents?" Lara asked.

Maggie nodded. "Yeah. And surprise, surprise. They're not at all interested. They said and I quote: 'It would be a complete waste of our time to meet with him.' They won't even do it as a favor to me." She paused for a moment and wiped something from her eye. "Now I have to give my boss the bad news. The bloke's gonna give me hell for it."

Sheesh. Family really sucks sometimes. It never ceased to amaze Lara how people could waste their limited precious time on earth neglecting things that truly mattered—like showing support for an only daughter.

"Mags, I'm really sorry," Lara said. Just then, her own smartphone buzzed with a text from Finn.

CAN'T MAKE DINNER TONIGHT
HAVE TO WORK LATE
RAINCHECK?

Lara groaned.

"What?" Maggie asked.

"Finn's working late again." Lara rolled her eyes. "Looks like I'm not going to tell him after all."

There was a soft rap at the door before it opened. Dr. Inaya

Saifi walked in with a broad smile, a stethoscope around her neck, and an electronic tablet in her hand. The petite Indian woman was always smiling with her eyes. Nothing could shake her sunny and good-natured disposition. Not even Lara's stubborn resistance to medical treatment.

The doctor gave Maggie a brief nod and then approached Lara on the table.

"I see you brought reinforcements this time," Dr. Saifi said, smiling warmly at Lara. She glanced down at her tablet, running her finger up and down the touchscreen. After a few seconds, her smile morphed into a concerned look. "In August, you came to see me and reported feeling unusually fatigued and lightheaded at times. You're still experiencing those symptoms?" She pointed to the screen as the date of Lara's last visit, her previous vitals, and a description of her symptoms appeared on the TV screen.

Lara nodded. "I've paid close attention to my diet. I've been eating more protein, making sure I get enough iron, and drinking plenty of water."

Dr. Saifi typed rapidly on her tablet as Lara spoke. "The nurse robot indicated you've been having nosebleeds and lost consciousness for quite a long time yesterday?" She scrolled up on the tablet to review the notes.

Lara shrugged her shoulders. "I was training my dog in the sun in the morning. Maybe I suffered from a bit of heatstroke. I looked it up online. I definitely had many of the symptoms—a throbbing headache, lightheadedness, and rapid heartbeat. I read that heatstroke can sometimes lead to loss of consciousness."

Just call me Dr. Kingsley. Lara suppressed a snarky smile.

Maggie looked up from her phone and narrowed her eyes at her.

Dr. Saifi grunted, put the stethoscope in her ears, and placed the cold diaphragm on Lara's chest. "What was her temperature yesterday after her fainting episode?"

Lara opened her mouth to answer the question until she

realized it wasn't directed at her. She pressed her lips together, her brow furrowing into a scowl.

Oh great. Now the real doctors are going to gang up on me.

Maggie cleared her throat. "Her temperature was slightly elevated, but not as much as I'd expect for a case of heatstroke. Plus, the outside temperatures hovered around forty-eight degrees that morning, hardly the typical conditions for heatstroke."

"I'm inclined to agree," Dr. Saifi said.

"But I did have a fever," Lara said, a defensive ring to her tone. "Maybe I didn't drink enough water?"

Dr. Saifi nodded, taking Lara's blood pressure. "It is definitely possible to pass out after experiencing high temperatures. The good news is your urine test didn't show any white blood cells and indicated good hydration. No obvious signs of infection."

"And the bad news?" Lara asked.

Dr. Saifi tapped her finger on her lips. "What troubles me are the bloody noses and fainting spells. There were also some traces of blood in your urine. The nurse robot indicated you experienced prior waves of dizziness and fatigue?" She peered at Lara's chart on the tablet. "And you collapsed another time about a week ago?"

Lara waved her hand dismissively. "That one was because of simulator sickness. I don't think these incidents are related."

Dr. Saifi shifted her gaze to Maggie, who shook her head. "That's certainly a possibility," she said, smiling.

Lara nodded in affirmation. *See. I knew it.*

"But highly unlikely," she added.

Lara sighed, her shoulders sinking.

"How have you been feeling since I last saw you?" Dr. Saifi asked.

Lara looked up at the ceiling, trying to recall the past month or so. "Well, I've been tired a lot lately, but I think it's mostly stress from not working."

"Stress from not working?" Dr. Saifi asked, chuckling. "I've heard about stress from working too much… but usually not the other way around."

Lara wrinkled her forehead. "I've been anxious about what to do with my life. I can't seem to get any work for my business. My boyfriend is pressuring me to do what he wants, but I'm not sure if it's what I want. Something has to change, but I'm not sure what."

Did I just call Finn my boyfriend?

Maggie looked up from her smartphone and grimaced at Lara.

Well, he is a boy… and my friend. What else am I supposed to call him?

She and Finn had yet to declare exclusive status. At the rate they had been bickering lately about Rob, they were more likely to break up than go steady.

A few moments of silence hung in the air. Another gust of cold air assaulted her from above. Lara waited on pins and needles for another question, but Dr. Saifi gazed at the tablet with increased intensity. "What do you know about your genetic history? Did your parents suffer from any health conditions you know of?"

"They died when I was eight. I have a few boxes of their stuff and recall seeing one or two marked medical, but I haven't gone through them yet. Maybe there's some information about their health. Did you find something in my DNA?" Lara asked, trying to see over the rim of the tablet.

"Hmm… I ran your latest DNA profile through our new diagnostic machine learning tool, which detects gene mutations and other genetic defects. The analysis of your genome produced some interesting biomarkers that I would like to investigate further."

Interesting? I don't like the sound of that.

An image of her DNA analysis flashed onto the video screen. Dr. Saifi pointed to several areas on the chart.

"What are biomarkers?" Lara asked, squinting at the screen, unable to make sense of what she was seeing. To her, it looked more like a timeline with random peaks and numerical identifiers.

"They are potential signs of abnormal conditions. Biomarkers are not definitive indicators of any disease or illness, but they are definitely something we want to look into further. They might be saying something important about your current and future health."

Future health? Shouldn't we just worry about the present first?

Lara's eyes widened, and she pulled back, staring at the needle on the counter. "What do you mean by look into?"

Dr. Saifi placed the tablet on the counter and crossed her arms. "First, I'd like to run a test to make sure your blood counts are in good order. My only human nurse is tied up at the moment, and we've received too many complaints about blood draws from the nurse robot. So, you're stuck with me today." She smiled broadly.

Lara winced, her pulse speeding up. *I knew it. She's going to take my blood.*

"I'd also like to do another round of whole-genome sequencing to analyze your full DNA sequence." Dr. Saifi turned toward the counter and reached for the pair of small latex gloves.

Lara's eyes widened. "But you already have my entire genome on file. And I've had a full sequence done every year since joining the military. What more can you learn?"

Dr. Saifi frowned. "By running another genome sequence, we may be able to detect some changes that are happening over time."

Lara shrank back. "Huh? Changes? I didn't realize my genome could change."

"The exact sequence of your DNA doesn't change much over time," Dr. Saifi said as she uncapped the needle of the syringe. "Changes to the DNA sequence of any living organism occur randomly and can accumulate as damage over time. For example, each time one of your cells divides, your genome is copied into the new cell. Sometimes mistakes are made during the copying process, and genetic mutations occur. Such changes can also happen when your cells repair damaged DNA. These types of changes are pretty rare."

"But then what's the point of sequencing my genome again if my DNA doesn't change for the most part?" Lara asked.

Dr. Saifi didn't miss a beat. "There are other aspects of our genomic data that can and do change quite a bit over the course of our lifetime."

"What sort of things?" Lara asked.

"Epigenetic changes can occur as a result of diet, environment, exposure to toxic substances, and of course, aging. Our environment and lifestyle can affect how our genes are expressed as traits—that is, what genes are turned on and off. These types of changes don't arise from genetic code but rather from other aspects of the chemical structure of DNA." Dr. Saifi paused to study Lara's face.

Lara wrinkled her nose. "My genes have on and off switches?"

Dr. Saifi took a deep breath. "You have two sets of genes. One set from each of your parents. Not all genes in your genome are expressed as traits at any given time. For example, even if you have brown eyes, you may still possess the genes that code for the trait of blue eyes. That means if you have children, you can pass on the genes for blue eyes to your kids even though you don't have that trait yourself. In other words, not all genes in your DNA are expressed as physical traits. Some of them are dormant. Does that make sense?"

Uhhh... maybe? Lara furrowed her brow. "But if my genome rarely changes, how does sequencing it again now help us?"

"We can observe epigenetic changes by examining the information layer on top of your DNA sequence, which contains tiny chemical tags. You see, your DNA is like the software code for your body, and the tags act as the operating system. The tags determine which genes or 'programs' are operational by switching them on or off. Some tags have positive effects, but others are mutations and can cause disease."

A lightbulb went off in Lara's head. "Does epigenetics account for differences in identical twins?"

Dr. Saifi gave her a broad smile. "Yes. Even though identical twins possess the same DNA code, they may exhibit significantly different phenotypes or traits. Especially if they grew up in different environments."

Lara nodded solemnly as Dr. Saifi tightened the tourniquet around her left arm. "Take a deep breath. You'll feel a slight prick," she said.

Lara winced as Dr. Saifi inserted the needle into her arm and began drawing blood. Lara hoped the test would prove what she already knew to be true. *I'm fine.*

Her smartphone buzzed again. Eagerly, she glanced down at her wrist to see a text from Rob:

AGENT CARTER FOUND SOMETHING BIG
HE WANTS US TO COME TO THE FBI
I'LL PICK YOU UP TOMORROW MORNING

ELEVEN

FBI Headquarters

October 3, 2028

THERE'S ACTUALLY A FULL-SERVICE STARBUCKS. Lara smirked and sipped her hot coffee, savoring the full-bodied hazelnut flavor. The FBI headquarters, with its bland and imposing facade made of poured concrete blocks, did not suggest the presence of modern amenities.

On the way inside, Lara had noticed some strange-looking netting lining the rooftop. Agent Carter explained the exterior of the building had fallen into a desperate state of disrepair. The upper floors were surrounded by safety netting to keep loose chunks of concrete from falling on the city streets below. And that was not the only structural problem.

The building's HVAC systems malfunctioned regularly, and water was seeping into the underground parking lot. Unfortunately, plans to build a new headquarters for the FBI had stalled for nearly two decades—they were tied up in the red tape of snail-paced bureaucracy and Beltway politics.

Across from her, Rob slurped his iced coffee through a straw like a kid. Lara had told him on more than one occasion how she felt about his love of straws.

Years ago, the D.C. Council had banned straws due to mass accumulations of plastic waste… until a company produced biodegradable straws from microbes in a lab. Lara wished the utensils had stayed dead. Rob wiggled his eyebrows at Lara and gave her a toothy grin in between drinks. She rolled her eyes, gave him a look of disapproval, and took another drink from her adult-appropriate cup.

"Did Agent Carter tell you what he found?" Lara asked, fidgeting with the smooth plastic lid.

Rob shook his head. "No, he didn't want to say anything specific over the phone. Only that he found sufficient evidence that would clear my name."

Lara gave him a half-smile.

That sounds promising.

She gripped her cup tightly in anticipation, putting a small dent in its side. It had been a long time since she'd seen Rob so hopeful. His persistent gloomy demeanor of late had her rather worried. She wasn't sure how he would cope with having his hopes dashed against the cliffs of disappointment yet again.

In the past year, Rob had suffered a few professional and personal disasters—his suspension and eventual dismissal from the FBI, his sudden breakup with Alexa, and the betrayal by his boss and friend, Harry Cogan.

And don't get me started on his dysfunctional family.

The interior of the FBI headquarters was mostly as she'd imagined it—a drab federal building packed with feds dressed in dark attire wearing short haircuts and stern expressions. After getting their escort-only badges, Agent Carter had taken them through the interior courtyard of the building where Lara encountered a pleasant surprise.

The ground level contained an outdoor seating area, complete with real grass. The soft splashing of a water fountain created a soothing undertone. Meanwhile, the second-floor mezzanine boasted a running track with green turf, apparently a popular spot for FBI agents who sought to squeeze in a midday workout. According to Agent Carter, the building also housed a two-story basketball court, a firing range, and a museum which highlighted the Bureau's many success stories. He promised them a tour if there was still time after they finished discussing the file.

I'd have to see it all to believe it.

Lara studied several groups of FBI agents huddled around the tables in the coffee shop, their chatter adding another layer of background noise. Some of them, most likely those who worked at headquarters, wore dark suits and had not removed their shades despite being indoors. Other agents with buzz cuts or tight buns wore tactical cargo pants, polo shirts, and navy FBI jackets. They were probably working in the field.

Despite the hot coffee, she shivered from the thought. *Anyone of them could be watching. Listening. Spying.*

"Are you sure it's a good idea to meet here?" Lara asked, wrinkling her nose. "We're right in the middle of the lion's den."

Rob looked around nervously. "Well, Carter didn't want to take the information outside the building. Meeting here is a much better idea than going up to his office. That is, if we want to avoid causing a scene with my former colleagues." He barked a laugh, not a small amount of bitterness revealed in his expression. "Now if I went up to my old floor? That would've definitely drawn some unwanted attention. The last thing we need is Harry figuring out we are coming after him."

"Wow. There must be some juicy information in that file," Lara said, pressing her lips together.

Rob nodded eagerly. "As soon as we're done, Carter plans to deliver it directly to the Director of the FBI for action. He says heads will roll for this." A grin appeared on his face.

Lara raised an eyebrow. "So, Agent Carter is finally willing to put his neck on the line?"

For the past several months, she'd held Agent Carter's lack of action on Rob's behalf against the kid. He was the only one who knew for sure that Harry had given the order to continue the surveillance operation on Sully. And he still wouldn't speak out.

He'd better come through for Rob, or I'll have words with him.

"He says the information is *that* good." Rob dipped his head toward the straw and took a drink, making a loud, sloppy sucking noise.

Ugh.

Lara glared at him. He slurped even louder and grinned at her mischievously.

"You don't think Harry would stop by for a coffee, do you?" Lara asked, her stomach fluttering at the notion.

"Nah, Harry hates Starbucks. He would never set foot in this place. He says their coffee is overpriced to attract yuppies, and it tastes like burned coffee beans."

He's kind of right.

Her eyes drifted to the pickup counter. Agent Carter stared down at his smartphone, waiting for his latte and tapping his foot on the floor. Lara's scalp tingled at the thought of what was inside the thick tan envelope under his arm. She wanted to run over, grab it from him, and tear it open. Wiping her clammy hands on her pants, she turned to eye the tables of FBI agents again.

Just then, the female barista slid a coffee toward the scowling Agent Carter, and Lara exhaled a sharp breath. Agent Carter grabbed the cup and marched over to their table.

"What took you so long?" Rob asked, rubbing his forehead.

"They messed up my order," Agent Carter said, grimacing as he pulled up a chair. "Not once but twice. It makes those automated machines look better all the time." He set the envelope on the table, took a long sip of his coffee, and then uttered an audible sound of satisfaction. "Wow. I really needed that."

"Are you going to show us what you found?" Rob asked, eagerness in his voice.

"Patience, grasshopper," Agent Carter muttered with a grin, pulling a thick file from the tan envelope and setting it on the table. The word *CyberShop* was scrawled across the top of the file folder.

Lara's heart sank when she recognized the writing. If she was not mistaken, it was the same folder the FBI evidence team had found while cleaning out Fiddler's laboratory.

The rogue scientist had gathered information on the drone show and CyberShop's activities to clear his daughter and son-in-law's names with the NSA. He'd paid a hefty nonrefundable deposit on the drones but reneged on the purchase. His sole request was that this folder of evidence be sent to the NSA.

A deeper pit formed in Lara's stomach as Agent Carter flipped it open. She recognized the first page. It was identical to the folder she'd already seen.

"Guys, this folder contains evidence of CyberShop's true identity as Justyne Marsh," Agent Carter said. "It also documents her involvement in providing stolen technology for the drone show."

Lara glanced at Rob's face as his hope dimmed, and she cringed.

"No paper trail on Harry?" Rob asked, a slight tremor in his voice. "But… we've seen this stuff before. You said…" His voice squeaked. "This is the exact folder I gave to Harry to send over to the NSA for Fiddler."

Agent Carter shook his head. "Nope. Not exactly the same. You might have seen the first several pages, but you definitely never saw the contents in the back of the folder. If you had, Rob, you'd still be working at the FBI. And Harry would be rotting in prison along with Justyne."

Lara sat up a bit straighter, placing her hands flat on the cool, hard surface of the table. "Let's just skip to the good stuff, then."

Agent Carter flipped past a few sections to a page of Sully's handwritten notes. When Lara saw the penmanship, she gasped out loud.

"Wait… that's Sully's handwriting." She read over the notes quickly, her eyes racing down the page. "These are his notes about his investigation into Harry Cogan."

Sully investigated Harry?

She glanced over at Rob. His mouth hung open in anticipation.

"What did he say about Harry?" Rob asked, his eyes bulging from his head.

"Sully knew about the FBI surveillance operation to monitor him. Harry was using the bugs to spy on Sully, but apparently, Sully knew all about them and used them to trick Harry."

Lara smiled to herself, her heart brimming with pride. *Sully outsmarted Harry.*

"Sully recorded every detail of Harry's movements and activities. He took many pictures as well," Agent Carter said. "Whenever Harry thought he was the one doing the stalking, sitting in his car outside Sully's townhouse, he was actually the one being tracked and photographed."

"But how?" Lara asked. "Harry would have known if Sully was inside the townhouse."

"According to his records, Sully used Fiddler's bionic bugs to follow Harry around, track him, and record him." Turning to Rob, Agent Carter added, "Do you remember how Harry talked about his wife and kids?"

Rob bobbed his head. "Yeah. Like all the time. And he had tons of photos all over his office and awards his kids had won."

"Well, based on Sully's records, Harry doesn't actually have a family," Agent Carter said, watching the shock form on Rob's face. "The home address he gave to the FBI? Fake."

Rob scratched his head. "But how—"

"Well, not exactly fake. He owned the house, and it looked inside like a real family lived in it. But it was all for show and a complete sham. Harry really lives in a one-bedroom apartment in Crystal City. He was leading a double life to hide his illicit activities. And Sully and Fiddler had it all figured out."

Lara and Rob exchanged spirited looks. This was better than either of them could have ever imagined.

"The rest of the file provides photographic and transcript evidence of meetings between Harry and D.C. Council members where he offered them bribes to support the drone show. There are also conversations between Harry and Linda Maxwell where they planned their next steps. Sully's investigation was thorough enough to put Harry away for years, if not the rest of his life."

"Any pictures of Harry with Justyne?" Lara asked.

"No. Harry appears to never have met with Justyne in person. At least, Sully didn't catch them in a meeting. Maybe they used Linda as the middleman to hide the connection."

Lara cleared her throat. "Middlewoman."

Agent Carter's face flushed slightly. "Of course, my mistake. Linda received the drone shipment at her warehouse, installed the encryption scatter devices on the drones, and launched them on the night of the drone show."

"Huh. I always wondered how Harry produced the drone swarm out of thin air. But I'm still confused," Rob said, his palm on his forehead. "Why would Fiddler send only a partial folder of information for delivery to the NSA? Why didn't he send the whole file with the parts implicating Harry?" He paused for a moment, his face sinking into further confusion.

Lara wrinkled her forehead. "Yeah, I don't understand why Fiddler didn't send over all the information he had."

"Maybe he was keeping it in his back pocket for some reason?" Agent Carter asked.

Still perplexed, Rob asked, "Carter, where in the world did you find this folder?"

Agent Carter flipped over the envelope to show them the postmark and the addressee. Rob's face went pale when he saw the envelope was addressed to him at the FBI.

"This file was sent to your attention less than a month ago," Agent Carter said.

The file was sent to Rob?

"Oh. Whoever sent it didn't know I was fired several months ago… so it never made it to me. How the hell—"

Agent Carter smiled broadly. "I found it in the mail room in a box of undelivered mail."

"You looked in the mail room?" Rob gaped at him, a look of awe in his eyes.

"Well, I was getting desperate. I tried finding evidence of Harry's involvement in our file room and on the servers. But I kept coming up empty. Harry must have done a thorough sweep of electronic and hard copy files. The mail room was the only place Harry wouldn't have looked. So, I checked it. You see, Harry saw the folder Fiddler sent over and thought he already knew everything Fiddler had found. And that's where he made his fatal mistake. He didn't realize that Sully and Fiddler had run a thorough investigation into his activities and not disclosed the information."

"But why would Fiddler send this to me several months after the fact?" Rob asked, a dumbfounded look on his face. "And how could he send it from prison at all?"

"Well, I don't think he sent it," Agent Carter said.

Rob scratched his temple.

"The clue is in the postmark," Agent Carter said, tapping his finger on the red stamp. "This was mailed from a post office near Foggy Bottom. Of course, we know Fiddler wasn't able to mail anything from there."

"His daughter, Anita Fiddler, has her medical practice in the neighborhood," Lara said.

Agent Carter nodded quickly. "Exactly. I haven't been able to track her down to confirm it, but it seems to be a safe guess that Anita sent the folder."

"Is there anything in this file about BlackDragon?" Lara asked, her pulse twitching.

Agent Carter frowned. "Not that I recall… though I did find one interesting photo at the back of the file. Maybe that's related to your Black Dragon." He flipped through the pages and pulled out a photo of a regal Chinese man dressed in a black trench coat. Another Chinese man, stocky and tattooed, stood next to him.

What?

Lara's mouth fell open. "That man was my last client, Mr.

Zhang. And the other man is Hai Xu, who ended up killing him. Hai was an operative of the Chinese PLA, and he was trying to get access to the same technology as Harry." Lara studied the photo closely. In the background, there was a blurry image of a Chinese woman with long black hair, probably in her forties.

Who is she?

Rob's eyes widened. "Didn't you work the case for Mr. Zhang long after Sully was dead?"

Lara nodded numbly.

Sully knew about Mr. Zhang?

"Do you think there's a connection between Harry and Mr. Zhang?" Rob asked.

"When was this photo taken?" Lara asked, flipping it over to see if it had a date stamp, but there wasn't any stamp or handwritten notes.

"Sully didn't mention the photo in his notes," Agent Carter said. "That's why I found it odd. Sully was otherwise so thorough with his investigation."

"Maybe he wasn't finished with this part," Lara said.

"Well, well, well... lookie, lookie who we have here..." a gruff voice called out from behind them. "My favorite ex-employee, his ambitious ex-girlfriend, and... of course. Agent Carter." The voice was laced with spite.

"Harry Cogan... good to see you, too." Rob's tone was neutral, but his face was grim.

Agent Carter looked up, his eyes widening and his face turning ashen. For a moment, he seemed paralyzed and uncertain about what to do. Without hesitating, Lara flipped over the envelope, shoved the notes and photos into the folder, and slapped it shut.

Was I fast enough?

A lump formed in Lara's throat as he moved into full view, Harry's lips twisting into a malicious smile. Then her heart nearly stopped.

He's the man from the black sedan. Harry has been following me. But why?

Harry's black, beady eyes stood out against his thick gray hair and bushy gray beard. He wore the customary navy suit over a white starched button-down shirt with his FBI badge clipped to his belt.

Lara rose from her seat. "We were just about to get going."

"I don't think so, sweetheart," Harry said, placing a strong hand on her shoulder and pushing her back down into her seat. He stood with a wide stance, one by one looking each of them squarely in the eye. "Since you're all here, I'd like to deliver a message from my big boss." His voice was husky and low enough so that no one else could hear him over the chatter. "If you'd like to keep your body parts intact and your hearts beating, and I mean all of you." He stopped and made direct eye contact with Agent Carter. "Whatever evidence you think you've found on me, you'll let it go."

"You think we're scared of your empty threats?" Lara asked, snarling at him.

Rob shook his head subtly, signaling to her to back down.

Harry took a step closer, towering over her, and winked at her, his lip curled. "Lara, you of all people must know my threats are not empty."

What does that mean?

"Please give Sanchez kind regards from his favorite dirty cop. Tell him he'll have to nail his colors to the mast before he ever gets the chance to nail me to the wall." Without saying another word, he turned on his heels and left the coffee shop, a cockiness in his step that gave Lara a chill.

Didn't Sanchez call Harry a dirty cop yesterday and say something about nailing him?

Rob stared at her, his face full of panic and unable to speak.

Lara's lip quivered. *Did Harry bug my townhouse?*

Agent Carter sank in his seat, nearly despondent. "We're so fucked."

TWELVE

Adoption Agency

Lara stood next to Sanchez in the lobby of Miracle Springs Eternal Adoption Agency, clutching a notarized letter which gave them permission to access any files related to the Langstons' adopted daughter. Her mind still raced from her visit to the FBI and the tense encounter with Harry earlier that day.

I don't get it. Why would Harry be following me?

"Dr. Pulido will be with you in just a few minutes," the receptionist said before rushing down the hallway and out of sight.

"Harry Cogan threatened you?" Sanchez whispered loudly. "And he wants to send me a message?" He puffed out his chest. "I'll send him a fucking message."

"Shhhh." Lara looked over her shoulder to make sure no one could overhear before responding. "That's not all. He bugged my townhouse and knows everything we've been planning thus far. Rob has already found three bugs on the first floor and is busy searching the rest of the house as we speak. Hopefully, we get them all."

"Cogan is definitely playing fast and loose," Sanchez said. "Gotta wonder what his endgame is…" The detective paused for a moment, as if he were considering the potential angles. "Anyway, he's bound to make a mistake. We'll get him when he does."

Lara grinned from ear to ear. "Oh, he's already made a mistake. Harry doesn't even realize he's overplayed his hand."

"You think Agent Carter will hand that file over to the FBI Director?" Sanchez gave her a skeptical look.

Lara nodded. "Oh yes. He texted Rob early this morning. Chimbo, an old buddy of theirs, works as a special assistant in the director's office. He promised to give the file to the director as soon as he gets in the office. It's only a matter of time before Harry has to face the music."

"I hope so… for Rob's sake," Sanchez said absentmindedly, his dark eyes focused on the screen of his smartphone. "God knows, we have our hands full with the Langstons." After a few moments, he cleared his throat. "By the way, we checked the paper butterfly for fingerprints. There was a partial that matched Molly. You were right."

And Loki found the clue. A surge of pride came over her.

"Any word on the babysitter? We need to talk to her."

Sanchez shook his head. "Still in Poland."

Very convenient.

He looked over at her, an eyebrow raised. "I just forwarded you Molly's genome in an encrypted email."

"Uh huh…" Lara stared back at the detective expectantly.

"Um… I was wondering if you could do whatever you did last time."

Lara shot him a baffled look. "What are you talking about?"

"Remember how you figured out Gavin's identity from the DNA on the cigarette butt? I was hoping you might work your magic again."

Now if only I had a magic wand.

"Magic?" Lara suppressed a groan.

A slight flush crept up the detective's neck. "Couldn't you just look up her profile in that public database Vik used last time?"

Lara sighed heavily. "I'm not sure that will be of much help here. We were trying to find out who the DNA belonged to by tracking distant relatives in an online public genealogy database. But we already know the DNA sample belongs to Molly."

"What if she has distant relatives in the United States or something?" Sanchez asked.

Lara rubbed her chin. "Good point. It couldn't hurt to check. I can have Vik take a look when he gets back from his honeymoon." A pang of guilt irked her when she thought about the unanswered texts from Vik.

I can't tell him about my illness over text.

A glass door whooshed open at the end of the hallway, and a young Latina woman in her thirties with striking features, long, smooth, dark brown hair, and bronze skin strode toward them, her heels clicking sharply on the tile floor. High cheekbones and shapely black eyebrows framed her large, brown eyes. She wore a white lab coat over an indigo blue sheath dress and a curvy figure.

Sanchez threw his hand out eagerly to greet her, smiling a bit too broadly. Lara stifled a sigh and fidgeted with her jacket.

The woman smiled slightly and extended her hand to the detective and then to Lara. "I'm Dr. Josephina Pulido, but you may call me Josie." Her grip was firm and confident. She motioned for them to follow her into the office at the end of the hallway. "My receptionist told me about Molly going missing. Obviously, I want to do whatever I can to assist you in your search," she said, holding the door open for Lara and Sanchez.

Moments later, Josie sank into her office chair behind a charcoal gray steel desk as Lara took a seat in a black leather chair next to Sanchez. The chair itself was small and modern, the frame creaking a bit as Lara settled. Burning incense on her desk gave off a musky sweet scent, sending a thin line of smoke curling upward. The morning light shone through the large panel windows on the right side of the office and reflected off many shiny surfaces. The sheer glass walls made Lara feel like she was in a fish bowl.

As Lara made herself comfortable, her eyes darted up to the exposed brick wall behind Josie. A giant oil painting with an eye-catching texture caught her attention. When she focused her vision, she recognized a fluffy white sheep with bright blue eyes on a bold orange background.

A painting of a sheep? That's odd.

Josie leaned forward, and the corners of her lips turned downward. "I'm not sure how I can help you. I haven't talked to the Langstons since Molly was a toddler."

Lara glanced at Josie's impressive academic credentials, an M.D. from Tufts University. It was framed and positioned on the corner of her desk, facing them. The diploma caused a question to pop into Lara's head. "Why did you decide to work at an adoption agency and not a hospital?"

Josie flashed her a knowing smile, as if she'd been asked that question before. "This is not your typical adoption agency. We not only service high-end adoptions, we also run a state-of-the-art in vitro fertilization center." She reached into her desk, pulled out a full-color brochure, and handed it to Lara. "With my specialization in reproductive endocrinology, I spend most of my time helping my clients have their own babies—naturally or by design. Basically, whatever our clients want in a baby, they can get it here. They can pick from thousands of combinations of traits."

Lara gaped at the brochure for a few moments, her mouth hanging open. The front cover showed a picture-perfect white baby boy with fair skin, blond hair, and blue eyes. Surrounding the picture, several words were scattered—high IQ, 20/20 vision, no baldness, perfect pitch, legs of a sprinter. She'd heard about people having designer babies in the news but had no idea it was possible to choose every detail.

"People can choose any traits they want?" Sanchez asked, a look of disbelief forming on his face.

Josie smiled as if on cue. "That's the power of genomic data. After sequencing the genomes of the entire U.S. population back in 2025 and ever since, that data has been stored in the National Genomic Data Repository. Using this database, scientists have performed advanced data analytics with machine learning and made major breakthroughs in identifying sets of genes that code for complex traits."

Lara raised her eyebrow. "How do you go about customizing a baby?"

Josie put her hair behind her ears. "There are two ways to choose the traits of offspring. We've done genetic mapping for decades for clients using in vitro fertilization to have children. We extract the eggs, retrieve a sperm sample, and combine each egg with the sperm in a petri dish to create a batch of embryos. Then we compare the genetic maps of parents and embryos. As the first order of business, we exclude all genetic disorders. Then we can choose traits by screening the embryos for them. The selected embryo is then transferred to the uterus for gestation and birth. Of course, this method is limited to the genetic information provided by both parents. If my clients want full customization, we can also use genetic modification techniques."

Like Fiddler did with the bionic bugs?

Lara furrowed her brow. "How is that different from genetic mapping?"

"Well, the sky is the limit with gene editing. We can create any combination of traits desired by parents. Plus, any genetic changes we create would be passed on to offspring, changing the hereditary future of a family. It's called germline engineering."

"Sounds like tampering with the gene pool to me," Sanchez said, a deep frown forming on his troubled face.

More like creating a different class of people... destined to be superhumans.

"But I thought germline engineering was illegal in the United States," Lara said.

"It was until last year. U.S. Congress passed legislation allowing IVF clinics with private funding to engage in germline engineering. Policymakers were afraid of China getting too far ahead of the curve and developing super soldiers or a fully enhanced population. Clinics with federal funding are still prohibited from getting into the game. Since we get all our research funding from private donors, our clinic is only one of two in the entire country that can provide these services."

"How much does it cost?" Lara asked, trying to hide her disgust.

"Standard IVF still costs around fifteen to twenty thousand dollars. Germline editing currently costs over one hundred thousand dollars, but I expect the price to come down as we finesse the technology and procedures over time."

The detective grunted. "Well, that's just great. Only the filthy rich can afford to buy designer babies at those prices. Why not give the wealthy more fucking advantages?" His face turned a light shade of pink, and his fists were clenched.

The doctor's mouth dropped a bit as if she were lost for words. She looked from Sanchez to Lara and back again.

Oh great. Here we go…

"Were you working here when Molly was adopted?" Lara asked, quickly changing the subject before Sanchez lost his cool.

Josie cleared her throat, nodded, and smoothed out her expression. "Yes, I was. Back then, I was working part time as an assistant in the IVF clinic. Of course, the director handled the adoption, and I don't recall any of the details. Several other infants besides Molly were adopted at the same time from the same village in China. We placed them all in amazing families."

Several infants?

Sanchez and Lara locked eyes, exchanging what-the-hell looks.

"Who was the director when Molly was adopted?" Lara asked, turning the page in her notebook.

"His name was Dr. Liam Nilsson."

"Do you have his contact information?" Lara asked.

Josie opened her desk drawer and flipped through a Rolodex. Then she handed Lara a card with his name, a phone number, and an email address.

"Great, thanks," Lara said, tucking the card in her jacket pocket. "Could you look up Molly's adoption file for us?"

"Of course." Josie turned to the LED screen on her desk and woke it up.

A holographic keyboard shined onto the surface of the steel desk, and Josie began typing, her fingers producing a dull thump with each letter. Lara watched as she opened up the adoption center database and entered Molly's name. A profile appeared on the screen.

Staring at the screen, Josie said, "I remember that Molly was abandoned at the side of the road as an infant. She was adopted from an orphanage in the countryside about an hour outside of Shenzhen, China, but her record doesn't list the name of the orphanage here..." She scrolled up and down on the screen. "Huh. That's strange. There's also no info on her birth or adoption in her file." Josie clicked a button and frowned when nothing happened.

"What's wrong?" Lara asked.

Josie's frown deepened. "Molly's profile is listed in the database, and I can pull up her basic metadata, but there's nothing further on her. When I try to access her complete file, there's nothing there. It's like it doesn't even exist. Maybe someone forgot to enter the information." After staring blankly at the screen for a few moments, Josie rose from her chair and walked over to the steel filing cabinets behind her desk. "No matter... we should have a paper copy on hand." Bending over to open the drawer marked with an *L*, she said, "Luckily, we were still keeping hard copies of our files back then. We stopped doing that five years ago. I'll just pull her file for you."

She dug through the filing cabinet, paused, closed the drawer, and opened another one. After a few moments, she gave up. "That's weird."

"What?" Sanchez asked, his eyes narrowing.

Josie's face paled slightly. "The hard copy file isn't here. It must have gone missing."

Sanchez and Lara exchanged wary looks.

Then someone must have taken it.

"You said earlier that your agency brought over several infants from the same orphanage," Lara said. "Do you remember names of the other families?"

Josie folded her arms across her chest and blinked at her. "Unfortunately, I can't look up files of other clients. We have to protect their privacy."

"I'm not asking you to reveal their personal information. But if you could remember their names, we could ask them a few questions."

Josie stared at the ceiling, her face scrunched with concentration. "Off the top of my head, I can only remember one name. The Jackson family adopted an infant around the same time as the Langstons. I think the girl's name was Chen Ling. They live in the D.C. area as well. Maybe the Langstons know them." She glanced at her watch and rose from her chair. "I'm really sorry to cut this short, but my next clients are due to arrive in a few minutes."

As Lara and Sanchez got up from their seats and made their way to the door, the colorful artwork hanging from the brick wall caught her attention again.

"Why do you have a large painting of a sheep in your office?" Lara asked, following Josie down the hallway.

"Oh that?" Josie turned to Lara and smiled, appearing relieved. "That's a painting of Dolly. It belonged to Dr. Nilsson. He donated it to the clinic, and since I like the colors, I left it hanging there."

"Dolly?" Lara asked.

"You know… the first cloned sheep back in 1995."

"Ah… yes, I recall reading about that at some point. Whatever happened to her?"

"She had six offspring but died prematurely of lung disease six years after her birth. Back then, clones still suffered from shortened lifespans. However, the science of cloning has come a long way after breakthroughs in China to lengthen telomeres."

Telomeres?

Lara was about to ask another question when Josie turned to them, said her goodbyes, shook their hands, and hurried back down the hallway. Both Lara and Sanchez made their way outside, stuck in a somber trance. For a few moments, they stood on the front stoop.

Sanchez muttered under his breath, "This place gives me the creeps."

"Me too," Lara said, pulling on her sunglasses to hide her eyes from the afternoon sun. She was about to begin unpacking the information they'd learned when her phone rang. She glanced at the screen.

"Hi Rob," she answered. "What's up?"

There was heavy breathing on the other end. "The folder. Went. Missing."

"What?" Her stomach tightened into knots, and her pulse began to race.

"Lara, it's gone," Rob said, his voice trembling. "The FBI Director never saw it. It disappeared into thin air."

This can't be happening.

Lara clutched her stomach. "But I thought you said Agent Carter gave it to Chimbo for direct delivery to the director."

"Chimbo said he put it on the director's desk but doesn't know what happened to it after that. Should have never trusted that idiot with such an important task. Listen, Lara, I'm at the office and a complete wreck. I've removed all the bugs, but gotta go home."

"Wait," Lara said, her mind spinning. "Uh… let's regroup. Meet me at Sully's storage unit tomorrow morning. We've yet to dig through all his files. Maybe we'll find something. You remember where it is?"

Time to find out what's in those boxes.

"Yeah. I can be there around nine."

"I've got an appointment with my therapist first thing in the morning, at half-past eight. But I'll get there right away afterwards. The storage unit key is in the ceramic pot on my desk in the office. You can get started without me, okay?"

"Copy that," Rob said before hanging up.

Detective Sanchez rocked back on his heels and crossed his arms. "We're gonna have to raise our game to beat this slime ball."

Amateur hour is definitely over.

THIRTEEN

Sully's Files

____

October 4, 2028

"I CAN'T BELIEVE that file went missing at the FBI." A dull thud sounded as Rob kicked the filing cabinet. He rose from his metal chair and began pacing in a tight circle, avoiding the stacks of files on the floor he'd already searched. "That was my ticket to getting my job back and getting justice."

Yeah. We should never have met in public.

Lara rubbed her forehead. "Harry must have taken action to ensure the folder didn't reach the director."

Or was Chimbo somehow involved in its disappearance?

Rob returned to the filing cabinet and flipped hastily through a stack of papers in one of Sully's files. After a few moments, he tossed it onto the cement floor of Sully's old storage unit, causing several slips of paper to fly into the air and float to the ground. Slumping onto the metal chair, Rob crossed his arms and glared sullenly at his feet.

A few feet away, Loki busied himself with a fresh bone on his dog bed, paying no attention to the sudden chaos around him.

For once, my holy terror of a puppy is staying out of trouble.

"How did Harry know we'd be at the Starbucks?" Rob asked, throwing up his hands.

Lara shrugged. "I don't know. Maybe someone tipped him off. Maybe he overheard something at the townhouse with the bugs. Harry has been a few steps ahead of us from the beginning."

Rob grunted.

Lara's own metal folding chair creaked as she shifted around. Staring at the unmitigated mess in the storage unit, she suppressed a groan. For the past few hours, Rob been desperately searching for evidence linking his former boss to Justyne or MacFarlan. After several heated exchanges, Lara had given up helping and left him to do the work on his own.

Instead, she'd been forced to sort through the leftover boxes of stuff from her parents. She attempted to steady her breathing before diving into the next one. She would have preferred to keep the boxes sealed shut for eternity, but now she needed information—old health records or some hints about her medical past.

Ever since her visit to the doctor, she couldn't stop worrying about what tragic fate might befall her at any moment. She tried her best to hold it together while reading through old, dusty files and parsing through her childhood memories for any signs of illness in her parents. Thankfully, Rob was too distracted to notice the tears welling in her eyes or the loud sniffling.

"This is the first time you've opened those boxes?" Rob asked, his forehead creased.

He noticed.

"Well, I didn't have them until a few months ago," Lara said, frowning. "The son of the executor from my parents' estate called up and said he'd found a painting along with a few boxes of records, while cleaning out the closet in his father's old office. Apparently, his father forgot to deliver them to me after my parents died. And now he's dead, too." Lara pointed to the painting wrapped in packing paper against the wall. "That painting was the only material possession leftover after their estate was liquidated to settle their debts. I didn't think they'd left me anything."

"And you weren't the least bit curious?"

Lara looked away, struggling to suppress another round of tears. "Why should I care about the past? My parents are dead and not coming back any time soon."

"But don't you want to know about them?" Rob asked, staring at her in disbelief. "I dunno… if I were you, I'd want to soak up every tiny piece of information."

Lara pressed her lips together. "I don't like to dwell on the past, okay?"

"Lara, it's not about dwelling on the past. This is about the present. Your parents are part of you. If you close that off, you—"

"Oh please… you sound like my therapist this morning," Lara said. "You know what? You can both go cry me a fucking river. I'm sick and tired of hearing about how I'm not coping properly or how I'm holding myself back." She threw up her hands. "From what? From the pain of their loss? From my complete isolation on the planet? My decisions about how to manage my feelings don't change the fact that they're gone from my life forever. Nothing will change that. Nothing will change that I'm utterly alone."

His eyes shiny with moisture, Rob remained silent, his face scrunched up as if he wanted to say something but held back.

"I'm doing the best I can, okay?" Lara added, sniffing hard and touching her nose to see if it was bleeding. A drop of red on her finger made her stomach sink.

"You okay?" Rob asked as a look of concern replaced the grimace on his face.

"I'm fine," Lara growled back. She was growing tired of being treated like a delicate flower. It wasn't very helpful, and it made her even more anxious about the test results.

"Are you sure? You do look a bit pale."

Lara clenched her teeth. "I said I'm fine."

Rob shrank back slightly. "Lara, we're not trying to cramp

your style. Can't you see we're all worried about you?" He was silent for a moment. "When are you going to hear back from the doctor?"

She balled her fists and glared at him. "Like I said yesterday, I'll hear back when the test results come in." Her tone was sharp, and she hoped he got the message.

Several moments of tense silence fell between them.

"So... how's the missing persons case going?" Rob asked, awkwardly changing the subject.

Lara sighed heavily. "Terrible. We have zero leads. No apparent motive. Almost no evidence. And we've heard nothing from the kidnapper."

"Any next steps?" Rob asked with an optimistic note.

"Not really. But Sanchez and I visited the adoption agency yesterday and picked up some strange vibes."

"How so?"

Lara crossed her arms. "The agency doesn't just help wealthy people adopt babies under suspicious circumstances. The in vitro clinic also allows people to pick out their biological baby's traits."

"You mean like design your own baby?" Rob asked, his face going slack.

"Yep. Apparently, Congress lifted the ban on germline engineering. So now rich people will get to buy superkids for thousands of dollars, and babies born naturally will be stuck being second-class citizens."

"Did you discover any useful information about Molly?" Rob asked.

Lara snorted. "Ha. We got next to nothing. Somehow, all of Molly's files have gone missing."

"Well, that's something, isn't it?" Rob asked.

She scratched her temple.

"Lara, read between the lines. Someone is trying to hide the truth about Molly's origins. That sounds like a giant clue to me."

"Possibly. Or it could just be colossal ineptitude on the agency's part. Sanchez and I will do our best to track down leads, but it's nearly impossible to get reliable information on organizations in China. At this point, we're dangerously close to a cold case. Unless the tip hotline turns up new information, we've got nothing."

Maybe I should give Hickerson a call.

"How's Finn these days?" Rob smirked.

"He's fine," Lara answered flatly, her gaze flicking upwards.

"Did you tell him you might be dying?" Rob asked, giving her a playful grin.

Lara rolled her eyes, recalling the tense conversation she'd had with Finn over the phone after her therapist's appointment that morning. "Yeah, I told him about my symptoms and the tests the doctor is running. But Sanchez had already beat me to the punch and told him about the fainting spell at the crime scene and the doctor's visit."

"Oof. I bet Finn was none too happy with you."

"That's a gross understatement. But he got over it pretty quickly when I reminded him how busy he's been."

Rob flashed her a mischievous smile. "I can't believe Finn let you come here... to spend time with me alone... in this small, cozy space. You never know what could happen..."

Lara cocked her head and then shook it slowly. "You certainly don't make things easy on him." Relaxing her shoulders, she let out a huge breath. "But for once, Finn is actually glad you're keeping an eye on me. He's picking me up in a bit, and we're going on a date. He promised not to make a scene when he arrives. I guess being perceived as an invalid has perks after all."

Rob chuckled. "He really needs to get over himself."

She said nothing, not wanting to start another argument. Instead, she stooped down to grab the last folder from the bottom of the cardboard box and placed it in her lap. Her head swirled in response to the quick movement. Breathing deeply, she held herself perfectly still and waited for the feeling to go away.

Okay, that's better.

She glanced down at the file, making slower movements to avoid stirring up her nausea. The folder was several inches thick and jammed with newspaper clippings and journal articles. When she opened it, several loose papers fell out and floated to the ground. She was about to reach down for them when the words on the first paper on her lap stood out like a neon sign.

Her body went rigid as she scanned the contents of the article. It was a scientific piece about blood disorders and gene mutations. Her father's handwritten notes filled the margins. At the top of the article, he'd starred his own question: *Do gene mutations cause inherited aplastic anemia?*

When she looked up, Rob was staring at her and rubbing the back of his neck. "What's wrong?" he asked.

"I found an article about aplastic anemia with handwritten notes in my dad's papers. It's a serious blood disorder caused by the bone marrow failing to produce normal amounts of red blood cells." Her head pounded harder and harder as she thought of her matching symptoms—fatigue, weakness, and bloody noses.

But I haven't noticed any bruising or unusual paleness. Her pulse sped up. *Is this a coincidence?*

"What notes did your dad write?" Rob asked.

Lara kept reading for a moment. "My dad was wondering whether inherited aplastic anemia is caused by a rare defect in a gene that regulates telomeres."

Didn't Josie say something about Dolly's telomeres?

Rob wrinkled his forehead. "Telomeres?"

I sure wish Maggie were here.

Lara raised her shoulders. "I really don't know what they are."

"Do you think your father had aplas… plastic…"

"Aplastic anemia," Lara said more firmly than intended. "Maybe? I have no idea. Several months ago, Lance Duncan told me my parents started a genetics company called Horizon Genomics. That's pretty much all I know about it."

Maybe Lance knows something more.

Rob winced at the mention of his former almost-ex-father-in-law.

Lara reached down to pick up the glossy paper from the ground and flipped it over in her hands. To her surprise, it was a brochure from Horizon Genomics.

My parents' company.

As she held it up for Rob to see, he raised an eyebrow.

She opened the brochure and read through the company's mission statement and description of services. Then she passed it to him, saying, "According to this, my parents' company focused on studying diseases caused by gene defects. In their mission statement, they planned to sequence genomes and collect genomic data in order to tailor treatments to a person's genetic makeup. They called it precision medicine."

Rob snapped his fingers. "Well, there you have it. Your parents must have been researching the cause of... that disease thingy."

"Aplastic anemia," Lara said.

"They must have been working to develop better treatments," Rob said matter-of-factly.

"Yeah..." Lara's head pounded harder as she speculated about her parents. She'd often experienced childhood memories and flashes of the car accident. But she rarely thought about who her parents had been as adults or what they did for a living. It felt strange to learn something new, something so important about them—so many years later. Her mouth went dry.

"Did you find anything interesting in Sully's files?" Lara asked, trying to distract herself.

Rob frowned deeply. "No luck yet." He rubbed his chin. "Didn't you say Justyne stole some files from Sully's storage unit?"

Lara scrunched her nose, attempting to retrieve the memory from the muddle of her mind. "Yup. Right before I took a blow to the head. She later told me about it at her office. Of course, then she attempted to inject me with a deadly dose of botulinum toxin." She shuddered. "I really don't want to see that woman again if I don't have to…"

Rob's face fell. "I bet she made off with all the evidence about the connections between her, MacFarlan, and Harry."

"Yeah, you're probably right. Maybe we need to set up that interview with MacFarlan after all. He might tell us something."

"You think Finn will let you travel with me to Kansas?" Rob asked.

Lara clenched her jaw. "Look, Finn is not the boss of me. He doesn't *let* me do anything. If we need to travel to Fort Leavenworth to solve your case, then he'll have to get on board or find another girl to date."

Lara's cheeks flushed as she turned away, her eyes falling on her father's painting carefully wrapped up in brown paper. *Her gut suddenly pricked with curiosity.* She got up from her chair, walked over to the painting, and ripped the paper down the center.

The tear revealed the Renaissance-era painting of a large fountain set in the countryside. Naked people were bathing in the fountain. She made a barf-face at Rob. *As bad as I remembered it.*

Rob gaped at it. "That's not original, is it?"

Lara ignored his question, used her smartphone to take a picture of the painting, and then spoke into her wrist. "Watson, what can you tell me about this painting?"

Her phone's screen came to life with an image of a British gentleman. "Of course, Ms. Kingsley, I would be happy to provide that information." A few seconds later, his voice chimed again. "The painting is called *Fountain of Youth*, created in 1546 with oil paints on lime wood board during the Renaissance period by the German painter, Lucas Cranach the Elder. The original hangs in the Gemäldegalerie located in Berlin, Germany. A handmade reproduction would be worth several thousand dollars." Watson stopped for an instant. "Is that all for now?"

Fountain of Youth?

"Yes, Watson, thank you."

"Huh," Rob said, half chuckling. "That's a strange painting."

Lara took a deep breath. "Yeah. Everything about it is strange."

A soft rap at the entrance of the storage unit made her look up. Finn stood in the doorway, grinning from ear to ear, his gray-blue eyes bright and eager. Her eyes widened at the sight of him dressed up as a medieval knight in black leggings, a white shirt, and a long two-colored tunic.

"Thou dost takest my breath away," Finn said, taking a deep bow. "Ready to go, m'lady?"

Rob raised his eyebrow.

"We're going to the Maryland Renaissance Festival," Lara said in a slightly defensive tone.

"What. Is. That?" Rob asked, an amused smile breaking out on his face.

He's enjoying this way too much.

"Um… it's a festival set in the medieval time period where people dress up in costumes, eat unhealthy food, and watch jousting matches and Shakespearean plays. At least that's what I hear," she said, nodding her head at Finn.

"Personally, I go for the turkey legs and the mead," Finn said, grinning broadly.

"What are *you* going to wear?" Rob asked, smirking at her.

"I'm going like this," Lara said, pointing to her outfit—black leggings, a turtleneck, and her new black leather jacket.

"We'll see about that…" Finn laughed, offering his arm to her. "Shall we, m'lady?"

Lara groaned as she turned back to glare at Rob. "If either of you tell Sanchez about the festival and costumes, I'll kill you. Got that?" She pointed at both of them with two I've-got-my-eye-on-you fingers.

Rob and Finn exchanged fake serious looks and nodded in an exaggerated manner. *Great. I'll never hear the end of this.*

"I'll come back and clean up this stuff later," Lara said, surveying the unit one more time. She stopped cold when she glimpsed a large yellow puddle on the cement floor next to her father's painting. The brown paper was now stained with wet splatters, and several drops of urine rolled town the canvas.

"Loki?" She yelled, swinging her head around. Her pup lay quietly on his bed and chewed his bone as if nothing had happened. Loki looked up at her and panted, his tongue hanging out.

Rob broke into laughter, his chest heaving. "Don't worry, Lara," he said, motioning with his hands. "I'll clean that up and take Loki back home. Go do your Renaissance thingy."

Lara sighed. "All right. Thanks."

"No problem." Rob headed for a roll of paper towels, and Lara turned to leave with Finn.

Just before she crossed the threshold, she noticed a picture face-down on the ground. She stopped, picked it up, and turned it over in her hands. Her heart jumped as she recognized her father sitting next to a Chinese woman holding a baby. Images from the past flooded her head, her nose filling with a memory of a foul scent.

Mothballs?

"What is it?" Finn asked, his face contorted with concern.

"Lara?" Rob stopped cleaning up Loki's mess and walked over to where she stood.

She showed them the photo. "This is a picture of my dad with a Chinese woman and her baby. I think it was taken the year he died." She stared up at the ceiling for a moment, sifting through the images coming to her. Something was familiar about the woman. "I might have met her before." She focused hard for a few moments but couldn't recall where. "Actually, I can't remember. It probably isn't important."

Shaking off a growing feeling of unease, Lara placed the picture on the nearest box and tugged on Finn's arm to leave.

FOURTEEN

Renaissance Faire

"How did your appointment with your therapist go?" Finn asked, a hint of caution in his voice as he pulled her hand gently, leading her down a dirt path. His longsword clinked against his shield as he walked.

Lara suppressed a scowl and lifted her long navy skirt to keep it from dragging in the dust. "Fine."

Finn chuckled. "Doesn't sound that fine to me."

She sighed. "Oh, she's been on my case about my past for our past few sessions. And it's getting old."

"What do you mean?" Finn asked.

"She wants me to deal with my parents' deaths, and I don't see her point," Lara said. "This isn't the sort of thing you get over. Ever. It just is what it is."

"I'm pretty sure she knows you don't stop grieving the loss… but maybe she thinks you're burying your feelings about it rather than confronting them head on."

"But what if burying my feelings works for me?" Lara asked.

Finn stopped for a moment and looked into her eyes. "Is it working?"

Lara looked away to hide the flush in her face. "How, pray

tell, did you start going to these Renaissance festivals?" she asked, changing the subject.

"What do you mean?" he asked.

Lara shrugged. "You just don't seem the type to like this sort of thing."

Finn covered his mouth with his hand, feigning insult. Then he grinned broadly and squeezed her hand. "My ex-wife was crazy about these festivals. Let's just say I was forcibly converted." Finn stole a glance at his smartphone as if he were expecting a call.

Uh... Lara bit the inside of her cheek, suppressing her irritation. Her blonde hair, tightly braided and held in place by layers of hairspray, tugged sharply at her hairline.

"I hope that doesn't bother you." He peered at her cautiously. When she said nothing, he continued. "At first, I went to spend quality time with her. Of course, I did enjoy drinking mead in the morning and not being judged for it. Before I knew it, I had purchased my own knight costume and everything. It's fun pretending to be someone else for a day."

"Yeah, sure," she said as cheerfully as she could muster. She glanced down at the satiny turquoise blouse bubbling out from under her form-fitting blue bodice and shuddered. It was lined with colorful frills that stretched down over her full skirt. The getup was courtesy of the artisan shops on the festival grounds.

I can't believe I'm dressed like a fairy.

"If this was your special thing with your ex-wife, why did you want to bring me?" she asked, a lump in her throat.

"Honestly?" Finn asked, finally putting his phone away. He stopped to look at her, his blue eyes twinkling. "I needed an excuse to see you parade around in a corset." He flashed her a toothy grin. "Now if only you hadn't pulled your shirt up so high. Then I could enjoy the view better."

"Actually, the lady at the store said this is called a bodice... not a corset." Lara said, giving him a playful nudge in the arm and blushing. "And, I wanted a serious answer."

Finn met her eyes, all playfulness discarded. "Okay. Serious answer?"

She nodded emphatically.

"You must be worried about your test results. I couldn't think of a better way to take you away from it all. I mean… how could you think of anything else when you're dressed up as a fairy? With me as your shining knight?"

Her eyes moistened, warmth spreading through her body.

He's right. I haven't thought about the test results at all. Or Rob's case. Or the missing girl.

Finn brushed a loose hair out of her eyes. He lifted her chin to his and kissed her gently.

When she pulled away, a deluge of worries came pouring back into her head. Ignoring them, she asked, "If you're supposed to be a knight, where's your shining armor?"

"You know how much this stuff costs?" Finn asked, staring at his phone again. "A quality breastplate costs four hundred dollars. Chain mail another two hundred. Leather arm bracers another seventy-five. And then there's the helmet, shield, and sword. The full ensemble costs about one thousand dollars. Instead, I rent myself a sword and shield every time I go, and call it a day."

Lara snorted. "One thing is for sure. You've done your research."

"Ten years of going to these things, and I've been to every craft shop on these grounds."

As they walked along the curved pathway, she gazed up at the tall pine trees surrounding the grounds. A ray of sunlight broke through the opening in the treetops. She breathed in the woodsy scents, which blended nicely with the savory smell wafting from a booth selling giant roasted turkey legs and the cinnamon and sugar aroma of elephant ears baking in an outdoor oven nearby.

Her thoughts drifted to the visit to Fort Leavenworth and her forehead creased. She turned to say something to Finn, but his face was glued to his smartphone and his fingers moved quickly across the keyboard.

Does he want to be somewhere else?

"Can I talk to you about something?" Lara asked, still bristling at his lack of attention.

Finn gave her a disapproving look and shook his finger at her. "Now we're not supposed to talk about stressful stuff."

Lara begged with her eyes. "Just one thing."

"Okay, one."

She pulled him off the path to let other people pass by and took a deep breath. "Rob and I need to visit Fort Leavenworth to interview General MacFarlan for his case. He's friends with Harry and may be able to tell us something about their connection."

Finn frowned deeply and said nothing for a few moments.

He's not going to let me go.

"Okay, then I want to come with you," Finn said.

Lara stepped backward and glared at him. "What? Why? Because you can't trust me to go with Rob?" A sudden wave of anger coursed through her body.

Finn held out his hand. "It's not what you think, Lara. I'm not asking because I'm jealous."

Oh?

"I'm suggesting I tag along because General MacFarlan will listen to me. And you'll have a better chance of getting the information you want."

Lara pinched her lips. "You don't think he'll listen to us?" she asked, her voice strained and high-pitched.

"Lara, you need to look at this from his perspective." Finn put his hands on his hips. "Why would he want to talk to you? General MacFarlan won't believe for a second that you or Rob can do anything for him even if he decides to talk."

Lara glowered at him and crossed her arms.

"Don't make me say it," he said.

Lara looked away.

"Fine, I'll say it. You're a disgraced military officer, and Rob was recently fired by the F—"

"And MacFarlan thinks highly of you…" Lara interrupted, waving her hand dismissively. "Blah, blah, blah."

"Yeah, there's that. Don't forget that my father's a two-star general. If I tell General MacFarlan I can make things better for him, he'll believe it."

Her posture slouched, causing the bodice to poke her in the ribs and squeeze the air out of her lungs. *Ouch.*

She glared at her costume, relieved she didn't live in an era where such clothes were mandatory. Standing tall again, Lara peered up into the thick pine trees in front of her. *Finn is right. Rob and I have no leverage.*

"When are you thinking of visiting the general?" Finn asked.

"Maybe tomorrow or the next day. It depends on when we can get access to Leavenworth."

"I'll clear my schedule and make some calls," Finn said. "Sound okay?"

I guess so.

Lara nodded and exhaled slowly.

Finn grabbed her hand, and they strolled on the dirt path through the woods, navigating the thick crowds. The grounds had grown more congested as people arrived to enjoy the festivities and feast on the delicious food offerings. Despite the late morning hour, many of them lugged around beer tankards, laughing merrily and stumbling around the hilly pathways.

In the thick throng of people walking toward them, Lara thought she spotted a familiar redhead strolling next to a young-looking bald man, both dressed in Renaissance costumes. Seconds later, the woman disappeared into the masses again. She glanced at Finn and caught him staring at his smartphone again. She poked him in the arm.

"What?" Finn asked, looking up at her.

Lara narrowed her eyes. "I thought I saw someone we know."

He stopped on the path and turned to face her. "Uh… yeah,

about that..." Finn winced slightly. "I invited Kaitlyn and her husband Bill to join us. I thought it would be fun."

No, it wouldn't.

"The more, the merrier," she said, forcing a smile and trying her best not to grit her teeth. She wasn't in the mood to pretend to be happy or pretend to like Kaitlyn.

Because I'm not happy, and I don't like Kaitlyn.

As Kaitlyn and Bill came into view dressed in full Renaissance regalia, Lara's heart sank. Looking even more beautiful than ever, Kaitlyn wore a floor-length purple and gold gown with long, flowing sleeves, rich brocades, and lavish trim. Her husband wore a plain beige medieval shirt, a brown belt, navy trousers, and brown leather boots.

Lara pasted on a big smile. "Hey Kaitlyn. Great to see you again!"

Finn shot Lara a nervous glance while giving Kaitlyn a short hug.

Lara widened her smile and bobbed her head excitedly. *God, I'm such a terrible liar.*

"Lara, this is my husband, Bill," Kaitlyn said, almost biting her words. Bill reached out his hand to Finn first, but barely smiled.

Huh. Were they fighting or something?

Lara studied the man carefully. Of all the possibilities, Lara would have never imagined a woman like Kaitlyn to be with such a lackluster man. Although Bill looked to be in his late twenties, there wasn't a single hair on his head. He obviously shaved his head bald rather than suffer his few remaining wisps. Kaitlyn was too attractive, smart, and well-connected to hook up with a guy like this.

He must have some redeeming qualities. Maybe he's rich? Maybe he's a spy?

"Nice to meet you." Lara shook Bill's hand but pulled away quickly. His hand was limp, and the expression on his worn face dull and lifeless.

He doesn't want to be here and isn't planning on hiding it. Fantastic.

"What do you do?" Lara asked, trying to be friendly. She bit her tongue as soon as the question tumbled across her lips.

Gah. All anyone cares about in D.C. is where you work and who you know. She prided herself on rising above that, but sometimes slipped into the habit like everyone else.

Bill cleared his throat. "I'm an accountant for the IRS."

Double whammy. Not rich. Or exciting.

"I take it you attend these things regularly?" Lara said, pointing to their extravagant costumes.

"We used to come with Finn and his ex-wife—" Kaitlyn hesitated, her eyes darting toward Finn.

"It's okay, she already knows all about it," he said reassuringly.

Kaitlyn turned back toward Lara. "Of course, I'm more into these festivals than Bill." She shot a look at her husband, who scowled but kept his mouth shut. Turning back to Lara, she smiled warmly and said, "I wanted to apologize for my behavior at the AVR room the other day. You could probably tell I was rather stressed because the admiral unexpectedly demanded access to the room at the last minute. And I'm not really supposed to let visitors in the room. Anyway, the admiral has a bit of a temper, and I worried that he'd pick up on the smell and lose his shit on me. But I never meant to make you feel bad about throwing up. It happens to most first-timers, including me."

Lara relaxed her stance, her lips parting. "That's okay. I'm just grateful that you were able to arrange it in the first place. At least I got to see my friend and his new wife for a little while."

"Anything for a friend of Finn's," Kaitlyn said, grinning.

"Hey, did you see they have virtual reality jousting this year?" Finn asked eagerly.

Virtual reality jousting?

"Really?" Kaitlyn's eyes lit up. "We should definitely go check that out."

Bill stared awkwardly at his feet.

Tugging at the frills on her bodice, Lara made a face. "I've had enough of virtual reality for a while. You guys go on ahead."

Finn and Kaitlyn exchanged nervous looks and their eyes darted back to Lara.

Then Kaitlyn gave her a reassuring look. "It's okay, Lara. Let's find something that we're all interested in doing."

"Maybe we should get some turkey legs instead?" Finn pointed to the food stops just down the way. "You can eat the meat right off the bone."

Lara grimaced at the thought of getting meat stuck in her teeth. She was about to say something snarky, when her phone buzzed. She glanced at the screen and shot Finn an urgent look.

"It's Sanchez. I have to get this. It's about the missing girl. Why don't you guys do that VR jousting thing after all? I'll catch up with you when I'm done with the call."

Finn's eyes lit up, and Lara motioned for them to go.

"Say hi to Danny for me," Finn said, grinning before he turned to head toward the VR booth. Bill slinked off after him, his face betraying intense disinterest.

Kaitlyn lingered for a moment, narrowing her eyes at Finn. "Are you sure, Lara?"

Lara nodded quickly, shooed her off, and answered the phone. "This is Lara."

"Got a moment?" Sanchez asked. "I've got an update on the case."

"Sure, I'm with Finn. He says hi, by the way."

"Listen, I don't have much time," the detective said gruffly.

"Okay, just tell me what you have," Lara replied in a flat business tone.

"Well, we found the kayak and two lifejackets," Sanchez said. "It was abandoned up near Great Falls Park, Virginia."

"Any idea where they headed after ditching the kayak?" Lara asked, her heart thumping.

"Not many traffic cameras in that area. The Virginia Police think they might have spotted the blurry image of the girl in the back seat of a car and a middle-aged woman on a camera at a gas station in a nearby town. She had long black hair and was petite. We think she could be Chinese."

"Any theories on their destination?" Lara asked.

Did they go to China?

"The gas station was about a twenty-minute drive from Dulles International Airport. Travel by air would be a pretty quick getaway."

"But why get gas if you're escaping by plane?" Lara asked.

"Maybe to throw us off. We've got DHS studying the camera footage at the airport for several days after the girl was snatched."

"What are the alternatives?" Lara asked.

"It's possible the kidnapper crossed several state lines. We've reached out to state police and put out Amber Alerts in Virginia, Maryland, West Virginia, North Carolina, and Pennsylvania. It's not much, but it's something."

"Well, that's a lot more than we had a few days ago," Lara said, exhaling sharply.

"Yeah… something to keep us busy at least. Who knows, this might end up being the break we needed in the case."

"I hope so," Lara said. *It's about time something goes my way.* "When I get off with you, I'm going to give Hickerson a call."

"The sleazy spook from the CIA?" Sanchez asked.

"Yep, that's the one," Lara said. "It was on our to-do list anyway for Rob's case, but now I have a better idea about how he can help us."

"How can *he* help?" Sanchez asked, not hiding his skepticism.

"I think he can help us figure out the China connection. I don't think it's a coincidence that Molly's adoption files are gone. Someone doesn't want us to learn about where she came from. Maybe if we did, we would have a better idea about who took her. Plus, Hickerson might be able to track down the name of the orphanage in China."

Sanchez grunted. "I don't like spooks. Especially not that one."

"Do you have any other brilliant suggestions?" Lara asked.

Sanchez cleared his throat. "After what he did last time, you're probably better off without his sort of help."

He could be right.

"Well, maybe so," Lara said, "but I'm willing to take the risk." She said her goodbyes to Sanchez, ended the call, and found Hickerson's number.

As she hit the call button, every ounce of her urged her to hang up.

But then Hickerson's voicemail picked up. She took a deep breath. "This is Lara Kingsley," she said. "Call me. It's important."

She hung up, Sanchez's warning echoing in her head.

FIFTEEN

The Anonymous Tip

October 5, 2028

"I'M SO sorry about this, Mags," Lara said, sinking into the front seat of the brand-spanking-new, electric-powered, silver Mini Cooper, complete with custom black stripes. She inhaled the new car smell and shuddered, recalling the explosion of Maggie's last Mini Cooper in the middle of downtown D.C. and their dramatic exit tumbling from the moving vehicle into oncoming traffic. For months after the incident, Maggie refused to buy another car and instead relied upon public transportation—until she got sick of the delays, rude passengers, and the occasional subway fire resulting from poor maintenance.

"No worries, mate. It happens," Maggie said, plugging the address into her GPS system. "I'm just glad your case is progressing." As soon as she pressed enter on the control panel, the car's engine whirred to life. A few moments later, the self-driving car pulled out of the parking spot and entered traffic.

They'd planned on enjoying a lazy morning at The Grind coffee shop before Lara received an urgent text from Sanchez about a major break in the kidnapping case while they were standing in line to order coffee. The text was followed by a demand to drop whatever she was doing and report to the Langstons' mansion ASAP.

"But I can't believe you've given into the dark side," Maggie said, grinning at her.

"What do you mean?"

"Babe, you're drinking iced coffee."

"Oh, this?" Lara said, pointing to her plastic cup before taking a sip from her straw. The cold coffee slid down her throat, leaving behind a bitterness undercut slightly by vanilla cream. "Well, it's all Sanchez's fault. If he wasn't in such a hurry for me to get over there, I'd drink hot coffee like usual. But I just wasn't in the mood for scalding my throat." Lara grinned from ear to ear.

"No kidding," Maggie said, laughing.

"Whatever you do, please don't tell Rob. He'll never let me hear the end of it. I gave him an earful the other day. Of course, he was slurping his like a child."

Maggie rolled her eyes. "So, you called me out for some emergency boy talk." She glanced at her watch. "We have about ten minutes before we get there. Let's get straight to the juicy stuff, shall we? I'm assuming you don't want to talk about Rob this time?"

Ugh. I'm pathetic.

Lara shrugged. "No, he's good. Things aren't going well with Finn lately. My emotions are all over the place. Something doesn't feel right between us."

She glanced out the window and glimpsed the first mansions of the Kalorama neighborhood passing by, memories flooding her mind. She swallowed hard at the memories and looked away. Lara had spent much of the first eight years of her life living in such a mansion surrounded by wealthy, well-connected people. That time in her life seemed surreal, as distant as a planet in outer space.

Staring at the houses, she recalled the attractive exterior of her own home—the manicured yard, the circular driveway, and the stately columns. Without warning, an image of Lara and her father playing catch in the backyard entered her mind. Instead of turning away from the memory, she leaned in this time.

It was right after he gave her the baseball glove for her birthday. His handsome face beamed with pride when she caught the ball for the first time. He'd said something about her being a natural. Maybe she'd play for a professional team someday. Lara's chest warmed for a moment. Then a painful pang stabbed her gut.

"Earth to Lara," Maggie said, waving her hand. "But I thought you went out on a date with him yesterday."

"I did." Lara grimaced at the thought. "But it ended up being a double date with Kaitlyn and her husband."

"And…" Maggie gave her a what's-the-problem look.

"Well, Finn never asked me if it was okay. He didn't even tell me about it until the last minute. They just showed up at the Renaissance Faire, and I didn't have much of a choice. Finn said he wanted to distract me from my test results."

"How did it go?"

"It went well, I guess. Kaitlyn was really nice. She made sure we did stuff I wanted to do. She even apologized for giving me a hard time for throwing up. But I still don't like her for some reason."

Maggie raised her eyebrow, "Are you jealous?"

Am I?

Lara frowned. "No, I don't think so. Why should I be? I mean… she's happily married, as Finn likes to point out. All the time. But when she's around, I feel like a total third wheel. There's this incredible feeling of ease between Finn and Kaitlyn. They get along so well, while things are bumpy and often awkward between Finn and me. It just doesn't feel right."

Should I be jealous?

"Aren't those two childhood friends? You just started dating Finn a few months ago. Maybe they just know each other much better."

Or maybe they're a better fit?

"Maybe. Kaitlyn's husband, Bill, wasn't thrilled to be there. I couldn't tell if he hates Renaissance festivals or if he was reacting to Finn and Kaitlyn having such a great time. Or maybe Kaitlyn and Bill are not as happily married as Finn thinks."

"Do you see a future between you and Finn?" Maggie asked.

"I'm not sure. He's quite different from Rob. In a good way. He likes to take charge of things. Rob always used to let me take the lead and complain about it later. At least with Finn, I know what he wants."

"But do you want the same things?" Maggie asked.

Good question.

Lara furrowed her brow, thought for a moment, and shook her head. "I think that might be the problem. He wants to ride the thrills of life while I yearn for that elusive feeling of home." She paused for a moment, a tingle stirring in her stomach. "You don't think Finn would cheat on me with Kaitlyn, do you?"

Lara's head began throbbing with a mixture of regret and fear as soon as she asked the question. She'd never fully been able to get over Rob's infidelity. She'd long forgiven him for the betrayal, but the unsettling shock of it all still lingered in her spirit. In addition to throwing her instincts for reading people and situations into question, it made it even more difficult for her to trust people. It was unfair to Finn.

"No, sweetie. I don't think he's the type to do that sort of thing. Do you have any reason to think he's being unfaithful?" Maggie asked.

I didn't last time, either. Is there such a type? Or is it just human?

"Not really… but he is spending more and more time at work lately… with Kaitlyn."

Maggie pinched the bottom of her lip. "I dunno, Lara. If you suspect something, I think you're gonna have to ask him straight up."

Uh… no thank you.

Lara grimaced. Through the windshield, she caught sight of the Langstons' mansion coming into view. The end of the urban cul-de-sac was shared by three stately homes. Despite the identical tall oak trees along the sidewalks, the matching stone walls and manicured bushes, the French-style house seemed strangely out of place among the traditional colonial homes on the city street.

Sanchez waited for her on the stoop at the front entrance of the house, glancing at his watch. When he looked up, he grimaced at the sight of Maggie's car and motioned for Lara to hurry.

As the car came to a stop, Lara put her plastic cup in the drink holder, grabbed the door handle, and said to Maggie, smiling, "Thanks for the ride… and the boy talk."

"Anytime, luv… and don't worry about Finn, okay? If he's the right bloke for you, it'll all work out."

And if he's not…

Lara closed the car door, waved goodbye to Maggie, and jogged up the stairs, swaying a bit when she reached the top. Sanchez nodded and held the door open for her, barely greeting her. As they entered the foyer, a cacophony of noises pulled her toward the sitting room like a magnet—the clacking of keyboards, voices, and the shuffling and footsteps of several people.

Inside, she glimpsed a state-of-the-art command center. The small sitting room was now packed with desks, screens, and computers. TV footage flashed across the screens with ticker tape. People in both police uniform and plain clothes sat at the computers, answering phones and logging tips as they came in. From across the room, Detective Franklin gave her a friendly wave.

"Wow, this is some operation." Lara's eyes widened as she took it all in. "I didn't realize…" A pang of guilt pierced her gut. Between working Rob's case and the doctor's appointment, she'd missed a great deal.

An eight-year-old girl is missing, and I let myself fall out of the loop.

In her absence, the detective had assured her the investigation was proceeding at full force. And he wasn't exaggerating. Still, she felt a heavy weight on her chest as if she could have done more to find Molly.

Sanchez extended his hand outward, moving it across the space. "As soon as we put out the reward announcement to the news media, we got more tips than we could handle at the station downtown. Julian suggested we set up an operation center here, and we gladly accepted his offer. He supplied all the equipment and even brought over some manpower from his company."

Sanchez motioned for her to follow him to one of the desks with a large video screen. He approached a young male police officer sitting at the first desk, who looked up at the detective expectantly.

"Could you roll the airport video for us?" Sanchez asked.

"Right away, Lieutenant." The officer opened a video file and pressed play.

Lara's body tensed as soon as the blurry footage of the airport security checkpoint began to play. A long line of people prepared for screening procedures. Lara spotted a middle-aged Asian woman with long black hair tied back in a ponytail. The woman placed her suitcase on the conveyer belt and then helped a young Asian girl with her bright pink backpack.

"Are those butterflies on the girl's backpack?" she asked, squinting to see better.

"Yep," Sanchez said. "The Langstons have identified the backpack as belonging to Molly. Even with the grainy quality of the video, we can see that the girl is Molly. That woman must be her kidnapper."

Her eyes glued to the video, Lara wrinkled her nose and tilted her head. "Molly seems too calm for having been taken from her parents by a stranger in the middle of the night. She *has* to know this woman."

Sanchez gave her a knowing smile and tapped his forehead in agreement. "The Langstons claim they have no idea why this woman would take their daughter," he said in a low voice. "They continue to insist Molly doesn't know her."

"Well, then they're lying," Lara said, her eyebrows creasing at the video footage. "Molly would be frightened if this woman were a stranger." She moved in closer to the video screen and rubbed her chin. "Why didn't airport security pick up Molly's name and picture from the Amber Alert when they checked in for their flights?"

Sanchez gave a nod as if he expected her questions. "Two reasons. First, she was traveling under a different name—her birth name, Mo Chu, combined with the last name Kong. We had no idea what her kidnapper looked like. Most of us assumed it was a guy."

Lara gaped at him, blood rushing from her face. "Molly traveled under her birthname? But how—"

"TSA identified the kidnapper as Yingyue Kong," Sanchez interrupted. "At least, that's what her passport says. Both Yingyue and Molly had authentic Chinese passports, identifying Yingyue as the girl's mother. She presented TSA with a signed letter authorizing the overseas travel from the girl's Chinese father, allegedly a Dr. Yishan Kong. From TSA's perspective, there was no reason to suspect anything was wrong. The second reason was timing. They made it on the plane two hours before anyone knew Molly was missing."

Are the Kongs Molly's birth parents?

"Oh, please don't tell me they flew to China," Lara said in a sarcastic tone.

"I'm afraid so. They departed on the last flight at 10:45 p.m. to Beijing the night Molly was taken. She was out of the country before her parents realized she was gone and reported her missing."

Well, that's just… a super nightmare.

"That's not all. I had to talk Mr. Langston off a crazy ledge earlier. He has a loony-toon plan to get his daughter back. I told him to go blow off steam and come back only when he's recovered his common sense. If he doesn't, it's gonna get ugly."

Loony-toon plan? Not sure I like the sound of that.

"What do we know about Yingyue Kong?" Lara asked, trying to stay focused on the facts of the case.

Sanchez nodded as if he was already a step ahead of her. "My team has built a detailed profile. Lucky for us, she doesn't appear to be a Chinese operative or affiliated with the PLA. Turns out she's the Director of Science at the Macrobian Institute of Life Sciences in Shenzhen, China."

Sounds like an operative to me.

"She's a legitimate scientist?" Lara stared at the detective unblinking.

"It appears so."

"Where's this institute?" Lara asked, trying to visualize a map of China and failing miserably.

Sanchez grabbed her arm, turned her around, and pointed at a bulletin board with a detailed map of China tacked to it. He pulled Lara by the arm and showed her the target city on the map.

"Shenzhen is a major city located between Hong Kong and mainland China in the Guangdong province," Sanchez said, pointing to a spot marked on the map. "The city is known for its high-tech industry. The institute is housed in the Shenzhen Science and Technology Park right here." He moved his finger to show her the exact location.

Lara narrowed her eyes at the detective. "How did you pull this information together so quickly?" She was not used to him sharing so much explicit detail.

Sanchez gave her a fake offended look and then smirked. "Well, that's the kicker. Mr. Langston knows the identity of the kidnapper after all."

Lara inhaled sharply and took a step back. "What?"

Sanchez nodded. "Mr. Langston owns a subsidiary company located in the same technology park. Right here." He pointed to the location. "Apparently, he's crossed paths with Dr. Yingyue Kong on several occasions but claims he has never formally been acquainted with her."

So, there's a chance Molly may have met this woman.

"How did you get the airport video footage?" Lara asked.

"It came in anonymously over the tip line by email."

"Why wouldn't someone want credit? The reward money is huge."

Sanchez shrugged.

"Have you traced the origins of the anonymous tip?" Lara asked.

"I hadn't thought about doing that," Sanchez said.

"Can you send me the email? I'll have Vik take a look when he gets back later this week."

"Sure thing."

In the foyer, the front door slammed, sending a sharp echo through the house. Startled, they turned to see Julian barge through the doorway of the sitting room, his eyes flashing and his jaw tensed. His gaze met Lara's, and his face twisted with anger. He marched toward her, shaking his fist at her face. "Remind me how much we paid you to find our daughter, and then I'll know how much to sue you for negligence."

Lara shrank back, her cheeks flushing. Before she could respond, Sanchez moved between them, puffed out his chest, and chopped the air with his hands.

"Sir, you need to back off and calm the fuck down," he said. "Your daughter went missing before Lara agreed to take this case. She's not responsible for anything that's happened."

Julian's mouth twisted into an ugly sneer. He pointed a long, thin finger around the detective at Lara's chest. "If you don't get our daughter back, you're done in this town. Do you hear me? Done."

Where have I heard that before? Powerful men and their threats. No, I don't think so.

Lara pushed Sanchez to the side to confront Julian directly, her fists clenched. She pointed her finger at him. "If someone is responsible for anything, it's you. Maybe if you'd been straight with the cops from the beginning, they would have focused their search at the airports and flights en route to China. Maybe Molly would already be home safe and sound. You want to fire me?

Then fire me. I didn't want to work this case in the first place. How about I just quit and leave you to your own devices?" She walked past him through the doorway and into the foyer, and then turned around, her ears burning hot. "You plan to tarnish my reputation? Go ahead. I'll happily repay the favor. How do you think this will play out in the press? Wealthy businessman obstructs investigation to find his daughter." Lara stuck her finger in the air, as if to take the temperature. "Hmm, not so good."

As she placed her hand on the doorknob to leave, rapid footsteps pattered down the stairs behind her. Cynthia appeared in the foyer with a tear-stained face and strode toward Lara, her lips trembling and her hands shaking.

"Lara, please don't go... we need your help. Molly needs you. Please, I beg you to stay."

Then she turned toward Julian with a mother's fierceness in her eyes. "You need to stop yelling at Lara. You think losing your temper will help us get our daughter back? Stop it right now." She turned back toward Lara. "Please. I'd do anything to have one more day with our daughter. Lara, you need to come through for us..."

Cynthia wobbled forward a few feet, her hands reaching out for something to steady herself, but found nothing. She collapsed onto her knees, burst into tears, and trembled uncontrollably. Julian ran toward her and sank to the floor next to her, putting his arms around her and holding her to his chest.

What would I do to have one more day with my parents?

As intense emotions came over her, Lara floundered her words, and the world seemed to slow down. She lifted her hand and then lowered it.

Sanchez motioned for her to rejoin them in the sitting room. Lara followed him reluctantly toward the bank of operations desks. Detective Franklin approached them with a worried look on his face.

"Did Sanchez tell you about Mr. Langston's crackpot plan?" Franklin asked in a low voice.

"No, he did not." Lara rubbed the back of her neck and raised her eyebrows. "He said there was a plan but didn't tell me any details."

Sanchez heaved a heavy sigh. "Because I was hoping Mr. Langston would drop it after calming down. He wants to assemble a team to forcibly retrieve his daughter from China. He said he can pull strings over at the Pentagon to make it happen."

Oh really.

Lara's mouth hung open, and she chanced a glance backward at Julian. Does he even know about my military experience? He can't possibly want me to lead that team. Not after his angry outburst.

Franklin smoothed his suit jacket. "If he asks you, don't even think about doing it, Lara. He'll be the least of your worries if Chinese authorities catch you."

"Any bright ideas on how to get Molly out of China, then?" Lara asked, biting her lip.

"I did some research," Franklin said. "Short answer, it don't look good. Getting her out legally depends on citizenship. If Molly really is a Chinese citizen, the situation becomes complicated. You see, the Chinese government doesn't recognize dual citizenship, which would make her U.S. citizenship null and void as soon as she crosses the Chinese border. In that case, we would need the Chinese government to cooperate to get her back. I suggested the Langstons reach out to the State Department, but they won't hear of it."

"Why not?" Lara asked. "The Langstons are powerful enough for the U.S. Government to care about their daughter's abduction. Surely, if Mr. Langston holds sway over people at the Pentagon, then he definitely knows someone at State who can help him—"

"Ms. Kingsley, I'm terribly sorry about before," Julian's voice sounded from behind her with a hint of forced remorse.

She spun around to see Julian and Cynthia standing side by side, their hands clasped. Cynthia's hand gripped her husband's so tightly, her nails dug into his skin. He motioned for her to come over to him. Lara shot a glance at Franklin and Sanchez before walking over to them, out of hearing distance of them and the other cops in the room. Sanchez returned a warning glare, shook his head slowly, and turned his attention back to the computer screens.

"We know it's not your fault that Molly was smuggled out of the country," Julian said through gritted teeth.

Right.

Lara pressed her lips together and said nothing.

"We're wondering… Cindy and I… well, after my sources told me of your military experience…" He glanced at his wife, and she nodded, encouraging him to continue. "We were hoping you would come to China with me to help get our daughter back." The tone of his voice was sickly sweet.

He's actually serious.

Julian lowered his voice. "We would fly over in my private jet and use my company headquarters in Shenzhen to stage the operation. I'll hire as many mercenaries as you think we'd need to find her. I'd put all my resources at your disposal to get the job done. You would be immensely rewarded." He stopped and seemed to study her for a moment. "Of course, I'll clear everything with the Deputy Secretary of Defense. He's a close friend of mine."

Yeah, right.

Cynthia stepped forward, grabbed Lara's hands, clasping them in her own. "Lara, please consider it. I beg you. We need to get our daughter back. We'll do anything."

You mean you'll ask me to do anything.

Her mind raced as she digested their request. Her chest tightened at the thought of the proposed mission. The personal and professional risks were enormous. If they were caught by Chinese authorities stealing the girl back, they could end up in a Chinese prison or worse. If the Pentagon didn't bless the operation and the Army found out, it would mean the end of her military career or worse. But Molly's picture and her floppy rabbit tugged at her heart strings.

She's only eight years old.

"If I agree to consider your idea…" Lara said, her eyebrows squeezed together.

Julian and Cynthia exhaled sharply.

"I said *if* and *consider*," Lara said, her eyes darting between their eager faces. "I'm not sold yet. First, you must agree to come with me to the State Department and see if they can help us. If that doesn't work, I'll consider your plan."

Julian's face twisted.

Cynthia squeezed his hand tightly and nodded. "We'll agree to that."

"And—"

"There's more?" Julian growled.

"Before I do anything further on this case, I want to interview your babysitter. I don't care what it takes, but you need to find a way to bring Alicia home from Poland immediately."

Julian scowled. "Is that all?"

"Yes." Lara pasted on a smile.

"Then it's a deal," Julian said, extending his hand to shake on it.

She took his hand and shook it. *That felt too easy.*

Turning around to hide her sense of unease, she walked toward the operation desk.

Sanchez moved closer and muttered in her ear, "You'd better hope the State Department can intervene. They don't mess around in China. They'll issue you an exit ban for next to nothing. And then you'll be stuck over there."

Lara gulped. Her smartphone buzzed. When she glanced at the screen, her heart thumped with anticipation.

"It's Hickerson," she said to Sanchez.

The detective raised an eyebrow.

"This is Lara," she said, pressing accept at the last minute.

"You called?" Hickerson said gruffly.

"Yeah."

"What's up?"

Lara filled in Hickerson on the situation—Molly's

kidnapping, the missing orphanage name on the adoption paperwork, and the identity of her abductor.

"Did you say your kidnapper is a scientist at the Macrobian Institute of Life Sciences?"

"Yeah. Does that ring a bell?" Lara asked with a hint of hopefulness.

"It might."

Lara's pulse spiked. "What bell?"

"Can't say just yet. I'll have to do some digging and get back to you."

"Thanks, that would be really great. We can use any help we—"

Hickerson hung up without saying goodbye. She stared at her phone.

I wasn't finished yet.

Sanchez gave her a knowing look. "Did your spook have any useful information? Or did he act spooky like spooks typically do?"

Lara pressed her lips together.

He may be a spook, but we need every bit of help we can get.

SIXTEEN

The Prison Visit

October 6, 2028

LARA WIPED beads of sweat from her forehead with her arm. Stale air pressed against her lungs, making it hard to breathe, and the faint smell of body odor was getting stronger with every passing minute. The hard metal chair limited the circulation in her legs, causing a tingling sensation.

Dire thoughts about her looming failure to resolve both of her cases went round and round in her head. There were still no leads on Molly's whereabouts in China. If MacFarlan refused to spill the beans on Harry, they'd be forced to talk to Justyne—or worse, Fiddler. Neither of whom would want to be helpful without some serious cajoling.

Nothing could possibly make the windowless, barren, dimly lit private visitation room at Fort Leavenworth any less uncomfortable—except, of course, being stuck in it alone for an extended period with Rob and Finn. They'd already exhausted the "safe" topics of conversation—the weather, the kidnapping case, Finn's job at the Pentagon, MacFarlan, and the weather again. The tension in the room was so thick she could cut it with a knife.

To distract herself from physical discomfort, troubling thoughts, and the increasing tightness of the room, she focused on the rhythmic tapping of her foot on the soft linoleum floor.

Next to her, Finn rested his elbows on the steel table in a stationary position, unflinching and focused. He wore his Army Class B uniform, hoping to use his military status and connections to persuade the general to help them. He'd been quite proud of himself for making the interview happen in the first place. But then his ego deflated, along with his mood, after waiting over ninety minutes—more than an hour past the agreed meeting time.

For the past ten minutes, Finn stared angrily at the door, apparently lost in thought. More likely, he was attempting to command the door to open and MacFarlan to walk through it.

Meanwhile, Rob paced back and forth, his fists clenching and unclenching, unable to sit still. His chances of vindication were now riding on the success of their chat with MacFarlan, and he wouldn't let Lara forget it.

Being cooped up with these two might be worse than solitary confinement.

She glanced at her wrist for her smartphone and remembered it was locked in a box in the visitor's center. Instead, Lara fidgeted with the spiral wire on her notebook. After several minutes, she'd twisted the end until it became flat.

"Finn, I thought you said MacFarlan agreed to see us over an hour ago," Rob whined, rehashing an earlier topic.

Finn frowned deeply. "Look, I called in some favors to make this happen. At first, MacFarlan refused to see us. I made it clear there was something in it for him, but it ultimately took an intervention from my father to deliver the message. His lawyer gave me the time and made arrangements with the prison. Obviously, something has happened to disrupt the plan."

Rob glanced at Lara as if he'd just remembered something. "Hey, what did Hickerson have to say for himself?"

Finn raised his eyebrow. "You talked to the spook again?"

Both Rob and Finn had expressed at various points intense desires to *have words* with Randall Hickerson. Well, not exactly words.

Several months ago, the CIA case officer had dragged Lara into the elaborate scheme to steal back technology from Spectral Industries, and she ended up witnessing the gruesome death of Calvin Westlock. Then Hickerson used her to set up General MacFarlan and swooped in to clear her name, but only at the last minute. Finn and Rob were still holding a grudge. Lara hoped the history with Hickerson might serve as leverage.

After learning the truth about his actions, Finn had threatened to break his neck, and Rob wanted to strangle him to death. Their dislike of Hickerson was one of the few things the two of them could agree on.

Lara didn't fully trust Hickerson, but was willing to leverage his connections in China if it would help get Molly back. "I thought he might be able to help me with the missing persons case. He probably still feels badly about how things went down with MacFarlan."

Lara caught herself justifying Hickerson's choices and making up a story to assuage their concerns. *But does Hickerson really feel badly?*

"Yeah right," Finn said.

"How can he help you with your missing persons case, anyway?" Rob asked.

Lara opened her notebook. "When Sanchez and I visited the adoption agency, Molly's files were expunged from the system. We don't know the name of the orphanage in China. Seven other babies were adopted from the same orphanage around the same time. I thought maybe Hickerson could figure out the name and location for me using his dense network of Chinese contacts."

"Did you tell him about our interview with MacFarlan?" Finn asked.

"Nope," Lara said. "He hung up on me before I got a chance to talk to him about it."

"Hickerson is a two-timing hustler," Finn said, pounding his fist on the table. "I wouldn't expect him to come through for you. He only helps anyone when it's in his interest."

Rob nodded in agreement.

Let's hope this is in his interest, then.

"I'm surprised the Langstons let you travel for my case," Rob said, changing the subject.

Lara shrugged her shoulders. "It's not like there's anything more I can do at the moment. Alicia is still in Poland with her father. There was a long waiting list for appointments with the State Department, but we're scheduled to meet with a case officer later this week."

"You'd think the Langstons could use their clout with the State Department and get in to see someone sooner," Finn said. "Have you thought about the possibility that the Langstons are somehow involved with their daughter's kidnapping?"

"Um, yeah," she said, rolling her shoulders and stretching her neck to release tension. "There's definitely more to the story. Molly gets kidnapped by someone who knows the layout of the house. Conveniently, the alarm system is shut off, and the parents are gone. Apparently, the girl doesn't scream or make any noise and acts like she knows her abductor at the airport. Then Molly's adoption records go missing at the agency. Now her babysitter, the only person who knows anything about the incident, is gone so I can't interview her. This whole thing feels like some sort of giant conspiracy."

"Not everything is a conspiracy, Lara," Rob said, chuckling.

"No? What about Sully's death? That's turning out to be quite a conspiracy. We're still dealing with the loose ends of that one. Not to mention we're sitting here waiting to talk to a guy who got us wrapped up in yet another conspiracy."

Rob held his hands up in surrender. "Sorry. I was just making a joke. You're right. We've been caught up in quite a few conspiracies lately."

"Are you feeling okay?" Finn asked, scrutinizing her face. He put his hand on her forehead to feel her temperature, and she swiped it away.

"I'm fine."

"You do look a bit peaked," Rob said, taking a few steps closer.

You're going to look peaked after I punch your lights out.

Lara rose from her seat and held up her hands. "Guys, seriously… if you don't want me to climb the wall and escape the room through that air vent right now, knock it off." She pointed to Rob and then to the chair. He obediently took a seat.

"We're just concerned about your welfare," Finn added. "I don't like the idea of you going to China on a dangerous mission when you're this tired all the time."

Lara shook her head vigorously. "There's an eight-year-old girl who is missing. I can't leave her parents hanging just because I'm tired. We need to get her back."

"But you could be seriously ill," Rob said.

Lara slammed her hand on the table, harder than she intended. A sharp sting reverberated from her hand to her elbow. "Hey, I have an idea. Why don't we talk about something else? How about the fact that both of you feel threatened by one another, and each of you would prefer the other didn't exist?"

Rob and Finn exchanged nervous looks and remained silent.

"Exactly, that's what I thought."

A chilly quiet descended in the room for several minutes. Then the door opened, and they looked up, expecting to see General MacFarlan dressed in his prison jumpsuit and secured in handcuffs. Instead, a short, pudgy man with thinning hair and thick glasses strode into the room holding a worn brown leather briefcase. After setting it on the floor, he lifted his pants over his thick belly, took a seat across from them, and slid his business card across the table.

"I'm John MacFarlan's attorney. I've just conferred with my client, and he declines to speak with you at this time."

"What do you mean he declines? We flew all the way to Kansas to speak to him," Finn said in a raised voice, and pointed a finger at the stubby man. "You said he was willing to talk yesterday. What's changed?"

"The circumstances have changed. If MacFarlan tells you the name of his accomplice, he fears for his life and his daughter's welfare. Yesterday, he received a threatening note, warning him not to be seen talking to you. If he talks, they will get him, even within these sturdy walls. Or worse, they'll go after his daughter."

"Threatening note?" Lara asked, her eyes wide. "From whom?"

The lawyer cleared his throat. "Someone who goes by the pseudonym BlackDragon. Sound familiar?"

Lara and Rob locked eyes. *BlackDragon?*

"But how could this BlackDragon person get him inside this prison?" Lara asked.

"MacFarlan says BlackDragon knows people who can get to him in here."

"Didn't you tell him we're willing to help out with his daughter?" Finn pressed, unwilling to give up. "If he can offer a solid lead, we'll set up a trust in her name with two hundred thousand dollars. We can also arrange for protection against this would-be assassin."

Rob gaped at Lara, presumably stunned over the amount of money Finn offered. She hadn't told him Kingsley Investigations was fronting the money to get information for his case. It was the only way to convince MacFarlan to share information. If someone had persuaded MacFarlan to break the law in exchange for help with paying for the medical bills of his sick daughter, he'd be willing to turn on his accomplice. For a price.

A muffled cracking sound in the distance made them look at each other.

"Did you hear that?" Finn asked, cupping his hand behind his ear.

"Hear what?" Rob asked, raising his eyebrow.

"Not sure what it was," he said. "But it didn't sound good."

The lawyer wrinkled his forehead. "I tried to convince my

client to cooperate despite the threat. But he won't budge. However, he did ask me to deliver a specific message to you, Ms. Kingsley." He glanced down at his paper to read the words. "He said he doesn't have any hard evidence on his contact at the FBI. But he says you know someone who does."

Who is he talking about? Justyne? Fiddler? Hickerson?

"MacFarlan admits he was working with someone at the FBI?" Lara asked, her pulse spiking.

"I'm sorry. That's all he was willing to say. He's probably said too much already." The lawyer got up and bent over to get his briefcase. With that, he turned around and opened the door. Before he could exit the room, the sound of footsteps pounded down the hallway and guards shouted, startling them.

Two security guards nearly ran into the lawyer as he attempted to exit the room. He scurried back inside and took cover in the corner. Lara, Rob, and Finn poked their heads out the door to glimpse the flurry of activity.

Another security guard raced down the corridor and approached them, his hand on his holster. "All of you. Get back in that room right now. There's a situation."

"What happened?" Lara asked as the double doors at the end of the hallway burst open. Two doctors dressed in white coats pushed a stretcher carrying a black man toward them. Blood oozed through a small hole in the prison uniform near the man's chest.

A gunshot wound in prison?

"Out of the way!" the security guard shouted. "We need to get this prisoner to a hospital right away."

As the stretcher rolled past the open door, Lara recognized the man.

It was General MacFarlan.

SEVENTEEN

To-Do List

October 7, 2028

"OUCH. YOU'RE. SQUEEZING. TOO HARD," Vik said, his voice squeaking.

Lara held on tight and refused to let him go. Still breathing hard, her heart pounded against her chest. When she'd heard him arrive at the front door, she'd raced down two flights of stairs, thrown it open, and barreled through it at top speed.

Two flights of stairs, and I'm out of breath?

Unable to contain himself, Loki jumped on Lara's legs. And then he did the same to Vik, sniffing him intensely. Then Loki ran around them in tight circles, barking happily.

"I missed you so much," she said, releasing Vik from her tight grip to see his grinning face. She eyed him curiously, taking in his new look—black skinny jeans, a black t-shirt, a dark gray hoodie, designer red-and-white sneakers. "Whatever happened to you? You've gone all hip and trendy on me."

Vik's brown eyes twinkled. "Shanaya happened. She thinks I should pay more attention to how I present myself."

Lara put her hands on her hips, giving him a skeptical look.

"Oh, I don't mind," Vik said. "These days I have more income to spend on clothes, and now I have a big discount. Shanaya just got a job as a fashion consultant, where she helps women develop their own sense of style." He grinned at her with pride. "You should get on her schedule. I know she'd love to dress you."

Uh oh, the fashion police are coming for me.

"She'll get fed up with me. I'm impossible," Lara groaned, staring down at her pink bunny slippers, grimy cargo pants, and raggedy t-shirt. It was all Loki's fault. She couldn't wear good clothes around him without getting a muddy paw here and there.

Where's the old Vik?

A lump formed in her throat. Lara didn't like how relationships sometimes changed people. And not always for the better. Her thoughts drifted to Finn, and she wrinkled her nose. She often wondered where to make compromises and where to draw the lines to keep her identity intact. Especially when she was uncertain about what she wanted in the first place. It would be too easy to get swallowed up in someone else's expectations.

The smell of freshly brewed coffee wafted through the library and tickled her nose. Lara motioned for Vik to follow her into the kitchen. "Come. I made us some coffee."

"I can't believe how big Loki has gotten in just a month."

Loki followed them into the kitchen and flopped down on his dog bed, his white teeth showing and a long pink tongue hanging out.

"Not just big. He's a holy adolescent terror. You wouldn't believe the trouble he gets himself into."

Vik gave her a knowing look. "I warned you not to call him Loki after the trickster god. You were inviting bad karma."

"Yes, I do recall," she said in a sarcastic tone. She walked over to the coffee pot and took two large mugs out of the cupboard.

Behind her, she could hear Vik playing tug-of-war with Loki and smiled. She picked up the carafe, poured two cups of coffee, and added cream. Grabbing the mugs, she walked toward the kitchen island. She pushed one mug to the other end and took a sip from hers.

A familiar warmth in Vik's eyes tugged on her heart. Lara's mouth changed to a pout. "You're never leaving me again, got that?"

Vik gave her a sideways grin. "Sure, boss. Whatever you say."

Lara made a face. "You have a new boss, now. How is Shanaya?"

Vik beamed at the mention of his wife and grabbed the mug. "She's great." His eyes dimmed. "But she's been worried about you since you collapsed in the simulator... and frankly, I'm worried, too."

Her cheeks flushed at the memory. "I'm really sorry to have caused a ruckus at your wedding. She's not upset about that, is she?"

Vik's eyes widened. "Oh no, of course not." He said it a little too quickly, averted his gaze, and sipped his coffee. "It was almost like you weren't even there." He flashed his teeth with a broad smile.

Lara grimaced. "Ha! You're funny."

Even in augmented virtual reality, Lara knew the incident would put a blemish on what was supposed to be Shanaya's perfect wedding day. Lara would never have imagined it possible for her to screw anything up as an avatar.

Vik plopped on a stool at the island and made direct eye contact. "Why didn't you respond to my texts while I was away?" The hurt look in Vik's brown eyes punched her in the gut.

Lara's face fell. "I'm sorry... I just didn't know where to start. And I didn't want to cast a shadow over your honeymoon."

"Getting information out of you is like... trying to take that toy from Loki," Vik said, taking another sip of coffee. "I want to hear everything. Don't bullshit me. I'll know if you're lying." He gave her a stern look—at least, the sternest one he could muster. "How are you doing?"

She suppressed a giggle. "I'm okay."

Vik narrowed his eyes. "You're lying."

Lara chuckled. "Okay, fine. Everything is somewhat terrible."

"Somewhat?"

"Okay, okay. Rather terrible. Worst news first?"

Vik nodded.

Lara scratched her head. *What is the worst news?*

"Well, I may have a nasty gene mutation, inherited from my parents." She looked heavenward and shook her fist to thank her parents for the parting gift. "I'm still waiting on test results. The doctor thinks it could be serious. I'm mostly in denial, but everyone else is treating me like I'm dying." She gave him a sheepish smile. "And that's what's killing me."

"What about treatments?" Vik asked, his lip trembling at the bad news.

And this is why I didn't tell him over text. Lara wanted everyone to stop gawking at her like she was on her deathbed.

Lara sipped her coffee. "Not sure yet. The doctor is running more tests before we decide on a treatment."

Vik's face went slack. He opened his mouth to say something but appeared unable to find the words.

Yeah, it sucks.

Lara sighed and continued. "Rob's case is going nowhere. We found a file with hard evidence detailing Harry's illegal activities and thought Rob's vindication was within our grasp. But then it went missing."

"What?" Vik gaped at her.

"Yeah. Apparently, Harry bugged my townhouse and overheard our initial meeting. He's been a step ahead this whole time, even knew about our meeting at the FBI headquarters. He's stalked me and must have been tracking Agent Carter as well. He obviously knew about the plan to hand over the file to the FBI Director and intercepted it."

"He bugged the townhouse?" Vik's eyes darted from one side of the room to the other. "Again?"

Lara nodded. "Don't worry. We destroyed them all. And I've

been scanning the whole house for bugs first thing each morning. He won't catch us with our pants down again. Not around here anyway."

He relaxed a bit but shook his head. "Unbelievable. You've had quite the month."

"Well, there's more," Lara said. "Finn, Rob, and I went to Fort Leavenworth to talk to MacFarlan."

Vik raised his eyebrows. "Uh… that must have been an interesting trip."

Interesting is right.

"At first, MacFarlan agreed to speak to us. Then he chickened out, refused to meet with us, and sent his lawyer in his place. His lawyer delivered a cryptic message. Next thing we know, two doctors were rolling MacFarlan on a stretcher down the hallway with a bullet hole in his chest."

"What?" Vik sat his mug on the table with a thud, a little coffee splashing over the rim. "How did that happen?"

"Apparently, MacFarlan received a threatening note from BlackDragon, warning him not to talk to us. After meeting with his lawyer, MacFarlan headed back to his cell, and a security guard shot him in the chest. The infirmary didn't have the capacity to save him, so they carted him off to the hospital."

"Is he dead?" Vik asked.

"As good as dead. He's in a coma and in critical condition. The doctors say it doesn't look good. The police think this BlackDragon character somehow got to one of the security guards. We may never get the chance to talk to him now."

Vik rubbed his forehead. "You're not thinking about visiting Justyne, are you?"

Lara wrinkled her nose. "I'd rather not. But it may come to that if we can't find any evidence on Harry Cogan. MacFarlan passed a message to me through his lawyer. He said that someone I know has hard evidence on the FBI insider. My best guess is MacFarlan is referring to Justyne. She must have a copy of the file or something."

"I wouldn't talk to her." Vik raised his shoulders. "She

probably won't help you anyway. If anything, she'll just get under your skin again."

"True that," Lara said, frowning at the memory of their deadly tussle. "Sanchez, Agent Carter, and Rob are coming over later this afternoon to discuss next steps. Agent Carter says he has some new information."

"Oh goodie, I get to see everyone again!" He clapped, but then his face became serious. "What else?"

"I guess this is good news… in a way. Kingsley Investigations finally has some paid work. Sanchez has me helping him on a missing persons case."

Vik gaped at her. "Wait. Our favorite detective… the cantankerous, stay-out-of-my-crime-scene Sanchez actually asked for your help?"

Lara cleared her throat. "Well, not exactly by choice. And this is where good news is bad news. An eight-year-old adopted Chinese girl named Molly was snatched from her bedroom about a week and a half ago. The girl's parents demanded I work the case in cooperation with the D.C. Police. You'll never guess who the parents are."

Lara had been waiting on pins and needles to break the information to him. Vik was the one person who would understand the significance.

Vik's mouth opened. "Who?"

"The Langstons."

For a moment, a look of confusion lingered on his face. Then, a glimmer entered his eyes. "But I thought they turned you down for that surveillance job… remember when…" He stopped himself before reminding her about Sully's death.

A sharp pang traveled through her body and something heavy pressed against her chest. Lately, with the anniversary of his death around the corner, she thought about Sully every day.

"But why would the Langstons reject you for a surveillance system and then later hire you to find their daughter?"

That is the million-dollar question.

Vik's eyes bulged as he seemed to put two and two together.

Then his jaw dropped. "You don't know the first thing about missing persons."

Lara pressed her lips together. "Thanks for reminding me... but you're right. I'm way out of my element. And we just found out the girl has been smuggled back to China."

No pressure. There's only the life of an eight-year-old girl on the line. And her wealthy, powerful parents to heap mass destruction upon my life if I fail.

"But how?" Vik's mouth was still hanging open.

"Cynthia Langston, the wife, claims she found an advertisement for Kingsley Investigations on FishBowl."

Vik looked confused. "We're advertising on social media now?"

"Nope," Lara said. "I've never advertised for Kingsley Investigations anywhere. Cynthia said the ad boasted about my skills in finding missing children. This puzzle has been bothering me for days. Either Cynthia found out about me another way and is mistaken about the ad, or someone placed an ad for Kingsley Investigations. I need you to find out if there was an ad, and I want to know who placed it."

"Will do, boss." Vik pulled out his smartphone and made a note.

Lara exhaled sharply. For the next few minutes, she filled Vik in on most of the details of the kidnapping case. After she finished, she smiled broadly at him. "I really missed you. Kingsley Investigations is not the same without you."

"No, you missed my mad skillz," Vik said, grinning.

"Yeah, those too."

He beamed at her. "Anything else?"

"Oh yeah, we're far from done. Sanchez sent me Molly's genome by email. Apparently after you identified Gavin Weir last time, the detective thinks we can conjure up answers for him."

"But she's a little girl, not a criminal with a record," Vik said, rubbing his chin. "The technique we used to find Gavin doesn't really apply."

Lara furrowed her brow. "I pointed that out to him, but he still wants us to check it out. Maybe she has relatives in the United States?"

Vik frowned. "I suppose that's possible. I can search the databases and see if I find anything."

"There's more. We identified the kidnapper as Dr. Yingyue Kong. She's a Chinese national and a scientist at the Macrobian Institute of Life Sciences. Dr. Yishan Kong, who signed a letter authorizing Molly's travel as her alleged father, heads the institute. Find out whatever you can about the Kongs and this institute."

Vik nodded and made a note on his smartphone.

"Also, I'm still trying to determine which Chinese orphanage worked with the American adoption agency to bring Molly over to the United States for the Langstons. Dr. Liam Nilsson was the director of Miracle Springs Eternal Adoption Agency at the time of Molly's adoption. See if you can track him down. Maybe he can tell us something."

"Miracle Springs Eternal?" Vik said, smirking at the name.

"One more thing. The video footage from the airport came in via an anonymous tip. I want to know who submitted the video footage to the tip line."

Vik nodded and made a note. "No problem, boss. Is that it?"

"Not quite," Lara said as a wave of fatigue came over her. "I need you to do some Internet research on two companies. Dig up whatever you can find on GenTech Industries. That's Mr. Langston's company. Then, I'd like you to look into Horizon Genomics for personal reasons."

"That's your parents' company, isn't it?"

"Yeah… apparently, they did research on aplastic anemia and gene mutations. And I want to know why. If I have the condition, they may have had it, too." Lara scrunched her face. "It might be hard to find information online, since my parents died in 2003. But they must have published their research somewhere."

Vik paused for a moment. "Wasn't Lance the one who told

you about their company in the first place? Maybe he knows something."

Lara pondered his words for a few seconds. "It slipped my mind in all the chaos. I'll give him a call."

Staring at his smartphone, Vik's eyes grew large. "Wow, this is a long list."

Lara raised her hands in the air helplessly. "If I could, I'd clone myself and create a team of minions to take care of it all."

Vik smirked. "You'd have to make sure to genetically modify them and turn off their stubborn genes. Otherwise they might start a mutiny."

"Good point."

They exchanged knowing looks and then burst out laughing.

EIGHTEEN

Trail of Evidence

Lara hovered over a plate of assorted donuts on her kitchen island, momentarily intoxicated by the cinnamon and vanilla aromas. She took a bite, relishing the sweet, sugary pastry. She breathed a bit easier as a familiar feeling of satisfaction came over her. *Enjoy it while it lasts. The sugar crash will come soon enough.*

Rob, Sanchez, and Agent Carter stood around the island, clasping steaming mugs of coffee. For a few moments, they just sipped hot coffee and munched on donuts. Without warning, Rob nudged her elbow. A huge grin plastered on his face, he motioned with his head in Sanchez's direction and put his hand in front of his mouth. She turned to see what was so funny.

Oh dear.

The detective had unwisely chosen the powdered jelly donut. Powdered sugar dotted his cheek and nose, and a large blob of red jelly rested on his chest, staining his white, button-down shirt.

Agent Carter narrowed his eyes at them and then peered over at Sanchez, an amused smile spreading across his face. Rob gave her a look of urgency, imploring her silently to say something. Agent Carter nodded in agreement.

Why do I have to tell him? She stole a glance at the detective who contently savored his coffee, oblivious to the back and forth. *For once, he's in a good mood.*

If Sanchez caught a glimpse of his reflection or noticed the jelly without anyone saying anything, there would be hell to pay. Especially for her.

She shot them an annoyed glare. Rob shuffled his feet and avoided her gaze, and Agent Carter pretended to be distracted, a sheepish grin on his face.

The detective finally looked up at them, his eyes large and inquisitive.

"What?" he asked, his eyes narrowing.

Lara handed him a napkin and pointed to his shirt.

When he looked down, his face flushed slightly. Then he snatched the napkin from her, moved to the sink, and rubbed his shirt, spreading the jelly around.

No, not that way… you're making it worse.

Lara took a deep breath as Sanchez reached for the wet rag from behind the sink and dabbed it lightly. Then her heart nearly stopped.

The house is way too quiet. She recalled how Loki had gotten into the trash bin the previous day and ripped everything to shreds. A sudden tremor rippled through Lara's system. *Where's Loki?*

She spun around in a panic, and her eyes landed on his dog bed in the corner. For once, Loki lay quietly, pretending to snooze—albeit with one eye open to keep watch over her guests. She checked her watch and let out a heavy sigh. She tapped her foot impatiently and glanced over at the sink. Sanchez was still attempting to clean his shirt.

C'mon guys. We don't have all day.

Sensing her growing impatience, Rob said, "Carter, I hope you have something for us. Our trip to Fort Leavenworth was a total bust."

"I take it General MacFarlan wouldn't talk," Agent Carter said, his words muffled by the remainder of his donut.

Worse. He'll likely never talk again.

Lara told Agent Carter everything that had transpired during their prison visit—the conversation with MacFarlan's lawyer and the general's cryptic message for Lara. "MacFarlan took a bullet to the chest just before we were about to leave," she said. "Someone working for this BlackDragon character must have gotten to him in prison."

"Do you think Harry was the one to shut him up?" Agent Carter asked, his face blanching.

Rob shrugged. "Has Harry ever gone by BlackDragon?"

"Not that I know of," Agent Carter said.

Several moments of silence descended around the island, followed by more sipping and munching.

"Did you get a chance to talk to the NSA?" Lara asked Agent Carter, eager to move things forward.

Agent Carter finished his coffee and cleared his throat. "Yes. I spoke to the head of counterintelligence at the NSA. The conversation was rather enlightening."

Lara raised an eyebrow.

Agent Carter continued. "The NSA closed its investigation on CyberShop after Frank and Anita were cleared of their involvement. There was no record of the case being reopened or Justyne working with anyone from that department. In fact, she was detailed to DARPA for causing so much discord in her home office. Upper management needed some time to figure out what to do with her. Apparently, Stepanov requested his own detail assignment to DARPA to keep an eye on her."

Detective Sanchez returned to the kitchen island, his face reddened and his chest puffed out slightly. He wore a large, wet, pink stain on his shirt. Lara's chest heaved again when she saw the white powder on his cheek. She took another napkin from the counter, shot Sanchez a determined look, and dabbed her cheek as a signal.

The detective's eyes bulged. He shook his head vehemently and waved dismissively.

Okay, then it's your problem.

"That means Justyne was never *officially* involved in any investigation?" Rob asked.

Agent Carter nodded. "That's correct. The NSA didn't want to reopen the CyberShop case after the embarrassment over Frank and Anita. Justyne was only pretending to work the case to get information from Rob."

Rob's face paled. "And I fell right into her trap. Like a fly to sticky paper."

"But didn't your boss tell you to work with her?" Lara asked, coming to his defense.

He stared at his feet. "Yeah, but never in writing. I should have known better."

"And those surveillance bugs you found," Agent Carter said, turning to the detective, who straightened his posture. "I traced the serial numbers. Before they were marked for destruction, they were used by a special agent working for Harry Cogan. You'll never guess who."

Rob slapped the counter. "Chimbo?"

Agent Carter nodded. "Yep. That could explain how the folder disappeared. Chimbo must have delivered it to Harry instead of the director."

Lara sank on her stool. "So, not only did we lose the chance to put Harry in jail, he now knows everything about Sully's investigation into his activities."

"I'm afraid so," Agent Carter said.

Rob slammed his mug on the island and threw up his hands.

"Let's look at the positives," Sanchez said. "I don't think Harry planned for the bugs at Spectral to be found. And we now know he's got a minion working for him. We can use that against him."

Lara rubbed her chin. "It's the biggest mistake he's made so far…"

"Should we put a tail on Chimbo?" Rob asked, a hopeful glint in his eye.

"With what resources?" Agent Carter asked, looking over at the detective.

"Sorry," Sanchez said. "Until we have real evidence of a crime, I can't commit department resources."

"I'll do it!" Vik said eagerly, bounding into the kitchen with an excited look on his face. Loki rose from his bed and raced over to greet him. "I'd love me a good stakeout."

Lara suppressed an eyeroll. "No, Vik. This isn't standard PI stuff. If you're made, it could be dangerous."

"I scoff in the face of danger," Vik said, forming his hands into a steeple and laughing manically.

Lara set her jaw and stood firm. "Remember, Sully likely got killed because he knew too much about the operation." *He knew a lot more than we thought.*

At the buzz of a smartphone, everyone glanced down at their electronic devices in unison.

"That's me, I'm afraid," Agent Carter said, scrolling through the messages on his screen. "Work is calling. I have to run."

"But we didn't get a chance to discuss next steps..." Lara said, a hint of disappointment in her tone.

"I'll support whatever you, Rob, and Sanchez come up with," Agent Carter said, grabbing a glazed donut for the road. Before they could say goodbye, he exited out the back door.

As soon as it closed, Loki pawed the back door and yelped.

Rob motioned with his head at Loki and then shot her a what-is-his-deal look.

"He needs to go potty," Lara said.

"I'll take him outside," Rob said as he stood. "I need some fresh air anyway."

Lara gave him a half-smile and watched him take Loki outside. Then she smacked her forehead. *Gah. I never got a chance to ask Agent Carter if he tracked down Anita.*

Vik grabbed a cake donut and popped the whole thing into his mouth. He chewed for a few moments. "So, I found some interesting stuff related to your missing persons case." Small pieces of donut flew from between his lips as he talked.

"I asked Vik do some research for us," Lara explained to

Sanchez, who looked surprised. Turning back to Vik, she asked, "What did you find?"

"I found the source of the ad for Kingsley Investigations on FishBowl." Vik laughed before continuing. "It's actually pretty good. Someone put some effort into making it look authentic. The ad described you as a seasoned expert in recovering missing children."

"What?" Lara's eyes bulged, her heart in her throat.

"Are you saying that Lara never placed an ad for Kingsley Investigations?" Sanchez asked, his face twisted in confusion. When Vik nodded, he glared at Lara and clenched his fists. "Why didn't you tell me this sooner?"

Her postured stiffened. "Because I didn't have any useful information. We're telling you now."

"Why would someone else place an ad for *your* business?" Sanchez rubbed his forehead.

And lie about my expertise? Someone wanted me to get involved in the case. But who?

"Did you find out who did it?" Lara asked Vik.

"I traced the ad to an IP address in China," Vik said. "It belongs to a computer located at the Macrobian Institute."

The news hit her like a bolt of lightning. Lara took a few steps backward, grasping her stomach.

The detective froze, his mouth open. "You mean The Macrobian Institute of Life Sciences in Shenzhen, China? The place where our kidnapper works?"

"That's the one," Vik said. "I'm not one hundred percent positive. But if I were on site at the institute, I would be able to know for sure if the ad was posted there."

Sanchez frowned. "You're telling me that someone at this institute put an ad for Kingsley Investigations on FishBowl… and the Langstons just happened to find the ad and demand that Lara work this case?"

Lara braced herself against the island. Her head spun in circles. Her knees felt weak. The coincidences were beginning to add up, and she didn't like the picture they painted.

That makes the trip to China even more dangerous. Am I walking into a trap?

"I found some other interesting connections," Vik said.

"What other connections?" Lara asked.

"Well, in my research, I discovered the Macrobians are a group of transhumanist intellectuals and scientists who seek to extend their lives indefinitely and discover the fountain of youth through science. The original Macrobians were an ancient tribal kingdom in the Horn of Africa who were known to have long lives. Their civilization was briefly mentioned in a book called *The Histories*, written by the ancient Greek historian Herodotus."

"Why are you telling me this?" Lara asked, her brow furrowed.

"Um… because I found it in a copy of the book on your shelf in the library."

Lara's mouth fell open. "That's my father's old book…" She'd long forgotten about the strange book she had put on the shelf in her library.

"There's more… Herodotus was the first figure to mention a water source capable of granting eternal youth to anyone who drinks from it."

"The fountain of youth…" Lara mumbled.

My father's painting.

Rob opened the back door, and Loki came bouncing back into the kitchen. After closing the door, he stood still for a moment, inspecting their faces carefully. "Did I miss something?" he asked.

Lara glared at Sanchez and Vik, warning them with her eyes to keep their mouths shut. If Rob knew what they'd discovered, he would start in with his concerns about the Langstons and her trip to China again. She didn't want to hear it.

Whatever the Langstons are up to, I'll handle it.

Rob's eyes lit up. "While I was outside, I thought of a way to get Harry."

"Do tell," Sanchez said.

"Harry doesn't know we know about Chimbo. And Chimbo

thinks we're on the same side. Why not use Chimbo to run a sting operation and draw Harry out of the woodwork? He won't even see it coming. And we don't need evidence of his past activities if we can catch him in the act."

Lara pressed her lips together. "That might work… but there are at least two problems."

"Oh?"

"We don't have enough information to make it happen. For example, does Chimbo work for Harry? How much does he know about Harry's activities? Is Harry still involved with the black market?"

"No problem," Rob said nonchalantly. "I'll get more information."

Lara bit her lip. "The other issue is that I don't have time to plan a sting operation right now."

Rob's face soured immediately. "Because of your other case?"

Lara nodded. "Yeah. I'll probably be heading to China sometime next week."

His expression tightened. "What am I supposed to do while you're busy with your other case? Just sit around and wait for you to come back?"

First, he's worried I'm doing too much. Now, I'm not doing enough.

Heat crept up her neck, and Lara reached for her wallet on the counter, pulled out her business credit card, and tossed it to him.

Rob didn't expect her sudden move and stood there like a limp noodle. The card clattered to the floor.

"There's my credit card," Lara snapped. "Buy whatever you need. If you've got a plan, get it done. Maybe Sanchez and Vik will help you."

Vik nodded eagerly and clapped his hands. "I'll help."

Sanchez snapped out of a daze and nodded. "Sure, sure. Whatever you need…"

Rob bent over to pick up the credit card and scowled at her.

As Lara was about to turn off silent mode on her smartphone, she noticed a missed call and felt the blood drain from her face.

When she recognized the number, her hand flew up and covered her mouth.

Rob glanced over her shoulder. "What's wrong?"

"My doctor called. My test results are in, and she wants me to come to her office tomorrow to discuss them in person."

"That don't sound good," Sanchez blurted.

No, it doesn't.

NINETEEN

Test Results

___

October 8, 2028

LARA AND MAGGIE sat in the office, waiting for the doctor to return with the test results. The results tab on the giant flat screen TV on the wall blinked at her, taunting her with news of her terrible fate. Dr. Saifi left to retrieve the tablet with Lara's results from the cabinet behind the reception desk. The ticking of an old-school clock hanging on the wall above the TV thudded loudly in her head with each passing second. She reached in her bag for a mint and popped it in her mouth. As the comforting flavor reached her stomach, it sizzled.

Lara shifted uncomfortably in her seat, trying to focus on her breathing. Maggie reached over and squeezed her hand gently.

Whatever it is, I can handle it. Right?

Dr. Saifi returned with the tablet under her arm and closed the door behind her. She made her way to her desk, sat down, put the tablet on her desk, and leaned forward in her chair. She scrolled up and down on the screen and glanced at Lara over the rims of her glasses. Her contemplative expression made Lara think she was preparing to share some bad news and wasn't sure where to begin.

Please don't be aplastic anemia.

"Just tell me everything," Lara said, resigned to her fate.

"The good news is that we have some preliminary answers." Dr. Saifi cleared her throat. "The bad news is that you may have a serious condition."

Lara exhaled sharply.

"I'll start with the results from your complete blood count test," Dr. Saifi said, staring down at the chart on the tablet. The TV screen on the wall lit up with a graph filled with numbers.

"Okay…" Lara said, gulping.

Dr. Saifi frowned slightly and pointed at the screen. "Your red blood cell and platelet counts are slightly below normal. And your white blood cell count is hovering at the lower end of the normal range."

Maggie squeezed Lara's hand again.

"What does that mean?" Lara asked, a slight tremor in her voice.

"Your low platelet count accounts for your bloody noses. And your low red blood cell level explains your fatigue, dizziness, and the blackouts."

Lara's face contorted as she tried to make sense of the new information.

Dr. Saifi continued. "These are potential symptoms of a blood disorder in which your bone marrow doesn't make enough new blood cells."

"Like aplastic anemia?" Lara asked, blurting it out.

Dr. Saifi's eyes widened, and her mouth opened. "How did you know?"

"A few days ago, I found some research in my father's old stuff about it. He was conducting research on the condition. I looked it up online, and it matches my symptoms."

Dr. Saifi nodded slowly. "I'm not yet one hundred percent certain. I've found indicators to suggest you may indeed have aplastic anemia. The condition is rare. Typically, we see it appear in children or young adults. Do you know if either of your parents had the condition?"

Lara shrugged. "No. That's why I was looking for their health records. All I found was some scientific research and a company brochure."

"Regardless of the origin of the condition, aplastic anemia is caused by mutations in certain types of genes. The gene type can give us a better indicator for the presence of the condition, its source, the prognosis, and potential treatments. That's why I ran another whole genome map of your DNA."

"I assume you found a gene mutation?" Lara asked.

Dr. Saifi nodded. "Yes. But it's important to understand that you can have the gene mutation without developing the condition. Aplastic anemia is a recessive disorder."

"What does that mean?" Lara asked.

"It means that you generally need two mutated copies of the same gene, one from each of your parents, to develop the disorder," Dr. Saifi said.

"If I have the gene, does that mean both my parents had the disease?"

Is that why they were studying it?

Dr. Saifi shook her head. "Not necessarily. If they were both carriers, then they were not affected by the condition, but passed the genes to you. In that case, you would have a twenty-five percent chance of developing the disorder. However, if one of your parents suffered from the disorder and the other was a carrier, your probability would increase to fifty percent. If both of your parents suffered from aplastic anemia, then your certainty would near one hundred percent. Inherited forms usually present during the first decade of life, so your case is quite rare."

"There are other ways to get aplastic anemia?" Lara asked.

"It can also be acquired from exposure to radiation, toxic chemicals, and certain drugs or caused by an autoimmune disorder or viral infection. But you don't have a gene mutation that suggests an environmental source for the condition."

Maggie interjected. "Dr. Saifi, may I ask what gene mutation Lara has?"

Dr. Saifi gave a short nod with a smile. "The geneticist identified a mutation on the ACD gene, which scientists believe causes hereditary aplastic anemia."

Maggie rubbed her chin. "That gene codes for the telomeres-binding protein, doesn't it?"

Telomeres? As soon as Lara heard the word, her mind began to race. Dr. Pulido from the adoption agency mentioned telomeres. Then Lara had also seen the term in her father's notes.

"Dolly!" she blurted.

Dr. Saifi and Maggie gaped at her, surprised by her strange outburst.

Lara's lip trembled. "The first cloned sheep died as a result of shortened telomeres. Does that mean I'm going to die, too?"

Maggie grabbed Lara's hand. "Hon, no, you're going to be fine. Everyone's telomeres shorten over time due to the aging process. That's why we age... why our skin develops wrinkles and our hair turns gray. Essentially, we're all dying slowly."

"Okay." Lara's cheeks flushed hot. She turned back to Dr. Saifi. "Sorry, you were saying..."

"Your friend is correct about the aging process, but the mutation in the ACD gene does lead to premature shortening of the telomeres. Excessive shortening of telomeres can lead to certain disorders, including hereditary aplastic anemia. This is the type usually diagnosed in adults."

"So, that's what you think I have?" Lara asked, her throat tightening with a lump. "Aplastic anemia caused by the shortening of my telomeres as a result of a gene mutation?"

"That's my best diagnosis at this time," Dr. Saifi said. "The disorder can develop suddenly or slowly. In your case, the onset is rather sudden. Without treatment, it will get worse and could become life threatening."

"What are my options?" Lara asked, clutching her sides.

"We would need to do a bone marrow biopsy to confirm a diagnosis of the condition. We can do that right here and send the sample to the lab. I'd also like you to get a blood transfusion today. That will get your blood cell counts back up to acceptable levels. You'll feel relief from your symptoms, but it's not a permanent fix."

Lara grimaced at the thought. "How do you do a biopsy?" A wave of nausea settled on her as she imagined the possible routes to getting material located inside of bones.

Not another needle.

"We'll have to extract red marrow from the back of your hip to measure your stem cells. If the number is low, we'll know you have aplastic anemia."

"What happens then?" Lara asked, bracing herself for the worst news. "Is there a cure?" She squeezed Maggie's hand harder.

Dr. Saifi frowned slightly. "A bone marrow transplant can often cure the condition—"

"But I'd need to find a matching donor first," Lara interrupted, her heart sinking. *No family members.*

Dr. Saifi nodded. "Once we confirm the diagnosis, we'll need to tailor your treatment based on your gene mutation. Given your situation, I'd like to explore options beyond a transplant."

"What sorts of options? Lara asked.

"If the biopsy comes back positive for aplastic anemia, we can try some new gene therapies."

Lara scrunched her nose. "Therapy for my genes?"

Dr. Saifi laughed lightly. "Not in the sense you're thinking. We would use gene editing tools to correct the mutation. Essentially, we'll fix the source of the condition and restore blood cell production in your own bone marrow. We could also explore some anti-aging therapies, which are focused on repairing the telomeres."

"Does this therapy stuff actually work?" Lara asked, wrinkling her forehead.

Dr. Saifi grinned. "Over the past decade, systematic collection of genomic data across the country has led to scientific breakthroughs and generated many new ways to cure diseases at the source of the problem by modifying DNA. The treatments are showing positive results, but only in some cases at this time."

Before he died, my father wanted to do that work.

Lara thought about the two cases on her plate for Kingsley Investigations, and the blood drained from her face. "Do I need to stop working?"

"You may want to avoid intense physical activity and anything that could result in injury for a while. But you should be able to assume your normal routines after today's blood transfusion." Dr. Saifi rose from her chair and motioned to the door. "Let's go have that biopsy and transfusion done right away, okay?"

As she got up, Lara's pulse spiked in anticipation of the pain.

Dr. Saifi turned to her. "Until we can figure out a long-term treatment plan, I'd like you to come in every few weeks for blood transfusions. That should keep you from experiencing another blackout."

"I'll make sure she comes in," Maggie said behind her.

At the doorway, the doctor stopped and glanced at Lara. "Oh, I almost forgot. After we entered your new genome profile into the national database, I noticed something strange. In addition to the records from your service in the Army, there was an updated genome profile in the database for you every year from when you were fourteen in 2009 until you joined the military. Do you know anything about that?"

Lara's mouth fell open. "What?"

"The profiles were submitted to your digital health record by a company called Horizon Genomics. Does that sound familiar?"

Lara stared numbly at the video screen which displayed her test results in full detail, including the company that sequenced her DNA. "That was my parents' company."

Dr. Saifi raised an eyebrow, and Maggie's mouth fell open.

But they died in 2003.

Lara's mind whirled for a few moments in response to the shocking coincidence. And then she recalled a fuzzy memory. "I remember having my blood drawn every year when I was a teenager. I wasn't sure why. They told me it was part of some pilot program to sequence the American population."

Dr. Saifi nodded. "Yes, I remember that… The U.S. Government tapped the foster care system for several years to generate data to support scientific research. They wanted to gather what they called longitudinal genomic data. That's long before they launched the national database."

Maggie's mouth fell open. "They treated foster kids like guinea pigs?"

Lara shrugged. "Yeah, as wards of the state, we didn't have much of a choice. I think they offered a small payment to participants, though." She gave Maggie a toothy grin. "That's how I bought myself some new tennis shoes."

Maggie's grimace deepened.

Dr. Saifi added, "And apparently, the DNA sequencing was outsourced to China. That means the Chinese probably have access to the data as well." Her tone was grim.

Lara's eyes widened. "But I thought you said it was Horizon Genomics that submitted the profile to my digital health record."

"I did. Horizon Genomics is a Chinese company."

My parents had connections in China?

TWENTY

Horizon Genomics

October 9, 2028

LARA SIPPED her watermelon banana smoothie, enjoying the sweet but slightly tart treat. At least this time, she had the good sense to add a protein supplement to balance out the hefty infusion of carbs. Since her blood transfusion, she was feeling more energetic than she'd felt in months. But she didn't want to press her luck.

God knows, I haven't had much good luck lately.

After her doctor's appointment, Lara had called Lance Duncan for information about her parents, and he suggested they meet at Smoothie King in-between meetings. Studying the brightly colored walls and giant posters of fruit at Smoothie King, she smiled at the memory of her first stakeout with Vik. They had waited in this tight space for hours, hoping to get information from Photonics CEO Lance Duncan on Project Gecko.

Across from her, Finn slurped a mango kale smoothie with an energy enhancer. He wore his official Army physical training uniform—running shoes, black pants, and a black jacket with diagonal yellow stripes, complete with the Army logo embroidered in yellow. While Lara met with Lance a bit later, Finn would go for his daily run.

Over the past few days, Finn and Lara had struggled to find quality time to spend with each other. While she was consumed by two cases, Finn had been working twelve-hour days at the Pentagon. And now they were multi-tasking and squeezing in time where they could find it—on the ride over to the smoothie shop and before her meeting with Lance.

She fidgeted with her hands, her fingers cold and clammy. Despite a whole thirty minutes in the car together, she had yet to tell him about her medical diagnosis.

Finn glanced at her and opened his mouth as if he was going to say something, but hesitated. "I know you've been avoiding me," he said, biting down on his lips. "Danny told me you got your test results yesterday. But I didn't get a phone call. Not even a text."

"I wanted to tell you in person," Lara said in a defensive tone, attempting to suppress her anger at the detective for tattling again. "And you've been so busy with work at the Pentagon, I didn't know when I'd get a chance to tell you." She swallowed hard, and her chest tingled with butterflies.

"You're the one balancing two major cases," Finn said, crossing his arms. Then he relaxed his posture and looked at her, his eyes wide and full of concern. "Are you going to tell me now?"

Lara avoided his gaze and fell silent for a moment. If her diagnosis was confirmed, there was no way she would be able to meet the Army's Standards of Medical Fitness. Without a cure, the disease would mean the end of her Army career. Even if she had a bone marrow transplant, Lara might not be cleared again for the battlefield. Would her relationship with Finn survive if she couldn't go back into combat, let alone stay in the Army?

"You're scaring me, Lara," Finn said, rubbing the back of his neck. "Is it really that bad?"

Lara nodded and proceeded to give him the bad news. As

she filled him in about the preliminary diagnosis of aplastic anemia, the outstanding tests, potential treatments, and prognoses, his shoulders slumped. He pressed his lips tight and listened to her calmly, not breaking eye contact. When she finished, he sat silently for several minutes as if he were running through all the implications in his head.

Taking another sip of his smoothie, Finn said, "If you really do have this thing, you won't be able to sign up for active duty."

This thing?

"Yep, that's correct," Lara said, her stomach twisting into a knot. "I'll probably have to separate from the Army altogether. My military career will be over."

Several moments of silence fell between them. Lara fidgeted with her straw. Her lip quivering, she asked, "You gonna break up with me?"

Finn's face contorted with confusion. "Why would I break up with you over this?"

Lara gulped, a lump forming in her throat. "I dunno... because I'm damaged goods... because you can't have your dream of deploying overseas together?"

"Oh Lara," Finn said with a compassionate tone, "that was just a dream. Probably a silly one at that. You actually think the Army would let us serve together? Ha! We'd probably get sent to opposite sides of the world—by accident due to some glitch in the planning system."

"Ain't that the truth," Lara said, exhaling a breath of relief.

She wasn't sure about the future of her relationship with Finn, but she didn't want it to end for a stupid reason.

"The truth is, I'm not worried about us managing separation due to a deployment. You're not at all like my ex-wife. She didn't have anything of her own, and her whole life revolved around me. When our dream to have kids fell apart, she began to resent my time away. And the constant fighting ended our marriage. If I get deployed, you probably won't even notice I'm gone." He grinned at her. "The time will just fly by, and then I'll be back."

Lara slapped him playfully on the arm. "Hey, that's not true."

Well, maybe.

Finn gazed at her. "One of the things I love most about you is your stubborn independence. But it's also the trait that drives me the most crazy." The sarcasm was hard to miss.

"What do you mean by that?" Lara asked, her eyes narrowing.

Finn held out his hands. "Lara, remember I love you when I say this. Don't punch me, okay?" He paused to make sure she agreed. "Lara, you don't listen to people who care about you. Once you have your mind set on something, you're as immovable as Mount Everest."

"What are you saying?" Lara asked.

Finn hesitated.

"Out with it," Lara said.

"Danny told me you're planning to go to China with Mr. Langston. And I don't like it."

Grr, I'm being ambushed.

Lara frowned. "It's not for you to like or not like. I was hired for a case, and I'm going to see it through. Plus, Mr. Langston said he'd get the op cleared by the Pentagon."

"I wouldn't be so sure about that. The Langstons haven't been straight with you from the beginning. Danny told me how they've misled you. Why? What's their agenda? And this team of mercenaries? They'll be working for Mr. Langston, not you. It's just not smart going into a contested environment like China without someone who has your six. It's not only dangerous, it's plain stupid. And I know you're not stupid."

Lara stared at her straw, as if she were expecting it to provide her with answers. Her thoughts drifted to her decision to check out the storage unit by herself during Sully's case. It was in the midst of trying to stop Fiddler from carrying out his plan. She had just refused to work for him. So, he kidnapped her in the parking lot of the storage facility. She nearly met a tragic end in a tank full of bionic bugs.

Finn does have a point.

Lara leaned back in her chair, her cheeks flushing hot. "You're not going to talk me out of it."

"I figured. And that's why I'm going with you," Finn said, his chest thrust out.

"What?" Lara's jaw nearly hit the table. "But what about your work at the Pentagon?"

"I'll make time."

"I'm not going to let you come with me."

"That isn't your decision. I've already told Mr. Langston I'm in, and he was over the moon about it."

Finn went behind my back?

Lara's hands began to shake, her pulse elevated. "You had no right! If something goes awry, it would mean the end of your Army career. You can't honestly think the Pentagon is going to sign off on this. Even if the mission is a success, how are we going to get in and out of China without the Army finding out about it?"

"You do realize I'm a Green Beret, right? Stealth is my middle name." He grinned at her.

"C'mon Finn, I mean it."

"This is non-negotiable. If you're going to China, I'm going to have your back. I'm coming with you, and that's final. Now it's your choice." He leaned back in his chair and crossed his arms. "Are you still going?"

Lara's ears pounded. She wanted to scream at him for risking everything for her and forcing her into such an impossible corner. *It was one thing for Lara to risk her own career, but shouldering the burden of Finn's life and illustrious career on top of it made her decision to go to China even harder.* If she failed, he would lose his dream job. Maybe even his life. *Is he expecting me to capitulate now? Because the risk is too great?*

At the same time, Lara understood she'd put him in an impossible situation with her decision. Finn knew he couldn't talk her out of it, and he wasn't the kind of guy to let her go on a dangerous mission without backup. From his perspective, it was an honorable move for which she should feel enormous gratitude. Instead, an intense pang of guilt stung her gut. I don't know if I can let him do this. Her chest tightened at the thought of backing out.

But I can't let Molly down.

"We're going to China then," Lara said, not blinking.

A shadow fell across their table, and she jumped slightly. A tremor passed through her body as she looked up to see Lance wearing a bespoke blue suit, holding a green smoothie, and smiling down at her.

"Thanks for meeting me here. Otherwise, I might have missed out on my daily fix," Lance said, glancing curiously at Finn.

She'd been so consumed with frustration over Finn she didn't notice the tall, handsome, middle-aged man with dusty blond hair come into the small shop.

"Uh yeah… sorry, I didn't see you come in," Lara said, her face flushing. The irony was not lost on her. The last time she'd come to Smoothie King to meet Lance, she'd nearly tackled him in line to ask him some questions. At first, he was quite rude to her, that is until he recognized her name. Later in his office, she learned that Lance and his wife had been good friends with her parents—back when they were young and idealistic and starting up tech companies in Silicon Valley.

"I didn't want to disturb you. You two seemed to be in the middle of something," Lance said, looking back and forth between them.

"Yeah. Um… this is Finn, my… uh, boyfriend." She noticed the corners of Finn's mouth turning upward. "This is Lance Duncan, CEO of Photonics, and a family friend."

Finn stood and shook his hand. "Sir, it's nice to meet you."

"I don't mean to chase you off," Lance said, moving toward his chair.

"Oh, I'm just Lara's chauffeur for the morning. I'm going for my daily run. Take your time."

She watched Finn leave the smoothie shop and let out a heavy sigh.

Lance took a seat across from her, his forehead creased. "You okay?"

She waved dismissively. "Oh, I'm fine." She didn't feel like talking about her health anymore. One disclosure of her terrible diagnosis per day was one too many.

Lance took a long drink of his smoothie. "So, you wanted to know more about your parents."

She took a deep breath. "Last time we talked you mentioned my father's company. Horizon Genomics. Since then, I found some of his scientific research in a box of his things. Apparently, he was looking into rare blood disorders related to shortening telomeres."

He tilted his head backward, eyes directed at the ceiling. "Ah, yes. Your father was obsessed with telomeres. He went on and on about them as if they were the secret to unlocking the universe."

Lara wrinkled her nose. "What are they exactly?" She'd been so distracted by her illness and fears about the accelerated shortening of her telomeres that she'd forgotten to ask Dr. Saifi about their significance.

"This is a topic I'm quite familiar with since I own several biotechnology companies engaged in genetics research. Telomeres are the DNA sequences at the ends of your chromosomes, designed to protect your genome from damage. They are made of thousands of repeated DNA nucleotides. Every time a cell divides to replicate itself, the telomeres lose several nucleotides and get shorter. When they get too short, the cells no longer divide, stop reproducing, and ultimately die. Over time, this leads to aging and death."

"Is it possible to determine how long your body has to live by examining your telomeres?" Lara asked, her hand trembling slightly.

"That's the current theory, but I'm rather skeptical about its validity."

"Why's that?"

"Some think the length of telomeres acts as a biological clock.

But many reputable scientists remain uncertain if the shortening of telomeres directly causes aging or merely the diseases that cause aging. As I recall, Ethan was desperate to figure out how to lengthen telomeres. He thought he was on the cusp of discovering the biological fountain of youth. Supposedly, longer telomeres lengthen human lifespans and postpone the onset of age-related diseases. But the science has not yet been proven."

"I found some research on rare blood disorders in my dad's old files," Lara said. "Do you know why he would be interested in them?"

Lance rubbed his chin. "Well, I'm sure it was related to his study of telomeres. Blood disorders are among the age-related diseases that may be caused by the shortening of telomeres. As far as I know, he was working on developing a measuring kit for telomeres and vitamin supplements to extend human lifespans and prevent the onset of such disorders. He was always on a soapbox about people needing to get serious about monitoring their biological clocks. He got into DNA lifestyle coaching for a while and had a few wealthy clients, mostly from Southern California."

Lara wrinkled her nose. "What's DNA lifestyle coaching?"

"Basically, he would encourage clients to exercise, eat a healthy diet, and measure their telomeres periodically. All in the service of extending life."

"How does measurement work?" Lara asked.

"You need to collect white blood cells from a tiny sample of blood. They're the only type of blood cells that contain DNA. Scientists isolate the DNA from these cells and measure the length of telomeres. Once you know your length, you need to compare it to a large population of samples to interpret it. Basically, you'll get a percentile that tells you if your telomeres are shortening at the average rate, or faster or slower than average. For example, if you're in the sixtieth percentile, sixty percent of people have the same or shorter telomeres than you. And only forty percent have longer telomeres. That score would put you above average, but still not in a group of people with the longest telomeres."

"How long are telomeres on average?" Lara asked.

"In young humans, telomeres are about eight thousand to ten thousand nucleotides long. As we age, the number goes down from there."

"Did my dad make any money measuring telomeres?"

"I don't think so," Lance said. "He told me it was challenging to market his services. Most people don't like to think about their own mortality, and research on telomeres was still in its early stages back then. But there were also some major technical problems with his approach."

"What sort of problems?" Lara asked.

"Although we inherit the length of our telomeres from our parents, there are actually only a few people with significantly short or long telomeres. In other words, they're not the best at predicting how long people will live."

"I assume he shifted gears when the life coaching didn't take off," Lara said.

He rubbed his hands together. "At some point, Ethan changed his course. He started a graduate program in molecular biology at Stanford and experimented with DNA at the university laboratory. Before he died, he wanted to become a geneticist. But your mom was not that happy about it." Lance smirked at the recollection.

"Probably because they were up to their eyeballs in debt," Lara said in a snide tone.

Lance's eyes widened. "Really? I never had the impression they were struggling financially."

"Then they must have been good at hiding it. When they died, they left me with nothing but a huge mound of debt."

And a weird painting.

"I'm really sorry to hear about that." He paused for a moment and looked at her contemplatively. "But you're doing okay now, right?"

"Yes, yes... of course."

Thanks to Sully.

Lara changed the subject. "You mentioned my dad spent time in the genetics lab at Stanford. What sort of experiments was he working on?"

Lance laughed at the memory. "Same crazy stuff. He once bragged to me he'd figured out a way to increase the length of telomeres by as much as one thousand nucleotides. He claimed that would lengthen the human lifespan by several years. All he needed to make the effort a reality was a major infusion of venture capital. Before he died, Ethan was trying to drum up funding for his ambitious proposal in Silicon Valley."

"Do you know if there were any takers?" Lara asked.

Lance shook his head. "Back then, it was still prohibitively expensive to sequence and synthesize DNA. And most venture capitalists didn't have the faintest clue about the economic promise of synthetic biology. They're kicking themselves in the ass now…" He sighed. "Your father was in many ways a man before his time."

"Do you know by chance if my dad or mom suffered from a rare blood disorder… like aplastic anemia?" Lara asked tentatively.

A surprised look fell across Lance's face. He thought about it for a few moments. "If they did, they never told me. Your parents were quite private and rarely shared personal information."

Maybe that's why he had no clue about their finances.

"Do you know what happened to Horizon Genomics after my parents died?" Lara asked.

Lance shrugged his shoulders. "Not sure. Maybe it got bought up during the settlement of their estate?"

Apparently by a Chinese company.

Lara slid the photo of her father with the Chinese woman and baby across the table. "Do you recognize this woman?"

He studied the photo for a few moments. Lara thought she detected a slight twitch in his eye. A slight twitch and then it was gone.

"Hmm… maybe?" Lance said, avoiding eye contact.

"Does anything come to mind about her?" she asked, her pulse fluttering.

"I think she studied microbiology at Stanford, along with your father. It's also possible she worked for his company at one point. My memories are faint, but she looks familiar. I'm sorry, I don't know much more than that." He handed it back to her and stole a glance at his watch. "Shoot, I have to run to my next meeting. If you have more questions, we could schedule another meeting. Just give my executive assistant a call."

"Thanks, I'll do that."

Without further ado, Lance got up, finished the last drops of his smoothie and dumped it in the waste bin a few steps away.

Turning back to Lara, he flashed her a crooked grin. "Let me know if I can help, okay? Anything for Ethan and Donna's kid."

Lara nodded and watched him rush out of the shop, but her stomach clenched.

What does he know that he isn't telling me?

TWENTY-ONE

The State Department

October 10, 2028

ALREADY LARA'S brief experience with the State Department had failed to inspire hope in a successful return of the Langstons' daughter. After forty-five minutes waiting for security screening, the lady at the check-in desk had to process her along with the Langstons to issue their non-escort badges, courtesy of Julian's high-level connections. Without an escort, they'd gotten lost several times in the endless labyrinth of lookalike hallways. Next to her in a row of chairs, Julian and Cynthia sat waiting impatiently for their turn to meet with the desk officer, who was running more than forty minutes late.

Above her, a clock ticked as every second went by, each tick becoming heavier, hitting Lara like a pound of lead. Her hands rested on a hard, cold plastic armchair. The seat itself was cushioned but slightly lumpy. The air tasted like dust, stale and dry, and her nose detected the faintest wisp of mold.

Tapping her pen on her notebook, Lara stared up at the silver-colored plaque on the wall across from the waiting area.

The engraved sign read Bureau of Consular Affairs Office of Children's Issues, Harry S. Truman Building.

Office of Children's Issues. It sounds so bureaucratic and cold.

Before the missing persons case, she'd never heard of such an office at the State Department and was immediately intrigued by the notion of what someone who worked at the office might actually do for a living. As far as she could see, there were no children anywhere.

"I've been meaning to ask you something," Lara said, looking cautiously over at the Langstons.

"What?" Julian snapped.

Cynthia poked him in the arm.

"When the detective and I visited the adoption agency, we couldn't get the name of the orphanage in China where Molly came from. Dr. Josie Pulido, the director, mentioned you might know the Jackson family. They adopted an infant from the same orphanage. If you could give me their contact info, I could—"

"We don't know any Jackson family," Julian snarled.

Why would Josie give me the name, then?

Lara's smartphone buzzed. She glanced at the screen, saw it was Sanchez, and stood, looking for a better place to take the call.

"Got somewhere more important to be?" Julian growled.

Cynthia kicked him in the leg.

"I have to take this call," Lara said, taking a few steps away from him. As she moved down the hall for some privacy, she threw him a glare and pointed to her phone. "It's related to your daughter's case, okay? There's nothing more important than getting Molly home safely."

He relaxed somewhat and motioned for her to go.

"This is Lara," she answered.

"Good. I'm glad you picked up," Sanchez said gruffly. "My contact at the Department of Homeland Security called to let me know that Alicia Novak, the Langstons' teenage babysitter, is finally back in the country. She arrived with her father thirty minutes ago at the Baltimore/Washington International Thurgood Marshall Airport. They've been detained by Customs and Border Protection as persons of interest in our kidnapping case. I've sent over a few of my officers to bring them down to the station for questioning."

"Can you detain them if they're not suspects?" Lara asked, furrowing her brow.

"Um... person of interest. It's a bit of a gray area. Don't worry. Mr. Novak knows his rights and has already threatened to sue me for unlawful detainment. Since he's only a person of interest, I've made it clear that his cooperation is entirely voluntary." Sanchez chuckled. "Well... not entirely. I might have said something about him coming into some trouble with his green card if he didn't help us out. Anyway, he's called in his lawyer and claims to have made contact with Mr. Langston as well. This could be fun." His tone ended on a cheery note.

Sheesh. I'd forgotten what a pain in the butt Sanchez could be.

Lara sneaked a peek at Julian, who continued to stare at the wall with a stony expression.

"I don't think Mr. Novak got through to Mr. Langston yet... because if he had, I'm pretty sure his head would be imploding by now. I'm at the State Department with him and his wife. I'll head over as soon as I'm finished here."

"Great. I'll get the father nice and warmed up and have them ready for you."

Awesome sauce. Now... how to break the news to the Langstons.

Lara turned and walked nimbly down the hallway. She hadn't even returned to her seat before Julian looked up at her expectantly. Lara gulped.

Here goes nothing.

"Any news?" he asked.

"Um, yes... it appears that your babysitter is back in the country and has been taken down to the police station for questioning."

Julian leaped from his seat, his neck turning red and his face twisted in anger. "I'll have that detective's badge."

Lara raised an eyebrow. "Why would you do that? Sanchez is

only doing his job… which is, by the way, getting your daughter back safely. That's what you want, right?"

"Alicia had nothing to do with my daughter's disappearance," Julian snarled. "She's already talked to the police and told them everything she knows. This is harassment."

"How do you suddenly know everything about your daughter's kidnapping?" Lara asked. "Were you there?" She paused for effect. "Or maybe you're upset because there's something you don't want us to know, and Alicia might spill the beans."

His ears turning fire-engine red, Julian clenched his fists and rolled up his sleeves. Cynthia rose from her chair and grabbed her husband's arm. He tried to lunge at Lara, but to his surprise, his wife kept him from reaching her with her strong grip. Lara took several steps backward to restore the space between them.

"You little—" he screamed, raising his fist at her.

"Uh, I wouldn't finish that sentence if I were you. Unless you want me to let you get Molly back on your own. Remember… we made a deal. If you want me to come with you on your little mission, then we do it my way. I'm speaking to Alicia."

A door opened, the hinges creaking loudly. Startled, Lara looked to see an overweight man with rosy cheeks and silver, thin-rimmed glasses peering out. "Mr. and Mrs. Langston?"

Julian and Cynthia whirled around to face him.

"Yes, that's us," Cynthia said.

"I'm Eric Salinger," he said, stepping only a few inches outside his door and shaking their hands. "I'm the desk officer for China and a member of the State Department's child abduction prevention team."

Prevention? It's too late for that.

Julian pointed to her. "This is uh… our private investigator, Lara Kingsley. We would like her to be present if that's okay."

Eric nodded. "Sure. Let's step into my office to talk about your situation."

Following Eric, the Langstons shuffled into the tiny, dimly lit office. Lara slipped through the door just before it closed. Julian and Cynthia took seats in the two wooden chairs across from the messy desk, leaving her without a spot. Lara lingered behind them, cramped between the back of the chairs and the wall.

Lara studied the office, eager to learn about the activities of the mysterious Office of Children's Issues. Behind Eric's desk, there were two sets of shelves stacked with tomes about international law, human trafficking, abductions, and human rights interspersed with stacks of white paper printouts. Multi-colored sticky notes marked important parts of the books that littered his desk.

After sinking slowly into his chair, Eric pushed aside several crumpled wrappers in his struggle to find a file on his desk among disorderly stacks of paper. When he finally found the file he was looking for, it was smudged with chocolate on the corners.

Apparently still wound up from their argument, Julian tapped his foot aggressively on the carpeted floor, creating a rapid series of dull thuds. Cynthia squeezed his hand, turned her neck slightly, and shot Lara a worried look.

Yeah. The last thing we need is another outburst.

Eric cleared his throat and glanced nervously at the Langstons. "I am truly sorry for your situation. Please be assured that the State Department will do whatever it can to ensure the safe return of your daughter. Unfortunately, China is not party to the Hague Convention of 25 October 1980 on the Civil Aspects of International Child Abduction." His voice wavered slightly.

Julian leaned forward, a scowl forming on his face. "I don't care about your conventions. Molly is our adopted daughter, and she was taken from us. My good friend Neil—he's your boss's boss's boss—he said you could help me get her back. I'm not here to listen to excuses."

Eric shifted in his chair. "Um… you said Molly departed the United States with a Chinese passport?"

Julian bunched his hands into fists. Cynthia placed her hand on his arm and spoke in his stead. "Yes, she was traveling as Mo Chu Kong under a Chinese passport."

Eric stared down at the paper in front of him and rubbed the back of his neck. "Well, that's a big problem. You see, as far as China is concerned, your daughter is a Chinese citizen."

Cynthia's lip quivered. "That's not possible. Molly is a U.S. citizen. We adopted her as an infant and have the paperwork to prove it."

Eric's jaw tensed. "The Chinese government doesn't recognize dual citizenships. We reached out to the Chinese Embassy here in D.C. prior to this meeting. And according to their records, Molly still holds Chinese citizenship. To them, her U.S. citizenship doesn't matter. It became null and void as soon as she crossed the border."

Julian's eyes bulged. "You're not seriously telling me that the U.S. Government can't do anything whenever Chinese foreign nationals kidnap an American citizen?"

Eric pushed his glasses back up his nose. "Mr. Langston, as I tried to explain before... China doesn't recognize dual citizenships. The Chinese government also does not adhere to any accepted practices with respect to international child abductions. Except for the territories of Hong Kong and Macau, China has not signed the convention." He paused and avoided further eye contact with Julian. "Was there evidence of Molly being taken against her will?" He directed the question at Cynthia.

Uh... No.

"She's a child," Julian growled. "Of course she was taken against her will."

Eric cleared his throat. "The government of China may not see it that way. In recent years, the Chinese government has demonstrated a pattern of noncompliance with its obligations. Moreover, the Chinese government has increased the forcible repatriation of people it considers to be Chinese nationals."

"Forcible repatriation?" Cynthia asked, her eyes widening. "After granting a legal adoption? But why?"

Eric shrugged his shoulders. "I don't know. Typically, China's kidnappings involve Chinese citizens who are adults, living abroad as citizens of other countries, and suspected of various crimes. I've never heard about this sort of thing happening to kids. We tend to refer these cases to the Department of Justice, which is more capable of handling law enforcement matters."

"Now for the life of me, I can't imagine why," Julian growled. "It seems the State Department doesn't want to figure a way out of this fucking mess."

Eric jumped slightly in his chair. "Sir, I'm very sorry for your situation. The State Department wants to do whatever it can to get your daughter back." He spoke in a measured tone, doing a poor job of hiding the fact that he was terrified of what Mr. Langston might do to him. "We can make a formal request for the Chinese government to return your daughter. And I'd be happy to do so. But I have to warn you against getting your hopes up. Even if China responds to a request for the return of a child, it may take more than two years for it to be resolved."

"Two years?" Cynthia gasped aloud. Her sad expression twisted with anguish, and her chest began to heave. A vein appeared in Julian's red neck as his face screwed up in anger.

"But China will most likely continue refuse to acknowledge Molly's status as a U.S. citizen and prevent her from leaving the country," Eric said.

Lara sat up straight in her chair. "Mr. Salinger, we came all the way down here to ask for your help. Surely, there's something the State Department can do to get Molly back. Perhaps at the very least, we could receive some information about Molly's welfare and location?"

Eric's gaze darted around the room. "Um… we can refer you to a list of attorneys who specialize in family law in China. They will be able to offer you legal guidance and possible options for resolving the situation with the Chinese government."

Julian leaped out of his chair and shook his fist. "A list of attorneys? That's what you can help us with? Do I look like a man who needs help finding a good attorney?"

Eric shrank back in his chair.

Julian turned to Cynthia and motioned for her to leave.

"We're done here. If we don't travel to China and get Molly back for ourselves, we'll never see her again." He glanced at Lara. "Just like I said in the first place."

Eric's eyes widened. "Mr. Langston, I strongly recommend against taking such drastic measures. If you attempt to take your daughter out of China, you may be detained indefinitely for reasons related to state security. They could impose an exit ban on you and your wife and anyone else traveling with you, prohibiting you from leaving China."

Julian gritted his teeth. "That's fucking insane. You're telling me a Chinese citizen enters our country, breaks into our house, kidnaps our daughter, and we can't do anything about it? Or perhaps the U.S. Government won't do anything about it." Julian threw up his hands. "I've had enough of this bullshit."

Eric stood, bumping into his desk, which squeaked with the sudden impact. "Sir, please... don't go to China. It would be a big mistake. If you break the law in China, you may tie the hands of the State Department from intervening on your behalf."

Julian shook his head and made his way to the door with Cynthia close on his heels. Within seconds, they disappeared into the hallway without saying goodbye to Eric. Lara lingered slightly behind and gave him an apologetic look.

"Thanks for trying," Lara said flatly.

"Please talk them out of that nonsense," Eric said. "The last thing we need on our hands is another diplomatic crisis with China."

Lara sighed. "I'm not sure I can." She walked toward the door, but stopped when she felt a hand grab her arm. When she turned toward Eric, his face was flushed red.

"Ms. Kingsley... please tell them if they are arrested or detained, they'll need to ask police or prison officials to notify the U.S. Embassy or nearest consulate immediately. They should at least grant this request. But I can't promise we can do all that much."

Lara nodded, pulling her arm back and leaving the office.

She walked down the hallway and exited the suite. She finally found the Langstons fuming by the elevator.

"I can't believe you wasted our precious time with that nonsense," Julian snapped.

Lara folded her arms across her chest. "Before we go risking our lives with a foolhardy mission in China, I thought it best to seek assistance from the government. Besides, I haven't exhausted all our options. I have a contact in the intelligence community, and he is currently looking into the exact whereabouts of your daughter. China is a big country. We can't just assume that Dr. Kong would take her back to her institute. Also, it would be good to understand why she was taken in the first place before we go in guns blazing."

"When can we expect to hear from him?" Julian asked.

"I wish I could say exactly. He is a bit unpredictable. But it will be worth the wait."

It had better be.

Julian pointed a finger at her. "You have twenty-four hours. If you don't hear from your contact before then, we're moving forward with our plan to go to China."

We'll see what your babysitter has to say first.

TWENTY-TWO

The Babysitter

As Lara walked into the lobby of the First District police station, the savory smell of buttery popcorn greeted her. Her mouth watering, she glanced over at the reception desk where an officer chomped eagerly on his mid-morning snack. Out of the corner of her eye, she spotted Sanchez standing across from her and waiting with a big smile on his face. Tucked under his arm was a manila folder and the plastic bag with the red paper butterfly.

"You ready for a good ol' smackdown?" Sanchez asked, clapping his hands and rubbing them together.

What's inside that folder?

Lara gave him a stern look. "Sanchez. Alicia is thirteen years old. This isn't going to be a smackdown."

"Good grief, Lara. I didn't mean I'd go after the girl. Her father's the one preventing her from talking. That's obstruction of justice. What do you want to bet that Mr. Langston paid Mr. Novak to keep her quiet?"

"I don't disagree with you. But if you go after him in the interrogation room with Alicia there, how do you think it will affect her?"

His smile waned. "Well, I wasn't thinking about that when I

made the flippant comment. I was thinking about how good it will feel when the truth finally comes out."

"Exactly. Unless you plan to interview them separately, which I'm sure Mr. Novak will prevent from happening, I think we should use a delicate approach. I know you think Mr. Langston is hiding something, and you want to get to the truth to get Molly back. But there is another young girl involved in this case. We need to keep her interests in mind even if her sorry excuse for a father isn't doing that." Lara shook her head in disgust.

Another case of family treating family like pawns.

"Yeah, you're right. Alicia probably feels terrible about what happened to Molly." Sanchez stopped and looked at her, his expression concerned. "By the way, does the doctor know what's wrong with you?" He cringed. "Uh… sorry. I didn't mean to bring that up. If you don't want to share."

"That's okay. It's only fair. You were there when I fainted. The doctor says I may have a serious blood disorder. We'll know for sure when the results of the bone marrow biopsy come in." She shuddered at the memory of the searing pain of the needle injection in her hip.

"Dang. I didn't realize it was something serious. That's terrible news." He averted his eyes and was silent for a moment. "Look, I'm sure something will work out. We've got the best doctors in the world, right?" He pasted a smile on his face as if his confidence would make it better. Deep crow's feet framed his face, and his brown eyes gave a soft twinkle.

Sanchez should definitely smile more often.

"Yeah, there are several options for treatment. Who knows? Maybe the doctors will be able to fix me up to be a bigger thorn in your side than I was before." She gave him a toothy grin.

"Now that's the feisty Lara I know," he said, smiling a bit too broadly. He motioned for her to head down the hallway toward the interrogation room. "So, you think you're the one to run the interview?" His voice was a bit gruff.

Uh oh. Ego alert.

Lara relaxed her stance and smiled. "No, I didn't mean to imply that. This is your investigation. You have many more years of interrogation experience than I do. As the lead detective, it's your call who conducts the interview. But if we want to get to the truth, we're going to have to make Alicia feel comfortable talking in front of her father. That's not gonna be easy."

"Good point," Sanchez said, shoving his hand in his pocket. "How about this? You take the girl, and I'll take the father. I'll get him to crack first, and then you can see if she knows something about Molly's kidnapping. Sound good?"

"Sounds good to me," Lara said, hiding her surprise.

I can't believe I have permission to participate.

"Here. You'll need this." He handed her the plastic evidence bag with the red paper butterfly. "Make sure you get the timing right on the big reveal, okay?"

Lara nodded.

Sanchez stopped in front of the interrogation room, grabbed the doorknob, and turned to flash her a mischievous grin. "And if the father won't let her talk, I've drummed up some incriminating evidence that may change his mind."

Lara raised her eyebrows. "Oh, really?" She put the evidence bag in her pocket. "What do you have?"

Way to bury the lead, detective.

Sanchez smiled broadly. "You'll see soon enough," he said, opening the door.

Crammed inside the small interrogation room, Mr. Novak sat squished between his fancy lawyer and his daughter. The well-dressed lawyer stood, his metal chair screeching against the floor, and introduced himself. "I'm Seth Goldstein from Cohen, Resnick, and Goldstein, representing Aleks Novak and his daughter Alicia. My clients plan to press charges for unlawful detention and harassment. I've already made a call to the police commissioner and the mayor."

Mr. Langston didn't waste any time bringing in the big guns.

Sanchez waved his hand dismissively. "Yeah, yeah, yeah. Have a seat. We'll get to that. I have a feeling your client will be changing his tune." The lawyer sat back down and glared at the detective.

Sanchez pointed to the remaining chair, indicating that Lara have a seat. He placed the manila folder on the table, ignored the lawyer, and looked directly at Aleks. "Mr. Novak, this is Lara Kingsley. She's a private investigator hired by your employer to get Molly back safely. I assume everyone in this room wants to do whatever they can to help her come home." He glanced at Alicia and gave her a warm smile.

The young blonde-haired girl wore a pink Disney princess sweatshirt and blue jeans. She was smaller than Lara expected for a twelve-year-old. The frightened look on her face called attention to her thin frame and pale skin.

Mr. Novak was a gray-haired man in his sixties and had sunken, pale gray eyes. The surface of his face looked more like worn leather than skin, like someone who'd spent too much time in the sun over a period of many years.

"Okay, let's get started. I'd like to ask you a few questions first, Mr. Novak. Is that okay with you?" Sanchez asked.

Aleks looked at his lawyer, who nodded in approval.

"You work for the Langstons?" Sanchez asked, flipping open his notebook, leaning over the table, and staring down the man.

"I've worked as their gardener for more than twenty years," Aleks said.

"And you live at the Langstons' estate?" Sanchez asked. He moved away from the table, slowly walking around the back of the room.

"Yes, I live in the servants' quarters with my daughter, Alicia." Aleks glanced at his daughter, and she squirmed in her seat, biting her lip.

"Is there a Mrs. Novak in the picture?" Sanchez asked, reversing his direction.

Aleks winced slightly. "Alicia's mother died of cancer ten years ago."

Sanchez flinched, his face losing a bit of its color. "Oh, I'm sorry to hear that." He paused for a moment, presumably to recalibrate. He stood still for a moment and crossed his arms. "Mr. Novak, where were you the night of Molly's kidnapping?"

"I already gave a statement to the police," Aleks said, glancing at his lawyer.

Sanchez walked over to the table, opened the folder, and pulled out a piece of paper. He tossed it on the table. "Yes, you did. I have your statement right here. But a lot has happened since the night in question, so I'd like to hear it from you again."

Aleks glared at him. "Fine. I was at a performance of Tchaikovsky's Third Symphony at the Kennedy Center."

Sanchez grunted. "Uh huh. Do you often attend events at the Kennedy Center?"

"No, I can't afford the ticket prices."

"Would you say that you have an active social life and are gone regularly in the evenings?" Sanchez asked.

"I'm a single father. So no, I'm usually at home with my daughter, helping her with homework."

Sanchez took a few steps forward, whipped a receipt for Mr. Novak's ticket out of the folder, and dropped it on the table in front of Aleks. He pointed at it. "Why didn't you tell the police Mr. Langston bought the ticket for you?"

"Uh… I didn't think it was important at the time."

Nice deflection.

Sanchez crossed his arms. "Why did Mr. Langston buy you the ticket?"

"It was a gift for my birthday. He knows I enjoy classical music."

"When's your birthday?" Sanchez asked.

"It was July 13th."

Sanchez tilted his head. "But the date on this receipt is August 27th. Why would Mr. Langston buy you a belated birthday gift?"

"Mr. Langston promised to get me a ticket on my birthday, but he had to wait until they were available for sale for the performance."

Sanchez grunted. "Don't you think it's a major coincidence

that his daughter goes missing on the night you happen to be at the Kennedy Center for the performance?"

"I didn't read too much into it. That was the only night the National Symphony Orchestra was performing Tchaikovsky's Third Symphony."

Sanchez furrowed his brow. "Why did Mr. Langston choose this particular performance?"

"Well, it's often called the Polish symphony because of the polonaise in the finale."

"Polonaise?" Sanchez asked, his neck flushing red and fists clenched.

I sure hope this wasn't his incriminating evidence.

"It's a slow dance originating in Poland. He thought I'd enjoy it more than another symphony, given my background. And I did." Aleks gave him a coy smile, as if he'd won the first round.

"Okay, let's talk about your trip to Poland," Sanchez said, clearly trying a different tack. He flipped back several pages in his notebook. "You left for Warsaw with your daughter the day after Molly's kidnapping. Why the rush out of town?"

"We had a sudden death in the family and needed to leave right away."

Sanchez turned to face Aleks directly and put his hands on his hips. "Who died?"

"A cousin of mine," he said, avoiding eye contact.

"You must have been close to this cousin if you hurried off to Poland at the last minute in the middle of a crisis."

"Yes, Igor and I were very close. Like brothers."

Sanchez grunted. "Hmmm…" He pulled out receipts for what looked to be plane tickets to Poland. Sanchez threw them on the table. The lawyer caught them with his hand before they slid off the edge. "Why did Mr. Langston purchase your tickets?"

"Because I couldn't afford the last-minute prices. He knew how much my cousin meant to me and wanted to do something nice. After twenty years as his gardener, he considers me more like family than an employee."

"That's all very heartwarming," Sanchez said, opening the

folder again. This time, he pulled out a stack of stapled papers that looked like phone records and slapped them on the table. There was a look of triumph in his dark brown eyes.

Aleks reached for the papers, his eyes widening. "How did you get this?" He stared at his lawyer, who fumbled with his glasses to inspect the documents.

"These are your cellphone records for the past six months. I got them the usual way. With a subpoena. There are no phone calls to anyone in Poland for the past six months." Sanchez stared down at Aleks and waited for a response, but none came. "Doesn't look like you were that close with any member of your family in Poland. Not to mention this supposed dead cousin of yours."

Aleks was about to respond, but the lawyer put his hand in front of his client, signaling him to remain silent. "These records prove nothing, detective. Mr. Novak could have made calls to Poland by other means. Mr. Langston often granted my client the use of his landline to make international calls."

Sanchez grinned as if they'd walked right into his trap. He grabbed the next stack of papers and threw them on the table, where they landed with a satisfying thwack. "Okay, here are the records for Mr. Langstons' landline for the past six months. No calls to Poland." The detective paused to let them absorb the new information. The lawyer's mouth opened slightly, but he said nothing.

"The judge also granted me an arrest warrant for obstruction of justice based on the evidence." He pulled out the warrant and laid it on the table. "But I was hoping you would cooperate voluntarily so that I didn't have to pull the trigger on this. You have one more chance to amend your official statement. Otherwise, you'll get to enjoy a taste of our first-rate accommodations. As a green card holder, I expect you'll also face deportation if found guilty. Still want to stick to your story?"

Lara suppressed a smirk. *Oh, he's good.*

The lawyer leaned over and whispered in Aleks' ear. For a few moments, they exchanged words in low voices.

Then Aleks faced the detective. "Okay, I will cooperate."

"Look, we don't want you to get into trouble for being loyal to your boss," Sanchez said. "We just want your daughter to tell us what happened the night Molly was kidnapped. Will you let my associate ask your daughter a few questions?"

Aleks nodded.

Lara leaned forward. "Hi Alicia. My name is Lara. We want to find Molly and bring her back home. Do you want to help her?"

With her pale blue eyes wide and full of fear, she nodded.

"I need to ask you a few questions about the night Molly went missing. Is that okay with you?"

Alicia bobbed her head slowly.

"Can you tell me about that night?" Lara asked.

Alicia glanced nervously at her father. "I don't know what happened to Molly. I was watching TV."

Aleks interjected. "It's okay, sweetheart. You can tell Lara everything you know. I won't be angry with you. We should do what we can to help Molly."

"I promise you're not in trouble, okay?" Lara said. "We're just trying to find Molly and get her back to her parents as soon as possible." Lara paused before asking the next question. "Did you turn the alarm system off that night?"

"Yes," Alicia said, not looking at Lara.

"Can you tell me why?"

"A girl from the neighborhood brought over Girl Scout cookies for the Langstons."

Mr. Langston mentioned an obsession with Thin Mints.

"Do you remember how many boxes?" Lara asked.

Alicia scratched her head. "I think there were two or three boxes."

"Do you remember what kind of cookies?"

Across the room, Sanchez raised his eyebrow.

"I think at least one box was Thin Mint. One was shortbread with fudge. They're called Thanks-A-Lots. I remember because

Molly asked if she could have some, and we opened the box. We both ate a few before she went to bed."

"Sweetie, why didn't you re-arm the security system after the cookies were delivered?"

A confused look fell across Alicia's face as she struggled to remember or find the right words. "Um… I don't remember. I think I got distracted. My phone rang in the other room, and I went to go answer it. I thought it might be the Langstons. Sometimes, they call to check up on us."

"Was it the Langstons?" Lara asked.

"No, the call came from an unknown number. When I answered, the caller hung up on me."

Huh. Interesting coincidence.

"Did you know the girl who delivered the cookies?"

Alicia nodded. "Oh yes. Her name is Emily Jackson. She's a few years older than me and lives down the street."

Emily Jackson? Lara's heart nearly stopped.

"Does Emily have an adopted sister like Molly?"

Aleks' body tensed, and he gripped his daughter's hand tightly.

Alicia winced and bit her lip. "I don't know. I've never met her family. We go to different schools."

Lara pulled the plastic bag containing the red paper butterfly from her pocket and pushed it toward Alicia. "Do you recognize this?"

The girl's face paled slightly. She shook her head quickly.

"Are you sure?"

"I've never seen that before," Alicia said, her lip quivering.

"Do you remember anything else about that night?" Lara asked.

Alicia shrugged. "I put Molly to bed a few minutes after eight. That's her bedtime. Then I came back downstairs and watched TV until I fell asleep on the couch around ten. When the Langstons came home… she was…" Her lips began to tremble. Tears welled up in her eyes.

"It's okay, honey. We're going to find her and bring her home safely. I promise. Can you answer one more question?" Lara asked.

Alicia bowed her head.

"Do Julian and Cynthia fight with each other?"

Aleks put his hand on Alicia's shoulder and leaned forward, glaring at Lara. "What does that have to do with anything?"

"Mr. Novak, I'm trying to find a missing girl here. I need to examine all possibilities."

"Well, then... I'll answer for my daughter. Alicia has no knowledge about the relationship between the Langstons." He tugged Alicia's arm and glanced at his lawyer. "I think we're done here."

"Thank you for your cooperation, Mr. Novak," Sanchez said. "You're free to go." He motioned to the door.

But I'm not done yet.

Lara glared at Sanchez, but he ignored her. The lawyer led Mr. Novak and Alicia out of the interrogation room. The detective reached for the door, closed it behind them, and turned to face her.

"I wasn't finished," Lara said, huffing at him.

"Yes, you were," Sanchez said firmly. "You did pretty good. I'm surprised Mr. Novak cooperated as much as he did. But I think we got enough."

Lara put her hands on her hips. "We didn't get enough to prove Mr. Langston's involvement in Molly's kidnapping."

Sanchez laughed out loud. "Yeah. We're not going to try to prove that. That's why I cut you off. My goal is to get Molly back to her family. That's all. For this case, that's what success looks like." He turned to look her squarely in the face. "We are not going after the Langstons. You got that?"

"Wait a minute. If we end up learning Mr. Langston kept details about Molly's disappearance from us, or worse, abetted his daughter's kidnapper, you're just going to let him get away with it?" Lara asked, a hint of indignation in her voice.

"You've got to be kidding me. What sort of Pollyanna world

do you live in? Do you think we have enough evidence to go after a man as powerful as Julian Langston?"

"We could collect enough evidence if we try," Lara said.

"If I attempt to bring Mr. Langston in for questioning, I'll be in deep trouble with my boss, the police commissioner, and the mayor. It would be career suicide."

Lara shook her head in disbelief. "And here I thought you were on the side of justice."

"C'mon. You know I am. But sometimes, you gotta choose your battles if you want to win the war. Let's focus on getting Molly home safely."

"Fine," Lara said, crossing her arms and scowling.

"But I'm curious about something. Why did you ask those questions about the Girl Scout cookies and the neighbor girl?"

"I'm not sure. My gut was telling me there's something off about that cookie delivery. Without it, the kidnapper would not have had access to the house without setting off the alarm. Alicia gave us a clue, but she didn't know it. Remember Dr. Pulido mentioning the Jackson family adopting a Chinese baby girl from the same orphanage as Molly?"

Sanchez nodded.

"That girl's name was Emily Jackson. Yesterday, Mr. Langston claimed he didn't know a Jackson family. Well, he knows at least one Jackson family. Why would he lie about that?"

Sanchez's eyes widened. "Ah, I see. Good work." Then he gave her an amused look. "Sometimes, you pick up on the most random crap."

"Oh, do you mean like the absence of lipstick on cigarette butts?" Lara said, reminding him of the clue that solved their last case. "The cookies weren't random. I think they were part of the plan."

The question is what plan and why?

"You're not going to try to steal their cookies, are you?" Sanchez said, chuckling.

"Not today," Lara said, smirking as her smartphone buzzed.

It was a text from Hickerson. "Hickerson wants me to come out to Langley to see him."

"Tell him I want to come with you," Sanchez demanded.

Lara eyed him nervously. "I don't know if—"

"Ask him now." The detective gestured to her phone.

Lara typed a text and pressed send. A few moments later, another text appeared on her smartphone.

NO. JUST YOU.

TWENTY-THREE

Metamorphosis

Lara waited at the long, gray conference table in the Sensitive Compartmented Information Facility (SCIF) at the CIA headquarters in Langley, Virginia. With one exception, the secure room was as bland and uninspiring as every other conference room she'd visited in federal office buildings. The main difference was the combination lock on the outside of the door.

The only notable feature of the room, a giant CIA seal hanging the wall, gave her goosebumps, reminding her of the Memorial Wall she'd seen on the way into the building. The famous wall paid tribute to those who died in the line of service as spies. She'd never forget her walk across the iconic dark gray and white seal on the marble floor. For a wistful moment, she'd wondered what it would be like to work at the heart of U.S. intelligence.

Not sure I have the stomach for it.

The steel door opened, the hinges scraping together softly, and Hickerson walked in holding a bright red file folder marked *Top Secret*. In the stale lighting, the gray circles under his eyes sagged, making him look rather weary. As he sat down in the seat across from her, Hickerson smoothed his few remaining wisps of hair and tucked his red tie behind the table.

"Sorry for the wait," he said, blinking his detached brown eyes at her. "I had to make sure we had your clearance on file. I've confirmed everything is in order, so now I can read you into Metamorphosis."

Lara raised her eyebrows. "What's Metamorphosis?"

He waved his hand dismissively. "We'll get to that in a moment. Obviously, I couldn't tell you anything classified over the phone. When you told me about the missing persons case, I wondered about a possible connection to a radical group we've been tracking in China and around the world for quite some time. They call themselves Macrobians."

Lara's eyes widened. "Vik told me they were a group of transhumanist intellectuals and scientists who are obsessed with living longer. Is there more to it than that?"

"Oh yes, much more. The Macrobians are a global community with branches in many different countries. At the CIA, we've been following the group due to the specific nature of their scientific activities, which are crossing dangerous ethical lines of interest to the U.S. Government. The Macrobians believe the human race can transcend its mental and physical limitations through the application of science and technology. Most Macrobians are eager to extend their lives. Some of them believe in attempting to achieve immortality using extreme measures. They're especially obsessed with advances in biotechnology, nanotechnology, and artificial intelligence. Above all else, Macrobians wish to become posthuman."

Lara wrinkled her nose. "Posthuman?"

"Basically, Macrobians wish to move beyond the human species as it currently stands to experience a quality of existence that has not previously been possible. They believe we humans are at an early phase in our evolution. We're not yet who we're supposed to be."

Lara scratched her head. "Um, I have no idea what that means."

"Well, to put it in less philosophical terms, they want to be free from disease and injury, remain young and vigorous, and exercise better control over their desires, moods, and mental states. Basically, they want to enjoy everything that life has to offer in a more enlightened state."

Lara smirked. "All of that sounds good. Sign me up."

Hickerson chuckled. "You may not like their methods of achieving it…"

"Something more than diet and exercise?"

"Indeed." He smiled politely. "They believe in leveraging science to the extreme without regard for ethics or safety. For example, they want to use germline gene editing and reproductive cloning to create new generations of superhuman offspring."

Lara blinked, her mouth suddenly going dry. "Human cloning?"

"Yes. In addition to using cloning for experimental purposes, the Macrobians want to develop a class of superhumans. I've read intel reports that suggest they seek to recreate some of humanity's best specimens through cloning by bringing the dead back to life. In fact, I wouldn't be surprised if they one day retrieved Einstein's DNA from his grave and transplanted his genetic information into an egg's nucleus to make a new baby Einstein."

What is the world coming to? Lara shuddered with disgust.

Hickerson picked a piece of lint off of his black suit jacket. "Macrobians also believe in our ability to do cryonics and upload our consciousness onto computer chips. That's how they plan to achieve immortality. Until they can reliably extend human life indefinitely—"

"Cryonics… that's not freezing dead bodies, is it?" Lara recoiled instinctively.

"Yep. If a Macrobian dies before they discover a way to achieve immortality, they will remain frozen until a later date. Some Macrobians suffer from disease and volunteer to be frozen prior to death. They hope to be reanimated someday when a cure is finally found."

Lara leaned back in her chair, her hand on her forehead.

"This is a real group? Like actual smart people believe in this nonsense?"

"I'm afraid so," Hickerson said. "The U.S. branch has gone mostly underground to evade attention from law enforcement authorities—especially the FBI. We're particularly interested in the Chinese branch of Macrobians because they face the least ethical constraints on their scientific research. Doctors Yishan and Yingyue Kong, your suspected kidnappers, are the leaders of the Macrobians in China."

Lara furrowed her brow. "I don't get it. Why do Chinese authorities allow such a group to flourish under their watch?"

"Because the Chinese PLA has a vested interest in the results of their research. It may help China's military develop superhuman soldiers and a superior, long-living civilian population. It's the perfect solution to their aging population, a devastating result of misguided reproduction policies of the past. We suspect that Macrobians might be working directly for the Chinese government." Hickerson stopped to study Lara's face for a moment. "Anyway, I wanted to read you into Metamorphosis because of the apparent connection between your kidnapping case and the Macrobians."

"You think their research has something to do with Molly's disappearance?"

"It might. We're not entirely sure. I mentioned before that Macrobians want to be free from disease and reproduce an enhanced human race."

Lara nodded.

"About a decade ago, we picked up some communications over the wire, indicating the Chinese branch started an experiment called Metamorphosis. We believe it has been underway ever since, but we have very little information about it."

"What sort of experiment?" Lara asked, uncertain if she really wanted to know.

"Yeah… okay, this is where it gets disturbing. We think the Macrobian Institute of Life Sciences may have cloned several baby girls from a single genetic stock. Maybe as many as a dozen babies."

"By genetic stock, do you mean a DNA sample or an actual person?"

"We don't know for sure. Anyway, we've been tracking the chatter on this experiment for years. We think it mostly has to do with gene editing and finding cures to genetic disease."

"What diseases?" Lara asked, sitting at the edge of her seat, her hands flat on the smooth, cool surface of the table.

"We think they're primarily studying rare blood disorders," Hickerson said.

"What do you think they do with the clones?"

"We believe the girls have been adopted into different families for the purposes of the experiment. They may travel to China for testing on occasion."

Lara's jaw dropped, her pulse surging. "Do you think Molly is a clone?"

"That's the scenario that makes the most sense to us. Especially since Yingyue came all the way to the United States to collect her. What other reason would she have to take Molly?"

"Do you think the Langstons knew all along that Molly was taken to China?" Lara asked, her heart sinking with the confirmation. "And by whom?"

"That conclusion seems to make sense as well." Hickerson avoided eye contact and said nothing for a moment.

Lara sat there paralyzed for what felt like several minutes, her mind racing... processing all the data. The Langstons had lied to her. About everything. She wasn't sure how deep the lies ran, but she guessed it began with the advertisement on FishBowl. For some reason, they'd dragged her into an impossible situation and now expected her to risk everything to travel across the world to retrieve their daughter.

Lara blinked rapidly as she tried to shake off her disbelief. She rubbed her eyes, and then looked up at Hickerson. "What do you think I should do? Quit working for the Langstons? Help them get Molly back?" She stared numbly at the conference table, her shoulders slumping.

"I know this is hard news for you..." Hickerson's voice softened. "But there may be something you can do. A way out of the predicament, so to speak."

Lara lifted her chin slightly.

"You could pretend you don't know what you know. Agree to go to China with the Langstons. Get Molly back. In the process, you could help us get more information on the Macrobians. If you did, it would be a tremendous service to the CIA and the U.S. Government."

Is he trying to recruit me?

Lara pressed her lips together and avoided his gaze. If she dropped the Langstons' case, she'd be putting Sanchez in a tight spot with the police commissioner. He wouldn't get his promotion and blame it on her. He might also refuse to help Rob find out who set him up at the FBI. Not to mention how one bad word from the Langstons might end any chance of her getting work for Kingsley Investigations again.

My Army career is already over. What choice do I even have here?

With a thin smile, Hickerson pushed a green file folder toward her, marked *Unclassified*. "Here is all the information you need to carry out your black op in China and get Molly home safely. I've cleared the release of this folder into your possession with my leadership, specifically for this mission. However, I ask you to treat it as sensitive information. Please don't share it with anyone who you think might be compromised or would interfere with the mission."

He knew I'd say yes... I guess CIA case officers know their marks.

"How would I pull it off?" Lara asked. "I promised the Langstons that one of my contacts in the intelligence community would help me help them. I can't exactly tell them what you've just told me or about your affiliation with the CIA. Who should I say I'm getting the information from?"

"You're a resourceful girl. I'm sure you'll concoct a credible story." Hickerson flipped open the folder and laid out the contents on the table in front of her. Lara's eyes bulged when she saw all the detailed information—a map of China with marked locations, building diagrams, satellite photos, and dossiers.

Hickerson pulled out the map. "We think Molly is currently being held at the orphanage and may be moved to the institute shortly." He reached for the diagrams. "Here are the exact locations and layouts for the orphanage, the Macrobian Institute, the private home of Yingyue and Yishan." Hickerson pulled a USB drive from his pocket. "This drive contains the virtual reality simulation data in case you want to view it all in 3D. I recommend using Hong Kong as your point of entry and departure and devise a viable cover story for your trip to China. The government officials in Hong Kong adhere to the Hague Convention on International Child Abduction. You'll have a better chance of getting Molly out of China without interference from State Security there. I have several of my assets placed within Hong Kong authorities to assist you if necessary."

Lara rubbed her chin, a feeling of uneasiness nagging at her. "Let me make sure I understand. You want me to take this information to the Langstons and lead the black op mission to China to get Molly back. And in the process, I'm to steal information for you."

"Yes."

"What sort of information?" Lara asked, pursing her lips.

"We want any scientific documentation you can find about Metamorphosis. Computer data, subject files, and Molly's original DNA sample."

Lara's eyes widened. "Her original DNA?"

"Molly's first sample was taken as a baby. We need it."

Lara wrinkled her nose. "Why?"

Hickerson shook his head. "That's classified."

"But I'm cleared to have access to sensitive compartmentalized information," Lara said.

"On a need-to-know basis," Hickerson said flatly. "You don't need to know. You'll need to bring a special container for DNA storage. Ask your friend Maggie to scrounge one from her lab.

And you'll have to figure out a way to keep your data collection effort a secret. We don't want the Langstons to know about it and prefer to stay off the Macrobians' radar."

That sounds complicated.

"And what if I get caught by the Chinese authorities?" Lara asked, her brow furrowed.

Hickerson gave her a probing gaze. "This is an unsanctioned mission. If you get caught, you'll be on your own and probably end up in prison."

Well, this sounds familiar.

Lara grimaced, her skin prickling slightly. "I suppose I should do this for you because I'm a patriot, and it's in the U.S. national interest, blah, blah, blah."

What's his real agenda?

"Aren't you going to help the Langstons bring Molly back to the U.S.?" Hickerson asked.

Lara sighed and hung her head. "Yeah."

Again, what choice do I have? She's an eight-year-old girl. I'm not leaving her over there.

"Okay, so you're already putting yourself at risk. What's a little more?" Hickerson paused to study her face. "You could always change your mind if it's too risky. We wouldn't hold it against you. Whatever information you bring back would be more than we have now."

Oh, he's very good at his job. Lara's eyes narrowed as she felt herself caving to his will. *Too good.*

"Okay, fine," she said through gritted teeth.

"Okay, you'll do it?"

"Yes."

"Good," Hickerson said, rising from his chair. "And let me know if you need anything further to support the mission— equipment, technology, information, etcetera. Whatever you need."

"Will do." Lara followed him through the door and said in a low voice, "By the way, Rob and I visited MacFarlan in prison."

Hickerson raised his eyebrow. "Why?"

"We're trying to clear Rob's name and get him his FBI job back. But MacFarlan wouldn't see us. He was afraid of someone calling themselves BlackDragon. Does that pseudonym ring a bell?"

Hickerson shook his head and motioned for her to follow him.

Would he tell me if he knew something? She sighed. *Only if he had something to gain.*

TWENTY-FOUR

The Test Run

October 11, 2028

ALL EYES LANDED on Lara as she entered the augmented virtual reality (AVR) room at the Pentagon. Before she could pull up her nose in time, a mishmash of male scents assaulted her—an odd combination of colognes mixed with stale socks.

Lara smiled nervously at the gaggle staring back at her in the familiar green glow of the lighting and made her way to the edge of the room. The space felt much smaller with so many people and the table crammed into it. She tried to seek refuge at the edge of the space, but the group moved to face her expectantly.

She swallowed hard at the sight of Kaitlyn. *How did Finn talk her into risking her military career to fly the chopper for this mission? I probably don't want to know. For another brief moment, she wondered if Kaitlyn had somehow helped Mr. Langston wrangle access to the Pentagon's AVR facility. If so, Lara would be indebted to her for yet another favor.*

As she took off her leather jacket, the intense staring made her feel self-conscious. Although she was accustomed to being team lead in the Army Special Forces, it had been a while since she'd gone into the field. She'd also never commanded such a motley crew—two experienced special operators, one top-notch Navy pilot, one reckless billionaire, and a gang of private sector mercenaries who looked more like thugs than soldiers.

The folding table standing at the center of the room contained the map Hickerson had provided. She'd given Finn the file the previous night and lied about its origins. From the looks of it, her team had made good use of their time until she arrived and had reviewed the contents. A quick glance at her watch indicated she was only a few minutes late. She exhaled sharply.

Finn smiled at her from where he stood next to Kaitlyn. He winked and gave a reassuring nod. Eyeing him apprehensively, Lara moved into the center of the square room to communicate her authority. Waiting in the wings behind him was a team of four burly dudes who acknowledged her with respect.

Who knows? I might be glad for the extra muscle at some point.

Ever since she agreed to the mission, she'd experienced jumbled feelings—a mixture of determination, unease, and excitement with a sprinkle of dread. Now that it was upon her, she wanted to get to work and bring Molly back home.

Julian took several steps toward her, extending his hand for a shake. "Ms. Kingsley, nice of you to finally show up."

As Lara suppressed a grimace, the smug look on Julian's face spread into a triumphant grin. "Thanks to Deputy Secretary of Defense and my very good friend," he continued, "we're going to give our little mission a test run on the most advanced AVR system in the world. I'm not sure what we would have done without him. Makes me wonder what I'm paying you for." His words were laced with ire.

He'd obviously not forgiven her for the detour to the State Department.

It was useless.

Lara flinched and swallowed hard. "Did you tell him about the mission?"

Julian raised an eyebrow. "Why would I do that?"

Dammit, he promised to get the DEPSECDEF's blessing.

Lara crossed her arms. "Then I assume you didn't tell him we're using this facility to practice an unsanctioned black operation," she asked, giving Finn and Kaitlyn a get-out-now-or-forever-hold-your-peace look to make sure they understood the implications.

They nodded subtly back to her.

"Of course not. I told him we wanted to simulate a few biotech experiments using VR to test the viability of the new virtual laboratories for GenTech Industries. I promised an exclusive briefing for the acquisition folks at the Department of Defense. He practically insisted we use the space and promised he'd have his assistant delete any digital record of it to protect our proprietary information." He paused for a moment, waiting for Lara to respond.

Without anything constructive to say, she bit her tongue.

"Finn told me your contact came through for us," Julian said flatly.

"Indeed, he did," Lara responded curtly. "My friend works for a private security firm in China and has some insider connections with Chinese intelligence. He was able to put together an impressive file of information for us, complete with commercial satellite imagery of the potential sites where Molly is being held." Turning away from them, she shivered slightly.

Am I overselling it? Anyone with a brain might ask how an American civilian would gain access to the information Hickerson had provided her without some intense scrutiny by the Chinese Ministry of State Security. If Mr. Langston could boast about his connections, why couldn't she?

Hopefully no one asks.

She avoided eye contact with Finn. Her insides cringed at the idea of lying to her boyfriend. She'd need to be careful her facial expressions or he might figure out she was spinning tall tales for Mr. Langston.

Her thoughts drifted to the lecture she'd received from

Sanchez about Hickerson. The detective had tried repeatedly to talk her out of what he called the "biggest fucking fool's errand on planet Earth." He wanted nothing to do with the operation, certain the fallout would be toxic for his career. He'd practically ordered Rob to steer clear of Lara until she returned with all her fingers and body parts intact. He added, "I can't save your ass this time, you know. China is way out of my jurisdiction."

He'll thank me when he gets the credit.

Sanchez promised to continue working the FBI case with Rob, Agent Carter, and Vik.

Hopefully, they have actual leads by the time I get back… if I get back.

"I'm very interested in hearing your plans for the mission." Julian gave her a guarded smile.

Lara studied her team. The hired guns wore eager faces and comfortable clothes in preparation for the test run. Kaitlyn was busy loading up the simulator with the digital files from Hickerson with Finn watching over her shoulder. A pang of jealousy rose in her gut.

Whose six does he have?

Turning to Julian, she said, "We're going to use the simulator to plot out the mission to rescue Molly and bring her back to the United States."

Lara walked over to the table and placed a hand on the map of the orphanage and the surrounding area. The run-down facility was located in a village in the countryside, about thirty minutes outside of Shenzhen by helicopter. To her dismay, it was called the Herodotus Social Welfare Institute, named after the historian who wrote about the Macrobians in the book owned by her father.

That can't be a coincidence.

"Does your contact have any idea about where they might be holding Molly?" Julian asked.

Lara bobbed her head, pointing to the images laid out on the table. "Based on the satellite imagery of the institute and the orphanage since the date of Molly's arrival in China, my contact's best guess is that they're keeping her at the orphanage." She pulled out several photos. "These are images of children coming to and from the orphanage with their caretakers. Unfortunately, the resolution isn't good enough to identify Molly. It was suggested we scope the orphanage out first. If she's not being held there, we'll pay a visit to the institute next. Of course, we won't know if they move her while we're en route to China. Mr. Langston, have you nailed down the travel plans?"

Julian pulled out his smartphone and scrolled down his screen. "We're departing on my private jet tomorrow morning and will arrive in Hong Kong sixteen hours later. From the airport, we'll fly with my company's helicopter to Shenzhen. Then, we'll set up operations at my company headquarters in the technology park near the institute. As soon as we're settled in, we'll make a trip to the orphanage to see if Molly is there."

Out of the corner of her eye, she saw Finn staring at her intently. He was shifting his weight back and forth, his hands deep in his pockets.

"Actually, I'd suggest sending a smaller team to the orphanage," Finn said, stepping toward the table and causing Lara to flinch.

Julian's body stiffened. Lara froze for a moment, unaccustomed to an outright challenge from a member of her team. On the battlefield, she was usually the one in charge even though she had to take orders from Command.

I guess Mr. Langston is Command now. And Finn is… acting like team lead.

"Too many people will draw attention and potentially tip our hand to the kidnappers," Finn continued. "If they take Molly into hiding in China, we'll never be able to find her. We need to maintain the element of surprise."

Julian crossed his arms. "What are you suggesting, then?"

Lara interjected quickly. "In that case, Kaitlyn and I should go there alone by helicopter. I'll play the role of a wealthy heiress looking to make a large donation to a Chinese orphanage. She'll

be my pilot and executive assistant. A wealthy philanthropist…
it's the perfect cover."

Finn cleared his throat. "Not quite. China is a bit old-fashioned. A single wealthy woman visiting an orphanage might raise suspicions. A wealthy couple would be better."

Lara shot him a glare, her eyes protruding. "I suppose you're volunteering for the husband role?"

Finn bobbed his head.

Lara's face flushed red, her hands shaking slightly. "Fine."

"I don't like it," Julian said, frowning deeply. "I want the whole team to go to the orphanage."

"Mr. Langston, trust me. It's better this way," Lara said, quickly getting on board with Finn's changes. "You can get the team settled in at your company headquarters. If you let us take the helicopter straight to the orphanage, we won't lose any time. As prospective donors, we can walk right through the front door and don't have to plan an elaborate break-in. If we see anything suspicious, we'll figure out a way to check it out under the cover of night without drawing any attention. I'd rather save the breaking and entering for the institute if needed."

"And while we're gone, the rest of the team can start scoping out the institute, the city of Shenzhen, and plan our escape route to the American Consulate in Hong Kong," Finn said, stopping when he saw the look of fury on Lara's face.

This is my mission.

"From there, we'll negotiate Molly's return to the United States from Hong Kong," Lara said.

"I don't want to ask anyone for permission," Julian grumbled. "She's my daughter. Plus, I thought China didn't sign that stupid convention."

Lara sighed. "Hong Kong's system of government is separate from mainland China, and their government adheres to the Convention. That's why I suggested we fly into Hong Kong in the first place. The city of Shenzhen in mainland China shares a border with Hong Kong. If we can smuggle Molly over that border and make it to the American Consulate, we'll have a better shot at getting her out."

"What about the border?" Finn asked, running his finger across the map. "There's a river along most of it, and fencing. Where do we cross?"

Moving the map away from him, Lara clenched her jaw. "My contact told me there's a land border area between Hong Kong and China called the Frontier Closed Area. In some areas, a flimsy chain-link fence serves as the only barrier to crossing. In other areas, the chain-link was upgraded to a more robust fence."

"Climbing over it shouldn't be a problem for us, right?" Finn asked, glancing at the crew of mercenaries.

The muscle shook their heads.

"Even while carrying my daughter?" Julian asked.

"Sir, we've carried far heavier loads in the Army than an eight-year-old girl," Finn said.

Lara cleared her throat. "As I was trying to say before, we won't have to carry her. There are some open spots along the border with signs posted, warning against illegal crossing." She pointed to the location on the map. "We'll aim to cross at such a location. In a worst-case scenario, we could hire some locals to help us travel across the border. The Hong Kong Police Force issues closed area permits to residents near the border that allow them to travel in and out of the neighboring cities. But I'd prefer not to open ourselves up to any breach of faith by the locals. We don't really know who to trust in a foreign country."

"Or who is working for Chinese state security," Finn said.

"Does your contact have anyone in Hong Kong we could trust?" Kaitlyn asked, entering their circle.

Yes, but I can't tell you.

Lara gritted her teeth. "Maybe. I'll look into it."

"What about a boat?" Finn asked. "We could have one ready on the riverbank."

"Too risky," Lara snapped. "If we leave the boat there for an extended period, the border guards are certain to notice. If we have someone wait and then drive up to meet us, we'll have to rely on comms. I'd rather not depend on a single point of failure. If our communication link goes down, everything could go terribly wrong." She turned to the group with a serious look on her face, looking each of them in the eyes. "The Chinese don't mess around, okay? If we get caught, we'll be going to prison and likely be tortured for information." She paused and glanced at Finn and Kaitlyn. "Especially those of us with security clearance in the military. Keeping a low profile will be critical." She looked at each of their faces again. "Got it?"

Everyone nodded solemnly.

"Okay, who's ready to take a spin in the simulator?" Kaitlyn asked. "We've got gear for three."

A surge of dread rose in Lara's chest.

No one stepped forward.

Ha. They must have already had a bout of simulator sickness themselves.

"Don't all volunteer at once," Kaitlyn said snidely. "This is the least scary part of the mission, so…"

Lara scanned the anxious faces of the mercenaries. "Fine. I'll go first."

If you want something done right, do it yourself.

Finn raised his hand halfheartedly.

Julian stepped forward. "I'll do it."

Lara moved toward the hooks on the wall and lifted a bulky backpack. Finn and Julian followed her lead. Lara lifted the weight of the pack over her head and connected the buckles, each with a loud click.

Her smartphone buzzed. Lara glanced at the screen and sighed heavily. Vik sent her a text:

I FOUND SOMETHING IN THE DATABASE
YOU'LL WANT TO SEE THIS RIGHT AWAY
MAGGIE FOUND SOMETHING TOO
WE'RE AT HER LAB. COME MEET US HERE

Lara texted back:

CAN'T COME RIGHT NOW
ABOUT TO GET IN THE SIMULATOR

Vik returned her text:

THIS CAN'T WAIT

Vik wouldn't insist if it weren't urgent.

"I gotta go," Lara said.

"What?" Finn asked. "Now?"

"Vik found something."

Julian towered over her, his eyes narrowing. "Who's this Vik?"

"He's my assistant."

"You're leaving us here to fend for ourselves?" Julian growled.

Lara put her hands on her hips. "Oh, you're in perfectly good hands." She glanced at Finn and Kaitlyn. "They know the plan and can run you through it. Would you rather have me babysit you or acquire clues that are critical to our mission's success?"

Julian looked like he might blow a gasket. "This had better be important…"

"Or you'll fire me. Yeah… I've heard that line before."

Julian's face turned red. "I want an immediate report on what your assistant has found."

"Of course," Lara said, lifting the AVR backpack over her head and setting it on the floor. She gulped as she left the room.

Hopefully, I can come up with something convincing.

TWENTY-FIVE

The Clones

____

When Lara arrived at the lab, Vik was sitting at a computer terminal, staring intently at the screen, oblivious to her arrival. She raised an eyebrow and smirked at his attire—fashionable black jeans with folded cuffs, cobalt blue leather tennis shoes, a Japanese anime t-shirt, and a charcoal-gray hoodie.

Must be another fashion masterpiece by Shanaya.

Lara glanced toward the back of the lab. It still smelled like a stinky toilet, but for once, Maggie's genetics laboratory was empty. It was located in the Department of Entomology at the University of Maryland and usually packed with students.

Good. We might need the privacy.

Maggie leaned against the humming sequencing machine, her head buried in a notebook. She was dressed in a white lab coat over gray slacks and a green turtleneck, her auburn hair tied up in a messy bun.

"Hey guys," Lara said tentatively, not wanting to startle them.

Both of them jumped and looked up at her wide-eyed. A slight smile formed on Maggie's face and then disappeared.

Uh oh.

"Hey, luv. I didn't realize you'd get here so quickly. Weren't you at the Pentagon doing a test run for your trip?"

"Um, I left as soon as Vik texted and took a Go-Go driverless cab." She glanced at Vik, but he looked away. "Because. It. Sounded. Urgent," Lara said in a deadpan tone.

Gee, I hope it was urgent.

Lara tapped her watch. "I leave for China with the team tomorrow, so time is of the essence. What do you have for me?"

Putting her hands on her hips, Lara looked from Maggie to Vik and then back to Maggie. Silent stares.

"Did you find something or not?" Lara asked, a bit too sharply.

Vik's eyes darted to Maggie, who motioned for him to go first.

"What the hell is going on?" Lara clenched her fists and took several steps toward Vik. "Spill the beans already."

"Um… I'm not sure where to start," Vik said, rubbing the back of his neck. "We discovered some mind-blowing stuff. Beyond belief actually… I'm still in shock and trying to make sense of it. What we found changes everything. We gave Sanchez a call, too. He's on his way over."

"Just start from the beginning, and we'll go from there," Lara said, her heart already thumping against her chest in anticipation.

Biting his lip, Vik still looked uncertain. "Okay… I know where the anonymous tip for the airport video footage came from."

Lara's pulse spiked. "Where?"

"Falls Church, Virginia. I'm pretty sure it came from a server at GenTech Industries. That's Mr. Langston's company."

The blood drained from her face.

"You think Mr. Langston submitted the tip himself?" Lara asked.

"It appears so. Or at least someone working for him." Vik paused, likely waiting for her to digest her shock. "But that's not all I found. You asked me to look into your parents' company…"

"Uh huh…" Lara motioned for him to continue.

"Your father sold Horizon Genomics before he died. And he sold it to GenTech Industries."

Lara's shaking hand flew to her mouth. Then she froze, the sound of her heart thudding hard in her chest and reverberating in her ears.

Mr. Langston bought my parents' company?

"There's more," Vik said, blinking his eyes rapidly.

"What?" Lara asked, bracing herself against the lab bench and staring wide-eyed at Maggie, who nodded slowly.

"After it was sold to GenTech Industries, Horizon Genomics moved its operations to China. Dr. Liam Nilsson is currently the CEO. I think you recognize the name?"

"Yeah, I do. He was the Director of Miracle Springs Eternal Adoption Agency when Molly was adopted." Lara sank onto the stool and stared numbly at the lab bench, her head whirling with the new information.

"I told you it was mind blowing…" Vik said, a look of guilt on his face.

"You okay, luv?" Maggie asked, approaching Lara.

Lara's mouth was dry. She heard the sound of Maggie's question, but hadn't quite registered it. She looked up, brow furrowed. "What?"

"I know it's heaps of news to take in," Maggie said gently, stroking her arm.

Lara's lip quivered. "Is that it? Is this why you called me down here?"

"Not quite," Vik said, hesitating. "I searched the GenDataBank genealogy database for matches to Molly's DNA profile as you requested."

"Did you find any of her relatives?"

"Uh… I found several exact matches."

"Exact matches?" Lara made a confused face. "More than one?"

How is that even possible?

"Yeah… that's the thing. I found seven different profiles in the database that match Molly's entire DNA sequence. Lara, that's seven exact matches to Molly's genome on separate profiles." Vik nodded slowly. "If this is right, Molly has seven twin sisters, living in different families as adoptive daughters around the country. If they're not octuplets, then they must be clones."

Clones? Her face remained slack. *Hickerson was right about Metamorphosis.*

"Wait... You don't seem surprised," Vik said, his eyes narrowing. "What do you know that you're not telling us?"

Damn. He knows me too well.

Lara shuffled her feet nervously and contemplated what to say.

Hickerson didn't forbid me from telling anyone.

Maggie crossed her arms and waited for Lara to speak.

Lara gave them a serious look. "Guys, I need to keep this confidential, okay?" Both Maggie and Vik nodded eagerly. "I went to see Hickerson at Langley yesterday. We talked extensively about a group called the Macrobians. Turns out the CIA has been tracking the activities of the radical transhumanist group around the world. They have branches in several countries, including a major presence in China where the group was founded. He mentioned a genetics experiment involving the cloning of baby girls called Metamorphosis."

Maggie's jaw dropped. "The Chinese are cloning baby girls? But what for?"

"Hickerson thinks they're running a research experiment in search of a cure for rare blood disorders," Lara said. "But the intent could be nefarious. He doesn't know for sure."

Maggie's eyes bulged. "By blood disorder, you don't mean aplastic anemia, do you?"

Lara shoved her hands in her pockets. "Possibly." She gave Maggie an uncomfortable grin. "Quite the coincidence, eh?"

The coincidences are definitely adding up.

Lara didn't like where they were pointing—back to her family history, her genetic past, and her current health situation.

She didn't like thinking about her dead parents and what things they were up to any more than she liked the idea of having inherited a serious blood disorder from them.

Vik creased his forehead. "You were diagnosed with aplastic anemia and didn't tell me?"

"Sorry, Vik," Lara said. "I meant to tell you right away, but I've been literally running back and forth between two cases. I think you understand why I didn't want to send you a text?"

Vik made a pouty face. "It sounds serious."

"It is, but there are treatment options. A bone marrow transplant could potentially cure the disease, but the doctor also wants to look into gene therapy. Due to my age and the fact that I don't have a family donor..."

Vik walked over to Lara and wrapped his long arms around her, hugging her tightly for a few moments. Tears welled in Lara's eyes as she held her breath. When he finally pulled away, Lara glimpsed the sheen in his brown eyes as well. Exhaling sharply, she said, "How about we get back to the case?"

Vik nodded, sniffing his nose. "Do you think Molly is one of the clones in this experiment?"

Lara bobbed her head. "That's the logical conclusion. Especially after what you've found."

"Do the Langstons know about it?" Vik asked, rubbing his chin. As the truth appeared to dawn on him, he began pacing around the lab bench.

"Not sure," Lara said. "We don't have any direct evidence of the Langstons' involvement in the institute, the experiment, or with the Macrobians. Well, except for his business relationship with Dr. Nilsson through my parents' old company."

Vik put his hand on his head. "If they know about it, you could be walking right into a trap."

Lara gave him a solemn look. "That's a distinct possibility."

He clapped his hands. "Then it's decided. I'm going with you," Vik said with an adamant look on his face. "I'm not taking no for an answer."

Lara chopped the air with her hands. "No. You're not."

Vik puffed out his chest and pointed his finger at her with a bravado Lara hadn't seen before. "Oh yes, I am."

Lara set her jaw. "No, you're not."

Vik planted his feet in a wide stance. "I mean it, Lara. If you say no, I'll quit my job right now."

She'd never seen him like this. Not once in all the time she'd known him. Words failing her, Lara stood silent for a few moments, unsure of how to react to Vik's forceful attitude.

"Does Finn know about Metamorphosis?" Vik asked in a defiant tone.

"Well, no," Lara said, a pang of guilt in her gut. "And we're not going to tell him about it."

He can't know.

If she'd told Finn, he might blow up the entire mission. Lara had too much at stake to risk disclosing the truth—a restored reputation for Kingsley Investigations, a promotion for Sanchez, money in the bank, and the detective's assistance to support Rob's case.

"Exactly what I thought," Vik said. "I'm going with you."

Instinctively, Lara shook her head again. In light of new evidence, it appeared Mr. Langston might be shady. It was possible he knew more about his daughter's kidnapping than he claimed. That was the best case. She had no idea what the worst-case scenario would be.

Molly is an innocent bystander in all this. She's a little girl.

"You need me to come with you," Vik said. "I can keep my eye out for you and make sure Mr. Langston isn't up to something."

I could use an extra set of eyes. And cover for my mission for Hickerson.

Lara grunted, still feeling unconvinced. "I didn't finish my story," she said, ignoring Vik's determined glare. "Hickerson gave me information to support our rescue mission in exchange for my assistance. He wants me to collect information about the Macrobians and their cloning experiment."

Maggie's eyes narrowed. "Crikey, Lara. You're working as a CIA asset now?"

"All the more reason I come with you," Vik said, apparently unwilling to drop his cause.

"What sort of information does Hickerson want you to get for him?" Maggie asked, her brow wrinkled.

"Scientific documentation on the clones. Hard copies or computer files. Whatever I can find. He also wants me to collect Molly's original DNA sample."

Maggie raised her eyebrow. "That will not be easy to hide. You'll need a special container to keep the test tubes secure."

"Do you have one I can borrow?" Lara asked, remembering Hickerson's suggestion.

Maggie hesitated for a few moments, as if she was debating whether or not to help Lara. Then she walked over to the cupboards on a lab bench and pulled out a small, rectangular, black ruggedized case. She placed it on the counter and opened it. Inside was an empty rack for storing several test tubes.

"You can use this one," Maggie said. "At least it's not too obvious."

"Oh Mags, thank you so much," Lara said.

"Look," Maggie said, "I know you won't listen, but this is madness. The Langstons are lying to you. They're up to their necks in this mess. For all we know, they could be Macrobians. How do you think they'll react if they find out you've been digging around in their business?" She paused, fidgeted with the hem of her shirt, and looked up at Lara with concern in her eyes. "I don't want you and Finn to get caught in the crossfire. This mission is as bad as a dog's breakfast."

Huh. Lara thought about Loki's bowl of dog food and was unable to grasp the comparison.

"I agree." Vik nodded vigorously. "But if you won't call it off, at least have the good sense to bring along some backup. I can cover for you." He flashed her an eager smile, as if a new line of argumentation came to him. "What if they store everything on password protected computers? Then you'll need me to get the information."

Nice bit of arm-twisting, Vik.

Lara threw up her hands in surrender. "Fine. You can go. But only on one condition."

"What's that?" Vik asked, a sparkle of excitement in his brown eyes.

"You need Shanaya's permission. I'm not putting you in harm's way without her consent. You got that?"

Vik nodded eagerly. "I'll go call her right now." He moved toward the lab exit and pointed to his smartphone.

Lara gave him a stern look. "And Vik, make sure you tell her the truth about how dangerous it will be. If she says yes, she'll need to text me. I'm not just taking your word for it."

"Sure, sure. I'll tell her everything…" Vik said, already headed toward the door, his voice trailing off.

When Vik was gone, Maggie approached her with a quizzical expression. "The name Metamorphosis reminds me of an experiment I read about in grad school. A team of scientists used a CRISPR gene editing tool to delete a single gene in a butterfly, and it altered other characteristics in unexpected ways. A tiny change produced a dramatic effect."

"Are you saying the edit had a 'butterfly effect'?" Lara asked, smirking at the irony.

The corners of Maggie's lips turned upwards. "Pretty much. By deleting a single gene, they effectively rearranged the colors on the butterfly's wings. They ran the experiment with other butterfly species and the same thing happened. Anyway, the scientists surmised from the experiment that mutations in one gene could lead to many other unintended effects in gene expression."

Lara wrinkled her nose. "Why are you telling me all this?"

"I'm trying to understand why the Macrobians would clone babies as an experiment. The butterfly study helped us understand fundamental rules about the function of genes. If scientists could crack the code of the butterfly wing pattern, then they could understand more about human genetics as well."

"Why butterflies?" Lara asked.

"Well, butterflies are extremely interesting for studying the functions of genes. As you know, a caterpillar undergoes metamorphosis to become a butterfly. Both the caterpillar and the butterfly share identical DNA or genotype."

Identical DNA? But they look so different.

Lara's eyes widened. "How does that work?"

"Remember when your doctor explained how gene expression can be turned on and off in response to environmental stimuli, leading to different physical characteristics or phenotypes?"

Lara nodded. "Yeah, she called it epigenetics."

"Well, it's the same for butterflies but a bit more extreme. In the early phase of its life, different parts of the butterfly's DNA are expressed to form the caterpillar. Metamorphosis is triggered by different proteins produced by the caterpillar's cells, to turn some genes off and others on, eventually transforming the caterpillar into a butterfly."

"Huh, that's fascinating. Do you think there's a connection between the metamorphosis of the butterfly and the experiment being conducted by the Macrobians?"

Maggie bobbed her head. "I'm guessing that Metamorphosis is about broadening our understanding of the human genome, the functions of certain genes, and how they're expressed in a person across different environments. Maybe that's why there are eight girls adopted into different families."

"Do you think they modified the genomes of the girls?" Lara asked.

Maggie thought for a moment. "If they're trying to find a cure for a blood disorder, they may have deleted different genes in each girl to control for different pathways of a disease or genetic defect. I'd have to study the DNA profiles Vik found to see if I can detect any biomarkers."

"Oh, would you do that?" Lara asked.

"Sure," Maggie said glancing at the clock. "I won't be able to get you any answers before you leave for China, though."

"That's okay. Something tells me this case won't be over once we bring Molly back home." Lara sighed, sinking onto the stool. "I'm at a complete loss about how to handle the Langstons."

"What about the Langstons?" a gruff voice asked from behind Lara.

Maggie's eyes grew wide. Lara craned her neck to see Detective Sanchez enter the lab with a dark grimace on his face.

Not in a good mood today, I see.

"Pull up a stool. There's much to tell," Lara said.

After Lara got done telling Sanchez what she'd learned from Hickerson and what Vik learned from his DNA fishing expedition, the detective stood silent for a few minutes, staring at the floor. Lara and Maggie exchanged nervous looks but allowed him the time to process everything.

Sanchez looked up and cleared his throat. "Uh… I think you should, um… I'd like you to go to China… I mean, if you're still willing. It's gotten pretty risky if you ask me, but I—"

"I'm going," Lara said.

Sanchez exhaled sharply. "Good."

Lara furrowed her brow. "I thought you didn't want me to go. Finn told me—"

"I just changed my mind," Sanchez said. "I'm not saying I'm ready to go after the Langstons or anything. I want to get to the bottom of this case. Only if you're, uh… willing to go. It's your call."

"I'm going to bring Molly home," Lara said. "That's the important thing. The Langstons are clearly hiding something, but I don't detect any bad intent. I think they just want their daughter back and are willing to go to any lengths to get her."

Sanchez shook his head. "There had better not be any more twists and turns on this case. I think I've had enough bombshells for one day."

"But I haven't told you what I found yet," Maggie interrupted.

"Wait, there's more?" Lara asked, gawking at her.

Maggie looked at the detective with uncertainty, but he motioned for her to continue. "I sequenced the DNA from the blood the police found in Molly's bedroom. I've determined that it can't belong to her."

Sanchez's jaw dropped.

Lara's body tensed. "What? But the police tested it and determined it was a perfect match to Molly."

"On its face, the DNA is an exact match to Molly's. But the forensics lab didn't measure the telomeres. You can't measure telomeres directly from DNA sequencing, due to their knotted structures. On a hunch, I used an established technique to determine the length of the telomeres and made a surprising discovery," Maggie said. "If you weren't specifically looking for the difference in telomeres, you'd never notice. The DNA came from a woman in her forties. Definitely not an eight-year-old girl."

Lara took a few steps backward. "What? Does that... was the blood on the wall from the kidnapper then?"

Maggie nodded. "Your kidnapper appears to be the original source of the clones. She's genetically identical to Molly and the others, only thirty-plus years older."

Vik marched back in the lab, a proud grin on his face. "I can go!"

Sanchez gave Lara a strange look. She glanced down at her smartphone to see a text from Shanaya, giving him permission to go with her to China.

"Look who is grinning like a shot fox," Maggie said.

Vik's eyes darted between each of their faces. "What did I miss?"

TWENTY-SIX

The Private Jet

October 12, 2028

LARA STOLE A GLANCE AT JULIAN, who was facing her and lounging casually in the cream leather armchair at the front of his private jet. Wearing a black turtleneck embroidered with the GenTech Industries logo and a pair of tan slacks, he was dressed more comfortably than she'd ever seen him. And yet, he held his posture tense, sipping a glass of Champagne in one hand and holding up a print newspaper with the other.

The front of the plane had two sets of four large, comfortable chairs facing each other, and Julian effectively took up all eight seats. Before takeoff, he had insisted no one else sit near him; he wanted to stretch and enjoy some peace and quiet. From the middle of the plane to the back, the same leather chairs were arranged in rows of four with two on each side of the aisle.

Lara's chair warmed her, despite the cool air that whooshed from the vents above. A nice baked-apple scent wafted through the cabin, courtesy of what she assumed to be a dry-scent diffuser in the air conditioning unit. The leather was soft, and the stuffing cushioned every part of her body. She repositioned herself, ignoring the barely audible creaking of leather, and discreetly looked at Julian again. His eyes moved slowly across the page as if he was deliberately reading each word.

Is he reading or just pretending to read?

On her stakeouts, she would pretend to read such a paper while hiding herself behind it. And she imagined she looked the same as Julian did at the moment. Lara suppressed a grin and shifted her gaze.

Her mind whirred at a steady hum with all the information she'd learned in the past few days. The Langstons had hired her to get their daughter back, but the kidnapping was not at all what it seemed. Even without positive confirmation, Lara was certain Julian and Cynthia knew about the abduction—who took Molly and where she was being held.

But why did they keep their knowledge a secret? They obviously wanted to get their daughter back. Did it have something to do with Molly's status as a clone?

She looked up at him again and jumped slightly in her seat. Julian was staring straight at her, his dark eyes locking with hers and then narrowing slightly. A jolt ran up her spine, causing her heart to pump faster.

She gave him a nonchalant smile, hoping he'd continue to buy her dutiful act of a hired employee and not realize she knew what she knew. But his eyes returned coldness with a flash of suspicion. She darted her eyes away from his, feeling as if lingering a moment longer might betray her innermost thoughts.

A few hours earlier, he'd been on her case, trying to learn what had been so important for her to leave the team at the simulator. Lara made up a story about the detective following a red herring that didn't pan out. But Julian wasn't buying it. Not one word.

I couldn't tell him any of it. Not about the clones. Not about the DNA match between Molly and her kidnapper. And definitely not about his company's connection to her parents and their biotech company.

Lara prayed he didn't notice the pink flush creeping up her

neck and filling her face. She stared out the window at the setting sun and the dark shadows descending upon the rolling clouds, breathing steadily to calm herself down.

I'm such a terrible liar.

She pressed her lips together and stared at her smartphone, acting as if she was distracted by the messages on the screen. She couldn't help scrolling through a series of heated messages between her and Rob from earlier in the day. Her stomach turned as she remembered their last conversation before her departure for China. Lara sighed heavily. Rob was so angry he'd barely listened to her instructions on how to care for Loki.

Hopefully he wrote down how much food to give him.

A lump formed in her throat, as she missed Loki with an unexpected fierceness. The magnetic force of her attachment to the dog had completely caught her off guard. She'd never felt such unconditional acceptance. As difficult as the strong-willed Doberman could be at times, he tugged at her heart strings like no human ever had.

"What's wrong?" Vik asked from the seat next to her, his eyes still glued to the action movie playing on his tablet. He finished his second glass of Champagne, set it on the table, and grinned at her. His head swayed slightly, and there was a strange flush in his face.

I told him not to drink that stuff so quickly. She'd tried to explain that sparkling wine absorbed into the bloodstream faster than regular wine. To no avail, apparently. Vik had protested vehemently, claiming he was used to having more than one glass of wine in the evening with Shanaya. Despite her warning, he refused to pass up the opportunity to try real Champagne. When Julian sensed Lara's concern, he seemed even more eager to share his bottle with Vik.

Lara groaned. "Oh, Rob is not happy with me."

"For abandoning his case?" Vik asked, stumbling over his words.

Oh great… he's drunk.

Lara eyed him with concern. "No, he understands I have to

bring Molly back home safely. He's angry at me for taking *you* with me." She rolled her eyes. "He says he needs your help more than I do."

"I doubt that." Vik's eyes widened. "But then he doesn't know most of it, does he?" He slurred through his disapproval. Lara glanced nervously at Julian to check if he was listening.

"If I'd told him everything, he would have forbidden me from going."

"You mean like Finn would have?" Vik whispered a bit too loudly.

Lara put her finger to her lips. "Shhhh. He can hear you."

"No, he can't," Vik said, swaying in his seat. "I'm whispering. Plus, he's not paying any attention."

Lara craned her neck to look toward the back of the plane. Finn was deeply engrossed in conversation with Kaitlyn. When they boarded, Kaitlyn had explained her intense dislike for fixed-wing aircraft and stated her strong preference for sitting in the back. Finn didn't want to leave her alone with the mercenaries so he offered to keep her company. He'd been sitting back there for three hours now, and they'd been gabbing nonstop. Kaitlyn's incessant giggling at Finn's jokes grated on Lara's ears like the screech of a dying bird.

A sharp pang rose in her stomach when she saw the broad smile on Finn's face. It had been a long time since things between him and Lara had been that light.

Ugh.

Finn was still annoyed with her for ditching them during the test run at the simulator. Especially when she kept dodging his endless questions about where she went and why. *Talking to him had been like an interrogation.*

She exhaled sharply at the memory. She wouldn't likely survive another round of meticulous questioning without copping to the truth. She'd decided against telling Finn for fear of how he might respond. She didn't think he'd follow her lead if he knew the truth about the Langstons.

Will he forgive me for not telling him?

She swung her head back around, not wanting to get caught gawking at them. Lara looked at her watch.

Only thirteen more hours. This is going to be a long flight.

"Don't worry too much. I showed Rob some stuff before I left," Vik said offhandedly.

"What stuff?"

"Some stuff on the Dark Web," he mumbled.

"What's he looking for there?" Lara asked, wrinkling her nose.

"Rob said he wanted to go over all my research into CyberShop and KillerBot to make sure we didn't miss anything about Harry." Vik rose from his chair and nearly fell on top of her.

"Where are you going?" Lara asked.

"I have to use the men's room," Vik said, tripping over her foot and struggling to reach the aisle.

Vik grabbed the back of her chair and pulled it backwards, her body moving with the sharp angle. Then he let go of it suddenly, and the chair bounced back into place, hitting her in the head. Scowling, Lara turned around in her chair to have some words with Vik, but instead felt sorry for the kid staggering back and forth down the aisle toward the back of the plane.

That's gonna hurt like hell in the morning.

She leaned back in her chair and closed her eyes for a few minutes. Her seat bobbed backwards, startling her. She looked up, expecting to see Vik returning to his seat. But it was Finn who was leaning on the back of her chair, a bright gleam in his eye.

"What do you want?" Lara asked, a bit too gruffly.

"Kaitlyn and I had an idea for the first phase of the mission."

I don't like the sound of this.

Finn had been coming up with new ideas for her mission ever since he'd demanded to come along with her. And without fail, Julian and the team of hired men hung on his every word, apparently intoxicated by the charismatic special operator and his many medals. Even though she too led teams in the Army Special Forces, the past few days had made her feel like chopped liver.

This is my mission.

"Uh huh…" she said without an ounce of enthusiasm.

He plopped into the seat in front of her and rested on his knees, looking at her over the top of the chair. Julian raised an eyebrow, now clearly paying attention. Finn folded his arms on top of the chair and leaned forward, gazing at her.

"We were thinking… maybe we should skip the initial scouting mission with you and I posing as a wealthy American couple seeking to donate to the orphanage. It seems like a waste of effort, with a high risk of getting caught."

We were thinking. Lara shot a quick glance to the back of the plane. Kaitlyn acted as if she were working on a crossword puzzle.

Yeah, right.

"We were thinking of taking a more aggressive approach," Finn said. "Let's send in two teams, use a decoy maneuver, break in, and search the place for Molly."

Lara frowned. The original plan was to use a scouting mission to decide if a break-in of the orphanage was necessary. If they thought it worthwhile, they would go in under the cover of night, minimizing the risk of getting caught.

How did I lose control of this mission?

She folded her arms across her chest. "Let me get this straight. You want to storm the orphanage during daylight in search of Molly, alerting the Chinese authorities to our presence and getting everyone thrown in prison in the process?"

Finn glared at her. "No. That's not what I'm saying. But we don't want to give them a chance to go underground with Molly after we gather information on her whereabouts."

"What are you proposing?" Lara asked, her voice wavering.

"We were thinking that since Vik is here, maybe you two could sneak into the back and search the orphanage for Molly while Kaitlyn and I distract the staff with our generous offer to fund the orphanage. Based on the satellite infrared images, it only looks like there are two personnel."

All this "we" talk. Where is Kaitlyn to pitch her own idea?

Lara bristled at the idea of Finn and Kaitlyn posing as the wealthy couple while she and Vik put themselves in danger. Her ears grew hot. She hadn't planned on putting Vik in harm's way so soon. And she took offense to Finn and Kaitlyn offering up his help as if he were trained for such an operation. It wasn't their place.

Finn wouldn't be so eager to have us "go in hot" if he knew what I know.

A pang of guilt reverberated through her chest as she wondered if lying to him was the right thing. Lara crossed he arms. "No, we're going to follow the original plan and scout the orphanage first. My contact said China's internal security agents scour even the most remote areas of the countryside for suspicious activities. And we're going to be just outside a major city. Even if there are no cameras, they'll have watchful eyes everywhere. Plus, I want to make sure our intelligence is accurate before we do anything drastic like break into the orphanage. What if there are more personnel than we think?"

Julian cleared his throat and came up beside Finn. "I'm inclined to agree with Major Stewart. I prefer a more aggressive approach. We'll have a greater chance of finding Molly before they hide her."

"Sir, I'd advise against a break-in during daylight hours. The risk of getting caught is too—"

"Whatever am I paying *you* for?" Julian sneered at her. He looked over her head and surveyed the team of mercenaries seated in the plane. Lara turned to follow his gaze. "Would any of you be willing to break into the orphanage during the day for a ten-thousand-dollar bonus?" he asked, receiving eager nods all around. He turned back to Lara with his lips curled. "It looks like you've been overruled. Or maybe we don't need you after all."

*Is he actually firing me? Right now? On the plane to Hong Kong…
after all his meticulous planning to involve me?*

She stared at him, meeting his eyes, refusing to blink, her lips
pressed firmly together.

He's toying with me.

After all, what would be the point of dragging her on this
mission in the first place, only to fire her? She remained silent for
a few minutes and contemplated her options.

*The Langstons are not worth risking life and limb. If only I'd told
Finn the whole truth, we wouldn't be in this mess.*

Lara wanted to kick herself for being so stupid.

When am I going to learn to trust people?

As she thought through the proposed plan, a silver lining
appeared. If Finn and Kaitlyn distracted the orphanage staff,
maybe she could steal some information for Hickerson.

It would be the perfect cover to get information.

"Okay, fine. Who knows, maybe we'll get lucky, find Molly,
and head home on the same night."

Finn smiled with relief. Julian nodded with satisfaction.

"I assume you've figured out our cover story?" Lara asked
Julian as he was about to head back to his seat.

Julian stopped and turned toward her, a sinister glint in his
eyes. "I informed Chinese authorities that I'm planning a major
tech expo in Shenzhen to be sponsored by GenTech Industries
and featuring high-level guests. For that reason, I'm bringing
over my security team to assess any potential threats. I also told
them we're planning a few visits in the countryside by helicopter
to make some charitable donations." He paused, lifting his chin
slightly. "Does that work for you?"

Lara nodded. "Sounds plausible to me."

Out of nowhere, Vik appeared in front of her, his skin flushed
red in odd places.

"What did I miss?" Vik asked, his eyes darting between their
faces.

Lara rolled her eyes.

TWENTY-SEVEN

The Orphanage

October 14, 2028

"MY HEAD HURTS," Vik whined.

So does mine. But for a different reason.

He stood close behind her and kept watch over the empty rice field and the footpath that led to the next village. He was supposed to be making sure they weren't being watched by anyone, not worrying about his headache.

"I told you not to drink so much," Lara snapped, leaning her body against the rickety door of the run-down orphanage. The intense humidity stifled her breathing, making her chest unusually tight. She swayed slightly under the heat of the sun, beads of sweat running down her face and body, drenching her clothing. A slight breeze sent a foul cocktail of body odor, pee, and human feces into her nose.

"I wouldn't have drunk the second glass if I'd known I was coming with you…" Vik replied in a defensive tone.

No, you should have skipped it because I warned you about the alcohol content.

"You could have stayed behind," Lara said, venting her exasperation. Her lungs couldn't seem to get a full breath of air, so she tried to breathe in more deeply, though it was a labored attempt. She needed Vik for backup, but she was sick of his complaining. The scorching temperatures and soaring humidity overwhelmed her, making her limbs feel heavy.

"Miss a brush with danger to nurse a hangover?" Vik rasped. "Never."

Brush with danger? If we're lucky, we won't end up getting tortured in a Chinese prison.

She shot him a glare and then gaped at his mostly dry face. "Aren't you hot?"

Vik furrowed his brow. "Why would I be? I mean… it's hot outside, but I'm okay. There's actually a nice breeze."

Nice breeze?

Vik grinned. "I'm used to this climate. Remember, I grew up in India… or maybe it's genetics."

Then I would like to edit intolerance to heat out of my DNA.

Lara pressed her lips together, attempting to suppress her anxiety. She blamed Finn for putting Vik in danger. But if she was being honest with herself, that ship had sailed as soon as she said yes to him coming along. And it was her fault Finn didn't know the truth.

This mission was extremely dangerous even if everything went exactly as planned. From the moment of take-off at Dulles, nothing had gone as planned, mostly due to last-minute changes by Finn and Julian. Breaking into the orphanage without proper intelligence was a foolhardy idea. Not to mention they were running the operation in broad daylight. When Finn suggested it on the plane, she didn't want to challenge him in front of the others. But it was Julian who had given her little choice to reverse course. After landing in Hong Kong, her team had hit the ground running, and she hadn't had a chance to talk with Finn in private.

It's almost like Julian wants me to get in trouble.

In the end, she decided Vik was safer with her breaking into the orphanage than staying behind with Julian and his group of hired thugs.

Pausing for a moment to wipe her forehead, she glanced over her shoulder past the rice field. In the distance, she glimpsed the spikes of corn stalks and thought about their uncertain exit plan. Not far beyond the first few rows of corn, the GenTech Industries helicopter stood hidden within the thick field, waiting for their return.

She prayed no one would find the concealed helo before their work was done, but that was probably naïve. Certainly, someone would have heard their approach, seen it fly through the air and land in the cornfield, wondered about the helicopter's origins, and reported it to Chinese authorities. With Finn's new plan to pose as a wealthy couple with Kaitlyn, they had no one to guard their only viable escape route. It was only a matter of time before someone showed up to investigate.

The clock is ticking.

She exhaled sharply as she went over the intel in her head. From the helicopter, Finn and Lara had surveilled the acres of empty farmland surrounding the grounds of the orphanage before landing. With the exception of an old wooden barn next to the cornfield they'd landed in, there was no other building structure within a mile radius. Not even a hut. Luckily, their visit coincided with the weekly rest day for the farm workers, which would help them avoid attracting any attention. As far as they knew, not a soul had stirred upon their arrival.

Lara found the absence of activity around the orphanage a bit uncanny. Perhaps the orphanage owned the surrounding land, and the locals knew to stay away. It was only an hour drive outside of the sprawling metropolis of Shenzhen, home to more than twelve million inhabitants, but far enough away to seem somewhat remote.

Despite the orphanage's abandoned appearance, the helo's infrared sensors detected the presence of two adults near the front of the main building, several children in the dorms, and a nursery with a few infants near the back of the building.

I thought orphanages were overcrowded in China. Apparently not this one.

As agreed, Finn and Kaitlyn would enter through the front door of the orphanage, posing as philanthropists seeking to donate to a worthy cause. After they set up the distraction, Lara and Vik would break in the back entrance and search the dormitory for Molly. The plan would also give Lara the chance to search for information for Hickerson.

That's what I'm counting on. Bringing home good intelligence was the main reason Lara had not fought hard about the change in plan.

A sudden gust whooshed past the side of the orphanage, followed by a screeching noise that pierced her ears, sending her pulse into high gear. Alarmed, she swung her head around to see where the grating sound was coming from. About hundred feet away, out in front of the orphanage near the foot path, an old rusty metal sign with the name Herodotus Social Welfare Institute swung back and forth.

Her smartphone buzzed with a text from Finn.

KAITLYN IS SITTING DOWN WITH THE DIRECTOR AND HIS ASSISTANT
YOU SHOULD BE CLEAR TO PROCEED

She responded:

GOOD COPY
ENTERING BACK DOOR NOW

This is our best chance.

A sprinkle of dull gray paint chips fell on her tennis shoes as she slid her lockpick up into the keyhole one more time and wriggled it around. Tinny sounds came from the old doorknob as it rattled under her touch. No dice.

"Lara… I think someone is coming," Vik whispered urgently.

Still fiddling with the doorknob, Lara cast a quick glance over her left shoulder. Vik's watery, bloodshot eyes were wide and alert, and he tipped his head backward toward the path.

Lara peered around him, and the sight of an elderly Chinese man hunched over sent a burst of adrenaline through her body. Carrying a large basket of green vegetables on his back, the man strode carefully down the hill on the footpath which headed straight for the orphanage. The urge to run for cover came over her, but she remained in place, nearly motionless, except the air moving in and out of her lungs.

We have zero cover.

Lara bit her lip and held her breath for a moment. If the man were to look up even for a moment, he would witness a very strange sight—a blonde-haired, white woman dressed in tactical gear attempting to break in the back entrance of the orphanage along with a gangly Indian man dressed in the same attire, keeping watch. It would be hard to miss and not easily forgotten.

"Does he see us?" Lara asked in a hushed voice, her muscles tense and on high alert. She turned back to the door to focus on her task. She rattled the pick again, but the lock wouldn't budge. The sound of her heartbeat thrashed in her ears.

"Not yet," Vik whispered. "He's bent over from the weight of this load and too focused on divots in the path to notice us. But he might see us when he gets closer. Better hurry."

Lara pulled the pick out of the lock, wiped her sweaty hands on her pants, and shook the tension out of her arms. She took a deep breath and tried to calm her nerves.

Okay, Lara. You've done this before. This ramshackle lock won't beat you. Not today.

She inserted the pick into the cylinder once more, feeling her way past each of the pins, and carefully set them one by one. Then she turned the lock.

Click.

The door opened with ease. Lara stepped inside quickly,

motioning for Vik to follow her. After he slipped inside, she closed the door behind them, sending another cloud of paint chips to the floor. Her arm across her forehead, she leaned her back against the wall for a moment to catch her breath. Then she turned to glance cautiously out the dirty, broken window pane.

Just in the nick of time.

The man stood on the path, a confused look on his face, shielding his eyes and staring at the back door of the orphanage. He must have noticed the sound of the door closing. Lara ducked out of sight and caught her breath. After a few moments, she turned around to survey the room.

What appeared to be a mud room was mostly empty, except for a coat rack on the wall and a leaky utility sink in the corner. A row of muddy boots lined up against the wall. The paint was peeling off the walls like a healing sunburn. There were two wooden doors leading from the room, one across from them and one to their left.

Lara squinted as she attempted to recall the layout of the orphanage from her memory of Hickerson's map. "That door must lead outside to the courtyard," she said. "From there, we should be able to look into the dormitory to see if Molly is there. Can you look at the map to be sure?"

Vik pulled out the rough map he'd drawn of the orphanage with details from Hickerson's satellite imagery. "Yup. If we got the layout right on this drawing, then the courtyard should be right through that door."

"Okay then. Let's go check it out." She walked across the room and motioned for Vik to follow. She waited for him to get behind her and then gripped the door handle. As she opened the door, the hinges let out a high-pitched squeak that pricked her ears.

She peered through the crack and listened for voices. Her heart was thumping so loudly, she could barely hear anything else.

"I think it's empty," Lara said in a low voice, opening the

door and entering the rectangular space surrounded by the buildings of the orphanage.

The ground was covered with a mix of dirt, gravel, and broken pavers. Several chickens scattered across the courtyard, their ammonia-like stench making Lara wrinkle her nose. A few beat-up toys lay strewn about.

She waved her hand for Vik to follow and then stopped him suddenly. She motioned to Vik and pointed to the three interior windows lining the courtyard. Vik opened his mouth to say something, but Lara put her finger to her lips. When she ducked down, he followed her lead.

A few angry clucks from the chickens erupted from the far corner.

"That window there must be for the admin office at the back of the orphanage," she whispered, pointing to the one just above their heads. "Those over there on the right belong to the dormitory. Stay low and follow me."

Lara crept along the wall toward the dormitory, her feet kicking up dust and crunching on the gravel. When they reached the first window, she signaled for Vik to take his position there. Then she crept further until she reached the second window. She nodded at Vik and gestured for him to follow her lead. She stood slowly and peered over the window sill into the dark room. Her mouth opened slightly in surprise. Vik stared at her, his eyes bulging in their sockets.

It's completely empty.

The large room contained two rows of eight cots. A large chest stood on either side of the room, presumably for storing clothes.

Lara crept back over to Vik's position.

"Where are the kids?" Vik asked. "Didn't we pick up heat emissions from at least ten kids?"

"We did. But it took about thirty minutes for us to land the helicopter and walk over here. We also lost some time finding cover to conceal it. They must be gone now."

"You think all the kids left during that short of a time window? Where would they go?"

Lara shrugged. "I don't know. But now we know Molly isn't here. Let's get back inside and search for intel."

Standing in front of the other door in the mud room, Lara texted Finn.

THE PACKAGE IS NOT HERE
SEARCHING THE REST OF THE BACK ROOMS
KEEP THEM BUSY

Finn replied:

DIRECTOR GETTING RESTLESS
NOT MUCH TIME LEFT

Lara put her finger to her mouth, motioned for Vik to get behind her, and then opened the door a crack. She exhaled sharply.

"It's an office," she whispered to Vik, opening the door further to reveal a row of metal filing cabinets lining the wall. They both stepped inside. In the middle of the room stood an executive-style aluminum desk with a ripped vinyl black chair.

"Must belong to the director," Vik said, closing the door behind them.

"Most likely," Lara said, frowning. She pointed to the Chinese characters on the labels marking the filing cabinets. "You don't read Mandarin, do you?" she asked, half joking, half hopeful.

"Nope."

As Lara approached the cabinets, she rubbed her chin. "If they alphabetized the files from left to right, Langston would be somewhere in the middle…" She pulled open the third drawer from the left and gazed inside.

"Oh, thank goodness. The files inside are in English," she whispered.

"That's a lucky coincidence," Vik said.

"A strange one," Lara said, taking a closer look. "Wait… there are some markings on these folders. She pulled out a file, and her jaw dropped.

"What?" Vik asked.

"These files are from the Miracle Springs Eternal Adoption Agency. See the stamp right here?" Then her eyes landed on the spot where the file for Mo Chu Langston would be, and her heart sank. "And of course, there's no file for Molly."

"Did you look under Kong?" Vik asked, peering over her shoulder.

"Mo Chu Kong… of course. That's brilliant, Vik!" Lara's eyes darted toward the files starting with K. Immediately, she spotted the file. And another. And another. "Wait a minute. There are several files with the last name Kong." Lara counted them. "Eight in total." She grabbed the entire stack and showed them to Vik. All the clones were identified with the last name Kong.

Vik slid out the file marked Mo Chu Kong and flipped it open. His eyes ran down the first few sheets of paper for a moment. "Lara, these aren't adoption records…"

"What are they then?"

"They're ownership contracts," Vik said slowly.

Lara's mouth fell open. "What?"

"See here," Vik said, pointing to the top of the paper. "This agreement states that Subject ID 657889500 remains the property of the Macrobian Institute of Life Sciences for the duration of the experiment. The institute agrees to place the clone into the care and custody of Julian and Cynthia Langston for eight years. The contract was signed by Mr. Langston."

"Wait, just Julian? Not both of the Langstons?"

"Only Mr. Langston signed the paper," Vik said.

Does Mrs. Langston know that Molly is a clone?

Vik continued, "After the clone turns eight years old, the Langstons are legally required to return it to the institute for the remainder of its life. If they fail to do so, the institute will report the clone as kidnapped to the Chinese government."

Lara winced at the pronoun *it*. "In other words, Molly was never legally adopted by the Langstons?" Lara asked, not believing her ears.

What does this mean?

Vik shook his head. "That's correct. This contract specifies that temporary adoption papers will be drawn up by the Miracle Springs Eternal Adoption Agency to facilitate transfer of the clone to the United States. The clones remain Chinese citizens and the custody agreement expires on her eighth birthday."

"Okay, this proves without a doubt that at least Mr. Langston knew who took his daughter from the outset," Lara said. She furrowed her brow. "Molly turned eight years old in July activating the return clause. But they didn't return her to the institute for some reason. Did Mr. Langston refuse to bring her back?" Lara tapped her lips. "Then Yingyue traveled to the United States and took her. Mr. Langston appeared to know about it and did nothing to prevent it. Why?" She paused, trying to pin down the contradictory thoughts speeding through her head. "He knew Molly had to go back to the institute per the contract."

Vik shrugged his shoulders.

"And then he led me right to the kidnapper," Lara said.

"Technically, this isn't a kidnapping," Vik said with a smirk.

"No, it definitely wasn't. Yingyue came all the way to the United States to collect her property." Lara raised her eyebrow. "Something doesn't add up here."

"Lara, it is possible that Mr. Langston knew who took Molly and why, but he couldn't divulge the details to you without appearing to be involved in the clone experiment or getting in trouble for an illegal adoption? Or maybe he didn't tell his wife about the whole thing and was terrified she'd find out. There doesn't have to be a bigger conspiracy here. But I agree, it definitely smells funny."

Lara nodded and remained silent for a few moments.

Vik flipped further through Molly's file. "Look here. This shows that Molly has been to China at least once a year...

apparently for medical tests. For genomic mapping…" His voice trailed off as he pointed to a sheet with the results of a medical test. "Holy cow."

"What?" Lara asked, looking over his shoulder. Her eyes widened when she saw the test result. "Then Cynthia must have known about the connection to China."

"Molly has the gene for aplastic anemia…" Vik said, dumbfounded. "What's going on here?"

Lara grabbed the file from Vik and handed him the remaining stack.

"Lara, do you think we should read through all the files in here?" Vik asked, motioning with his head to the door on the other side of the office. "Someone could come in here at any moment."

Finn would warn us, right?

"Yeah… good point," Lara said glancing at her smartphone. There was no text from Finn warning them.

"Do you need to find anything else for Hickerson?" Vik asked, setting the stack of files on the floor.

"Yeah… let's search the files for any other mention of Metamorphosis. If we start at opposite ends, we can cover ground quickly.

Lara placed Molly's file on top of the stack and moved toward the filing cabinets. She opened the top drawer and thumbed through the files, looking for something… anything that might sound familiar.

After a few minutes, she sighed. "Did you find anything?"

"Nope… no mention of the experiment," Vik said, furrowing his brow.

Loud voices coming from the hallway startled them. Lara swung her head around, looking for a place to hide.

No time to escape the office without detection.

She ran toward the small door in the corner and threw it open. It was a supply closet.

"Quick, get inside," Lara said, shoving him into the tiny space.

They both crowded inside and managed to close the door behind them just in time.

The office door opened, and heavy footsteps entered the room. Then she remembered, and a jolt of adrenaline coursed through her body.

We left the stack of files on the floor.

Lara peered through the keyhole and glimpsed a tall Scandinavian-looking man with curly gray hair. A younger Chinese woman with wavy, black hair came in after him and circled the desk, coming within a few feet of the stack.

What if they see it?

"What I'd like to know is how those bloody Americans found this orphanage," he said in a gruff tone. "And less than half an hour after we moved them."

Were the clones here or something?

Lara studied the older man. There was something familiar about him, but she couldn't put her finger on it. He must have been in his late sixties and was plainly dressed, minus a luxury watch and cufflinks.

"Should we call her?" the woman asked. "To warn her to look for anything out of the ordinary at the institute?"

The man nodded grimly. "I told Dr. K taking the clones there was a dumb idea. Especially the one she had to collect herself."

Lara's heart began to pound. *Molly was here.*

"Yingyue insists keeping her in the open was the best way to protect her," the woman said. "She's a Chinese citizen. Mr. L won't try to take her back in the middle of a large city."

They know Mr. Langston plans to get Molly back?

"Your mother is a bit too arrogant for my taste," the man growled.

The woman put her hands on her hips. "Oh c'mon. You know the girl has to undergo the procedure like the others. We can't exactly treat her here under these conditions. And Dr. K doesn't like it when you call her my mother."

That's Dr. K's daughter? Lara's scalp prickled as a muddled connection tried to form in her brain.

The man grunted and picked up the phone. "You go take care of those Americans. I'll handle Dr. K."

"Can I have a look?" Vik whispered, motioning to the keyhole.

Lara moved aside to let him see.

"Wait… I recognize him from the photo," he murmured.

"What photo?" Lara hissed.

"From the file I put together for you…" Vik creased his forehead. "Remember? Right before we left?"

"Sorry, Vik… I think I might have been a bit distracted by all the bombs you dropped on me."

"That's Dr. Liam Nilsson," Vik said, "the former director of the adoption agency."

Oh.

"And the CEO of Horizon Genomics," Lara said, her jaw dropping.

"Oh crap… he put the phone down and is walking toward the filing cabinets," Vik said, cringing. "He's gonna see the stack of files we left out there. If he does, we're toast." He grabbed her arm and covered his face.

Lara typed a text into her smartphone as fast as her fingers would allow.

HELP!

ASK FOR THE DIRECTOR

NOW

Then she pushed Vik aside to peek through the keyhole. Dr. Nilsson was about to turn in the direction of the stack when the door opened, and the woman stuck her head inside the office. "Dr. Nilsson, the Americans are asking to speak to you again."

Dr. Nilsson gasped with irritation. "Fine. I'll get rid of them myself." He turned and strode toward the door. Before leaving the office, he muttered, "If you want a job done right…"

Do it yourself.

Lara and Vik exchanged close-call looks and exhaled a

collective breath of relief. As soon as he was gone, Vik and Lara piled out of the closet, grabbed the stack of files, and headed toward the back door. Out of the corner of her eye, Lara spotted something red on the desk.

A bowl of red paper butterflies.

TWENTY-EIGHT

The Tour

October 15, 2028

"I CAN'T BELIEVE you withheld important information about the Langstons from me," Finn growled, walking across the pedestrian zone in Shenzhen's Science and Technology Park.

I should have told him. But now is not the time for a full confession.

"Well, I didn't really know for sure before we left for China… but I had my suspicions that they must have known who kidnapped Molly." Lara kept pace with him as they continued toward the institute.

"Yeah, we've gone over this." Finn deepened his scowl. "And your point is…"

After the break-in at the orphanage, Finn insisted on seeing what she and Vik had found in the office. Lara managed to show him Molly's medical file, minus the ownership contract, to appease his curiosity, keeping the rest to herself. If he saw the other files, he would immediately realize how much more she knew about the girl's disappearance than she was letting on.

Once she showed him Molly's file, it didn't take long for Finn to put two and two together about the medical tests. At first,

Lara denied having suspicions about the Langstons' knowledge of the kidnapping. As usual, her lies had come off clumsy, and he refused to believe her. When she confessed, his temper flared, and he became angrier than she'd ever seen him.

Lara gave him a pained stare. "I already said I'm sorry. And I've explained why I kept it from you. I was worried you'd share the information with Kaitlyn. What if Mr. Langston found out we know? If he knew about the kidnapping before the trip and didn't tell us, he can't be trusted."

"It feels like I'm the one you don't trust," Finn snarled.

Lara gulped, guilt gurgling in her stomach as if she'd eaten spicy food. *He doesn't even know half the truth, and he's furious. What happens when I tell him the rest?*

The truth was shocking… and woefully incomplete. If she told him anymore, Finn would likely become distracted with partial details and confront Julian, throwing the operation into chaos. Lara wanted to keep their mission in China as simple as possible. Rescue Molly and get home safely. Except now, they would technically be kidnapping her and returning her to the Langstons, who had no legal custody claim. Things had suddenly become incredibly complicated.

Lara's determination to bring Molly back to the only home she knew overrode everything else. She could figure out the rest later when she didn't have to worry about spending life in a Chinese prison. She didn't trust Finn to share her view if he knew the truth. Quickening her pace, Lara passed by Finn, giving in to the urge to escape the situation.

He'll never forgive me for this.

Finn caught up to her and pinched Lara's arm before they reached the entrance of the Macrobian Institute of Life Sciences. She yanked her arm away, charged forward, and thrust open the glass door. Knots in Lara's stomach tightened at the unexpected sight of two armed security guards standing at both sides of the entrance.

Armed guards?

Hickerson hadn't mentioned the institute having such a

robust security presence, but perhaps there had been recent changes. Thankfully, if they aroused any suspicions at the institute, they would invoke the cover story and claim they were scoping out the facility as a potential venue for the tech expo.

When she gave the guards a second glance, something familiar caught her eye, stopping her dead in her tracks. The two men wore black exoskeletons and sturdy helmets with heads-up displays, rather overkill for a scientific institution. Memories of her last case flashed through her mind. They made her think of MacFarlan, Rob, Sanchez, and the next generation battle suit being developed by the Pentagon for the U.S. military.

Huh. Just like the ones from Project Gecko.

The sound of trickling water distracted her, and she turned her gaze toward the lobby where various people were rushing about. A giant, round, limestone fountain decorated the middle of the space. Four white, nude statues surrounded a white pedestal. They were obscured by spouts of water, leaping into the air at the center of the basin. She was about to turn away when she noticed something carved into the base of the fountain. It was an infinity symbol with the letter *h* and a plus sign.

What does that stand for?

Finn tugged on her arm, bringing her out of her daze. When she saw him tapping his watch impatiently, she shot him an angry glare.

As they stomped over to the front desk, she surveyed the people moving around the lobby. The high ceilings, white floors, and glass walls gave off an airy, light, and modern vibe—a stark contrast to the strong security presence. Institute personnel were dressed in uniforms consisting of turquoise tunics and white pants. They wore white badges on lanyards hung around their necks. Lara spotted more armed guards dressed in the same exoskeletons and helmets milling about, keeping a close eye on things. Several more were stationed in front of the airtight steel doors that led away from the lobby.

An army of security cameras covered every inch of the facility.

And those are just the obvious ones. I bet there are hidden ones, too.

Each of the cameras would be outfitted with facial recognition technology as well as sound and infrared sensors. Almost every inch of Chinese cities was covered with them and connected to a national database, feeding the surveillance pipeline with new data. Upon entry into the country, Chinese authorities uploaded passport information and photos for all foreigners into their system in order to keep track of visitors' movements.

At the front desk, a young Chinese woman in a turquoise dress looked up and smiled warmly. "May I help you?" she asked in a stilted accent.

"We're here for the tour at ten," Lara said.

"Do you have reservation?" she asked.

"Yes, under Kingsley... Lara." Vik suggested they use false names, but a cover would be useless if the Kongs were expecting them. And the facial recognition algorithms embedded in the security cameras would have already identified them anyway. Lara was certain the records of the Chinese authorities would mention the given reason for their visit to Shenzhen. A tour of the institute would make sense in light of their mission to plan for the tech expo. Using a false name would only attract more attention, or worse, blow the whole mission.

The woman glanced at her screen, her face lighting up. "Yes, I see here you have reservation for two. May I see some ID, please?"

Lara pulled out her passport and handed it to the woman.

"IDs for both persons, please."

Lara nudged Finn, who retrieved his passport from his pocket and slapped it on the counter. She shot him a stern glare.

"You are all set," the woman said, placing their passports on the counter. "Here are tour badges. Please wear around your neck. You wait over there by the fountain. Tour guide will see you shortly."

After stuffing the passports in her bag, Lara put the badge around her neck and handed the other to Finn. With a deep frown on his face, he just stood there, his feet planted in front of the reception desk. Lara nudged him to move, and he took a few heavy steps toward the meeting spot and put the badge around his neck. He grabbed her hand, squeezing hard, and they walked toward the fountain.

This is going to be. So. Much. Fun. She stole another glance at the armed security guards. *At least we're doing it my way this time.*

Her thoughts drifted back to the mission. When they'd finally convened the entire team at the GenTech Industries headquarters after their visit to the orphanage, Lara informed everyone that Molly was moved from the orphanage and was most likely being held at the institute. Of course, Julian was ready to storm the building with guns blazing.

Luckily, Vik discovered the daily tours of the institute's facilities via his Internet research. Lara latched onto the idea, suggesting it was important to confirm the layout of the facilities and the level of security. Then she had to spend the next hour trying to convince Julian that another scouting mission would increase their chances of rescuing Molly without any casualties or mistakes.

This time, empowered by his newfound knowledge about the Langstons, Finn sided quickly with Lara. Julian backed down and allowed them to attend the tour in order to conduct reconnaissance on the institute.

During the tour, they would be able to scan the grounds for entry and exit locations, choose the transit pathways, and if possible, steal an employee ID, preferably with high-level access, to help them gain access to secure zones during their operation.

She glanced at Finn's face, hopeful that his dark mood might lift soon. His light blue eyes brooded under a deeply furrowed brow.

Will he ever be able to forgive me?

Without warning, he pulled his hand away from her, and the knots in her stomach tightened. Finn's eyes grew large, and Lara shifted her gaze to see what or who he was looking at. A beautiful Chinese woman with wavy black hair and a long nose approached and smiled broadly.

Why is he gawking at her? Wait... is she?

She extended her hand to Lara. "Hello, I'm Mei Xing Kong. I'll be your tour guide for today." Her voice sounded familiar. A slightly puzzled look came over Mei Xing's face when she shook Finn's hand, but she gave him a quick smile.

"Nice to see you again," he said, continuing to gawk at her.

Lara froze. *Nice to see you again?*

"Dr. Kong, my sister and I wanted to stop by the institute to see what your movement is all about... before my wife and I reach a decision on our donation."

Sister?

Lara did a double take. *Dr. Kong? I thought she was Dr. Nilsson's assistant.*

As soon as Mei Xing turned away, Finn leaned closer to Lara and whispered, "She's the woman from the orphanage."

Oh my God.

The blood drained from Lara's face. "Did she just recognize you?"

Finn nodded. "Apparently."

"Well, then she saw you with your 'wife' Kaitlyn yesterday." Lara made quote signs with her fingers. "So, we'd better try hard to sell this sibling thing. And your newfound interest in transhumanism." She wiggled her eyebrows at him, but his face remained slack.

I guess it won't be that hard to act like siblings.

A group of tourists formed in the lobby, wearing the telltale tour badges. Mei Xing motioned for them to form a circle around her. Lara glanced at the white institute ID hanging from the bottom of her shirt. The text was in English. The badge marking identified Mei Xing as a personnel member with the highest level of security access. Lara nudged Finn in the arm, and he returned a subtle nod as an acknowledgement.

Between the two of them, he had the best pickpocket skills. Since she'd done the breaking-in on the previous day, it was only fair that he be the one to steal the ID. In her view, criminal activities should be divvied up equally among team members.

But will he get a good chance to swipe the ID?

"Welcome to the Macrobian Institute of Life Sciences," Mei Xing said. "Today, I'll take you on a tour of our state-of-the-art scientific facilities and introduce you to the global transhumanist movement of the Macrobians." She gave them a warm smile before continuing. "Unlike in other countries, Macrobians are quite welcome in China, where we cherish the Buddhist concept of liberation from suffering, or nirvana. Above all, Macrobians believe in human transcendence from suffering. We seek to extend and enhance human life. We plan to do so through the advancement of science and technology. Please walk this way."

Mei Xing motioned for the group to follow her toward a set of double doors—notably without armed guards posted. She pushed open the door and led them into a massive auditorium. "This facility is devoted not only to science but also to the education of next generation scientists. For this reason, we have a cutting-edge theater where we feature high resolution and fully immersive films."

Mei Xing led them back out of the theater and down a hallway with several doors. Between each of the doors, a glass window showed a laboratory classroom furnished with the latest in VR technology. Finn followed closely behind the tour guide, his face pinched with concentration.

He's waiting for the perfect moment.

Lara held her breath as he was about to seize the moment, his body tensing. Right before Finn was about to jerk out his hand, Mei Xing turned around to face the group and gave them a broad smile. Her eyes landed on Lara's face, lingering for a few moments. Then one of them closed for a second.

Did she just wink at me?

Without losing a beat, Mei Xing turned and pointed to the doors. "We offer free classes in the evenings and on weekends for those who wish to learn science and become believers."

Lara raised her hand, primarily as a distraction for Finn, but her curiosity had also gotten the better of her.

Mei Xing pointed to her and nodded.

"Do you run into any problems with Chinese authorities, given your religious beliefs?" Lara asked.

The tour guide gave her a half-smile. "As you know, the People's Republic of China allows for freedom of religion, but that is not relevant to Macrobians. Transhumanism is not a religion, but rather a philosophy devoted to extending human life and defeating death. Macrobians come from all faiths, but many of them here practice Buddhism." She pointed across the lobby at another set of double doors—also lacking a guard presence. "You may be interested in visiting our cafeteria to get a better idea of our sense of devotion," Mei Xing said.

Lara made a mental note. *The airtight steel doors have guards, but the rest do not.*

"To support our lifelong health, we eat a diet high in omega-3s," Mei Xing added. "In our cafeteria, you can only order boiled fish and milk. Today, we're serving mackerel and salmon."

Lara pulled up her nose at the thought of it as Mei Xing led the group toward the airtight steel door, nodded at the guards, and placed her ID on the keypad. Lara frowned when she noticed the fingerprint and retina scanners enabling biometric identification, but Mei Xing didn't use them.

How are we going to get past those?

The lock disengaged, and the door hissed open. She hurried the group through the door and led them down a long hallway which dead-ended into another hallway. She made a right turn and motioned with her hand. When they reached a large window, Mei Xing stopped. On the other side of the window was a nanotechnology lab like the one she'd seen at George Mason University.

Mei Xing pointed to the window. "This is our Nanotechnology Center. Here, we are focused on improving the delivery of medicine and gene therapy to cure disease." She pointed to the end of the hallway. "The lab in that direction is our Cybernetics Center where we explore ways to control the human brain. That's where we're studying human-machine interfaces and conducting our implant studies."

"Implant studies?" Lara asked, wrinkling her nose, her mind drifting to her last case.

Like Nate Brooks' neural and vision implants?

Mei Xing bobbed her head. "We're using science and technology to augment the five senses and boost cognitive capacity by placing technology inside our bodies. We've recently developed eye lenses that extend our eyesight to detect more wavelengths of radiation, such as infrared and ultraviolet."

Behind her, a strange clacking sound echoed down the hallway. Startled, Lara turned to see a young man in his twenties bouncing by on carbon-fiber blades.

Mei Xing smiled as he walked by. After he rounded the corner, she cupped her hands to prevent her voice from traveling further. "That was Tom, our head IT guy. He replaced his limbs voluntarily with those blades. Macrobians consider prostheses to be superior to human legs because they often enhance our performance."

Lara's eyes bulged. *Cutting off perfectly good limbs?*

Mei Xing led the group to an elevator and pressed the button. The group piled inside. Finn stood next to Mei Xing, eyeing her ID. Lara's pulse raced, and her cheeks flushed. Feeling somewhat claustrophobic, she held her breath until the door opened again on the second floor. When fresh air blew against her face, she exhaled sharply.

"Let's go to the right, please," Mei Xing said. They reached another glass window. Inside a dark room were rows of glass tanks illuminated by glowing blue light. In each tank, there was a shadow in the form of a human body.

Wait. Is that...? Lara blinked her eyes to see clearly. *That can't be.*

"This is our Cryonics Center," Mei Xing said.

Lara shuddered. *Dead bodies.*

"As Macrobians, we don't believe in the limitations of death,"

Mei Xing said. "For this reason, we use cryogenic preservation. By placing bodies in low-temperature storage immediately after death, we believe we can achieve technological progress that will make it possible to revive them. Someday, we believe humans will achieve immortality through mind uploading."

Wait, what?

Lara and Finn exchanged troubled looks.

Are we in a science fiction film?

"Uploading will allow us to transcend our physical bodies by transferring or uploading our minds to computers. It is very much like rebirth."

"I suppose you'll be able to download your brain into a new body then too?" Lara said, not hiding the deep skepticism in her voice.

Mei Xing gave her a pensive look. "Actually, yes. That's the hope."

Lara stared through the window at the tanks. Naked dead bodies appeared to be suspended in a thick teal-blue liquid. In the far corner, the sight of a tank containing a blonde-haired woman with a serene look on her face put Lara in a trance like the call of a siren on the high seas. The vision was both calming and unsettling at the same time. The woman had chosen death in the hopes that she might one day have her life back.

Lara wasn't sure how bad things would have to get before she'd decide to freeze herself to death. *Hopefully, it never comes to that.*

Finn tugged her arm and motioned for her to come. The tour group was already on the far side of the hallway, listening to Mei Xing talk in front of another window.

"This is our last stop on the tour. Our Genetics Laboratory." The tour guide pointed through another wide window in the wall. It looked similar to Maggie's lab, full of lab benches, cupboards, lab equipment, and stainless-steel fridges.

Lara elbowed Finn, who acknowledged her nudge. They noted nearby airtight steel doors and counted the surveillance cameras.

We're gonna need that ID. But how do we get past the biometrics entry pads if they are activated?

"One of the most important goals of Macrobian science is to eradicate aging as a cause of death," Mei Xing said. "The Genetics Laboratory is where we explore why DNA ages and gets damaged. Our scientists are looking for ways to reverse these processes."

That's where I need to go for Hickerson.

Lara raised her hand. "Do you practice medicine at the institute?"

Mei Xing nodded. "We have a state-of-the-art medical center located just beyond the Genetics Laboratory, where we apply our scientific advances to help people overcome disease. To protect the privacy of our patients, we don't take tour groups to our medical wing."

That must be where Molly is getting her procedure.

"What sort of procedures do you do here?" Lara asked.

Mei Xing raised her eyebrow. "We focus primarily on gene therapy, but we're equipped to do everything from minor procedures to major surgery."

"Do you study reproductive cloning?" Lara asked.

A look of uneasy surprise fell across Mei Xing's face. "No, Macrobians frown upon creating multiple copies of a human being. However, we do study germline engineering for the purpose of human enhancement."

Lara pressed further. "I'm confused. If you're okay with uploading and downloading your brain into other bodies and freezing people for revival, why would you be against cloning?"

Finn nudged her, presumably signaling to her to knock it off.

"Again, such an effort would go against the Macrobians' ethical code. Now if you would follow me, we'll return to the lobby to conclude your tour." Her tone was curt.

"Actually, I have one more question," Lara said.

Mei Xing gave her an annoyed look.

"I noticed a high degree of security throughout the facility, including biometric identification measures. You swiped your badge, but you didn't use the retina or fingerprint scans once."

Mei Xing frowned. "Well, you do have an eye for detail. Unfortunately, our biometric system went down after a recent update. Our entire IT department is scrambling to fix it. I assure you all we take security very seriously. I expect it to be up and running shortly."

I sure hope their IT department can't get the system back online. If they do, we're screwed.

A few minutes later, the group reconvened in the lobby. After Mei Xing thanked the group for their attention and said her goodbyes, Finn pulled Lara aside.

"What were all those cloning questions about?" Finn whispered.

Lara shrugged. "I don't know. Something bugged me about the whole thing. The Macrobians like to think so highly of themselves, but what they're doing to little girls here is sick and twisted."

Finn took a step back. "What do you mean what they're doing to little girls? I thought they just kidnapped Molly. Do you know more than you're telling me?"

Oh fuck.

Lara felt her face grow pale as she realized she'd told him too much.

Again. Now is not the time to tell him about Metamorphosis.

"Um... no, I just..." She fumbled before regaining her composure. "Well, you saw Molly's medical file. When I was in the back room, I heard Mei Xing and Dr. Nilsson talking about a procedure. She's obviously part of some experiment."

Finn narrowed his eyes and grunted in response. He wasn't buying her explanation.

"Did you get the ID?" Lara asked, changing the subject quickly.

"Yep."

Lara's eyes widened. "But I didn't even see you take it."

Finn gave her a slight grin. "I think that's the point."

As Lara surveyed the lobby one more time, her eyes landed on a giant piece of artwork hanging on the wall, opposite to the auditorium. She swayed slightly, nearly losing her balance.

How did I not see that before?

"What's wrong?" Finn asked.

"I have a copy of that painting in my storage unit at home," she said, her lips trembling.

"Exactly the same one?" he asked.

"Yeah. It belonged to my father."

TWENTY-NINE

Breach

———————

October 16, 2028

LARA GLANCED NERVOUSLY over Vik's shoulder. The computer code flew across the screen as he typed, but she couldn't make any sense of it. A flash of lightning illuminated the pitch-black interior of the van, causing her body to tense.

She peeked out the window and saw an ominous cluster of clouds warning of the oncoming storm. The weather forecast hadn't indicated any potential for a thunderstorm, but subtropical climates could be notoriously unpredictable.

Whatever happens, we need to beat the storm.

Rain would be an unwelcome complication for their mission. Even if it didn't take long to breach the back door, her team would get drenched, all the way to the skin. And they would leave a wet trail of their movements in the institute for the security guards to detect and follow.

Biting her lip, she continued to stare out the window and wondered what other unforeseen complications would occur before the night was over. The white van was tucked in the dark alley behind the institute. For additional cover, the outside of the vehicle was disguised with authentic Chinese characters denoting an air conditioning company. The nearby streets and large pedestrian zone occupied by the technology park were relatively empty—at least for a metropolis like Shenzhen at 11:55 p.m. Every few minutes, a passerby walked by the alley entrance, causing a spike in Lara's blood pressure.

After checking once more to make sure she had all her gear, Lara craned her neck to survey her team. Barely visible, Finn and Kaitlyn sat in the back of the van ready for action, along with the four mercenaries hunched in a tight circle. Everyone was dressed in matching black skin-tight suits, tactical gear, body armor, black masks, push-to-talk radios for comms, and night-vision goggles.

"I'm almost in the system," Vik said, typing as fast as he could. Beads of sweat rolled down the side of his face. He let them fall to the keyboard as he kept working. "Just need a… few more minutes."

Giving him some space, Lara leaned back and wiped her sweaty hands on her pants. For the past thirty minutes, Vik had been attempting to hack the surveillance system of the Macrobian Institute of Life Sciences. Security measures had proven far more robust than expected, and they were quickly falling behind schedule.

A sudden clap of thunder broke the tense silence. Seconds later, the rain pattered hard against the roof, drowning out the tapping of Vik's fingers. Lara sighed heavily.

Is the rain a bad omen?

She stole a peek at her watch. Though digital, Lara could swear she heard it ticking, reminding her of their limited window of opportunity.

The plan for the breach depended on the accuracy of Hickerson's notes, which suggested the next shift change in security personnel would take place around midnight. A team of eight armed security guards protected the facilities at night. The number of guards at the institute were fewer than during the daytime, but enough to complicate their mission. Except for the shift change when the total number reduced to four. Since two security guards remained in the control room at all times to monitor the cameras, her team would only have to deal with two patrolling the huge expanse of the institute. The shift change would offer them the ideal timing for breaching the facility and rescuing Molly without being noticed.

However, none of this mattered if Vik couldn't hack the advanced surveillance system. It would be impossible to evade the motion infrared and audio sensors integrated into the security cameras that covered every inch of the facility.

"Got it," Vik said proudly, sitting up straighter in his chair. "I've managed to spoof the surveillance system. And I've confirmed that the biometric system remains offline."

"What does spoof mean?" Lara asked, furrowing her brow.

"It means I put thirty minutes of video and audio footage on a continuous loop for the next hour. I also managed to disable the infrared and motion sensors. As far as security personnel will know, the system is working perfectly. They won't be able to detect our presence without physically patrolling the hallways."

"You sure the AI-monitoring system won't detect the anomaly of the continuous feed?" Lara asked. "Any malfunction or change in normal patterns could cause the system to send a remote alert to the security team and prompt a reaction."

"I've disabled all the sensors that transmit real-time data, so the AI-monitoring system won't know anything is out of order. I made it blind, deaf, and dumb."

"Good work, Vik," Lara said, patting him on the back. She grimaced as her hand came away damp from the sweat soaking through his shirt. Suppressing a gag, she dried her hand on her pants and pulled on her tactical backpack.

Vik rose from his seat and grinned, apparently eager for another brush with danger.

She avoided his gaze. "Vik, I've changed my mind about you coming with us. You should stay behind in the van and provide overwatch for the teams." Pressing her lips together, Lara grabbed the black case Maggie had given her to collect DNA.

Vik's face broke into full protest. "But what if you need me onsite for technical issues?"

Lara shook her head. "With the delay and the rain, the mission just got a hell of a lot more dangerous. I think you should stay here."

"What about…" He flicked his head toward the black plastic case, to which she shot him a stern glare.

They'd originally planned for Vik to help her collect samples and information from the genetics lab. But her instincts nagged at Lara. She had a bad feeling that something was about to go terribly wrong.

"How much more dangerous is it for me to go inside with you than stay in the van? Out here, I'll be a sitting duck for Chinese authorities." Vik cocked his head to the side.

Lara thinned her lips. *He has a point. It might be better to keep an eye on him.*

"Okay, fine," she said, groaning. "But you're sticking with me, okay?"

Vik smiled broadly and took the black case from her.

She turned to the rest of her team and studied the motley crew for a moment.

Pulling out a small tablet from her hip pack, she pointed to the medical center on Hickerson's digital map. "We believe Molly is being held somewhere around here." She touched the screen and zoomed in. "There are some exam rooms and a few hospital rooms with beds here. This is on the opposite side of the institute from the Genetics Laboratory."

"Do we still have time for both objectives?" Finn asked, tapping his watch.

She took another look at her watch and flinched. 12:01a.m. "Okay. Slight change of plans. We'll split into two teams of four each, Alpha and Bravo," she said, looking directly at Finn. "You lead Bravo Team." She handed him one of two IDs from her hip pack. "Here's the duplicate of Mei Xing's ID. Don't lose it. The airtight steel doors with access control panels are located everywhere. Without Vik, this mission would not have been possible in the first place."

I still don't know how Hickerson missed the airtight doors.

Vik's face flushed. "That was the easy part. Making the AI-monitoring system incapable of detecting the duplicate ID was the hard part."

She reached into her hip pack and pulled out Molly's floppy pink bunny and tossed it to Finn. The mercenaries eyed it suspiciously, and Finn gave her a strange look as he took the stuffed animal.

He doesn't know there could be more than one girl.

Swallowing hard, Lara said, "You might need it. The bunny belongs to Molly. She'll recognize it."

Eager to move on, she pointed to the two mercenaries closest to her. "Stew, Mack... you're coming with me and Vik. The others will go with Finn."

Both men wore buzz cuts and had a few scars on their faces. Stew was the taller one. He had a lanky, athletic build and was quick on his feet. She had a few conversations with him over the past two days, and he seemed like a decent guy. Mack was short and built like a truck. He had a crass mouth on him, and she didn't like him much. But if she had to run her part of the op without Finn by her side, she needed the extra muscle power.

"We're going in unarmed, but we've got the muscle and skill on our side. Whatever happens, we need to avoid any shots being fired." She looked each of them in the face. "We don't have official top cover if anything goes wrong. Got it?"

They nodded in unison.

"Bravo team will breach the back door and head to the medical wing to look for Molly. Alpha team will follow behind and search the genetics laboratory for samples." She waited for Finn's affirmative response. "Okay, let's get this done in less than thirty minutes. Rendezvous at the van."

"Copy that, Alpha One," Finn said, giving her a cocky grin. He'd clearly forgotten his anger from the day before. Or perhaps he was just finally back in his element and enjoying the adrenaline rush.

He'll always be a special operator at heart.

She smiled. There were only a few people she'd follow into battle, and Finn was one of them. He was smarter than any other man she'd ever met. And lethal as hell. On the battlefield, she always could count on him.

"Okay, let's move out."

Without wasting another second, Finn picked up his gear, opened the back door of the van, checked for any bystanders, and then motioned for his team to follow him. One by one, they jumped out of the van and made their way through the torrent of rain gushing down the alley and flowing into the drain at the end of the street. As Stew and Mack jumped out of the van after them, they landed in the deep puddles, sending water everywhere.

Lara climbed out of the van and helped Vik jump to the ground before closing the door and locking the van. Rain pelted her face and her suit as she scurried toward the back entrance of the institute. Lara and Vik huddled next to Stew and Mack at the base of the stairwell along the wall of the building, waiting for the breach.

Positioned on the landing to the back entrance, Bravo team placed the charges and took cover, breaching the door in seconds. As his team entered the building, Finn held the door open for Lara. She grabbed the door from him. Before disappearing into the darkness, he reached for her face and kissed her lightly on the cheek.

Lara's team filed into the building in darkness and closed the door behind them, shaking the water off. Small puddles formed on the tile floor. They pulled on their night-vision goggles and took out their infrared illuminators to see in the dark. Several meters away, Lara could hear Bravo team break off in the direction of the medical wing, their wet shoes squeaking on the tiles.

She spoke into her radio, to test the comms. "Bravo One, see you on the other side, over."

"Roger that, Alpha One. Proceeding to the target."

Vik pulled out the tablet and scrolled down the screen to pull up the map from Hickerson. He pointed to the hallway on the left and glanced down at the map again. "We're on the first floor," he whispered. "We just need to proceed down that hallway, through an airtight security door, and grab the elevator to the second floor. Then it should be the second door on the left."

Is this the right way?

Feeling slightly disoriented, she hesitated for a moment and then nodded. Since they entered the back of the building, they were closer to the Genetics Laboratory than she remembered on the tour where it had been their last stop.

No choice but to trust Vik's navigation.

She pulled out the ID and scanned it against the control pass. The security door hissed and then slid open. At the elevator, Lara pressed the call button, moved to the side of the door, and motioned for her team to wait around the corner. When the elevator dinged and the door whooshed open, she peered around the edge to confirm it was empty. After motioning to her team, they piled into the elevator, dripping pools of water on the floor.

A few moments later, the door opened. Mack held the elevator door while Lara swept the area for guards. Then she waved her team out and strode down the hallway past one door. When Lara reached the second door, she shined her illuminator on the nameplate.

MACROBIAN INSTITUTE OF LIFE SCIENCES

GENETICS LABORATORY

"This is it," she said, scanning the stolen ID with the door's pass. The lock clicked open, and then the airlock door hissed.

She pulled the heavy, steel door open and motioned to her team. "We're in. Quick, let's go."

Stew pointed back toward the security door. "I'm going to stand watch at the end of the hallway and make sure no one is coming."

"Good idea," Lara said. She handed the ID to Mack. "Stand guard outside, watch for signals from Stew, and let us know if there's trouble."

"Yes, ma'am," he said, his posture stiffening as he took his position outside the door.

Vik and Lara entered the lab on their own, closing the door behind them. They were searching the lab with illuminators when a chirping noise disrupted the silence.

"Alpha One, do you read me, over?"

Lara pressed her radio button. "Copy, Bravo One. What's your sit rep?"

"We've reached the medical wing and are commencing the search for the target," Finn said. "What's your status, over?"

"At the Genetics Laboratory. Beginning our search, over."

"Copy that. Will update when target found, over."

"Roger."

Lara surveyed the room in the dim light provided by her illuminator. The lab was smaller than Maggie's, but the setup was similar with a row of lab benches dividing the space down the center of the room. Along the walls, there were storage units with upper cupboards, countertops, and lower drawers. Several computer terminals were scattered about with corresponding stools. On the counters, Lara recognized equipment for gene sequencing and synthesis. In the corner, there was a large stainless-steel refrigerator, about twice the width of a normal fridge.

"Let's go through the files first," Lara said to Vik, pointing to the drawers. Her heart raced at the thought of finding the whole truth behind Metamorphosis and its connection to Molly.

She strode to the far end of the lab, opened a drawer located along the wall, shined the illuminator on the files, and thumbed through the folders one at a time. Vik opened the drawer on the opposite end and did the same. Lara squinted in the faint light. The print on the folders was small and difficult to read without better lighting. It took some concentration to understand the labels.

But at least they're in English.

Several minutes passed, and she discovered nothing of interest.

"Have you found anything yet?" Vik asked in a low voice.

"Nope. Not yet," Lara said.

Finally, her eyes spotted the familiar word. "Wait, I think I have something." She pulled out nine folders, each labeled Metamorphosis. Other markings included subject ID numbers but no names.

She flipped open the top folder and scanned the first page.

"What is it?" Vik asked, looking over her shoulder.

"Looks like a project summary."

"What about the others?" Vik asked.

"The rest are case files," she said, counting them. "Eight in total, one for each subject."

Vik pulled off his backpack. "Here, put them in my bag. You don't have room in yours."

Hickerson will be so happy.

As she stuffed the folders in Vik's backpack, her radio chirped again.

"Alpha One, do you copy, over?" Finn asked.

"Copy, Bravo One. What's your status?"

"We have a problem. There are eight hospital rooms, each with an eight-year-old girl, over."

Lara furrowed her brow. "What's the problem?"

"They are all identical to the target. No way to tell which one is her, over."

So, they did create eight clones. Lara winced in disgust.

"I may have found information that could help. Stand by." She reached for Vik's backpack, pulled out the Metamorphosis files, and flipped frantically through them, scanning quickly across the pages. When her eyes fell on the names Julian and Cynthia, she was certain she'd found what must be Molly's record. At the top of the page, she saw the subject ID number.

"Bravo One, are there identifiers on the nameplates?" Lara asked. "A nine-digit number?"

"Copy. Each door has a different number. Nine digits."

"Okay, try Subject ID 657889500."

"Wilco, Alpha One. We're entering the room with the matching subject ID number. The girl is awake and sees us coming. Will transmit the convo over radio." There was a moment of silence. "Hi there, sweetheart. Is your name Molly?" Finn asked in a gentle voice.

Silence.

"Are your parents Julian and Cynthia Langston?"

Silence.

Lara pressed her radio button. "Bravo One, try the bunny, over."

"Copy," Finn said. Sounds of a backpack zipper transmitted over the radio. "Is this your bunny?"

"Yes," said a small, distant voice. "That's Ollie."

"Alpha One. We've found the target," Finn said, his voice charged with energy.

"You sure?" Lara asked.

"Her eyes lit up when she saw the bunny, and she grabbed it away from me. It's definitely her."

We have Molly.

Vik stared at her with wide eyes. "They found her already?"

Lara nodded and pressed her radio button. "Bravo One, return to the van with the package. Alpha team will be there shortly, over."

"Good copy," Finn said.

Lara stuffed the files back into Vik's backpack and turned toward the back wall, her eyes falling on the stainless-steel refrigerator. "Let's get the case ready," she said to Vik as she scanned the ID on the keypad to the fridge.

Time to find Molly's original DNA sample.

After a loud hiss, the door opened, and the fridge light illuminated the darkness. Nitrogen gas blew out of the fridge, blocking the view for a moment and gushing cold air over Lara's body. When the gas cleared, she spotted a total of six shelves covered with racks of test tubes labeled in tiny print.

The fridge was wide enough for both her and Vik to stand side by side. *How are we going to find anything in here?*

His arm brushing hers, Vik studied the rows of tubes with tiny print. "At the orphanage, Molly was under the name Kong," he said. "Maybe they're stored alphabetically like last time?"

"Or by the subject ID number," Lara said, still trying to get her bearings among hundreds of tubes. Her eyes rested on the middle row first. She stared at the label on the first test tube and then the next. "Okay, they're not in numerical order." She studied both tubes again and found the last name of the samples in fine print. "They're alphabetical by column!"

"What letter are you at?" Vik asked.

"I'm in the H's."

"Then the K's must be to your right."

Lara's eyes scanned the next columns quickly.

I's... J's... K's... Wait, what?

She jerked her head back, her pulse spiking. As she squinted to make sure she was seeing things correctly, her heart began to throb.

How can this be?

"Did you find it or something?" Vik asked, trying to get a clear view over her arm.

Lara wanted to back away, but she couldn't move her body. It was as if she was paralyzed. Her mind raced for answers as her eyes darted between the tubes.

How is this possible?

"What's wrong, Lara?"

She raised her hand slowly and pointed at the first tubes in the column.

"Holy crap," Vik said. "Why do they have a sample of your DNA here?"

Lara's lip trembled. "Not just mine... look at the one behind it."

"Wait... Ethan Kingsley. That's your father..."

Lara nodded as if in a daze. "Look at the one behind it."

Vik's jaw dropped. "Donna Kingsley. They have your mother's DNA, too?" As he yanked his hand away, his sleeve caught on the edge of the rack.

Trying to free his arm, Vik jerked his hand, pulling the rack out further. Before Lara could react, the rack tilted forward and slid out of the fridge, falling onto the floor below. Tubes of DNA flew in every direction, and the sound of glass shattering filled the air.

THIRTY

Total Recall

Reeling in shock, Lara stared down at the disorganized jumble of more than three hundred tubes laying strewn about on the floor. A few tubes rolled across the linoleum floor, coming to a stop on the other side of the lab.

What is my family's DNA doing here?

"I'm so sorry, Lara," Vik exclaimed, a horrified look on his face. His hands in the air, he stumbled backwards. Glass fragments crunched under his feet as he grabbed the countertop next to the fridge in an effort to find better footing.

She waved her hand dismissively. "We don't have much time. Let's try to find Molly's DNA sample and get out of here." Lara lowered herself to the floor, careful to avoid shards of glass from broken tubes. She placed the black case next to her, unfastened the sturdy latches, and folded it open. Then she picked up a handful of tubes of DNA, turning them over in her hands, one by one, and studying the labels. But if she was being honest with herself, she wasn't looking for Molly's DNA anymore. Her mind had only one track.

I need to find my family's tubes. That is, if they're not busted.

Vik clamored about, trying to avoid stepping on any more of the tubes, and then nearly slipped on one. Finding a safe place to put his feet, he bent over, picked up the rack, and set it gently on the floor next to her.

Giving him a half-smile, Lara placed tubes she'd already inspected into the rack in no particular order. There was no point in trying to disguise their intrusion anymore.

The cat is way out of the bag.

Vik got down on his hands and knees to help her. Together they made quick work of sorting through about thirty tubes before the lab door opened and closed with a loud thud. Startled, Lara looked up to see a grim look on Mack's face.

"Ma'am, we've got company," he said. "You'd better get what you came for fast because we need to exfil. Now."

Now can the cat escape without getting caught?

"I need a few more minutes," Lara said, a tremor in her voice.

"Ma'am, we don't have a few more minutes. The institute's security guards have detected our presence and are headed this way. Grab whatever you can, and let's get out of here."

Vik's face turned sheet white. Panicking, Lara fumbled with a fistful of DNA tubes, dropping all but one.

Should I just toss a bunch in the case and hope I get lucky?

She glanced down at the two remaining tubes in her hand. For a moment, she thought her eyes were deceiving her. Looking down, she read the names again to confirm.

DNA samples for myself and my mom.

Her hand trembling, she placed them into two empty slots in the plastic case.

"Ma'am, we have to go," Mack said, waving his hand urgently. "Right now!"

She had no choice but to leave the others behind. Lara sprang to her feet and reached for Vik's arm to pull him up. He was still holding a single tube and staring wide-eyed at it.

"Molly's tube..." Vik said in disbelief.

Oh, thank God.

Lara grabbed the tube from him, glanced at the label to confirm, shoved it in the case next to the other two, and closed the lid, snapping the latches shut. "Vik, we need to get the hell out of here."

Mack nodded in violent agreement and motioned for them to hurry. Lara raced across the lab. Vik followed after her, carrying the black case. Mack tossed her the ID and grabbed the door handle. She caught the ID with one hand and then swiped it at the control panel. As soon as the door beeped and hissed, he flung it open and held it for them.

The lab door banged shut behind them. Lara glanced down the hallway, hoping to return the way they came.

Coming from that direction, Stew marched toward her with an apprehensive look on his face and waved his hands. "That way is blocked by two guards," he said. "We're gonna have to find another way out."

Behind Stew, Lara glimpsed two Chinese security guards running in their direction through the glass door at the end of the hallway.

Mack moved quickly down the hallway in the opposite direction. Lara raced after him, Vik and Stew trailing closely behind them. When they reached the airtight door, she dug in her pocket for the ID. Her body tensed, and a sharp pang stabbed her chest. All she felt was the soft fabric interior of her suit. A terrible realization dawned on her.

I lost the ID.

Stew gave her a what-the-hell look.

Lara looked around her, whipping her head back and forth, and staring at the floor to see if it fell out of her pocket. "I must have dropped the ID exiting the lab."

Did I even put it in my pocket?

"You go back to the lab and find that ID. Mack and I will head the guards off and cover for you while you search," Stew shouted, running toward the airtight door at the other end of the hallway. "We're gonna need that ID to get out of here in one piece." He headed toward the security guards, Mack tightly on his heels.

Lara made her way down the hallway, scanning every inch of

the white linoleum floor for the white ID card. Her heart pounded through her chest and a lump formed in her throat.

"Where the hell is it?" Lara asked.

"You don't think you dropped it in the lab, do you?" Vik asked, setting the black case on the floor.

Oh crap.

Lara's heart sank. "We can't get back in the lab without the ID…"

Vik pressed his face against the glass window and stared down at the floor in the lab. When he pulled away, his pale face and wide eyes told her everything she needed to know.

The ID is locked in the lab. We're trapped.

The airtight door at the end of the hallway opened, making a hissing sound. Two armed security guards wearing exoskeletons and combat helmets barged through the door, their guns drawn. The two mercenaries assailed the guards, colliding into them with their bodies and knocking the guns to the floor. A fist fight broke out between the mercenaries and the guards.

Keeping an eye trained on the violent scuffle down the hallway, Lara pressed her radio. "Bravo One, do you read me? We have a problem. Need assistance, over."

"Alpha One, copy," Finn responded. "We're almost at the van. What's your status, over?"

Lara gulped before speaking. "We're trapped in the hallway on the second floor outside the Genetics Laboratory between two airtight doors. Need backup and the cloned ID, over."

A loud thump and a hiss from behind made her jump. Lara spun around to see two more armed security guards headed their way from the other direction. They shouted orders in Chinese and drew their guns at Lara and Vik.

She turned to confront them, placing herself in front of Vik, shouting into her radio, "Bravo One, we're surrounded. Four tangos. I repeat four. Two on each side. We need help. Now."

Rallying herself for a fight, Lara clenched her fists. Suddenly, the security guards slowed their advance, came to a stop, and lowered their guns.

What the hell? Why aren't they moving in?

A groan of anguish came from the other side of the hallway. Lara whipped her body around to see Stew lying stunned on the floor, his head bloodied. Though he was still alive, he appeared to be out of commission. Lara's eyes darted about frantically, looking for a way out of their predicament. Then she spotted the pistol lying on the floor near the wall.

"Vik, go try to help Mack if you can," Lara said, eyeing the two security guards on her side. "Maybe make a distraction. I'm gonna take on these two."

"How?" Vik asked, his eyes bulging.

"Never mind that," Lara said, pivoting to get another look at the security guards. They remained in their positions with their guns lowered.

Why are the guards just standing there?

Lara looked over her shoulder to see Vik stumbling in Mack's direction, his hands shaking. A wave of guilt washed over Lara for putting him in harm's way and not being able to snap him out of it. The other two security guards attacked Mack with renewed ferocity, clearly more confident in their numbers advantage.

The gun on the floor caught her eye again. This time, without hesitating, she dove for the pistol, grabbed it, rolled over, and bounced back up on her feet. She turned to face her adversaries. Rather than putting up a fight, the guards just stood there frozen in place, their faces seized with fear.

Why aren't they shooting? Or threatening me? Or anything?

"Drop your weapons," Lara commanded the guards.

They didn't respond.

She took a few steps toward them and pointed her gun at the taller security guard's chest. "Drop the gun now, or I'll shoot."

The tall security guard lowered his gun and placed it on the floor.

"Now, step back and put your hands on your head," she said.

The tall security guard obeyed. Lara trained her gun on the other security guard. "Put your gun on the floor."

His hand trembling, the other guard also laid his gun on the floor.

"Move a few steps back and put your hands on your head."

He obeyed.

Lara approached the guards cautiously, holding her gun out. When she reached the two guns lying on the floor, she bent over and picked up each of them with her free hand, one by one, walked them back several feet, and flung them on the floor. An uneasy feeling came over her.

She turned to see the other side of the hallway. Mack had regained control of the fight with one security guard down. Vik had come out of his stupor and was unhooking the guard's ID from his shirt. He turned and looked down the hallway at her, giving her a proud grin. Then his face went slack, and his eyes became dark.

A gush of cool air brushed past her face, causing her loose hairs to flutter. Vik's mouth opened wide, and the words came tumbling from his mouth as if in slow motion. "Behind… you… Lara…"

She turned her head. Out of the corner of her eye, she saw several more security guards come up behind her. She turned slightly to see a familiar looking Chinese woman in her forties, dressed in a white lab coat.

The blood drained from Lara's face. Before she could react, a security guard grabbed her arm, holding her in place. Then she felt a sharp pinch in her neck like a needle. Within seconds, she slumped forward. The gun in her hand dropped to the floor, making a clunking noise. Her eyelids drooped, and her limbs became heavy like weights.

So tired. Can't… move…

Her entire body went limp. She felt herself being carried a few feet and then placed on a stretcher.

She wanted to shout, to warn Vik and the others. But her tongue grew thick in her mouth, and nothing came out except for a grunt. The distant echo of muffled voices resonated in her head.

The hiss of the airtight door and then the squeaky rolling of wheels filled the air. The stretcher traveled down a labyrinth of hallways. Her eyesight blurry, Lara focused on the sounds she could recognize. The whooshing of access control doors. The pounding of footsteps. Muted voices speaking in Chinese.

The noises came to an abrupt stop. Strong arms lifted her into something that felt like a medical recliner. Bright lights blazed down on her from the ceiling, completely blinding her. She held her eyes shut to avoid the painful pinch.

Someone tied thick straps around her arms and legs and secured them tightly. Then they secured her head to the back of the chair, restricting her movement. A door open and closed. Footsteps receded from the room. Silence.

She was alone.

THIRTY-ONE

The Other Side

October 17, 2028

LARA DOZED in and out of hallucinogenic sleep for what felt like several hours. Her dreams were filled with blurry images of her childhood mixed with distorted scenes from the orphanage and the lab. When she finally opened her eyes, it felt as if they were stuffed with cotton. She blinked a few times in an attempt to generate tears, but her eyesight remained fuzzy.

What did they give me?

She tried to lift her head, but something prevented her from moving it. Then she remembered the straps. Lara moved her eyes as far to the right as she could. From the far corner of her right eye, the room appeared to be bare and offer her little information about her location. The white walls suggested a hospital room, but she couldn't see any of the usual machines or furniture.

Maybe I'm in the Medical Center?

Her mouth was parched, so dry she could barely swallow. She closed her mouth in an attempt to build up saliva, but none came. She squirmed in the recliner with discomfort. A growing pressure on her bladder caused intense pain in her abdomen. Lara squeezed her legs together in an attempt to hold it. A little urine trickled out, and she worried she might empty her bladder.

How long has it been now?

A door opened, and Lara's eyes jerked toward the sound, a slight tremor passing through her body.

A Chinese woman wearing her black hair in a tight bun and a pair of tiny eyeglasses entered the room and began rustling about behind Lara. As she moved about, the pungent odor of mothballs wafted past Lara's nose. Memories flooded back to her.

The woman from my father's picture.

Squeezing her eyes shut, Lara lay motionless, the sound of her heart pounding filling her ears.

My father knew Molly's kidnapper?

"Welcome to the Macrobian Institute for Life Sciences, Lara," the woman said, coming around Lara's chair and smiling, her hands in the pockets of her lab coat. "I am Dr. Yingyue Kong, the Director of Science here and the medical physician on staff. I'm deeply sorry that your stay with us today will be brief. I would have so much liked to have gotten reacquainted." Her voice was light and soft. Almost soothing.

What does she mean by brief?

Lara stopped breathing for a moment. She wanted to say something but words failed her.

Yingyue seemed to notice her reaction and gave her a knowing smile. "I knew your father well," she said, the wrinkles around her eyes becoming sharper. "We were good friends." She paused, her eyes gleaming at Lara with nostalgia. "You may not remember this, but we met a few times when you were a little girl."

"I remember," Lara rasped, her throat hoarse. "You taught me how to fold paper animals in the Chinese tradition."

Yingyue's eyes lit up in recognition. "I did teach you *zhezhi*, but it was your father who folded paper with you. He would sit with you for hours while you made all kinds of animals. He talked about it at the office all the time. Sometimes he'd bring me one of your creations. I treasured every one of them."

"Why did you take Molly?" Lara asked, cutting to the chase. "Did Mr. Langston refuse to return her to you as promised?"

Yingyue said nothing and disappeared behind Lara's chair for a moment. Running water poured from a faucet behind her and then stopped abruptly. She returned with a plastic cup of water. Lara's mouth salivated in anticipation.

Yingyue hovered over her, gazing into Lara's eyes. "You're thirsty," she said, tipping the cup toward Lara's lips.

Lara moved her head eagerly toward the cup. Yingyue rested it against her lips and tipped it slightly, allowing water to trickle into Lara's mouth. Her eyes watered in response to the cold liquid touching her parched throat and dry tongue.

After a few moments, Yingyue removed the cup. Lara attempted to follow the cup with her head, but she was restrained by the strap. The woman disappeared out of sight. When she returned into view, the cup in her hand was gone. Instead, she pulled around an IV stand on squeaky wheels and prepped the drip for insertion.

A gush of adrenaline surging through her body, Lara cringed with fear at the sight of the machine.

"Don't worry, darling," Yingyue said reassuringly. "This won't hurt a bit."

"What are you going to give me?" Lara squawked, staring wide-eyed at the IV bag.

"I'm preparing you for your journey to the other side," Yingyue said softly, rubbing Lara's arm on the inside of her elbow.

Other side? She doesn't mean death, right? Lara blinked her eyes rapidly as she pondered it. *No, if she was going to kill me, wouldn't I be dead already?*

"But what's in the IV?" Lara asked, her sense of urgency growing.

"I'm going to inject you with heparin. It's an anticoagulant to keep your blood from clotting."

"Why do I need that?" Lara's eyes widened further.

Yingyue ignored the question and inserted the drip into Lara's arm.

Lara winced at the sharp pinch of the needle, trying to concentrate on getting information from the woman. "Why are you doing this to me?" she asked, her voice trembling.

Yingyue ignored her question. "This should take about forty-five minutes to make it into your bloodstream... maybe an hour," she said. "Next, we pack you up with ice, and we'll transfer you to the cryonics facility."

Ice? Cryonics facility? But that's...

"Why are you taking me *there*?" Lara asked, clutching the arms of the chair.

Yingyue's soft features dimmed with sadness. "Sorry. I'm so used to speaking to believers that I forget myself sometimes. When I said the other side, I assumed you'd know where you were going." She rubbed her chin. "How to best explain this? In his last will and testament, your father requested we cryonically preserve your body in the event that you developed aplastic anemia." She paused for a moment, as if waiting for her words to register. "As soon as we learned about your symptoms, we began putting a plan in motion."

Who is this "we"? What plan?

Lara's eyes grew wide as she realized her father had known about the condition that would afflict her. "How did you know about my symptoms?"

"You visited your doctor in August?"

Lara nodded.

Yingyue gave her a slight smile. "Surely, you know that all health records are digital and stored in online databases. You might not be aware, but the U.S. Government has neglected to secure this information against cyber vulnerabilities for decades. Your health information is extremely vulnerable to hacking. One of our hackers exploited a vulnerability in the database to place an alert on your record. When you started experiencing symptoms and visited your doctor in August, we learned about it immediately and began carrying out your father's instructions."

"How did you know about the contents of my father's will?" Lara asked, fishing around for a way to worm herself out of her predicament. The executor of her parents' estate had never mentioned any odd provisions about cryonics.

"He left a copy of his will with the Macrobian Institute," Yingyue said.

But how did she know I'd come to China?

"I don't believe you," Lara said, trying to shake her head. "My father wouldn't have wanted this for me."

Yingyue's lips turned upward slightly. "He wanted you to live a long and happy life and made provisions for that to happen. He paid two hundred thousand dollars for the luxury cryonics plan before he and your mother died."

My father paid for cryonics?

Lara's eyes bolted open, any remaining blurriness zapped by another shot of adrenaline. Her forehead pressed hard against the strap as she turned toward Yingyue with wide eyes. "But don't I have to be dead first?"

Yingyue shook her head. "Not entirely. We've developed a new method of cryonics that has a higher potential of resurrection on the other side after reanimation. We're going to freeze your body while you're still alive."

Lara shuddered in disbelief. "You're going to have me die in order to live?"

"In principle, yes. You will die from the extreme cold temperatures. Before we lower you into a vat of liquid nitrogen, we will replace the water in your cells with cryoprotectant. It's mostly painless."

Lara wrinkled her nose. "Cryoprotectant?"

"It's a chemical mixture… like human antifreeze. It prevents your organs and tissues from forming ice crystals and shattering. That would obviously hinder our ability to bring you back."

"But I won't survive for long without water in my cells," Lara said. "Won't that cryo-stuff kill me?"

"If it doesn't, your body will freeze lying on a bed of dry ice. When you reach minus 130 degrees Celsius, we will transfer you to a large metal tank filled with liquid nitrogen. Your body will be stored at a temperature of around minus 196 degrees Celsius, remain fully intact, and not age while you await reentry."

My father wanted this for me? Lara's thoughts raced.

As if reading her mind, Yingyue continued, saying, "Don't worry, Lara. This will allow for your rebirth. Your father didn't want you to have to suffer through the long process of waiting for a bone marrow donor, only to have it fail."

Lara raised an eyebrow. "But I thought bone marrow transplant could cure aplastic anemia."

"How many blood transfusions have you had?" Yingyue asked.

"Only one so far," Lara said.

"Did the doctor explain that each transfusion lowers the chance for a successful transplant?" Yingyue asked. "Did she also mention the success rate for bone marrow transplants from non-related donors at a later stage in life?"

"She was still running a few tests before I left. Then we were going to talk about my options."

Yingyue frowned. "For patients younger than twenty, the five-year survival rate is about eighty percent with a bone marrow transplant from a family member. From there the rates go down based on age and donor. You're thirty-three years old and don't have access to a family donor. Even if you have a successful transplant someday and survive, the disease can reoccur, especially if you have the gene mutation that causes the disease in the first place."

"My doctor said I inherited a gene mutation."

Yingyue nodded. "Yes, I've reviewed the results of your bone marrow biopsy. You have a gene mutation on the ACD gene, something you inherited from your parents." She paused as a wistful look came over her face. "The disorder is two to three times more common in Asian countries. I also inherited the condition from my parents."

"Did my parents develop the disease before they died?" Lara asked, ignoring the connection between them.

Yingyue nodded. "Your father experienced severe adult-onset aplastic anemia. Shortly after being diagnosed, he discovered a major shortening of his telomeres, which suggested he didn't have many years left. It was his dream to find a way to fix the gene mutation someday. Unfortunately, his life was cut short by another tragedy."

"When did he learn about his illness?" Lara asked.

Yingyue frowned. "Shortly before your parents died in that car accident."

Lara squinted, concentrating on retrieving her scattered memories of the accident. For most of her life, she'd worked hard to block them out. Now more than anything, she wanted to remember every detail. Right before the collision, her parents had been arguing. Lara didn't understand what they were saying at the time. Her memories were jumbled, and the words mixed together. Whatever they were saying scared her, so she pretended not to listen. Instead, she stared out the window, looking for mountain lions in the dark forest.

Were they arguing about his illness? About cryonics?

"Did you know my team was going to break into the institute tonight?" Lara asked, struggling to make sense of how the mission went wrong.

Something flickered in Yingyue's eyes, but she didn't acknowledge Lara's question. Her black eyes became distant and cold. "Your father's plan outlined the terms under which you and your parents are to be revived… only at a time in which scientists have discovered a cure to your illness or a way to upload your consciousness onto a computer, liberating your soul from the frail human body."

"My parents are frozen?"

Yingyue moved away and out of Lara's line of sight. "Your

tank will be situated next to your mother's in the cryonics facility."

Images of the cryonics tank with the lonely, familiar woman from the tour filled Lara's mind. *Was that my mother?*

Yingyue set a clock on a tray next to Lara's face. "I'll come get you in about an hour."

"What about my father?" Lara asked, straining her voice. "Where's his body?"

Yingyue moved across the room and opened the door.

"Wait," Lara croaked. "How did you know I'd come to China? Were you the one who placed the advertisement for Kingsley Investigations?"

Yingyue turned around with a curious expression.

"Why are you doing this to me?" Lara asked.

"You may not understand this now, but you will when you return, Lara. I'm doing this to save you." She paused to look at Lara one last time. "I'll be back soon."

THIRTY-TWO

The Escape

As soon as the door slammed shut, Lara squirmed in the chair, trying to get free.

If only I could get one of these straps loose.

The material was resistant to both tearing or stretching. After several minutes, the skin under the straps turned red, stinging severely, and she had a small cut on her right arm. A few drops of blood trickled to the floor.

Resigning herself to failure, she leaned back in the chair, wishing she could wipe her sweaty forehead. She glanced at the clock, and her heart thudded dully in her chest. More than twenty minutes had already passed. Yingyue would be back in less than forty minutes. If her head weren't restrained by a thick strap, it would have been spinning.

This is how I spend my last minutes? Tied to a chair with heparin running through my veins? I'm supposed to believe my father put this whole thing in motion?

Absolutely not. A painful lump rose in her throat.

She pressed her head against the chair as her mind raced through the information she'd learned from Yingyue. She didn't remember her parents, especially her father, as irrational or even religious people. Then again, she was only eight years old when they died. Lara had to reject the notion that her father would have chosen such a terrible end for his only daughter. Killing her to save her life was not rational. It was not something a loving father would do. Unless…

Was my father a Macrobian?

As soon as the troubling thought surfaced in her mind, it went around and around. It was the only answer that made sense. Her father, maybe even her mother, must have joined the lunatic transhumanist group for a time. She could imagine them wanting to contribute to the advancement of science and technology through their startup company Horizon Genomics. Or maybe they became members because her father became ill with a genetically inherited disease and they hoped for a cure. But at some point, when things got too extreme, they must have changed their minds. Perhaps her parents had fallen out with the institute at some point. Lara's body tensed as a new idea popped into her head.

What if the Kongs had my parents killed in the car accident?

Lara wanted to shake her head at the notion but couldn't. Instead, she stared up at the ceiling, and her mind went numb. She'd dreamed up a conspiracy worthy of a daytime soap opera in an effort to explain her circumstances. But even the fictional facts didn't add up.

Are the Langston's involved? Are they Macrobians, too?

She recalled Cynthia's dramatic reaction to Molly's kidnapping. Lara didn't think she would ever put Molly in harm's way for the sake of some conspiracy, even if they were members of the Macrobians. *No. If the Kongs wanted to get me to China, why wouldn't they just kidnap me in the first place? Why did they take Molly and lure me here?*

None of it made any sense…

I'm going to die in this awful place.

None of it mattered. She wanted to kick something. Hard.

A faint noise at the door startled her.

Is someone there?

Her body tensed, and she lay completely still, her bladder

nearly ready to burst. Silence. When she heard nothing, her breathing returned to normal. She was about to return to her circular analysis, when the door opened and closed with a soft click. Lara blinked her eyes but could see nothing. She held her breath for a moment.

The air rippled in front of Lara, opaque wrinkles forming in the rough shape of a person. Then, a thin layer of material fell to the floor, revealing a young, familiar Chinese woman. Lara squeezed the arms of the chair as adrenaline spiked her chest. Unable to hold it any longer, a stream of warm liquid ran between her legs, soaking through her black cargo pants and dripping on the floor.

When she finally regained her wits, Lara recognized her as the tour guide from the day before—Mei Xing Kong.

How does she have an invisibility cloak? What is she doing here?

Her heart still knocking against her chest, Lara opened her mouth to speak but, in her embarrassment, found no words.

Putting her finger to her mouth, Mei Xing set a large black duffle bag on the floor next to Lara. She walked behind Lara's chair for a moment and came back with a fistful of paper towels. Bending down, she wiped up the urine from the floor and dumped the soiled towels in the trash bin. Then, she unzipped the bag and ruffled through it for a few moments. When she stood back up, she had a shiny, metal object in her hand.

Lara jerked her head backward, her eyes focused on the movement of the metal object with laser-like precision. She gripped the arms of the recliner, her knuckles turning white from the tightness. When her eyes focused, she gasped at the sight of a large pair of scissors.

Mei Xing raised the scissors to Lara's face, the tips pointed toward her eyes and cutting edges open for action. Lara attempted to yank her face away, but the strap held her head stubbornly in place. As the shiny metal scissors brushed past her eyes, Lara screwed them shut and pulled her face taut. Seconds later, she felt the cold blade slide between the strap and her forehead. A soft snip. Lara's head was finally free.

"I'm going to get you out of here," Mei Xing whispered.

Why couldn't you have said so a bit sooner?

Lara exhaled sharply and studied Mei Xing. The girl couldn't have been more than twenty-five years old, but to Lara, Asian people often looked young for their age. She assumed Yingyue and Yishan Kong were her parents, since they shared the same last name. And Mei Xing worked at the institute. But for some reason, she wanted to help Lara escape.

"I need you to keep quiet," she said in a stern but kind voice. "She'll be coming back for you soon." A smirk moved across her face. "Thanks to your little stunt, the institute is crawling with armed security guards. For all I know, her thugs are lurking outside the door of this room."

Lara detected a hint of amusement, which made her relax.

"Why are you helping me?" Lara whispered in a hoarse voice, leaning forward to get a better look at the duffle bag on the floor.

Mei Xing put a finger to her lips and cut through Lara's arm straps. "Shsst. We can't talk about that here." She gently removed the needle from Lara's arm, and blood trickled from the tiny hole.

Lara shook out her arms and rubbed the tender skin where the straps had made small indentations. She stared at the mysterious young Chinese woman scurrying about.

Mei Xing dug through the duffle bag as if she was looking for something. Then she pulled out several jars of pills.

"How are you feeling?" Mei Xing asked, pouring out pills from each of the jars and filling a glass with water.

Lara eyed her nervously. "Um... fine, I guess. All things considered."

"When was your last transfusion?"

She knows about my illness, too?

"Maybe a week ago?" Lara frowned. With all that had transpired, it felt like several months ago. Her world had been turned upside down by her sickness and the kidnapping case. And now the possibility that they were both deeply intertwined somehow. She felt tired, and her heart ached for home and a sense of normalcy—to see Maggie, catch up with Rob and Sanchez, and play with Loki.

"I'm going to give you some vitamin B-12, folic acid, and iron to tide you over," Mei Xing said, handing Lara a few tablets and a glass of water. "You'll need your strength." Then she walked toward the cabinet at the back of the room and opened all the drawers, one after the other. In the last one, she found gauze and Band-Aids.

Lara swallowed the pills and gulped down the water.

Mei Xing wiped the blood off Lara's arm with gauze, took a folded piece and pressed it tightly, and then secured it with a Band-Aid. "You're gonna need these after that heparin injection," she said, handing Lara a few more Band-Aids. "To stop the bleeding..." She paused to look at Lara, her intense black eyes full of curiosity. "The American philanthropist couple seeking to donate to the orphanage was a distraction, wasn't it?"

Lara nodded sheepishly. "You knew about the break-in?"

"I wasn't sure until now." Mei Xing's eyes flashed with understanding.

"How did you figure it out?"

"Dr. Nilsson discovered several files missing and went ballistic. The visit by the American couple was the only thing we could point to as a possible breach. We don't advertise our location or services at the orphanage. Any visitors would have to know we exist in advance. For me, that's what gave them away at first. But there was also something off about the chemistry between those two."

Lara bit her lip, and a twinge of jealousy pinched her gut. "Isn't Yingyue your mother?" she asked.

"Uh yeah... but I don't call her that anymore. Maybe I should... she acts more like my mom than my boss these days. When she asked me to conduct the group tour yesterday, I was so furious that I threw a teenage-level fit about it."

Mei Xing cut through the straps around Lara's legs.

"I used to run the tours at the institute before I went off to medical school in the States. But now that I'm an actual doctor, I didn't think I'd get stuck doing it again. A total waste of assets. But she wouldn't budge, so I had to do it. After all, she's my boss. But she could ask me because I'm her daughter. I've never seen anyone else with an MD lead a tour group."

Lara raised an eyebrow.

"I should have known something was up when she asked *me* to lead the tour. Afterward, I spent several hours in the security office, getting lectured by Yingyue for being so reckless." She wrinkled her forehead for a moment and looked at Lara. "I take it you're the one who stole my ID?"

Lara held her palms out and shrugged her shoulders. "Yeah, Finn took it… sorry about that."

Mei Xing tilted her head. "Don't worry about it. It was probably all by design anyway. They must have known you were planning to rescue Molly. Dr. Nilsson was in such a rush to get the girls out of the orphanage that morning…"

Did Mei Xing know, too? The young woman seemed nice enough. After all, she was saving Lara's life. But to Lara, her explanations felt a bit staged. Mei Xing had to have known something about Molly's kidnapping.

How else would she know to help me? Why is she doing this? Should I trust her?

Lara frowned deeply as a tangle of worries crept into her mind. She thought about Vik, Finn, and Kaitlyn and the large contingent of armed security guards.

Did they get out okay?

As if reading her mind, Mei Xing said in a gentle tone, "Your friends are fine. I overheard Yingyue telling someone they made it out. You were her target, and she didn't want that many bodies on her hands." She shot Lara a grim look, and Lara shuddered.

I was Yingyue's target.

"Though I'm sure she already made that crystal clear," Mei Xing added wryly.

No, not really.

A spike of adrenaline shot through her tired muscles as she

remembered the black plastic case on the floor in the hallway before she was taken.

Dammit. I lost the case with the DNA samples.

"What's wrong?" Mei Xing asked.

"I lost my case of DNA samples we came here for."

Mei Xing smiled slightly. "No, you didn't."

Lara's eyes bulged.

"I retrieved the case for you," she said, pointing to the black duffel bag.

Lara swung her legs over the edge of the medical recliner. She bent down and rustled through the bag, pulling out the black plastic case. She flipped it open quickly to check on the contents. The three tubes were still there. "I don't get it. Why are you helping me?" Lara asked, looking up at her, still baffled by the girl's motivations.

"Short answer? I detest the Macrobians and almost everything they stand for," Mei Xing said. "The longer answer is more complicated. Your father's plan to freeze your body until a cure can be found is complete lunacy." She put both hands to her chest, as if pained by the idea. "Death is not a given. Not for you. For one, you can survive on transfusions. A successful bone marrow transplant might be a long shot, but it's still possible. Plus, scientists are close to developing gene therapies to correct mutations like the one you have. They're still experimental and don't always take, but the point is, we're rapidly making progress on genomic science. There could be a breakthrough any day now… I wasn't going to stand around and do nothing while they killed you."

Lara didn't know what to say.

"I know what it's like to be entangled in some pretty bad family dysfunction," Mei Xing said. "I spent the past eight years studying medicine at Stanford and just came home to rejoin the family business. When I saw what they were doing with the Cryonics Center, I didn't know what to do about it. I wasn't going to let…" She stopped, her voice trailing off. Her eyes moistened, and she turned away.

What isn't she telling me?

"Have scientists even figured out how to successfully reanimate a body after cryonic preservation?" Lara asked, her heartbeat finally settling back into its normal pace.

Mei Xing shook her head vehemently. "We're not even close. I never believed in any of the transhumanist bullshit. Of course, I support the advancement of science and technology to improve the human condition. But what they've been doing here since I left..." She visibly shuddered. "They're experimenting on humans without their consent."

"Do you mean Metamorphosis?" Lara asked.

"You've heard about it?" Mei Xing asked, her eyes protruding.

"I have my sources," Lara said.

Mei Xing narrowed her eyes. "Is Hickerson from the CIA one of your sources?"

Lara felt a wave of dizziness coming over her. *How does she know Hickerson?*

"I guess so," Lara said. The mention of his name hit her like a meteor tumbling into the atmosphere from outer space.

"Hickerson approached me during my final years of graduate school at Stanford. He wanted information about Metamorphosis, but I had no idea what he was talking about." Mei Xing exhaled sharply.

"Hickerson recruited you?" Lara asked, already certain of the answer.

Mei Xing nodded. "He's the reason I had to come back to Shenzhen and see for myself what was going on here." A tear rolled down her cheek. "It's far worse than I imagined."

"How so?" Lara asked softly.

Mei Xing sniffed. "About nine years ago, Yingyue began using reproductive cloning to create copies of herself for the purpose of an experiment she called Metamorphosis. She recruited families with the Macrobians to raise the clones as adopted children. And I suspect she didn't stop at the first batch of eight clones."

There are more than eight?

"Why so many?" Lara asked.

"A larger sample size for scientific research. Because they're genetically the same, identical twins make ideal test subjects for experiments. Clones are no different, except where they came from. You probably already know this by now, but Molly was one of the eight original clones."

Original?

Lara nodded.

"Anyway, at first, I thought the purpose of Metamorphosis was to find a cure for aplastic anemia, a condition my mother also suffers from. At least that would be an honorable goal… even if I don't agree with conducting the experiment. But it turns out that's not the real objective at all."

"What is it, then?" Lara asked.

Tears rolled down her cheeks. "The Macrobians want to find the secret to immortality. They're using the clones to study the factors that shape the lifespan." She sniffed. "Twins are similar in terms of life expectancy. However, identical twins will have very different lifespans depending on environmental exposures, lifestyle, and physical activity. Yingyue wants to identify the gene or group of genes that contribute to a longer life."

"And how will she do that?" Lara asked.

"Eight years ago, they determined that one of the girls would serve as the control group or the first clone. The girl was put in a family that would limit exposure to any hazardous environmental toxins, guarantee a healthy lifestyle, and ensure a good amount of physical activity."

"And the others?" Lara asked.

"Each of the other clones were placed in similar environmental and lifestyle settings. However, they had their genomes modified, each in different ways, in order to help isolate the genes that contribute to longer life. Yingyue says she's getting close to locating longevity genes that will allow humans to live longer. But the girls are only eight years old." She paused. "The experiment will last for several decades."

"Is Molly the control clone?" Lara asked.

Mei Xing nodded. "Good guess. She's critical to every aspect of the experiment."

"I'm confused," Lara said. "You mentioned the experiment started out as a means to cure aplastic anemia… and now it's evolved to be more about extending human life. That's a pretty big leap, isn't it?"

"Actually, not at all," Mei Xing said. "Interestingly, blood disorders and longevity appear to be genetically related. Yingyue discovered a gene mutation that causes a rare blood disorder if a person possesses both copies of the gene."

"So, if someone inherits the gene mutation from both parents, they get the blood disorder," Lara said, proud of herself for remembering the doctor's explanation. "Like aplastic anemia."

"Yes, but I'm not talking about aplastic anemia. For this particular disease, the mutation prevents regulation of a protein that dissolves blood clots. But the interesting aspect is when a person only gets one copy of the gene mutation, it leads them to have lower levels of the clotting protein. Mysteriously, this seems to lead to a longer than average lifespan and much longer telomeres. If Yingyue succeeds in confirming her theories, she'll have discovered a genetic fountain of youth."

Lara sat silently for a few moments, contemplating what that might mean for the world. People who could afford it would have their genomes edited to live stronger, healthier, and longer lives. Instead of recruiting individuals from civilian populations, governments could grow armies of superhuman soldiers from enhanced clones. She shuddered.

This will change everything.

"You're not afraid of what Yingyue will do to you when she finds out you helped me escape?" Lara asked.

"I don't intend for her to find out." She bent down to pick up the invisibility cloak from the floor. Mei Xing glanced at her watch and made a face. "We have to get out of here. Are you ready?"

Lara grabbed the black case. "Ready as I'll ever be."

THIRTY-THREE

Reunion

Mei Xing pulled the invisibility cloak over herself, opened the door slowly, and peered outside. She signaled that the coast was clear, held the door open for Lara, and pointed down the hallway toward the airtight door. It was standing open.

"You know the way out from here?" she asked.

Lara nodded.

"Well, then… good luck." Mei Xing reached her hand out from under the cloak. "Till the next time we meet."

Next time?

Lara shook her hand and watched Mei Xing disappear under the cloak as she walked away in the opposite direction. Lara crept down the hallway toward the open door. With each step, her heart thumped in her throat. Passing through the airtight door, Lara walked down the hallway until she reached an intersection. On her right, she eyed the elevator she had used with her team to reach the Genetics Laboratory. To her left, there was a door to a stairwell.

I need to get to the first floor. Then I need to turn right and walk all the way to the other side of the building. But I'm not using the elevator this time.

As she grabbed the handle of the door to the stairwell, the

sound of moving fabric pricked her ears. Out of the corner of her eye, she glimpsed two armed security guards dressed in black. Before she had a chance to run for it, they grabbed her arms, zip-tied them behind her back, put a gag in her mouth, and pulled a sack over her head. Lara heard the black plastic case thump to the floor.

She struggled wildly as the two men carried her down the stairs and into a long hallway. A door opened, and muggy air from outside rushed into the building. Over the din of the city streets and honking of traffic, she could hear a light pitter-patter of rain. Seconds later, rain drops landed on her bare skin.

Wait a minute. We must be at the back entrance.

Once outside, the two men opened the door of a van, rolled her body inside, and slammed the door shut. She heard them place something next to her.

Is that my case?

Quiet once more, the rain clinked gently against the roof of the van. With the sack cutting off fresh air, she took in short breaths and tried to get her mental bearings. The driver and passenger doors opened and slammed shut. The engine started, and tires squealed as the vehicle peeled out of the alley behind the institute.

Forty minutes later, Lara still lay tied up in the fetal position in the back of a van, straining her ears and trying to discern clues from the sounds. From the muted voices in the front, she could tell there were two men, maybe the same two men who had taken her. At first, the driver tore up the city streets as if fearful of being followed. At some point, they crossed through a control point. Lara assumed they passed through the border between Shenzhen and Hong Kong. The border guards didn't bother searching the vehicle.

Mei Xing is helping me escape, right? Somehow this didn't feel like much of a rescue to her. More like another kidnapping.

Lara went over every part of her conversation with Mei Xing, analyzing the girl's possible motivations. *Was the gag necessary? Why would she rescue me and then sell me out?*

Rain spattered hard against the windshield, and the wipers oscillated back and forth at a fast pace. The van came to an abrupt halt, the tires screeching. The passenger door opened. A moment later, the side door slid open. She could hear someone climb into the back of the van. A pair of strong arms pushed her and began rolling her toward the edge. Another pair of arms dragged her.

Without warning, she rolled past the edge and dropped down onto the wet cement with a thud. Pain shot through her hip and shoulder where she made contact with the cement. The crack of robust plastic on cement sounded next to her. Then the side door slammed shut, followed by footsteps and the slam of the passenger door. The driver revved the engine and then took off, the tires squealing behind him.

They just left me here? In the middle of a street?

Heavy traffic whizzed up and down the street, splashing muddy rain in Lara's direction. The rainfall drenched through the sack cloth and ran down her face, the taste of dirt on her tongue.

Heavy footsteps were followed by loud voices shouting. Seconds later, she felt as if she was surrounded by people. A foot nudged her. Lara moaned loudly to let them know she was alive.

The sack cloth scraped her face as someone yanked it off her head. She looked up frantically into the stern eyes of a middle-aged U.S. Marine in uniform. Behind him stood several others, looking alert, armed, and dangerous. They stood ready to shoot if necessary. The Marine untied the gag in her mouth.

Lara coughed desperately for air.

"Ma'am, I'm Sergeant Simmons. Are you a U.S. Citizen?" he asked.

"Yes, I'm Lara Kingsley..." Lara croaked and nodded her head vehemently. "Please help me."

He retrieved a pocket knife from his belt, flicked it open, and cut through the ties around her arms and legs. "Are you hurt? Can you get up?" He reached out his arm to help her up.

Lara nodded and grabbed his arm, lifting herself from the

street. Another younger Marine came around and picked up her plastic case. She exhaled sharply when he opened the case and saw the tubes. His eyes bulged.

"Those are important DNA samples for a case officer at the CIA," Lara half-lied. Only one of the specimens was for Hickerson. The other samples belonged to her and her mother. "Randall Hickerson. He's a senior CIA case officer for China. He asked me to collect information for him. I almost lost my life over those tubes."

Hopefully, Vik got the paper files out.

"We'll have to verify that with the CIA Station Chief," Sergeant Simmons said, motioning to the guard to open the gate. "Let's go inside the Consulate and get you checked out. You'll be happy to know there are some friends eagerly waiting for you."

Inside the Consulate, Lara spotted Vik and Finn waiting in the lobby. Finn was pacing around in circles, and Vik was obviously unable to keep still. Both of them had dark bags under their eyes and distraught faces, like they hadn't slept a wink in days.

When they saw her, their eyes lit up, and they ran toward her with open arms. Finn picked her up and hugged her tightly. Then he set her down gently. Seconds later, Vik pounced on her, causing her to wince.

"Ouch," Lara said. "Not so hard… everything hurts."

"Sorry," Vik said, giving her a half-smile.

"Are you okay?" Finn asked, his light blue eyes bloodshot. "We thought you were dead." There was moisture in his eyes, but he'd never admit it.

So did I.

Lara shuddered at the memory of Yingyue and her thoughts of being frozen to death. "Where are the others?"

Finn's face fell. "They've already returned home."

"What?" Lara asked, taking a step back, her face aghast.

"Mr. Langston said he got what he came for, took his private jet, and flew back to the United States," Finn said.

He has some nerve. Lara clenched and unclenched her fists. "He just left me behind?"

"Kaitlyn wanted to stay behind and wait with us, but I told her to go home to avoid trouble at work. Vik and I have been trying to get the diplomats to do something to rescue you, but we reached a dead end in the negotiations. The Chinese authorities denied your presence in Shenzhen and wanted to play hardball." He paused and looked at her, a slight grin forming on his face. "But apparently, you didn't need our help after all."

"How did you ever get out of that place?" Vik asked.

Lara sighed heavily. She didn't really feel like recounting her terrifying journey so soon, but she owed them an explanation. Especially Finn. She pulled them further into the lobby, found some chairs, and told them the whole story from start to finish. She skipped over any details that would indicate to Finn the extent of her prior knowledge about Metamorphosis or Molly's true status as property of the institute. Vik made disapproving eyes at her but said nothing to contradict her. Lara also didn't tell them about Mei Xing's relationship with Hickerson.

By the time she finished, Vik's jaw looked permanently open and glued to the floor. Finn gripped the arms on his chair as if he were riding the world's tallest rollercoaster.

"But why did Mei Xing help you?" Vik asked, rubbing his chin. He shook his head. "I don't buy her anti-Macrobian spiel. There's got to be a reason why she'd go against her family to set you free."

Yeah, she's an asset for the CIA. But that's not for me to tell.

"And why she did it in the way she did," Finn said. "How did she get those guys to help her?"

Some of Hickerson's contacts?

"Yeah, that was no fun. I thought I was being kidnapped all over again."

Vik gave her an eager look. "Are you hungry, by chance?"

Just then, Lara's stomach gave off an angry growl.

The three of them burst out laughing.

"I think she is," Finn said.

Vik gave her a look of relief. "That's great because I haven't been able to eat a thing since we made it out yesterday... and now that Lara's okay, I might start chewing my own hand."

Lara laughed. "Now, we can't have that." She looked around the lobby. "Do they have anything good to eat here?"

THIRTY-FOUR

Accolades

___

October 24, 2028

A FAKE SMILE pasted on her face, Lara stood on the granite stairs of the majestic John A. Wilson Building located in downtown Washington D.C. Keenly aware that all eyes were on her, she fidgeted with her skirt and smoothed her shirt under her suit jacket before resuming her stiff posture.

The bright afternoon sun glared down on her like a stadium spotlight, causing her to squint. She wished she'd worn her sunglasses. Especially since it might have served another useful purpose—to hide the truth in her eyes from inquisitive minds around her.

This ceremony is a complete sham.

Down a few stairs in front of her, Mayor Wanda Peters leaned forward against a wooden podium. She was delivering a moving speech about the traits of heroes and acknowledging the hard work of the Metropolitan Police Department to secure the rescue of Molly Langston.

Only a few weeks away from her reelection bid, Mayor Peters had jumped at the chance to capitalize on the safe return of a young girl to help support her key campaign issue of fighting crime in the District—it was a compelling story.

We brought Molly home.

Pride welled in Lara's chest, distracting her from the nauseous pit in her stomach. She'd broken several laws, put her Army career at risk, nearly gotten her friends killed, almost got turned into an ice cube, jeopardized diplomatic relations with China, and mostly screwed up her mission to get information for the CIA. From her perspective, outside of bringing Molly home alive, the trip was a bust.

Upon their return to D.C., the news media made a large fanfare about her team's brave mission to China to bring back the Langstons' kidnapped daughter. Lara's newfound fame led to multiple requests for TV interviews and several calls a day seeking to hire Kingsley Investigations—so many that Lara considered disconnecting the line.

The irony of her previous shortage of work resulting from the Project Gecko case was not lost on her. *Get a client killed protecting national security, lose business. Save a kidnapped girl while jeopardizing national security, get business.*

On one hand, the District often gave the perception of a small town. And yet, there were unlimited opportunities for reinvention. *If you're hot, you're hot. When you're not, you're not.*

She'd turned down every one of the interviews to avoid having to lie about the details of the mission and keep reports in the dark about the maverick methods the team used to get the job done.

Before returning to the United States, Lara and Finn had met with State Department officials at the American Consulate in Hong Kong to contain the fallout of their stunts. After much negotiation, they agreed to a set of alternate facts to explain how they were able to convince Chinese authorities in Hong Kong to release Molly to the Langstons. Nothing would be gained by either country if the details of their activities on Chinese soil were to come to light. The facts could be viewed as a breach of Chinese sovereignty, something the Chinese government would not be able to tolerate if it went public.

Lara didn't like the idea of political spin but agreed it was in the best interest of all parties involved. To protect their careers in the military, Kaitlyn and Finn couldn't afford to have their actions become part of the public record.

Despite the tidy ending to what could have been a fiasco, the unanswered questions about the Langstons bothered her. Her tolerance for spin stopped with them getting away with what they'd done to mislead the police and put her life at risk. Even if they didn't pay for their crimes, Lara wanted to know the truth of their involvement. The full truth.

Rubbing her sweaty hands on her skirt, she stole a glance at Detective Sanchez standing to her left. He stared straight ahead, his posture rigid and full attention focused on the mayor giving her speech. Dressed in a navy suit and red tie, and clean-shaven, Sanchez looked unexpectedly handsome and proud. The crinkled set of crow's feet around his eyes matched the slight upturn of his mouth.

To her right, Julian and Cynthia Langston huddled closely with their daughter Molly—the centerpiece of the mayor's narrative. Lara had tried to make eye contact with them several times to get their attention. But no such luck. They were avoiding her, and with good reason after Julian ditched her in China. The police commissioner stood tall and proud next to the Langstons.

The large audience standing in front of the building below consisted of the who's who in D.C. politics and a fleet of video cameras. The mayor's loud voice boomed over the microphone, drowning out the non-stop click-clicks of the cameras taking photos. A high school band in uniform waited in the wings, ready to play the next musical number.

Lara's eyes grazed the many smiling faces in the crowd. Then she spotted Vik, Rob, and Finn near the front with wide, toothy grins. When their eyes met, Vik made a face at the ridiculous pomp and circumstance of the ceremony. She gave him a slow, knowing nod.

It's all for show.

Even though most people would see through it for what it was—a political target of opportunity for the mayor—they wouldn't really care. Playing the political game was the norm in the Beltway and as key to political survival as breathing air.

Lara perked up when she heard her name. Without warning, Mayor Peters turned to her and motioned for her to come forward.

Her face flushing hot, Lara walked down several steps, planting herself next to the mayor. The mayor put her arm around her and began talking about Lara's career in the Army Special Forces and her work as a private investigator helping to fight crime on the streets of the nation's capital. The spotlight made Lara want to shrink herself to the nanoscale.

"It is for these reasons that I, along with the Metropolitan Police Department, have decided to award Ms. Kingsley with the Medal of Honor." Lara's mouth fell open slightly, and her eyes widened. She glanced behind her at Sanchez, who grinned back at her.

He knew about this?

The mayor paused as the audience clapped in response. "This award is the MPD's highest honor. It is reserved for police officers and civilians who perform an act of exceptional bravery, above and beyond the call of duty. Ms. Kingsley traveled to China at great risk to herself and her team. With this medal, we recognize her extraordinary bravery and heroism."

I don't deserve a medal.

The mayor turned to Lara and shook her hand. "Thank you for your service to your country and to this city. We are forever in your debt." Then she pinned the medal on Lara's jacket and motioned for Detective Sanchez to come forward. Lara pasted on another fake smile to hide her disgust.

I need to barf in a bucket.

"Today, we also wish to recognize one of MPD's finest

detectives, who worked tirelessly to bring Molly safely back home. Detective Mario Sanchez, we are awarding you the Medal of Valor for your exemplary service to the District." She paused to smile at Sanchez. "I also have a sneaking suspicion you'll be a top contender for Detective of the Year."

A sheepish grin on his face, Sanchez shook the mayor's hand. Then she pinned the medal on Sanchez's uniform. "As we close this ceremony, please join me in celebrating these fine people, their accomplishments, and their service to our great nation's capital."

The crowd whooped and applauded. After a few moments, the mayor gave the band the signal, and they broke into *The Grand Flag.* Then she turned to Lara and the detective, shook their hands one more time, and begged an apology for her premature departure. Moments later, the mayor scurried back into the building with her entourage of interns, staffers, and reporters.

As the band music came to a close, the audience dispersed, many of them returning to work in the mayor's office. Others walked back to nearby buildings. A few tourists lingered to snap more photos.

Sanchez glanced down at his shiny new medal. "I'm not so sure I deserve this."

"Ditto," Lara said, giving him an embarrassed smile.

Sanchez put his hands in his pockets and cleared his throat. "Um, I don't know… how to thank—"

Lara put her hand on his arm and smiled. "You don't have to thank me. I did what I needed to do to bring Molly home."

He rubbed the back of his neck. "But um, I heard that you almost…"

Lara motioned dismissively with her hands. "At least I didn't get stuck in a tank of Fiddler's beetles. Let's just leave it at that."

Not much worse than almost getting frozen to death in a tank of blue goo. But bionic bugs are up there at the top of the list.

Sanchez gazed at Lara, his eyes full of warmth. "I owe you one, okay?"

"Let's just solve Rob's case, and then we're even," Lara said, turning away from him, suddenly remembering something she wanted to do. She searched for the Langstons. And of course, they were gone. Her smile waned. "I wanted to talk to the Langstons. But they've been avoiding me since I got home."

"Didn't they pay you for your services?" Sanchez asked, giving her a suspicious look like she was about to ruin his day.

"Oh yeah. They paid me in full." Lara narrowed her eyes at him. "But I think you know why I want to talk to them…"

Sanchez rubbed his forehead. "You're not going to cause trouble for me, are you? You know the D.C. Police Department considers this case closed."

Lara put her hands on her hips. "They were lying about… well, almost everything. I don't think they should just get away with it like nothing happened. Do you?"

"You think I want to go stirring the pot? After all this?" He waved his arms around. "The police commissioner is considering me for promotion to Captain. That means if I play my cards right, I'll be heading a new Future Crimes unit by the end of the year. Can you please let this go?"

Lara shook her head in disbelief. "I can't believe receiving a medal and a fancy promotion would change your mind about serving justice. That's not the Sanchez I know."

Sanchez crossed his arms. "That's not fair. Tell me… if you were me, would you go after the Langstons? What charges do you want me to bring them up on?"

Lara shrugged. "I dunno. You're the detective. Obstruction of justice? Filing a false police report? How about fraud?"

Sanchez scoffed and dismissed her suggestions with a wave of his hand. "You're grasping at straws, Lara. A fraud charge requires intentional deception of a person for financial or personal gain."

"Isn't that what Mr. Langston did, though?" Lara asked, raising her voice. "He kept the truth about Molly's kidnapping from the police and convinced me to risk my life and get his daughter back under false pretenses. And she's not really their adopted daughter, so in essence we kidnapped Molly and illegally brought her back into this country. He wasn't just playing with my life and career. We're talking about Finn... Kaitlyn... Vik. You're telling me that kind of bullshit wouldn't count as fraud?"

"Sure, it could. But that's not the point," Sanchez said. "What's your evidence? You can't expect the district attorney to fend off the battery of well-paid lawyers without a solid case. The DA isn't going to waste political capital going after one of the District's most powerful families for a bad police report and a little obstruction. And definitely not without solid evidence."

"What are you two arguing about?" Rob asked, climbing the stairs toward them.

Sanchez and Lara exchanged irritated looks.

"Nothing," Lara said, staring at her feet.

"That didn't sound like nothing from down there."

"Where are Vik and Finn?" Lara asked, changing the subject.

"Finn had to go back to the Pentagon for some work stuff. He said he'd swing by for the party at Wicked Bloom later tonight. Vik got hungry for falafel and went to track down a food truck a few blocks away."

Surprise, surprise. Vik got hungry. And Finn is working.

Finn had also been avoiding her since they returned. He couldn't seem to shake her dishonesty, and Lara didn't blame him for it.

Rob slapped her on the back, causing her to glare at him. "I'm glad you're back," he said. "I made some progress with the case. Sanchez and I can't wait to get back to work. Right, detective?"

Sanchez grunted unenthusiastically.

Something in the distance caught Lara's eye, distracting her. Two blocks away, she spotted familiar smoke rings and a man in a trench coat, walking briskly.

Hickerson showed up for the ceremony?

"We might have found something on Harry," Rob said eagerly.

His words barely registered. "Yeah, uh…" Lara said, walking down a few steps past Rob and Sanchez. Then she turned back to them. "Sure, we'll get to that later. I have a few loose ends to tie up first. See you later tonight, okay?"

Without another word, Lara started walking in Hickerson's direction.

"But I want to fill you in on the case," Rob said, his voice trailing off.

Lara waved her hand. "I gotta go. See you both at the party tonight, okay?"

THIRTY-FIVE

The Photo

Lara hurried after Hickerson down 14th St NW and toward the National Mall, alternating between an awkward power walk and a haphazard jog. Her speed constrained by her skirt and high heels that bit at her feet with every step, she desperately longed for her leggings and tennis shoes.

Hickerson's trench coat whipped around his body as he traveled at an impressive clip. She wondered if this was another one of his cat and mouse games. He always seemed to be one step ahead of her, and she didn't like it. His manipulations would end today if she had anything to say about it.

Where's the spook going, anyway?

Lara saw him start down a cement path. It was the one that curved around the National Museum of African American History and Culture in the direction of the Washington Monument.

"Hickerson," Lara shouted as she stopped, hoping to get his attention.

Midday traffic drowned out her voice. Hickerson kept marching down the path as if on some sort of mission.

"Hickerson!" She yelled more loudly this time, cupping her hands around her mouth to project her voice through the noise.

He tilted his head, slowed his pace, and appeared to glance sideways over his shoulder. With a small movement of his hand, he motioned for her to follow him and then continued up the path toward the Washington Monument.

He knew I was tailing him all along.

Lara was about to surge forward in his direction when someone grabbed her arm from behind. She whirled her head around and her stomach lurched. Anita Fiddler stood there in a long wool coat, her blonde hair fluttering back and forth in the wind. Her skin was paler than Lara remembered and her blue eyes notably bloodshot.

"What are you doing here?" Lara asked, her sense of urgency rising at the same rate as her pulse. She craned her neck to see Hickerson disappear around a corner.

What if Hickerson leaves?

Anita's lips trembled slightly. "I read about your case in the paper and came to the ceremony." She hesitated. Appearing to notice Lara's preoccupation, she grabbed her arm again. "I really need to talk to you."

"But you have my number," Lara said flatly. "You could have called." Immediately, she regretted the curtness of her reply.

It's not her fault Fiddler is her father.

Anita winced. "Yes… I know… but my father…"

Lara shuddered as memories of John Fiddler surfaced. "What, about him?"

"His life… may be in danger," Anita said, her voice wavering. "That's why he asked me to send that file to Special Agent Martin at the FBI."

The file!

Lara wanted to smack herself in the forehead for forgetting a critical detail related to Rob's case—the Foggy Bottom postmark on the envelope. She'd not been able to refocus since returning from China. Her one-track mind was still obsessed with the Langstons. "Yes, you sent that file to Special Agent Martin for your father?"

Anita nodded. "It had been in my safe since my dad went to

prison. He asked me not to open it. I have no idea what was inside the envelope. And then out of the blue, he told me he needed to send it to the FBI. The last time I visited him, he was hysterical and spouting all sorts of mumbo jumbo about the file. He said Sully told him about BlackDragon's identity before he died. Whoever that is…"

Lara's postured stiffened at the mention of Sully's name, her heart now pounding. *Did BlackDragon have Sully killed?*

"Do you know anything more about the file you to Special Agent Martin?" Lara asked.

Anita frowned. "My dad said something about the file containing new information. He mumbled something about Sully not being finished with the investigation into BlackDragon when he died."

"Did he tell you anything more?" Lara asked.

Anita shook her head. "No. But were you able to use the file?" Her eyes lit up with a trace of hope.

Lara hated to crush it but saw no sense in shielding her from the truth. "The file got lost in the mail room at the FBI. When we finally found it and read through its contents, it went missing before we could turn it in to the FBI Director for action. I'm afraid it's gone."

Anita's eyes dimmed, and tears welled. "That was his last copy."

Crap.

Her lip quivered. "I'm worried about him."

Trying to forget what Fiddler had done to her, Lara gave her an empathetic smile. "If you want, I could have Detective Sanchez check on him for you." She regretted the offer as soon as it came out.

I want nothing to do with Fiddler.

Anita wiped away a tear. "Oh… that would be great."

Lara glanced at her watch. "Look, I have to run, but it was good to see you again."

Anita nodded and waved goodbye. Without wasting another moment, Lara took off up the hill toward the monument, a tingle of guilt swelling in her chest. Ten minutes later, she reached the base of the monument, huffing and puffing. After spotting Hickerson with a dark glare on his face, she bent over to catch her breath.

After a few moments, she stood and walked over to him.

From the lofty vantage point, depending on which way they looked, they could see the Lincoln Memorial, the White House, the U.S. Capitol, or the Jefferson Memorial. Acting as if he didn't know her, Hickerson walked toward the circle of American flags lining the edge of the monument's base and looked down on the Lincoln Memorial. He took out a cigarette, lit it, took a drag, and blew his signature rings into the chilly air.

Lara followed his lead and positioned herself next to him. She wrinkled her nose at the smell of cigarette smoke and prepared to sneeze.

"What took you so long?" Hickerson growled.

"Sorry. I got ambushed."

He grunted. "I don't have much time. We've analyzed the files from your trip."

"Oh? Find anything interesting?" Lara asked, fairly certain he wouldn't give her a straight answer.

"Yes and no. Most of it we'd already inferred. But it's good to have confirmation of our theories."

Another perfect non-answer.

Lara held out her palms. "Sorry I wasn't able to get more information… we ran out of time. Because as it turns out, they knew we were coming." She shot him a knowing look. "But then, you probably knew that… didn't you?"

Hickerson motioned dismissively with his hand. "We have more information now than we did before. In any case, you exceeded my expectations."

Well, that's nice.

"You knew, didn't you?" Lara snapped, her temper rising.

Hickerson raised an eyebrow but his face remained slack. "What did I know?"

"You knew what I'd find in that refrigerator."

"I don't know what you mean."

"Don't play dumb with me," Lara said, bitterness in her voice. "There are always twisted motives behind your spy games." She paused to gather her energy. "You didn't need me to collect the DNA samples, did you? You could have just hacked the online database storing all the genomic data for Metamorphosis."

Hickerson raised his finger to his mouth. "Don't mention the code name here."

"Whatever." Lara threw up her hands.

"You're wrong about the mission," Hickerson said. "We needed Molly's original sample. It wasn't in the database."

Why didn't he just have Mei Xing get it for him? Will he tell me about her?

"Stop dancing around the truth," Lara said. "You wanted me to go see what was in that fridge. You knew I'd find samples of my family's DNA. Don't pretend to deny it. Now I want to know why."

Hickerson shuffled his feet and puffed hard on his cigarette. His face remained slack, and he said nothing.

Lara put her hands on her hips. "Look, I'm over it, okay? We're done here. Either you come clean with me right now… or I'll tell the press all about the secret experiments and your illegal mission to have me conduct espionage in China for you."

Hickerson took a step back, giving her an aghast look. "You wouldn't dare. You'll lose your clearance. You might even go to prison."

"Are you so sure I wouldn't dare?" She smirked at him. "Do you know me as well as you think you do, Mr. Case Officer? Think about it. What do I have to lose? My Army career is already over now that I'm damaged goods. Even if the Chinese can prove I broke into the orphanage and the institute, they don't want that information to go public. They'll probably deny anything happened. But I think U.S. authorities will be interested in your actions on behalf of the CIA." She stole a glance at his face. Still blank. "I'm pretty sure you're not supposed to recruit American citizens to do your dirty work off-book. I also think the State Department would be interested in your ongoing surveillance activities on the Macrobians in China. Tell me… whose career do you think would blow up more if I spill the beans to the press? Mine or yours?"

When you have nothing to lose… you're dangerous.

Hickerson stood silently for several moments, as if weighing all options. He finished his cigarette, tossed the butt on the ground, and crushed it with his foot.

The corners of his mouth twitched. "Okay. There was more to the mission than collecting information and DNA."

"There you go," Lara said, plastering on a smile. "See… was it that hard for you to tell me the truth?" She studied his reaction, but he revealed nothing. Lara huffed and crossed her arms. "Next time you want me to be a pawn in your evil game, let me in on it. I'll be a better pawn if I know why I'm doing what I'm doing and what I'm doing it for."

Hickerson sighed, studying her face for a few moments with what appeared to be fondness. "You remind me of another strong-willed woman, you know."

"Who?" Lara asked.

"Your sister." His lips turned upward slightly as he said it.

Lara stared at him for a moment, not sure if she understood what he said. "My what?" She asked the question mostly out of instinct. Her brain had already processed the words, but the world stopped moving. It was as if nothing and no one else existed. Just her and Hickerson.

I was an only child. My parents died when I was eight.

Hickerson gazed at her with serious, thoughtful eyes. "I think you heard what I said."

She gaped at him, unable to formulate words, her mind racing with possible candidates and scenarios. She would have noticed her mother being pregnant. Then it must have been her father. He must have had an affair.

But with whom?

Lara's heart nearly stopped. *The photo of Yingyue with her baby?* It had fallen out of her father's files when she was searching the storage unit with Rob.

No, that can't be. A memory flashed through Lara's mind.

Hickerson scrutinized her face. He must have seen the lightbulb come on in her eyes, and said, "Mei Xing Kong is one of my newest agents in China. I recruited her several years ago when she was studying medicine at Stanford. I know her as Mia Kingsley."

"How is that even possible?" Lara rubbed the back of her neck, but it did nothing to relieve the growing tension throughout her body.

"Before he died, your father had an affair with Yingyue. She had a baby girl before she moved back to China."

Swaying slightly, Lara reeled from the new revelations about her family. *My father had an affair and kept my sister a secret from me.*

Lara wrinkled her forehead as she contemplated everything. "Yingyue knew we were coming to the institute to get Molly, didn't she? You knew from Mia we were walking into a trap and said nothing," she said, beginning to put the pieces together.

Hickerson waved off her accusation. "After the break-in at the orphanage, Mia told her mother about your team's plans in order to gain her trust. After her many years of rebellion during her studies at Stanford, we needed to convince Yingyue that her daughter was back in the fold and a willing member of the Macrobians… that Mia had finally seen the light and had come back to become part of the family business. Her desire to sell out her own sister to please her mother worked."

Mia knows that I'm her sister?

Lara shrank back slightly. "Did you plan on me getting frozen to death in the process?"

"No, that was definitely an unexpected complication."

"Complication?" Lara said, her voice screeching slightly.

"As soon as Mia learned about Yingyue's plans for you, she alerted me, and we came up with an escape plan. I activated several of my agents in Shenzhen and Hong Kong, they broke into the institute, and we got you out." He shrugged his shoulders. "All's well that ends well, right?"

Lara thought back to her escape, how she was tied up, gagged, and thrown into the back of a van by some Chinese thugs—presumably Hickerson's agents. Now she understood why her rescue went down more like a kidnapping.

Mia couldn't let Yingyue know she was involved.

"Let me get this straight." She pointed a finger at his chest. "You leveraged Molly's kidnapping as an opportunity to develop your asset... to insert her back into the institute where you'd have watchful eyes deep inside the operation. And then you leveraged my involvement to allow Mia to gain even more trust."

"Yes. And it worked. Yingyue confided in Mia about her plan to put you into a deep freeze. Or do you wish we hadn't interfered? If we hadn't, you'd be floating in one of those tanks right now." Hickerson looked away, narrowly avoiding the flames blazing from Lara's eyes.

He used me. Again.

He pulled another cigarette from the pack in his coat pocket and put it in his mouth. It hung there limply on the edge of his lip, and he made no move to light it.

"Were the Langstons involved in Molly's kidnapping?" Lara asked.

"I don't know. You'll have to ask them yourself."

Lara crossed her arms and glared at him. "If Yingyue confided in Mia, surely she told her daughter about why she was taking Molly."

"I have a theory."

Lara tilted her head. "Do share."

"The location of Julian's company in Shenzhen is a few steps away from the institute. That can't be a coincidence. From years of research, we have reason to believe that the Langstons belonged to the Macrobians at one point in time, maybe were even among the founding members and served at the highest level of leadership. Given the importance of

Metamorphosis, we don't think the Macrobians would place one of their precious clones with just anyone. Mr. Langston must have agreed to take Molly and understood his obligations with regard to her health and testing as part of the experiment."

"And you think he changed his mind about Molly taking part in the experiment?" Lara asked, remembering Cynthia's desperate state of mind.

"That's a decent hypothesis," Hickerson said.

"Maybe they had a falling out with the Kongs and refused to take Molly to China," Lara said absentmindedly. "And then Yingyue came to the United States to take Molly back."

Hickerson nodded. "Also possible."

"Who is this Dr. K?" Lara asked.

"Dr. K is used to refer to Yingyue or to her husband, Yishan Kong. They insisted all group members use the nickname. We believe it's part of creating the cult of personality driving the devotion of the Macrobians. We've been attempting to learn more about Yishan for years, but he is an elusive target. For all we know, Yingyue and Yishan may be one person. Mia hasn't detected a single sign of life for him."

"But Mia talks about Dr. K as if he's real…"

"It's expected of all institute personnel to revere Dr. K. One of her high priority missions over there is to get us information on Dr. K's identity, network, and activities."

"You sure Mia is not a double agent? Maybe she's working for Dr. K against you," Lara said.

Hickerson raised his eyebrows. Lara thought she glimpsed a flicker of doubt in his eyes before his face went blank once more. For several minutes silence fell between them.

Why is Hickerson so interested in the Macrobians? The group crossed ethical lines, but they were operating within Chinese law. Cloning babies to cure disease was troubling, but would it be a top priority of the CIA? She thought back to the night they breached the Macrobian Institute.

The guards were wearing exoskeletons. Similar if not identical to the one I once wore during my last case. Her instincts fired on all cylinders.

"There's more to this, isn't there?" Lara asked.

"What more is there?" Hickerson asked, blinking at her.

"You dragged me into this mess a while ago." She paused for a moment, running through the facts in her head. "It was your idea to get me involved with the Project Gecko case last spring. You're the one who convinced Mr. Zhang to hire me. You knew about my family ties to China already then, didn't you?" Lara rubbed her chin. "Yes, Mia said you recruited her when she was a student at Stanford."

Hickerson didn't respond.

"There's a connection between Project Gecko and the Macrobians, isn't there? Let me see if I can figure it out. The Macrobians are buying technology from the black market in China… technology stolen from the U.S. Like the exoskeletons the security guards were wearing. They were identical to the one made by the Pentagon for Project Gecko. And then there was Mia's invisibility cloak. The PLA sent Hai Xu to coerce the Spectral CEO into getting access to the technology for China, but that plan failed. If the Macrobian Institute has gotten access to the technology another way, it's possible that the Macrobians were the interested party behind Hai's machinations in the first place. That means there would likely also be a connection between the Macrobian Institute and the PLA."

How did the tech leak to China after Hai died?

"Was Hai working for Yingyue?" Lara asked.

Hickerson eyed her with respect. "You know… you have a real knack for putting things together from small observations. You might consider a career in tradecraft and maybe come work for the CIA someday."

"Just be straight with me for once."

"Okay, fine. You're right about most of it. We came across the Macrobians while tracking shipments of black market technology around the world. We think Yingyue's institute has ties to the PLA, but we're not sure. It was the PLA that sent Hai to D.C. to steal the technology, but somehow Yingue got access to it even after the failed mission. She must have another source. That's what we want Mia to find out for us."

Lara wrinkled her forehead. "Illicit trade on the black market coming from the United States? That sounds more like the FBI's domain. What's the CIA's interest?"

Hickerson cleared his throat. "Um, yeah… we're cooperating with the FBI. It's really their investigation."

"Right…" Lara said, cocking her head. "I'm thinking the CIA's involvement must have something to do with China's plan to gain technological advantages over the United States by stealing critical defense technologies. You're interested in the Macrobians for more than a few links to the black market. I bet you want to know if the Chinese government plans to exploit their clone experiments to develop superhumans for the battlefield."

Hickerson gave her a slight smirk. "Like I said… you'd be a great spy." He glanced at his watch. "I have to get going." He turned to leave.

Lara grabbed his arm. "Wait." He craned his neck and looked at her expectantly. "You said the CIA is collaborating with the FBI on the case. Is that how you first met Harry Cogan?"

"I think I've said enough," Hickerson said, lighting his cigarette and walking across the base of the monument toward 15th Street NW.

Lara followed him. "Tell me what you know about Harry. Please…"

He lifted his hand in the air and waved. "Take care of yourself, Lara."

She watched him go. When he was out of hearing distance, she spoke into her wrist. She stood there, staring after him for a few minutes. Then an idea formed in her head.

"Watson?" Lara asked.

"Ms. Kingsley, how may I help you?" a friendly British voice called out.

"Please find the photo of my father with the Chinese woman and the baby."

"One moment… here we are… is this the photo?"

Lara glanced at her screen. "Yes. Send it to Lance Duncan with the following text: I know what you know. Meet me at Wicked Bloom tonight around eight."

"Right away, Ms. Kingsley."

It's time for Lance to tell the truth about my father.

THIRTY-SIX

Wicked Bloom

Lara heaved open the heavy glass door and shuffled into Wicked Bloom, her eyes staring numbly ahead. Even on a normal day, Lara didn't like fanfare in her honor. And this wasn't a normal day. The ceremony led by the mayor followed by Hickerson's startling disclosure about her long-lost sister had pushed her way over the edge.

After Hickerson's abrupt departure, her mood had plummeted. She'd spent more than an hour wandering aimlessly around the National Mall, trying to recover from her shock.

Her bladder eventually brought her back to reality. Not wanting to face the usual hassle in the District of using bathroom facilities without buying something, she decided to head over to the bar early.

I really need a drink. Or maybe five drinks.

She desperately wanted to climb in bed, pull the covers over her head, snuggle with Loki, and pretend none of the events in the past month had happened.

Like that would help anything.

She thought about cancelling the party, but she didn't want to let anyone down. Especially not Amber, one of Wicked Bloom's owners and a longtime friend. When Amber learned Lara had successfully closed her big kidnapping case, she insisted on hosting a party to celebrate. Just like she'd once done for Sully. That party was the last time Lara had seen him before he dropped dead in front of her at the ballpark. Her chest ached painfully for a moment.

Hopefully, this party isn't as momentous.

It felt premature to celebrate, like she was jinxing herself. The case wasn't quite closed. Not for Lara. But, only a handful of people knew the whole truth—as much as there was to tell.

Still in a daze, Lara opened the door to the bar, turned right, and slammed right into a giant poster sign. She stumbled back and hit her elbow on the door frame. A shock of pain shot up her arm, and she rubbed her elbow as she regained her bearings. Now that she was snapped out of her stupor, she looked around. The bar was completely empty. And unrecognizable. Apparently, Amber had gone all out and decorated the bar with green and white streamers, red roses, and golden balloons. The smell of something sweet baking wafted from the kitchen, filling the main room. A poster advertising special cocktails themed around her mission to China stood in front of her. On a lighter day, she might have laughed out loud at the drink names. Instead, she suppressed a groan.

Shenzhen Sour. Hong Kong Affair. Macrobian Iced Tea.

Lara hurried toward the bathroom and took care of business. When she came out, she nearly bumped into someone who was walking out from the kitchen toward the bar.

"Oh sorry," Lara said in a daze, not seeing her friend until a familiar chuckle reached her ears. She took a step backwards.

"The lady of the hour has arrived," Amber said, glancing at her watch. "Sweetie, you're an hour early."

"I need a drink," Lara said, this time letting her groan be heard.

"That bad, huh?" Amber said, motioning to the bartender who hurried about, getting ready for happy hour. "A pint of Blue Moon for Lara." Amber stopped and flashed a toothy grin at Lara. "Or did you want some of that iced tea? Finn called ahead and gave me suggestions for the drink names. We mixed that one up just for you. But he wouldn't tell me why."

Finn is such a funny guy. He still hadn't forgiven her for lying to him. She didn't blame him. Maybe this was a sign. Lara grimaced. *Nope. Nothing ice-related for me.*

Amber grabbed Lara's arm gently, pulling her toward the bar, and patted the bar stool. "Sit down and tell me everything."

Lara slumped onto the stool, accepted the smooth glass pint, leaned her elbows on the bar, and told Amber the convoluted saga from the beginning—her inherited gene mutation, the strange photo of the Chinese woman with her father, Molly's kidnapping, her suspicions about the Langstons, the ceremony, and the revelation about her sister. She left out most of what happened in China, in particular the breaking-and-entering and nearly getting turned into an ice cube.

By the time she got to the part about her newfound sister, Amber's jaw hung in midair for several moments.

"How do you feel about that?" she asked.

Feelings. Ugh.

Lara pressed her lips together. "Honestly? I don't know. How am I'm supposed to feel about discovering I have a sister? My emotions are all over the place. Shock. Anger. Confusion. Mostly, I feel betrayed by my father."

"Do you think you'll get to see her again?"

Lara shrugged. "No clue. I'm not gonna return to China anytime soon if I can help it." She took a long drink of her beer, the fresh citrus taste quenching her thirst. "But if you don't mind, I'd like to keep this between us."

"You're not going to tell your friends?" Amber asked, raising an eyebrow.

Lara shook her head.

"Not even Vik?"

Guilt rose in her chest about keeping the discovery from her most loyal sidekick. *He'll kill me when he finds out.*

"It's too soon. I want to be certain about it before I spring it on everyone. The guy who told me about my sister is probably lying again."

I'd have to be a complete idiot to take Hickerson's word about anything. Actually, I'm already an idiot for trusting him at all.

"Who is lying to you again?" a familiar deep voice asked from behind, causing her to jump a bit on her stool.

That was a bit too close for comfort.

She turned to see Rob's crooked smile and tousled brown hair. He wore blue jeans, a V-neck t-shirt, and a brown leather jacket. Taking the stool next to hers, he leaned in close to her. Almost too close. His citrus-scented cologne wafted past her nose. The familiarity sent a happy feeling to her brain. For a brief moment. Then the doom and gloom returned.

"I'll have your best whiskey neat," Rob said to the bartender. "She'll have another…" He waved his hand around. "… whatever she's having. Put it on my tab. We're celebrating this girl tonight. A real hero." Rob slapped her on the back, and Lara rolled her eyes.

Someone shoot me now.

"I'm glad you're here early, Lara. We can catch up on the case. Without interference from your hotshot boyfriend."

Excellent. I need a distraction.

Lara gave him a warning look, signaling he should behave himself. "You said you found something on Harry?"

Rob nodded. "While you were off traipsing across China, I went digging around on the Dark Web."

Traipsing?

Rob rubbed his chin. "Vik passed along his research from the CyberShop case and gave me some suggestions about where to start looking."

Lara pressed her lips together, suppressing a hint of irritation. "Yeah, he told me on the plane over. Did you check out the TechNow message board where Justyne communicated as CyberShop with John Fiddler as KillerBot?"

"Yup, plus a few others. But I have a key advantage over Vik's work."

Lara raised her eyebrow. "And what's that?"

"I know about BlackDragon, the supposed big boss of the illicit trade ring, and he didn't."

Lara whipped her head to him. "You think BlackDragon is Harry's boss?"

Rob pursed his lips. "Maybe. I hoped I'd find something interesting with the new lead. I started by tracing the communications between CyberShop and KillerBot. Then I stumbled onto several conversations with BlackDragon. I kept coming across another pseudonym for someone who interacted quite a bit with BlackDragon."

"What pseudonym?" Lara asked, clasping her hands tightly around her beer.

The bartender set a glass of whiskey down in front of Rob and slid another cold beer her way. Rob picked up the glass and threw it back, drinking it down in one gulp.

"I really needed that." Rob motioned to the bartender for a refill.

"Easy there, tiger… we've got all night," Lara said, grinning. She took a gulp from her second beer, enjoying the cold fizzle. She'd need to slow down if she wanted to avoid getting tipsy before the others arrived. "What did you find?"

"As soon as I came across the new screen name, I knew I was on to something," Rob said, his eyes teasing her.

"C'mon, Rob, you're killing me here. What's the new name?"

"Chimbo4ever." He watched for her reaction.

Lara's eyes lit up. "Wait a minute… that's not your buddy Chimbo, is it?"

"If he took Chimbo4ever as his pseudonym on the Dark Web, then he's even dumber than I thought. My guess is the name belongs to Harry, and he's sending me a message. I asked Agent Carter to look into it at work, but I haven't heard from him in a few days. In my research on the Dark Web, I found a pattern of interactions between BlackDragon, CyberShop, and Chimbo. Of course, CyberShop's communications dropped off completely after Justyne was arrested."

"So, presumably, Justyne and Harry were communicating with BlackDragon, whoever that is. Is that everything?" Lara asked, a wave of disappointment coming over her. They were barely better off than before she'd left for China.

"Not quite," Rob said, his face splitting into a proud smile. "I found several posts between Chimbo4ever and BlackDragon in Chinese."

Chinese?

Lara's eyes widened. "Does Chimbo speak Chinese?"

"Not that I know of," Rob said. "But Harry does…"

Harry speaks Chinese?

"So, Harry was communicating with BlackDragon under this Chimbo4ever pseudonym?"

"It would appear so."

"Then Harry can't be BlackDragon…" Lara mumbled as memories from China flooded her mind. She sat up a bit straighter when she made the connection. "I forgot to tell you something. The security guards at the Macrobian Institute were outfitted with exoskeletons just like the ones made by the Department of Defense."

Rob's eyes widened.

"Not only that, someone working at the institute turned up wearing an invisibility cloak," Lara said, scratching her forehead.

"Maybe the institute is a customer of the black market ring?" Rob asked.

That means Harry is connected to Yingyue somehow.

"That's what I was thinking." She looked at Rob.

He gave her a strange look. "You didn't tell me who was wearing the invisibility cloak."

Lara swallowed hard. "Oh, just someone who works there." Looking away, she took a long drink of her beer. "So, did you find any tangible leads?"

"What aren't you telling me?" Rob asked, his eyes dead serious.

Such. A. Bad. Liar.

"Um…" Lara winced and looked at him with pleading eyes.

"Can I tell you another time? I'd rather not get into it right now. I'll tell you when I'm ready… I promise."

Rob tensed slightly. "You're not in trouble again, are you?"

"No, it's not that. I just learned something about my family. I'm still trying to process it."

Rob relaxed. "Okay. Whenever you're ready."

Lara gave him a half-smile. "What else was Harry doing on the Dark Web while posing as Chimbo?"

"Sorry… I lost my train of thought earlier. Harry appeared to be talking with an associate on a message board, something about visiting an old friend called Hazel. The associate warned Harry about the visitor log. And that was it."

Lara wrinkled her nose. "What does that mean?"

"Well, I figured it must be some sort of code. I made a list of places that have visitor logs and require sign-ins and sign-outs by law, and there aren't that many. The White House. Nursing homes. Psychiatric facilities. Rehab facilities."

"And prisons," Lara added, a lightbulb going off in her head.

"Exactly. And it turns out that our old friend Justyne is an inmate at the medium-security Federal Correctional Institution in Hazelton, Pennsylvania."

An old friend called Hazel. Harry was talking to BlackDragon about Justyne.

"That's only a few hours away," Lara said.

Rob nodded excitedly. "Yeah… I started tracking Harry's activities and following him around. The surveillance operation was pretty boring, but I made good use of the downtime, researching on the Dark Web from my car. Then, three days ago, I got lucky."

Lara perked up.

"Harry visited Justyne at the prison," Rob said, deadpan.

Lara's mouth fell open. "You followed him all the way out there?"

Rob bobbed his head. "I took pictures and sent them to Sanchez. He's working on getting a warrant for the visitor's log. If we can show a pattern of visits, then we can establish a link between Harry and Justyne. And once we get the Dark Web posts translated from Chinese to English, we'll have a connection between Harry and BlackDragon."

"But that's circumstantial," Lara said, frowning. "Not enough to put him behind bars."

"Yep, but it's something. More than we had."

"Why do you think Harry visited Justyne in prison?" Lara asked.

"Not sure. It looked like he was bringing some snacks with him. Apparently, she likes her candy bars."

"What kind?" Lara asked.

"Snickers, 3 Musketeers… you name it. Keyword chocolate."

Lara made a face, and her stomach growled. She reached for one of several small bowls of honey roasted peanuts spread out across the bar, taking a moment to munch on the salty, sweet snack. "Maybe she doesn't need to stay skinny in prison." Through the haze of her mind, she suddenly remembered something she needed to tell Rob. "I bumped into Anita."

Rob stared at her, dumbfounded. "When? How?" He wrinkled his forehead and added, "Why?"

"She came to the ceremony and followed me. Anita confirmed she's the one who sent you that folder. Fiddler asked her to send it. He's afraid for—"

"Did she have another copy?" Rob interrupted, a manic look glinting in his eyes.

"No, that was the last copy, and she never read it," Lara said. She waited for a few moments while the awful truth settled. "So, what's the next step for the case?"

"Now we need Harry to incriminate himself somehow. It's gonna be the only way we nail him. After a few weeks of digging, Agent Carter can't find anything more at the FBI. With the exception of the missing folder, there are no emails, documents, or even a paper trail suggesting impropriety. Nothing. That's why he's still working at the FBI, and I'm not. He made sure any remaining evidence points toward me."

"So… how are you planning to get him?"

"I want to run the sting operation I was talking about. I've laid much of the groundwork. While tooling around on the Dark Web for the past few weeks, I created my own pseudonym and started participating on the tech message boards."

"Oh, please tell me you didn't go with Droneman again." Lara did a face palm.

"C'mon Lara… you never give me any credit." Rob glared at her. "I interacted with a number of shady characters and claimed to have access to a wide variety of advanced biotech that I wanted to offload, hoping to get a bite from either BlackDragon or Chimbo4ever."

"And did you?" Lara asked, leaning forward.

"Yep. Word got around, and Chimbo4ever took the bait. But he wants to see a demo of the biotech before he makes a purchase."

That sounds familiar.

"So, what's your plan?" Lara asked.

"I want to draw this Chimbo4ever character out into the open. If I'm right about his identity, we can implicate Harry in the theft of proprietary biotechnology."

"But how?"

Rob grinned at her. "Well, first I need access to some hot, new proprietary biotech from a major company. Then we set up a demo and try to get Harry to come out of the woodwork to buy the stolen tech. If Harry shows up, we'll make sure the cops are on hand to take him down."

Lara furrowed her brow. "And where are you going to get the biotech to pull off the demo?"

Rob glanced at her nervously. "Uh… I was hoping you could help me with that."

She jerked her head. "How the hell am I supposed to come up with proprietary biotech?"

Rob dipped his head. "Um… maybe you could ask Lance to help us?"

Lara put her beer down on the bar and stared incredulously

at Rob. "You want me to ask your former almost-father-in-law for help clearing your name?"

Lance did say to ask him for help.

"He really likes you. I think he might even feel responsible for you a bit... now that he knows you're his friends' kid. It couldn't hurt to ask him."

Lara took a deep breath. "I guess I can ask him... but I just don't see him wanting to get involved."

"But you'll ask him?" Rob asked.

"Yeah. I'll talk to him." Lara paused to think, but didn't tell Rob that Lance might stop by the bar later about another matter.

"You're the best, Lara." Rob broke into a broad grin.

She rubbed her chin. "But before we attempt a sting operation, don't you think we should first visit Justyne in prison? Maybe she'll give us evidence to implicate Harry. I mean, she's paying for his crimes, and he's walking around as a free man. I bet things aren't peachy between the two of them."

Rob frowned. "I did look into that. Turns out it's not that easy to visit an inmate. We would have to be on an inmate's approved visiting list first. That means we would have to fill out some paperwork, and Justyne would need to sign off on it. What if she refuses?"

Lara's face fell.

"There is another way, but it's not easy either," Rob said. "We can visit Justyne if we're her lawyers... or at least if we can prove that we are lawyers. Know any sleazy lawyers who would be willing to help?"

Lara's shoulders slumped. "No, I don't."

Another dead end.

THIRTY-SEVEN

Missing Puzzle Pieces

Loud voices erupted at the front entrance of the bar, startling Lara. While Rob stared into his whiskey glass, Lara set her beer down on the bar and turned to see the source of the ruckus. Vik, Shanaya, Maggie, and Sanchez tumbled into Wicked Bloom with big smiles as if they'd already been drinking. Lara noticed a new warmth between Sanchez and Maggie since their breakup. When Lara's eyes met Maggie's with a raised eyebrow, her friend's face flushed.

Oh, they're back together again.

"Now that we're here, the party can finally get started," Vik said, beaming at her expectantly.

Lara slipped off the bar stool, gave Vik a limp high-five, hugged Shanaya and Maggie, and offered an awkward combo of a handshake and hug to Sanchez.

"Thanks guys, for coming out," Lara said, pasting on a smile. "It really means a lot." Her tone was intentionally cheery, but as the words came out of her mouth, they sounded forced.

Fake it until you make it, right?

Vik gave Lara a strange look, appearing to read her thoughts.

"Wouldn't miss it for the world, luv," Maggie said, glancing at Sanchez. "Plus, it gets me away from my parents for a bit. They're driving me up the bloody wall."

Sanchez grimaced and headed straight toward the bar to order a drink. Vik made a fork-to-mouth hand motion and headed to the bar with Shanaya to order something to eat.

"Your parents aren't staying with you at the apartment, are they?" Lara asked, slightly horrified at the idea.

"Oh, hell no. They're at the Ritz Carlton. But they keep insisting on dragging me to their hoity-toity meetings with the who's who in science. Usually, I don't mind networking. But this is embarrassing. If feels like they came here to parade their daughter around to all their scientist friends."

"I take it that's a problem for you?" Lara asked.

"Yes and no," Maggie said, a flash of guilt on her face. "On one hand, it's nice my parents finally recognize my work. On the other hand, it makes me feel like they think I can't run my own life or make it on my own. And let's not talk about the grueling demands on my social schedule. Last week, I had less than two hours to get any work done in the lab. My boss is on my back about it. Mostly he's bloody pissed that they won't make time for him. And not a day has gone by where he didn't let me forget about it."

Lara winced. Then a slow smirk formed. "Are you and Sanchez back together again?"

Maggie looked away. "Remember when he came by my lab? You know... before your trip to China?"

Lara nodded.

"Um... well, my parents were completely off their rockers that day. Mario took me out for a drink so that I could vent. That turned into drinks... and..."

Lara shuddered and raised her hand, signaling for her to stop. "Yeah, I got it." She didn't want to hear about how they hooked up. Lara's stomach sank. She wasn't sure why it bothered her that Maggie and Sanchez were back together. They'd been off and on since her case to catch Sully's murderer.

Maybe she wanted someone more stable for the detective than her flighty friend.

"Where's Finn?" Maggie asked, changing the subject. "I thought for sure he'd be here by now."

Lara looked at her watch and sighed. "He's running late. Probably got caught up in some work thing. That's been happening a lot."

"You two doing okay?" Maggie asked.

Lara shrugged. "I don't think we're being straight with each other. I haven't been honest with him about the Langstons and what I know about the Macrobians and such." She averted Maggie's gaze, hoping her friend wouldn't notice she was keeping secrets from her as well. "I don't know what he's keeping from me, but something's definitely up." Suddenly, she remembered something. "Hey, did you take a look at the DNA samples from China or the DNA profiles of the clones?"

"Not yet, hon. But I'll get to it. I promise."

Out of the corner of her eye, Lara saw a familiar, handsome man with blond hair and a grim look on his face enter the bar. Maggie must have noticed Lara's eyes widen because she turned to see who was coming.

"You didn't tell me that hottie billionaire was attending your party," Maggie whispered.

"Mags, he's happily married… so don't get any ideas."

Lara slid off her stool and went over to greet Lance. She reached out her hand to shake his, but he didn't take it.

Instead, he motioned for her to follow him to a quiet corner.

Oh, he's definitely not happy to see me.

"I don't appreciate being summoned," he growled.

And yet, here you are.

"Well, I don't very much appreciate being lied to," Lara retorted. "Especially when you claimed you wanted to help me."

Lance made a pained face. "I said I'd help out Donna and Ethan's kid, not tarnish your father's good name and reputation."

"My father's dead and doesn't care a lick about either of

those. Don't I deserve the truth?" She paused for a moment to let him absorb her words.

He remained silent.

"When you told me about Yingyue being a grad student at Stanford and working at my father's firm, you also knew they were having an affair, didn't you?"

Lance hesitated for a few moments before answering. "He never told me about it, but I guessed as much. Especially when Yingyue got pregnant and had the baby without a significant other in the picture."

Lara's mind flashed back to her parents fighting in the car, minutes before the deadly accident. She closed her eyes to focus on the words in the background, the words she'd suppressed all these years. Maybe because she was too young to understand. Maybe because she was too young to handle the breakup of her family. But all this time, she'd suppressed the memory. And now, it came back to her like a high-res video playing in her head.

"I told you to fire her," her mother said, tears rolling down her cheeks.

"You know I can't do that," her father replied. "How would she possibly provide for the baby? I can't just leave them on their own."

"Yes, you can," her mother shouted. "You have your real family to think of. But I should know better by now. You only ever think of them."

The sound of tires screeching and metal crushing filled Lara's ears, followed by a spinning sensation as the car rolled and then came to a sudden stop. She threw her eyes open and stared at Lance, feeling peaked.

"I remember it now."

"What?" Lance asked, a confused look on his face.

"I remember what my parents were fighting about before they died. They were fighting about her. And the baby. My sister Mia."

Lance took a deep breath and exhaled. "Lara, I'm sorry I didn't tell you... I thought you might be better off not knowing the truth. Your father asked me to be Mia's godfather, but then Yingyue took her back to China. I've not been in contact with her."

"Not even when she was at Stanford?" Lara asked.

"No." He tilted his head and gave her a contemplative look. "By the way, how did you find out about Mia?"

Lara frowned. "I'd rather not say… if you don't mind."

He nodded quickly.

"I'm still trying to put all the pieces together," she said. "Do you know if my father was a Macrobian?"

Lance's face remained slack for a moment. Then he must have decided against holding back any longer. "Yes, he was a founding member of the group in Silicon Valley."

"Well, that explains his will and testament then," Lara said grimly. "As his last dying wish, he wanted me to be cryonically preserved until a cure can be found for aplastic anemia."

Lance took a step back and stared at her in shock. "No, that's not possible."

She nodded vehemently. "When I was in China, I was taken prisoner by the Macrobians. My father's mistress, Yingyue, prepared to have me frozen to death. Apparently, my mother is cryonically frozen in tanks at the Macrobian Institute. My dad wanted me to be stored next to her."

Lance's mouth hung open, and he waved his arms emphatically. "No. I don't believe it. Your parents joined up strictly for the science, not the cultish aspects of the group. I distinctly remember your father railing against that cryonics bullshit." He paused and looked into her eyes. "Trust me. Don't let that crazy woman taint the image of your father. He was a good man, and he loved you very much."

Then why would Yingyue try to freeze me? Why would she tell me those things?

"Listen, I have to run," Lance said, glancing at his watch and moving toward the door.

From across the room, Lara could see Rob staring at them

intently. "Wait. Before you go, I need to ask you something," Lara said, brushing a loose hair from her face.

"What is it?" The corners of Lance's lips turned downward at Sanchez approaching them, holding a beer in his hand.

Lara motioned with her head toward Sanchez, who gave her a curious look. "Detective Sanchez and I are working on a plan to clear Rob's name."

Lance grimaced at her.

"Look," Lara said. "I know you agree Rob is innocent and should never have been fired from the FBI. His boss framed him, and we've been unable to dig up any tangible evidence."

Lance took a few steps back and lowered his brow. "I'm really sorry for Rob's situation. But how do you expect me to help?"

Lara took a deep breath. "We want to put together a sting operation to implicate Rob's boss, but we need access to some advanced biotechnology."

"And you expect me to cough up some biotech for your op?" Lance asked, scratching the back of his neck.

"That's what we were hoping."

"Lara, I know I said I'd help you in any way I can. But this crosses the line. After Calvin Westlock died, I made a promise to myself never to mess around with that sort of thing again. If something were to happen to you or the detective, I'd hold myself responsible." He fidgeted with his hands and then said, "We'll catch up more another time, okay?"

With that, Lance walked toward the exit. Lara's shoulders slumped as Rob approached her, his eyes full of hope.

Lara avoided eye contact. "He said no."

Rob didn't respond.

A thought formed in her head. "But I might have someone else to ask..."

"You're not going to do what I think you're going to do," Sanchez said.

"Huh?"

"I don't want you running off to the Langstons to harass them, okay?"

How did he know what I was thinking?

Tapping his foot, he waited for her to acknowledge.

Lara crossed her arms and pressed her lips together.

"I mean it. This case is closed," Sanchez said, waving his hand around.

"Uh huh..." Lara said halfheartedly. She opened her mouth to make her case to visit the Langstons when Sanchez's phone dinged.

He glanced at the screen, and his face paled. "Crap, I gotta run."

"But you just got here..." Lara said, unable to hide the disappointment in her voice. "We need to talk—"

"My sister said something's happened with my mom," he cut her off, a panicked look on his face. "I need to get to the hospital right away. We'll have to talk later."

Lara watched him run out of the bar.

—about the Langstons.

THIRTY-EIGHT

The Confession

October 25, 2028

LARA KNOCKED LOUDLY on the door of the Kalorama mansion for the third time. Waiting for an answer, she clenched and unclenched her fists. Perhaps she should have called first, but she didn't want to give the Langstons any advanced warning. They might have called Detective Sanchez, or worse, the police commissioner, to tattle on her.

When he finds out about this, Sanchez will not be happy with me.

After waiting several minutes, she spotted Molly through the narrow window, coming down the stairs in the foyer, making her way to the front door. The eight-year-old smiled at Lara, unlocked the door, and poked her head out, her silky, straight black hair falling off her shoulder.

"Hi Lara," she said.

"Sweetie, are your parents home?" Lara asked.

Molly nodded and held the door open for Lara to enter. "They're in the backyard. That's why they didn't hear you. Wait here. I'll go get them."

Lara listened as the pitter-patter of Molly's feet made it all the way to the back of the house. The back door opened, and Molly called to her father out in the yard. After a few moments, Julian came into the house, the door slamming behind him. He strode down the hallway and entered the foyer with a stern look on his face.

"Is there something wrong with our payment?" Julian asked, frowning at her.

"Oh, everything is fine on that front," Lara said, smiling warmly in an attempt to break the ice between them. "I just have some follow-up questions about our trip to China. And since you left Hong Kong in such a hurry, we didn't get a chance to talk."

Julian avoided her gaze. "I'm not sure what there's left to talk about. You brought our daughter back, and for that, we're forever grateful."

"Yeah… about that. I need to clarify several pieces of information I learned in the investigation before and after the trip to China."

Julian raised an eyebrow. "And where is the illustrious Detective Sanchez? May I assume you're here on official police business?"

Lara shook her head. "Not exactly. He doesn't know I'm here. I thought it might be wise to exercise some discretion."

"Fine, if you insist." He frowned and then grunted. "If this will take more than a few minutes, I'd prefer to sit down."

"I think it might," Lara said.

Julian grimaced and motioned for Lara to follow him into the sitting room next door. He offered her a seat on the couch and then took his place in an arm chair across from her.

Molly entered the room, carrying a tray with a plate of cookies and two glasses of lemonade. "My mom thought you might be thirsty," she said, smiling at Lara and setting the tray on the coffee table.

"Thank you. That was very kind of her." Lara leaned forward and grabbed two cookies and a glass of lemonade. "What kind of cookies are these?"

"Shortbread cookies dipped in fudge," Molly said. "They're called Thanks-A-Lot cookies. I like them the best of all."

The same Girl Scout Cookies delivered the night of Molly's kidnapping?

Before taking a bite, she stared closely at the cookie, and her eyes widened. They were embossed with Chinese characters.

Chinese? Is Cynthia trying to tell me something? Her skin tingled as a sheen of sweat formed on her face. Then an idea came to her. Does she want me to confront her husband about his knowledge of the kidnapping? Does she guess he was involved?

Julian shooed his daughter out of the room and then turned to Lara. "What do you want to discuss?"

Trying to keep focused, she took a deep breath. "I'd like to start with the anonymous tip," Lara said, flipping open her notebook to remember exactly what she'd written down. "My assistant tracked the source of the video footage to an IP address in Falls Church, Virginia. Specifically to a server at GenTech Industries. Do you know anything about that?"

Julian rubbed his forehead. "Sorry, I'm not a computer person. I don't understand what that means."

Yeah, right.

"That means someone at your company acquired the surveillance footage from TSA and sent it to our hotline. And I'm guessing it was someone with a great deal of clout in this town... I'm thinking it was you, sir. You're the one who reached out to DHS to get the video and then emailed it to our control center from your company."

Julian stared aghast at her.

Lara didn't wait for him to object. "Clearly, you don't know enough to cover your own tracks. There's no point in denying it because I have several other pieces of evidence to suggest that you knew all along who kidnapped your daughter. In fact, maybe you were even involved in the plan."

"That's fucking absurd."

Lara leaned back on the sofa and stared at him with defiance. She didn't actually know for sure if Julian orchestrated the kidnapping. Based on the information she'd learned in China, she was operating on a hunch. "What's absurd is that you thought I wouldn't get to the bottom of your involvement in this case and still hired me. I'm a private investigator. This is what I do."

His face turning bright red, Julian jumped up from his chair and pointed to the door. "I don't know who you think you are, but I run this fucking town." He shook his finger at her, trembling with rage. "If you want to keep your reputation intact, I suggest you leave now and never speak of this again." He stomped his foot and pointed to the door.

Lara crossed her legs, sending a clear signal she wasn't going anywhere. She remained seated and glared back at him with all the ferocity she could muster. "You see, that's where you've underestimated me. Unlike you, I don't give a flying fuck about my reputation in this town. I don't have anything to lose here. So, I think you'd better sit down, Mr. Langston. That is, if you know what's good for you."

He crossed his arms and glowered at her from his spot. "Leave now, or I'll call the police. I'm friends with the police commissioner and the mayor. You must be crazy if you think you're going to string me up on charges for obstruction and making a false report to the police. You'll be sorry for trying to frame me. You're done in this town."

"Frankly, I don't care about the powerful friends you keep. My guess is they will scatter like a flock of terrified birds when they find out you used your own daughter as a pawn. You let her get kidnapped and taken overseas for some reason. Why? They'll be even more shocked when they learn your daughter is one of eight clones, the centerpiece of a Chinese genetic experiment called Metamorphosis run by the Macrobians. What kind of monsters are the Langstons? That's what they'll be asking. They won't give a shit about me. Because I'm a nobody, as you've already pointed out."

He gave her a defiant look but said nothing.

"Don't you make your money off of improving people's

health and wellbeing?" Lara continued. "Hmm, I wonder how your human experimentation on children will go over with your customers. You think when the press gets a hold of this news that your company's stock won't plummet?"

Julian threw up his hands. "My daughter's a clone. So what? You don't have any evidence that I knew about it. I'll end up looking like the victim, a brokenhearted father who learned he was horribly duped by the adoption agency."

Lara flashed him a cheeky smile. "You see, that's where you're wrong. I have hard evidence that Molly is not your legally adopted daughter but rather that she belongs to the Macrobian Institute and is a Chinese citizen. I stole the files from the orphanage during the operation you insisted we conduct with zero advanced intel in broad daylight… you know, the files you probably worked hard to hide deep in the Chinese countryside. And my contact who helped us plan the op? Yeah… he's CIA. He'll vouch for everything I know about you."

Hopefully, he doesn't call my buff. She knew she couldn't count on Hickerson to do anything that wasn't in his interest.

Lara detected a slight pallid color in his face as he resumed his seat. She paused for a moment to study his face. A look of defeat settled in his eyes. "And I bet that your wife doesn't know the full extent of your involvement in Molly's kidnapping or her status as an experimental clone. It's your signature on the contract. I'm guessing you kept it a secret from her. What would your wife do if she found out? So, Mr. Langston, I don't know who you think you are, but I do know you'll be sorry if you don't fully cooperate with me."

After a few moments of tense silence, Julian growled, "What do you want from me?"

"Well, first, I want some answers. Let's start with the past and work our way forward, why don't we? You bought my father's company, Horizon Genomics, in June of 2003. Why?"

Julian's eyes bulged from their sockets. He'd clearly not expected this line of questioning. His mouth hung open, but no words came out.

"You knew my father, Ethan Kingsley, didn't you?"

Mr. Langston, still floundering, gaped at her for a moment. "Uh… I only knew of him. He died before I got the chance to meet him. We were fellow entrepreneurs at the start of a new era in biotechnology. We got into the business when synthetic biology was still time and resource intensive. When he offered to sell me his company for pennies on the dollar, I snapped it up. He died tragically in a car accident only a few weeks after we closed the deal."

"Why did Horizon Genomics sequence my DNA every year from 2009 to 2013?"

"I have no idea what you're talking about. If Horizon Genomics engaged in such activities, I was not aware of them."

"You can't seriously think I believe you," Lara said.

"I don't care what you believe. I run a billion-dollar, multi-national company and do not track the inner workings of all my subsidiaries. If Horizon Genomics sequenced your DNA, it must have won the contract to do so. The U.S. was heavily outsourcing its sequencing to China at the time. Not the best idea for privacy, national security, and such… but quite cheap."

"You and your wife belong to the Macrobians, don't you?" Lara asked, switching gears suddenly. She'd chosen a shock-and-awe strategy in the hopes that he might confess everything. "That's why you were entrusted with a clone baby. And not just any clone baby, but the control for the experiment."

Julian sighed. "Yes, we were founding members. We left the group last year after a falling out."

"What happened?" Lara asked.

"I agreed to parent one of the eight clones, which meant that we had to bring Molly to China each year for testing. Cynthia had no idea why we went to China regularly. In the eighth year, the clones were all supposed to return to Shenzhen for the remainder of their lives. But Cynthia had fallen in love with our daughter, and I changed my mind. I wanted out of the experiment for my wife's sake and was prepared to do anything to make it happen. But that's not how it works with the

Macrobians. Dr. K refused to let me leave the arrangement and threatened to make our involvement in the group public. As you pointed out, that would have sent my company's stock plummeting."

"So, you made a deal."

Julian nodded, staring down at the floor and saying nothing.

Lara furrowed her brow, searching her mind for reasons why Julian would allow his daughter to be kidnapped. "Mr. Langston, what sort of deal did you make?"

"I agreed to do the testing, but this time, instead of us traveling to China, Yingyue would come to collect her from our house to make it look like a kidnapping. To hide the truth from my wife."

"But it wasn't a kidnapping. Molly knew about her trip to China?" Lara asked.

"Yes, Molly knew about it. She thinks of Yingyue as an aunt, and we told her about a special trip. We explained that the trip needed to be a secret, even from her mother. And that's why she was leaving out the window and through the woods. They left shortly after eight in the evening to make the last flight to Hong Kong leaving that night."

That's why she wasn't afraid. That's also why the bed was still made.

Lara wrinkled her nose. "I still don't understand. What sort of deal did you make to get Molly out of the experiment?"

"Yingyue said she would let Molly leave the experiment if I could lure you to China, and she could keep *you with her*," Julian said in a flat voice.

Keep me? Her pulse spiked when she thought of Yingyue preparing her for the cryogenic tank.

Lara's jaw dropped. "Wait, what? You made a deal to keep your daughter in exchange for *me*?"

Julian stared at her blankly. "I'd do it again to protect my family."

"But if Yingyue wanted to have me so badly, why didn't she have me kidnapped herself?" Lara asked.

"She said that was too risky. It's not an easy task for a Chinese national and a member of the Macrobians to bring an adult American woman, an Army Special Forces officer no less, against her will to a foreign country on the other side of the world. That's the sort of thing the FBI and CIA would pick up on right away. When I begged her to let Molly out of the experiment in August, Yingyue saw a target of opportunity. If helped her get you, and she would give me what I wanted."

"You hired me so that I'd go to China to help you, be held hostage, and then be frozen to death?" Lara asked.

"Technically, my wife hired you. Obviously, Cindy didn't know anything about the deal I made with Yingyue. She would never have allowed Molly to be taken out of the country on her own. Making my wife think she'd hired you to get Molly back provided a cover for my involvement. It was a small price to keep our daughter here and my wife happy, don't you think?" He paused, a slight smirk appearing on his face.

Oh, I think Cindy has her suspicions.

Lara sat in silence for a few moments, digesting the information. She'd suspected something like this, but it was another thing to hear Julian confess it to her.

"Mia helped you escape. All's well that ends well, right?" Julian said.

Upon hearing Mia's name, Lara froze for a moment. It hung in the air like a thick fog. No one except Finn, Vik, and Hickerson knew about Mia helping her escape from Yingyue's clutches, and only Hickerson knew her American name. At least that's what she assumed. *Crap. Yingyue must know about Mia working for the CIA. I need to call Hickerson.*

Lara put her hand on her forehead, her heart thumping wildly. "I found my DNA in the fridge at the Institute. Did Yingyue want me for some sort of experiment?"

Julian held out his hands. "I don't know why she wanted you… just that she did, and it was worth more to her than keeping Molly."

"How did the institute get access to my physical DNA? Did you give that to them as part of your deal?"

Julian gave her a smug look. "They don't need a physical sample anymore."

Lara furrowed her brow. "What do you mean they don't need my DNA sample?"

"All they need to synthetically reproduce your physical DNA in a lab is your genomic data. And conveniently, they can find your full DNA sequence in the U.S. National Genomic Database."

Lara's mouth fell open, her lip trembling, her mind racing for the next question. She knew Julian would tolerate her interrogation for only a little bit longer. Lara swallowed hard and shifted in her seat, trying to keep her emotions in check. "Okay, so the plan was to trade me for Molly. To get me to China, you hired me as a private investigator to help find your daughter. I'm not a lawyer, but that sounds like we can add accessory to trafficking and attempted murder to the long list of possible charges."

Fury rose in Julian's eyes. "What are you playing at? I thought you just wanted answers."

Lara narrowed her eyes. "I meant what I said. I'm not here to make trouble. Just reminding you about the secrets I'll be keeping."

"Well, I assume you want something from me… in order to keep quiet about all of this."

Lara nodded. "I need your help with another case I'm working on with Detective Sanchez. If you help me, you have my word I will not expose your involvement in Molly's kidnapping. I'm pretty sure I can get Sanchez to stay quiet as well."

Not only would the detective say nothing about the crimes, he would likely wring her neck for even having this meeting. *What Mr. Langston doesn't know can't hurt him.*

"What sort of help do you need?" Julian asked, his forehead wrinkling.

"We're trying to draw out a dirty FBI agent who peddles stolen defense technology on the black market. My colleague and I want to set up a sting operation, but for that, we need to demo some advanced biotech. Do you have anything we could borrow for this?"

A look of surprise and relief fell across his face. "That's all?"

Lara nodded.

Julian pursed his lips. "Let me give my R&D director a call. I think we might have something that could work. Anything else?"

"One more thing. We need to visit a female inmate in federal prison who has deep ties in the illicit trade ring behind the theft of commercial and military technology. We think our dirty FBI agent has been paying her regular visits at the prison. She might be willing to give us incriminating information on our suspect. But we can't pay her a visit without advanced approval. However, if I were to accompany a lawyer, we could probably get in. Do you know a lawyer who would be willing to help us?"

Mr. Langston nodded stiffly. "Yes, I think I know just the man for the job. Is that all?"

"I think so. If you could help us with these two things, we would be indebted to you for helping us cinch the case," Lara said.

Not sure justice for Rob makes up for the Langstons' crimes, but I'll take it.

"I'll see what I can do." Julian got up from his chair and looked at Lara. "For what it's worth, I'm glad you escaped. I didn't know Yingyue wanted to kill you."

Yeah, right.

Lara got up from the sofa and walked into the foyer. Turning back to Julian, she shook his hand and said goodbye. Once outside on the landing, Lara spoke into her smartphone.

"Watson, call Rob."

"One moment, Ms. Kingsley."

The phone rang a few times, and Lara worried it might go to voicemail.

"Hey Lara, I was just going to call you," Rob answered. "How did it go with the Langstons?"

"We got the tech."

"Really? How did you get him to say yes?"

A few threats and a strong arm.

"I can be persuasive when I want to be," Lara said, wincing at her fudge.

She would eventually tell Rob everything. But for now, they had to focus on solving his case.

"Well, I just got some bad news," Rob said.

"What's that?" Lara asked, not sure if she wanted more bad news at this point.

"MacFarlan is dead. That means we have no choice but to do the sting operation."

"Don't forget about Justyne," Lara said. "She might have a beef with Harry and be willing to give us something. Mr. Langston also agreed to hook me up with a lawyer to get us inside the prison."

"Yeah, but do we really want to depend on her to come through for us?"

Probably not.

THIRTY-NINE

Sting Operation

October 27, 2028

ADJUSTING her comm's earpiece so it didn't pinch, Lara glowered angrily at the long bank of video screens in the cockpit of the windowless van. She and Rob were sitting in the concealed rear compartment, prepping for his long-awaited sting operation.

Lara's face tightened as she inspected the shiny new vehicle, fully equipped with the latest in video, camera, and audio surveillance equipment plus a long list of extras—night vision, thermal imaging, GPS, police and CB radios, telephone connection, computers with wireless Internet, and a combo printer/scanner. On the roof of the van, there was even a 360-degree periscope capable of capturing video and photos from all possible angles. It had that new car smell mixed with Rob's cologne. Though it was a larger van, all the equipment made the space tight. She couldn't avoid brushing her arm or leg against Rob every time she moved.

All courtesy of Rob's shopping spree and my line of credit.

Loki sniffed eagerly at her feet as if he'd located a hidden treasure. Lara glanced down, scowling at the leftover crumbs from something Rob must have eaten earlier.

Despite her anxiety about the sting operation, she couldn't forget what Mr. Langston said about Mia. If he knew Mia helped her escape, her sister's life was in danger. She tucked a few loose hairs behind her ear and peeked at her wearable smartphone. Her jaw tightened. Still no calls from Hickerson. As soon as she'd left the Langstons, she'd left messages, warning him that Mia's cover might be burned.

Would Yingyue actually hurt her own daughter? Lara nodded to herself. That woman was capable of anything.

Lara's eyes shifted back to the monitors. On the first video screen, she could see Vik fidgeting with the zipper on his bomber jacket. He stood next to Detective Franklin, who was dressed down in jeans and a sweatshirt for the undercover mission. Franklin had reluctantly agreed to step in for Sanchez, who remained at his mother's bedside in the hospital.

Between Vik and Franklin, there was a waist-level stack of boxes. The GenTech Industries desktop DNA printer, loaned to them by Mr. Langston, sat on top of the stack. The second video screen showed the door to the warehouse where Chimbo or Harry would arrive for the demonstration.

She glared at Rob and sighed heavily while Rob fiddled with the volume of the video feed from the tiny camera installed inside a button on Detective Franklin's shirt.

"Bravo One, can you hear me?" Rob asked, testing the comms.

"Got you coming in loud and clear," Detective Franklin replied in a low voice.

"Good. We're about twenty minutes out, but stay alert for any unexpected company."

"You think Harry's actually gonna show for this?" Franklin asked.

"I'd give it a fifty-fifty. If Harry doesn't show up, he'll at least send his minion, Chimbo."

Lara eyed Vik nervously, her stomach sizzling with a severe

case of heartburn. She'd objected at first to his direct involvement due to the potential danger, but Vik convinced Lara he could handle playing an active role in the sting operation. He'd cleverly reminded her about his swift recovery from his panicked state at the institute and his successful escape. On both counts, he'd come out ahead of her.

I'm the one who got caught.

In the end, Vik was the only one who knew how to operate the DNA printer with any competence. He'd spent some time around Maggie's DNA sequencer and synthesizer in her laboratory and felt confident he could explain how it worked. Unlike Rob or Lara, he would also not be recognized by Harry or Chimbo. It drove Lara crazy that she had to stay in the van with Rob for surveillance and as emergency backup instead of being in the middle of the action.

Rob looked up from the control panel and grinned at her like a little boy on Christmas morning, trying out his new toys for the first time.

"I still can't believe you spent seventy thousand dollars," Lara said, giving him a hard smile. "Do we really need all this?"

Rob shrugged nonchalantly. "You threw your credit card at me and didn't want to be bothered with the details. You told me to get it done. Then you went off to China and were out of pocket for days. So, I had to make decisions without you. I'm sorry you don't like them."

Lara crossed her arms. "I told you to set up the sting operation… I didn't say to spend my entire fortune."

Clenching his teeth, Rob waved his hands around. "Lara, I worked for more than ten years at the FBI. This is how we do sting operations, okay?"

Lara scoffed at him. "Well, this is not how PIs do sting operations. Try sitting in a beat-up car with a camera and audio amplifier." Suddenly, Loki's ears pricked up. She paused for a moment and watched Loki, who sat at alert, his body tense. "Did you hear that?"

"I can't hear anything over your incessant complaining," Rob said. "We're not gonna catch Harry with a few pieces of used surveillance equipment. Lara, he knows what he's doing... and we need to act like we do, too."

Loki let out a low growl.

Giving her dog a quick look, Lara turned back to Rob and threw up her hands. "And spending tens of thousands of dollars is your proof you know what you're doing? This operation feels slapped together at the last minute. We've not thought this through. Something is bound to go wrong... even with the fancy equipment."

Rob glared at her, pinching his lips. "Look. We had a limited window of opportunity with Chimbo, okay? I wasn't going to lose that because you were off gallivanting across China with your boyfriend."

"Are you freaking kidding me?" Lara asked, baring her teeth. Her ears filled with heat, and her cheeks flushed. "You make it sound like I was wasting my time in China while you were here doing the important work. I helped secure the safe return of an eight-year-old girl against all odds. And oh yeah... I nearly got killed doing it."

Rob's nostrils flared. "I'm sorry you think I crossed some invisible line of permission. I did what you told me to do, and now we need to focus on the operation. Maybe look at this van as a long-term investment in your business. After all, how many PIs can say an FBI agent set them up with top-of-the-line surveillance capability?"

"Okay, to be clear, you didn't 'set' me up." Lara made quote signs with her fingers. "Kingsley Investigations paid for this stuff, not you." Loki nipped her ankle, but she pushed him away.

"But I picked it out and set it up based on my years of expertise," Rob said in a defensive tone. "You couldn't have done it yourself."

Lara rolled her eyes. "All that expertise and you went out

and bought a white van? Could you be any more predictable, Droneman?"

Rob winced at the use of his old call sign. "You think a black van would be better? We might as well announce we're with law enforcement from a megaphone."

Lara pulled up her nose. "What's hilarious is that you think you were being stealthy just because you put fake HVAC company lettering on the outside. But it's so freaking obvious."

"Why don't we talk about the second-rate technology you rounded up for this operation," Rob said. "DNA printers are so yesterday."

"Maybe if you hadn't burned your bridge with Lance by breaking his daughter's heart, we wouldn't have to beg Mr. Langston for help."

Loki yipped at the side van door, but Lara paid him no notice.

"Sure, sure. I'm to blame for everything," Rob growled. "Just put it on my tab of the long list of things you can't forgive me for."

Lara flinched, her ears pounding. "You're just too thick to understand this DNA printer is a cut above the rest on the market. Not only does it get better accuracy than the current models, the strands are ten times longer than the best printer today, and it produces DNA at a faster pace. That means less stitching together of segments in the lab—something that requires skill and practice. This printer is so advanced, you can use it to store information in DNA—making this machine in high demand by the IT sector."

"Oh, so you're saying even a moron like me could produce DNA using this machine," Rob said.

A lump formed in her throat as regret washed over her.

We shouldn't be fighting like this. Not here.

Before Lara had a chance to respond, the side door of the van slid open with a loud thunk. Lara jerked her head to see a dark shadow of a man standing in the opening. Loki bared his teeth, growled, and barked. He tried to lunge forward but was held back by his leash, which was tied to Lara's chair. A jolt of adrenaline shot through her body as she stared into the calloused eyes of Harry Cogan.

Harry held a gun in his right hand, trained on her chest. In his left hand, he held a small remote with a red button, his thumb hovering over it. Her heart pounded in her chest. Lara knew what the remote was for. She'd seen plenty of trigger devices for bombs in her time in the military.

Where are the explosives that go with that remote?

"Nice van," Harry said in a low voice. "A half-decent attempt at out-copping a cop, but not good enough, I'm afraid."

Rob leaned forward, and Harry raised his left hand.

"Don't try any fast moves," Harry said. "If you do, I've strapped enough C4 to the bottom of the van to blow us all to smithereens. And I'd prefer to keep my body parts intact if at all possible."

"What the fuck do you want?" Rob asked, gritting his teeth, his face a shade paler than before. Loki tried to launch himself at Harry again but was jerked backward by his leash. He yelped as he flopped to the floor, but got back up, alert and growling in Harry's direction.

"Isn't that clear? You should have ended your investigation weeks ago and gone about your merry way. I tried to warn you what would happen, but you thought you could outsmart me. I know all your operational signatures."

"What do you mean?" Rob asked.

"It wasn't hard. You used the same tricks on Fiddler. The half-baked pseudonym. The offer of access to advanced technology. The demo. I anticipated each move down to every last detail. And all this time, you thought you were conducting a sting. I used Chimbo's pseudonym specifically to lure *you* here." Harry laughed. "I played you from the start."

"Did you sell technology to the Macrobian Institute in China?" Lara asked, searching his face for a reaction.

How's that for a distraction?

A tiny muscle in his cheek twitched, but Harry said nothing in response.

"Why were you stalking me several weeks ago?" Lara asked, pressing further.

A glint of something appeared in Harry's eyes. His roguish smile sent shivers up and down her spine.

He shot her an apologetic smile. "Lara, I'm really sorry you got caught up in this. It wasn't part of the plan. I'll have some explaining to do."

Part of what plan?

Harry grimaced. "I've always had a soft spot for you, Rob, but that ends today. I'm cleaning up loose ends—you are the last target on my list."

Harry was about to shut the van door, when Lara shouted, "Wait!"

He slid it back open and looked at her expectantly.

"Who is BlackDragon?" Lara asked.

"Wouldn't you like to know," Harry sneered.

"If you're going to kill us anyway, what's the harm in telling us?"

"Better safe than sorry." Harry smirked at her. Loki growled and tried to lurch at him. Fearing what Harry might do to him, Lara pulled the dog back.

"Agent Carter is on to you," Rob said. "If you kill us, he'll bring the weight of the FBI down on you. You'll never get away with it."

Harry brushed Rob's threat away like it was a fly. "Agent Carter won't be talking to anybody."

Lara winced at the thought of Agent Carter's grim fate.

Harry gave them a malicious grin, lifted his trigger hand in the air, and then slammed the van door shut. His footsteps pounded the pavement as he ran away from the van, putting distance between himself and the vehicle. Rob and Lara locked eyes and leaped to their feet. She bent over, removed Loki's leash, and reached for the side door, her palms sweaty.

"We need to get out of here," Lara said, grabbing the handle of the side door. She tried to turn it, but it wouldn't budge.

She looked at Rob, frantic fear overwhelming her senses. "It's jammed."

FORTY

The Boss

"Lara, let's go," Rob shouted, hitting a button on the console and pushing the back doors as they swung open. "Now!"

He jumped out, motioned urgently, and held his hand out for her. Lara whipped her body around Rob's chair as fast as she could, grabbed his hand, and jumped down to the street. Seconds later, Loki leaped from the van and sprinted toward the warehouse, his leash dragging behind him.

"Loki, no!" she shouted, her stomach lurching in her dog's direction. She stopped to watch as Loki disappeared into an alley, barking wildly at something. Cupping her hands, she screamed, "Loki, come!"

Rob yanked Lara's arm so hard it nearly came out of its socket. He pulled her with him and sprinted in the opposite direction toward a parked car. When they reached it, he shoved her behind the car and pushed her down onto the cement, protecting her with his body. As they both covered their heads, the van detonated into a massive fireball, sending debris into the air.

The back bumper landed only a few feet from them and tumbled a few times, coming to a stop only a few inches away from their location. Moments later, the gas tank exploded in a secondary blast, adding to the blaze that ravaged the van and all the expensive equipment inside it.

Amidst the noise and vibrations, Lara peered around the corner of the car. Her heart pounded through her chest, fear coursing through her body. *Where's Loki?*

Rob jumped to his feet and pulled her up. "Quick, Harry's getting away." He scanned the area, looking for signs of Harry, and then pointed to the alley between the warehouse and another building. "He must have gone that way." Drawing his gun, he ran down the alley at top speed. Loki's barks echoed in the distance.

That's where Loki ran.

Pulling out her pistol, Lara followed after Rob, close on his heels. When they reached an intersection with another alley, he pointed two fingers in a different direction.

"You keep going that way," Rob said. "I'm going to see if we can head him off around this corner."

"Good idea," Lara rasped, her chest heaving. She sprinted down the alley, keeping her eyes wide open for any signs of movement and hoping for a sign of her dog. When she reached the edge of the building, she pressed her body up against the side and peeked around the corner.

Two gunshots rang through the air, sending tremors through her body. *Where are Vik and Detective Franklin?*

Following the noise, Lara turned right and ran along the building as fast as she could. As she poked her head around the next corner, she saw Rob on the ground, slumped against a dumpster. He held his right arm tightly to his chest as blood trickled through his fingers from his shoulder. His face was as pale as a ghost, but it betrayed more than shock and fear. His brown eyes were also full of rage.

Lara edged out from the cover of the building and caught sight of Harry ten feet away. Looking like an executioner, he was facing Rob with his body rigid and his gun pointed at Rob's head.

Lara burst into the open space, screaming, "Put your gun

down, or I'll blow your head off!" She planted her feet and aimed her gun at the back of his head.

Turning to look at her, Harry kept his gun trained on Rob. A cruel grimace formed on his face and something sinister flashed in his eyes. "Wrong again, sweetheart."

A twig snapped behind her, and an unfamiliar musky, male scent wafted past her nose. From behind, Lara felt the barrel of a gun press hard into the bottom of her neck and a thick arm wrap around her neck. She craned her head slightly, moved her eyes as far as she could, and glimpsed a familiar short man in his late twenties. The kid was none other than Rob's former teammate, Chimbo.

Police sirens wailed in the distance, causing Harry to move slightly.

Where are Detective Franklin and Vik? They must have heard the noise. And where's Loki?

"Lara, you don't need to die today," Harry said, an eerie smoothness to his tone. "You're not my target. You don't need to be collateral damage. Put the gun down, and I'll let you go free."

Yeah, right.

Keeping her eyes on Harry's face, Lara contemplated her options. If she attempted any maneuver, she'd have to be fast enough to catch Harry off guard and not get shot by either of them. To do that, she needed to remain as calm as possible and appear compliant until the exact second before making her move.

"Lara, don't listen to them. They'll kill you, too," Rob cried.

Lara took a deep breath and lowered her gun, as if to surrender. Chimbo released his grip on her neck and backed away slightly. Then she raised both hands in the air and slowly bent over to place the pistol on the ground.

Harry shifted his attention back to Rob as the sirens grew louder. Lara had only a few seconds to make her next move. One miscalculation and both she and Rob would be dead.

Placing the gun on the ground, Lara peered behind her to get a better view of Chimbo. He was standing two feet away from her with his gun pointed at her back.

Without hesitation, Lara straightened out her body and pivoted to the left. She ducked down low and swung her left leg around, making contact on the back of his calf and knocking him off his feet. He stumbled backward, his gun arm flailing. As he lost his balance, he fired a shot, but it missed her. She brought her right leg around and up and kicked him in the left arm. The gun fell out of his hand and skittered across the pavement, coming to a stop a few feet from them.

Chimbo and Lara both scrambled for the gun, Chimbo on his hands and knees and Lara diving through the air. She crashed on the cement, and he managed to grab it first. But not before Lara's hand clamped tightly around his. She kneed him in the groin, catching him off guard. He recovered quickly and grabbed her hair, pulling so hard, tears sprang from her eyes. Her hand released the gun, and he was about to get the upper hand.

An unmistakable growl came from behind them. Before they could react, Loki sprang into the air and landed on Chimbo, sinking his teeth into his arm. Chimbo screeched in pain.

"Get him off me! Get him off me!" he screamed.

"Loki, leave it," Lara shouted.

Loki released Chimbo's arm, leaving the kid in the fetal position, holding his bloodied arm. He looked up at Lara, his ears alert and hair on end, waiting for her command.

Lara glimpsed the gun on the ground and was about to jump for it.

"Don't move," Harry snarled from behind. "Call your attack dog off now if you want him to live."

She froze for a moment and looked down at her pup. "Loki, go," she said, pointing her trembling hand. His ears drooping, he gave her an uncertain look. "Go on! Go find it!" Reluctantly, Loki slinked away and disappeared into the alley. Lara exhaled with relief.

She turned around slowly to face Harry. He stared directly in her eyes, his gun pointed at her chest. The roaring of engines and police sirens sounded near the perimeter of their location. Brakes screeched, and doors slammed.

Backup.

"Surrender now, Harry, before someone else gets hurt. You're surrounded. There's no way out," Lara shouted.

Harry gave her a strange look and took aim at her. Unable to reach the gun several feet away, Lara faced him head on and braced for the hit. In the last second, Harry shifted his aim toward the ground where Chimbo was lying and fired two shots. For a moment, Lara stood there in shock, staring at Chimbo's lifeless body. Red splotches appeared on Chimbo's chest.

Then he turned to Rob and aimed the gun at his head. Lara lunged forward as Harry pulled the trigger, screaming, "NO!"

Click. Click.

Lara tumbled to the ground, startled by the lack of a gunshot. Confused, Harry stared at his gun for a moment, the color draining from his face at the realization. He was out of bullets. Harry lowered his arm, sprinted past Lara and around the corner, and disappeared.

She got up, walked over to Chimbo, crouched down, and felt for a pulse. He was dead. Then she rushed to Rob's side and inspected his wound.

"Are you okay?" she asked, her voice quivering.

"I think so." Rob gave her a delirium-induced grin. "I was right about Harry. Now if only we'd proved it sooner…" His voice trailed off.

Detective Franklin came running around the corner along with Loki. Her dog ran over to Rob and began licking him, causing him to laugh through his pain.

"Which direction did Harry go?" Franklin asked, breathing heavily.

"He went that way," she said, pointing to the corner, still in a daze about what had happened. Lara slumped her shoulders, certain they wouldn't catch him. Harry was smart enough to have a decent escape plan, especially if he planned to eliminate his accomplice. Tears welled in her eyes as she thought about how close she came to losing Rob.

Franklin motioned for a few uniforms to chase after Harry.

Suddenly, panic spread throughout her body.

"Where's Vik?" she asked Franklin, pain in her chest from the adrenaline.

"Safe and sound, sitting in one of the cruisers. He whined about it, but I told him to stay put until the danger passed."

Lara heaved a breath of relief. "Thanks for taking care of him."

"No problem." Detective Franklin grimaced. "Um… I have to tell you something else. While Vik and I were waiting in the warehouse, I got a text from the medical examiner."

"From Caroline Stevens?" Lara asked.

Detective Franklin nodded.

"Why?"

Rob's eyes opened and squinted at them with interest.

"She found a dismembered body in her recycling bin this morning," Franklin said, not hiding his disgust.

Dismembered body?

Lara's eyes bulged. "What? Who?"

Looking at Rob and then back at Lara, Franklin paused as if he were about to deliver some bad news. "I'm sorry, guys. I'm afraid someone *got rid* of your friend, Agent Carter."

Shit. Caroline must be beside herself.

Lara hung her head, a pit forming in her stomach. "Harry mentioned we wouldn't be hearing from him again. I was hoping it was bluster." Turning to Rob, she said, "I'm so sorry… I know you were friends."

Rob slouched against the dumpster and groaned, tears welling in his eyes. "I knew something wasn't right when I didn't hear from him… I should have reached out, but… he must have found something on Harry. That's the only reason Harry would play his cards in the open, burning his career at the FBI, and going on the run." Rob covered his face with his hands.

"What?" Lara asked.

He looked up, swallowing hard. "We have plenty of proof that Harry's the dirty cop since he killed Chimbo and possibly Carter, but we still don't have evidence to clear my name."

"Proving Harry's bad news doesn't get you off the hook with the FBI?" Lara asked, her eyes widening.

Rob shook his head. "They can always say we were in it together. Maybe I'll get even more heat over this."

Lara touched his good arm. "Don't lose hope. We're not done with this case. Not by a long shot. We might have one more card to play… Justyne may still have a copy of Fiddler's folder."

Two EMTs came running down the alley with a stretcher and medical supplies.

"That's supposed to make me feel better?" Rob asked, wincing in pain. "You're pretty much saying that my vindication at the FBI rests in Justyne's hands… I'm sure Harry would have struck a deal with her in exchange for her silence."

Well, hopefully she wants revenge on Harry now.

FORTY-ONE

Sweet Revenge

October 28, 2028

LARA FIDGETED with her sleeve as she sat in a chair in the visitor's area watching the short, balding man argue with the six-foot-tall warden of the Federal Corrections Institute in Hazelton. Staring at the back of the lawyer's head, she contemplated whether or not Mr. Langston had broken his word to help her. She couldn't imagine this man, who had introduced himself to her as Douglas L. Jones, esquire and attorney at law, to be a proper employee of the Langstons. He simply didn't look the part.

Maybe he's the guy who handles their dirty work.

The lawyer wore a coffee-stained white shirt, a worn brown wool suit with patches on his sleeves, and a gold Rolex watch that was probably a fake. He had apologized to Lara for his ragged appearance, claiming a woman had spilled coffee on him earlier that morning and he didn't have an extra shirt in his car.

Pretending to read a magazine, Lara overheard him demanding an exception for the unplanned visit and claiming his client had decided to hire new counsel. When the warden balked at the request, the lawyer warned of the potential consequences of denying inmates access to legal counsel.

But this will only work if Justyne wants to meet with me.

Lara's stomach tied itself in knots as she considered the odds of Justyne's cooperation. The interview was their last shot at vindicating Rob. The last known copy of Fiddler's folder was missing or destroyed. General MacFarlan, Agent Carter, and Chimbo were dead. That left Justyne and Fiddler as the only two people known to have incriminating information on Harry. Even if Lara were willing to confront Fiddler to ask for his help, she didn't think the crazy scientist was up to the task. After bumping into Anita, Lara had made some calls to make sure Fiddler was okay and learned that the old scientist was spinning out of control and had to be sedated.

Justyne is our last chance.

Lara looked up to see how things were progressing. She lifted her eyebrow as the lawyer pulled out his bar card and handed it to the security attendant. After a few moments of negotiation, Mr. Jones motioned for Lara to join him at the booth. She leaped from her seat, her pulse jumping slightly.

Justyne agreed to see me?

"And this is my assistant, Ms. Lara Kingsley. She'll also need to be present in the meeting with Ms. Marsh."

"Ma'am, I'll need to see your driver's license," the security attendant said in a nasally tone.

Lara produced her driver's license from her wallet and gave the attendant as innocent a smile as possible.

After a few moments, the attendant said, "Okay, please have a seat and wait while we process the request. Of course, we'll have to check with the inmate for final approval."

Lara stood there paralyzed for a moment, her brow furrowed at the words she just heard. Then she realized they'd only passed the first obstacle. Her shoulders slumping, she followed the lawyer back into the visitor's seating area and took a seat.

Rubbing the back of her neck, she glanced at her smartphone to see if she'd missed any calls. Hickerson had still not gotten back to her about Mia, and that meant her newfound sister remained in danger. Her stomach churned at the thought of something happening to Mia before Lara got a chance to know her better. At first, Lara had acted to warn Hickerson, believing she owed Mia for saving her life. But the idea that she was no longer alone in the world had grown on her.

Another hour passed before the attendant called on them again. The lawyer rose from his chair and approached the booth. A moment later, he returned, holding two green plastic cards in his hands.

"Ms. Marsh agreed to see us," he said, a hint of surprise in his eyes, handing her a visitor pass. "We'll be meeting her in one of the attorney meeting rooms. They've already retrieved her from her cell."

The guard standing at the security door motioned for them to follow him and gave the attendant in the booth a nod. Just then, Lara's smartphone buzzed with a text from Rob.

DOES IT FEEL LIKE HARRY'S CLEANING HOUSE?

She replied:

WHAT DO YOU MEAN?

Rob texted:

MACFARLAN. CARTER. CHIMBO.
WHO ELSE KNOWS ABOUT HIS TIES TO THE BLACK MARKET?

Justyne, Linda, and Fiddler. Interesting theory, but would Harry kill them off too?

"Ms. Kingsley, are you coming or not?" the lawyer asked, standing by the door with his brow furrowed.

"Yeah, sorry."

The attendant buzzed them in, and they entered a long hallway with several doors, each marked with a number and a sign warning them about the presence of security cameras. The security guard pointed to the last door at the end of the hallway.

The guard cleared his throat. "These rooms are monitored with video surveillance cameras with no sound for attorney-client privacy. The inmate is cuffed to the table and will be unable to harm you. If you have any issues or concerns, just knock hard on the door, and I'll be right there."

Lara followed the lawyer into the room. Slumped in her metal chair, Justyne sat on the other side of the table wearing a bright orange jumpsuit. Her black hair was neatly tucked into a tight bun. For once, Justyne's face wore no makeup but, instead, several fresh bruises. She stared sullenly at Lara with the same piercing blue eyes and grasped an unopened Snickers bar in her hand.

Wait, didn't Harry bring candy bars for Justyne…

The lawyer pulled out both chairs, the metal screeching against the linoleum floor, and then took a seat across from Justyne.

Lara sat down next to him and offered Justyne a half-smile. "What happened to your face?" she asked.

"Lara, it's so nice of you to come see me," Justyne said, ignoring the question and gritting her teeth. "I've missed our little chats." Her tone was laced with chilling sarcasm.

"Did you get in a fight or something?" Lara asked, disregarding Justyne's nasty attitude.

"When I saw you requested a meeting, my heart nearly leaped with delight." Justyne gestured to the lawyer and shook her head. "And to think, all the trouble you went through to make this happen. It's just too bad that I'm not in the mood to help you with whatever you came here for." Justyne smiled defiantly.

"Where did you get that candy bar?" Lara asked, not allowing Justyne to get under her skin.

Surely, she didn't agree to meet with me just to tell me this. She wants to talk about something.

Justyne ignored the question. "I heard about your little trip to China. Did you see the exoskeletons we sold to the Macrobian Institute?" She grinned, opening the candy bar. "MacFarlan gave Harry the blueprints right before his arrest, and we re-engineered them to be even better. Now we're the sole supplier of the suits on the Dark Web. Even the Russians are buying them from us."

I won't let her get to me.

Lara nodded dismissively. "I wouldn't eat that if I were you," she said, pointing at the candy bar. Her face remained slack despite the number of thoughts racing through her mind.

Well, that's confirmed, then. Yingyue was a customer of Harry's.

"What's it to you?" Justyne asked, her eyes narrowing.

"Didn't Harry give that to you when he came to see you a week ago?" Lara asked, tilting her head and pointing to the candy bar.

Justyne lifted an eyebrow, thickly grown in after months of not getting waxed. "And what if he did?"

"Have you eaten one and lived to tell the tale?" Lara asked, giving Justyne a slight smirk.

"No, I haven't." Justyne wrinkled her forehead and inspected the chocolate bar. "I've spent most of the past week in solitary confinement, if you must know."

"Well, then I wouldn't eat that if I were you," Lara said, crossing her arms and giving her a hard smile.

"Harry wouldn't try to harm me," Justyne snapped, raising the candy bar to her mouth.

"Would you be surprised if I told you MacFarlan and Chimbo are dead?" Lara clasped her hands together.

Justyne's eyes bulged. She dropped the candy bar, and her hand froze in place, hovering over the table. "What?"

"Someone got to the general at Fort Leavenworth… paid off a guard to shoot him. He died a few days ago. And Harry shot Chimbo right in front of me. He tried to kill Rob, too. I'm pretty sure he's coming for you next."

Justyne's eyes widened.

"Just how certain are you about Harry's loyalty? Aren't you in here because of him?"

"No, I'm in here because of you." Justyne pointed her long, thin finger at Lara.

Lara shrugged. "Meh. Not really. I did solve the case in the end, but it was Harry who delivered Fiddler's folder of evidence about you to the authorities. So, he's the one who got you locked up… admittedly, you didn't help yourself that much when you tried to kill me. But Harry has gotten off scot-free. And all he does for you is bring you candy bars? My question for you is, why aren't you willing to rat him out?"

Lara paused to watch Justyne's facial reaction. The woman's face remained emotionless, but her color was several shades paler. Licking her lips, she eyed the candy bar one more time.

"Can we cut through the crap and get down to business?" Lara asked.

"Okay," Justyne said, her tone a few notches cooler. "Why are you here?"

"I'm here because I need to clear Rob's name."

"And I suppose you think I can help with that."

"Yes," Lara said. "I think you have information that could help us."

"Wouldn't you rather know why I killed Sully?" Justyne asked, blinking her eyes.

I'm not taking the bait. I'm not taking the bait.

Lara's body tensed. *It doesn't matter why Justyne killed Sully. He's dead, and nothing can bring him back.*

A malicious smile split Justyne's face. "I killed Sully because he was getting too close to figuring everything out."

Lara ignored the taunt, but her mind drifted to the piece of paper with three names. *KillerBot. CyberShop. BlackDragon.*

"So, you admit that you and Harry were working together to sell stolen technology on the Dark Web."

"Sure, why not." Justyne tilted her head and winked at Lara. "But good luck proving it."

"I need you to help me prove it," Lara said.

"After Sully was out of the picture, Harry asked me to follow you—to see if you knew what Sully had on him," Justyne said, her tone boastful.

"And that's why you wanted to work with me so badly," Lara said.

Maybe she'll cooperate better if I follow her lead.

"You were much harder to trick than your boyfriend. He bought everything Harry fed him—hook, line, and sinker. The perfect fall guy for our operation. Rob didn't even see it coming, did he?"

Lara's ears felt hot, her blood pressure rising. "Takes a patsy to know one. Aren't you the perfect fall girl for Harry, too?" she asked, watering the seed she'd planted earlier. "What has he promised you? Why are you protecting him?"

Justyne frowned deeply. The irony was apparently not lost on her.

Lara continued before she could respond. "You took a file from Sully's storage unit, didn't you... that night when you hit me over the head? It was the evidence he had on the black market operation you, Harry, your sister, and MacFarlan were building, with ties to Russia and China."

"My big boss wanted to get rid of you from the start," Justyne blurted.

BlackDragon?

"Who's your big boss?" Lara asked, a shiver running down her spine. "BlackDragon?"

"I resisted the order until you finally connected all the dots," Justyne said. "Initially, I didn't think you posed much of a threat. And I was really starting to like you... until you nosed around my office and found Sully's remote. That's when I knew I had to get rid of you."

"If your big boss wants me dead so badly, why didn't Harry just kill me during our confrontation yesterday?" Lara asked. "He had every opportunity to get rid of me, but he shot Chimbo dead instead." Lara shuddered as she thought about how close she came to getting shot to death. And to losing Rob.

"The big boss must still have plans for you. Otherwise, yes… you would be dead."

What plans?

Ignoring the barb, Lara pressed onward with her mission. "Do you have Sully's file or not?"

Justyne sat silent for several moments.

Lara paused to wait for a response, but none came. "Well, if you don't talk, I'm sure Fiddler will help me." She started to get up from the table.

"Fiddler's dead," Justyne said, a nasty smirk forming on her face.

Lara froze midair, gaped at her, and sat back down, sinking into her chair. "How come I didn't hear anything about that?"

"The news hasn't made the rounds yet. He died this morning. My sister Linda heard about it and called me to tell me someone had replaced his sedative with… wait for it… botulinum toxin." She smiled broadly.

"Do you think Harry has any of the toxin leftover? If so, I bet you and your sister are next," Lara said with confidence.

Justyne's smile disappeared.

"Harry is tying up loose ends and is likely on his way out of the country. I bet he thought you'd have eaten that candy bar before today. Do you think he went to see Linda, too?" She studied Justyne's face.

For the first time during their conversation, there was real fear in Justyne's eyes. All of a sudden, she looked smaller in her orange jumpsuit and metal chair. Her lip quivered, and her free hand began to shake.

Justyne's eyes narrowed. "If I help you, I'd want something in exchange."

"What do you want?" Lara asked, hoping she could make it happen.

"I want you to test that candy bar for poison, and make sure Linda is safe."

Lara nodded, relieved at her requests. "Sure, we can do that."

"And I want my sister Linda transferred to this prison to

serve the rest of her sentence here. If you can make that happen, you'll get your folder."

"I want to see the folder first," Lara said.

Justyne slapped her hand flat on the table and met Lara's eyes. "No sister, no folder." She wasn't backing down.

"How do I know you still have it?" Lara asked.

"I guess you'll just have to trust me… like old times." Justyne flashed her teeth, a nervous edge to her smile. "Oh, and if you can't make it happen within a week, the deal is off the table."

"A week? But there's no way I can make it happen that quickly."

Justyne pointed at the smartphone on Lara's wrist. "You better get to it, then."

FORTY-TWO

The Funeral

November 3, 2028

DRESSED in thick black coats over their Sunday bests, Lara huddled with Finn under a large black umbrella, reciting the Lord's Prayer with the large crowd. The deep, sad sound of nearly fifty people speaking in unison seemed to penetrate her skin down to the bone, the rhythm of the prayer vibrating through her body. Barely touching each other, they stood just close enough to keep themselves dry from the bitter cold downpour.

Next to them, Rob and Maggie squeezed together awkwardly under another umbrella, and further down, Vik and Shanaya snuggled under theirs as newlyweds tended to do.

The sea of wet, black clothes, umbrellas, and solemn faces around them matched the dreariness of the occasion. They gathered at the St. Mary's Catholic Cemetery for the Rite of Committal to mourn the passing of Sanchez's mother and commit her body to the earth. Maria Sanchez had fought hard during her last months, but eventually succumbed to the cancer.

I need to talk to Sanchez about Justyne.

A deep melancholy pressing on her shoulders, Lara peered over at Sanchez and his large family. They were standing in a cluster behind the Catholic priest dressed in his official robes.

Lara had called Sanchez as soon as she left the prison. But he didn't pick up right away, so she called Detective Franklin instead. His partner was the one who told her the bad news about Sanchez's mother passing away and asked her why she was calling during his time of need.

Dammit Maggie. You think you could call me with the news.

Lara found it strange how life often ran its own course, without rhyme or reason, as if to remind humans they were not in control of anything and planning a future was futile. The timing of Sanchez's mother's death could not have been worse for Rob's case. The promise of his vindication now hung in the balance of Justyne's whims. And she'd given Lara a tight deadline, one that didn't work well with the natural course of events.

Lara stared down at her hands, trying to keep her eyes from welling up. It was her second funeral in the past two days; the first one was for Agent Carter. Somehow the first one was much harder. Agent Carter was young. And a good friend of Rob's. But apparently also Caroline's fiancé.

At the funeral, Lara learned that Agent Carter had just proposed to her after several years of an on-and-off-again romance. She shuddered at the memory of consoling Caroline, who became hysterical during the service and ran out of the church. Caroline had been the one to find what remained of Agent Carter in her own recycling bin. That gruesome image would be seared into her brain forever.

The fact that Lara had missed the one-year anniversary of Sully's death on October 19, 2028, further dampened her mood. In all the chaos of the past few weeks, it had completely slipped her mind. Although she'd been on the plane headed back from China on the day, she felt guilty for not doing anything special yet. Lately, she felt scattered about everything. Since her conversation with Justyne several days ago, only one thought could keep Lara's attention for very long.

I need to talk to Sanchez.

When she spoke to Detective Franklin, Lara relayed everything she'd learned from Justyne and the demands she made in exchange for providing them evidence against Harry. Detective Franklin came by her house immediately to pick up the candy bar Justyne gave Lara for testing. He also called Linda's prison to see if she'd received any packages and learned from the warden that a man matching Harry's description had delivered a box of candy bars. Thankfully, it hadn't made it through inspection. Franklin requested they hold off on delivering the goods to Linda until further notice and send him one for testing based on an open case he was tracking.

Unfortunately, Franklin had suggested they wait for Sanchez to work the prison transfer angle. Unlike his partner, as a junior detective he didn't have any clout with the D.C. Mayor or other key players they would need to rally to make it happen. But Sanchez had been offline for the past few days, making funeral arrangements and managing his family. The clock was ticking, and they had only one day left to meet Justyne's deadline.

Father Michael delivered the final blessing over the grave from the refuge of a giant golf umbrella. Lara tried to listen for once, but the loud patter of the raindrops on her own umbrella drowned out his words.

Standing at the head of his family as the eldest son, the detective's face was stoic, revealing none of the pain residing within him. Next to him stood his four siblings from oldest to youngest. Behind them stood their spouses and a gaggle of children. A large group of uniformed police officers including the police commissioner and Detective Franklin gathered beside the family to pay their respects.

After sprinkling the open grave with holy water and incense, Father Michael motioned to Sanchez. With a solemn face, he grabbed the spade, shoveled wet soil onto her grave, and said his final goodbye. Then he handed it to his younger brother. His three sisters each dropped single white roses onto their mother's casket below, tears trickling down their faces.

The rain slowed to a drizzle. When the priest concluded the ceremony with a prayer, the crowd offered their condolences and dispersed. After some time passed, Sanchez came over to Lara, his head hung low, his clothes drenched with rain. Maggie took her umbrella and held it over him while Rob sought shelter under Lara's umbrella, crowding Finn.

How cozy this is.

"Detective, I'm extremely sorry for your loss," Lara said.

The others joined in offering their condolences.

Sanchez brushed off their well wishes. "Guys, thanks for your thoughts, but I'm okay. My mom was suffering, and it nearly killed me to watch her in that kind of pain for so long. Now she's at peace. I'll be fine, okay?"

The group nodded solemnly.

Sanchez turned to Lara and gave her a half-smile. "I heard about the failed sting operation. Thank God no one got hurt." He clapped Rob on the back. "Really sorry about being unable to clear you, man. I definitely wanted to help you get your job back and put that dirty, son-of-a-bitch cop in jail."

"We might still have a chance," Lara said, seizing the moment. "That's why I wanted to talk to you. There's a new possibility to vindicate Rob."

Finn jabbed her in the ribs, signaling for her to stop. She glared at him long enough to catch his look of disapproval.

Sanchez will appreciate the distraction. He wants to think about something else.

"I'm listening," Sanchez said with an attentive look.

Lara bit her lip. "I visited Justyne in prison several days ago. She claims she has a copy of the folder of evidence Fiddler gathered on Harry. The one she stole from Sully's storage unit. The same one Agent Carter found in the mail room at the FBI. We think the information will demonstrate Harry's role in the drone show and help clear Rob. It was good enough for Harry to destroy it... and to take out Agent Carter for, so..."

Rob winced at the mention of his friend's name.

Sanchez gave her a skeptical look. "What does she want in return?"

Lara took a quick breath. "She wants her sister Linda to be transferred to her prison so they can serve out their time together."

Sanchez frowned. "Hmm… I don't like it."

"She gave me until tomorrow to make it happen," Lara added, ready to wince at the detective's angry response.

"Tomorrow? How the fuck are we supposed to get that done?" He looked at his watch and shook his head. "Why don't we just go ask Fiddler for the information? He might be easier to deal with."

"Yeah, that's the problem. He died in prison the morning we visited Justyne. Apparently poisoned with botulinum toxin."

Sanchez raised an eyebrow. "We're dealing with that stuff again?" He rubbed his chin. "You sure this isn't some sort of elaborate setup by Justyne? There are a lot of dead bodies piling up and forcing you to ask her for help."

"I thought about that," Lara said. "She'd have to know I'd come to her for the information in that folder. It's possible Harry even told her we were after it. But he might not know for sure she has a copy. I don't think she'd tell him about it. After all, it's her insurance policy against him."

Sanchez rubbed the back of his neck. "I'm not sure I can pull this off. Prisoners can be transferred for any number of reasons, but generally not to group friends and family members together."

"They'll both be in prison under constant surveillance," Lara said. "What does it matter?"

"I'm not sure I want the two of them together again," Sanchez said, furrowing his brow. "What sort of scheme will they come up with next?"

Franklin poked his head into their huddle. "Are you all talking about Justyne and the prison transfer?"

Rob nodded, an overeager expression on his face.

Looking over his shoulder at the crowd of mourners, Finn grimaced in disgust at their poor taste.

I've become a murder case junkie just like them.

Franklin continued. "Cuz, I've got some news that you'll want to hear. Despite being a basket case, the medical examiner, Dr. Stevens, managed to test the candy bars from both Justyne and Linda's care packages and found them positive for botulinum toxin."

Lara gaped at Franklin, surprised Caroline had the gumption to return to work in her state.

Franklin gave her a sheepish smile. "When I told her what the test was for, she went back to work immediately after the funeral. Apparently, she's gunning for Harry Cogan for whacking her fiancé."

I saved Justyne's life.

"Botulinum toxin?" Sanchez asked, his mouth hanging open. After thinking about it for a moment, a smirk crept onto his face. "I guess that's some poetic justice for ya. I'll give the mayor a call and see if there's anything she can do." He surveyed the group and gave them a partial smile. "Great work, guys. Thank you all for coming. I have to go be with my family, but I'll see you around."

After saying their goodbyes, Finn pulled Lara by the arm, dragging her away from the group until they had some privacy. The rain had finally stopped, and she collapsed the umbrella and shook it off.

Glancing at Finn's clenched jaw, a knot formed in Lara's stomach. They still hadn't spoken properly since they returned from their trip to China. She feared the writing was on the wall for their relationship. Neither of them wanted to admit it. But the expression on his face said they were dealing with much more than normal relationship woes.

"What were you thinking?" Finn asked gruffly.

"What?" Lara asked.

"You bombarded Danny with your case stuff. At his mother's funeral." He raised his voice.

Lara shushed him. "He didn't seem to mind."

"That's because Danny is a decent guy," Finn said, his voice still loud. Lara glanced nervously at where Rob and Maggie stood. "He'd never call you out in front of your friends."

Lara crossed her arms. "Look, Sanchez and I have been working together a lot longer than you've known him. And we've been working together for weeks to get something on Harry. He's not the kind of guy to let that slide in the wake of his mother's death. If I hadn't told him today, he'd be furious with me later."

Why is Finn so mad at me?

Several minutes of awkward silence descended between them. Lara's thoughts were jumbled, and her emotions were reeling out of control. Amidst the muddle, a thought started to form.

Finn is not the right guy for me.

Since they had started dating, she had the impression Finn was trying to make her the solution to his problems. He didn't accept her for who she was. And it wasn't just that. Finn was constantly trying to solve her problems. His way. Interfering with her cases by cozying up to Sanchez. Nagging her about Rob at every turn. Pressuring her to go active duty. Forcing her to hang out with people she didn't like. Pushing his way onto her China trip. Changing her mission plan.

I need to break up with him.

He was suffocating her, and in return she was shutting him out. She hadn't shared her gut instincts about Mr. Langston being involved, the discoveries about the clones, or their relationship to Molly's kidnapper. She'd kept it all to herself because she didn't trust his reaction. She feared he would take everything into his hands and not give her the chance to have any input. And then, there were her fears about Kaitlyn and whether something might be going on between her and Finn. She didn't think she could endure another betrayal of trust.

Please be the good guy I thought you were, Finn.

"Why don't we talk about what's really bothering you," Lara said, breaking the deafening silence between them.

Finn gave her a pained smile. "I'm sorry I've been so distant. I didn't mean to shut you out... the truth is that I have something I need to tell you. And you're not going to like it."

I knew it.

Lara's heart sank. She felt her mouth go as dry as sandpaper. *Is he going to tell me he's cheated on me with Kaitlyn?*

She rocked slightly, preparing for the devastating punch in the gut, bracing for a ton of bricks to fall on her head. "What is it?"

Finn opened his mouth to respond but hesitated for a moment.

"Just tell me," Lara said, her heart now pounding.

"Well, I've been called up to go on an extended tour overseas," Finn said, avoiding her gaze.

Huh?

Lara's mouth fell open. It was not at all what she was expecting. "What? But I thought—"

"I thought I'd finish out the position at the Pentagon, too. But they need me to lead a special forces team in Yemen to support Task Force Jasmine. I have specialized knowledge that will support the mission. And now that I've signed up for active duty, I don't have much choice. Kaitlyn has been called up as well, and her husband is not happy. That's why I've been talking to her a lot lately... helping her deal with her situation and trying to figure out how to tell you."

Lara nodded numbly and said nothing for a few moments. *What am I supposed to say?*

Finn's eyes dimmed. "Of course, I didn't expect we would have to be apart for the full nine months. I was hoping to finagle a way for you to join me on the task force, but then we learned about your illness."

How do I break up with him now?

His chin dipped down. "I don't like leaving you when you're sick."

Lara stood straighter. "Sick?" She made a face. "I may not be able to go into combat, but I'm definitely not sick."

"You know what I mean," Finn said, grimacing.

Lara groaned. "In case you haven't noticed, I've managed things just fine despite my condition." She paused for a moment, searching for the right words. "Why do you keep trying to shove a round peg through a square hole and then get mad at me because it won't fit?" Lara asked.

"Huh? I don't understand."

"You're always trying to change me or steer me in a particular direction." Lara took a deep breath.

"What are you trying to say?" Finn asked, his eyes widening.

Lara took another deep breath. "Finn, we've been friends for a long time. Then by chance, you and I both became single at the same time. After failed relationships on both sides, it seemed like a good idea to see where things might go."

Finn thought for a few moments. "But you don't think things are working out between us."

"Not romantically, no," Lara said, looking at him directly in his eyes. "You're one of my best friends on the planet, and I would do anything for you. I'd follow you in battle without a second thought. And you're probably the hottest guy I know. But I want to stop having to hide things from you to keep you from getting upset at me."

He closed his eyes, and his face fell. Moisture collected around his eyelids. He pressed them tighter, and a single tear rolled down his cheek.

She took his hands in hers.

He opened his eyes, obviously trying to hold back tears. "I think you're right. I've been thinking the same thing, but didn't know how to tell you. We're just not a good fit."

"That doesn't mean we can't be the best of friends," Lara said.

He gave her a crooked smile, a hint of relief on his face. "I'll always have your six, Queen Bee."

FORTY-THREE

Office of the Inspector General

November 7, 2028

LARA FOLLOWED Rob tentatively down the long corridor, her high-heeled shoes clacking on the marble tiled floor of the Department of Justice building. Even while recovering from his bullet wound, Rob's long legs still outpaced hers. A fresh lemon scent filled her nose as she strode toward the conference room. Around a corner, she noticed a lady cleaning the floor with a pail and a mop. Suddenly aware of the slippery floor beneath her feet, she slowed her pace, putting further distance between herself and Rob.

Passing by several tall solid oak doors with ornamental plaques, her hands became sweaty. She studied the room number on the next plaque and realized they were almost at the room where Rob would learn about his fate. A jolt of anxiety rippled through her stomach as she contemplated the range of potential outcomes of the meeting.

In her experience, the justice system was not always fair. Although it was built on the rule of law and supposed to operate based on the principle of objectivity, life was simply too complex to fit into neat boxes of the law as conceived of by a bunch of lawyers. When it came to powerful people, the legal system demonstrated plenty of gray area. But for those poor souls without much power, however, the system often proved to be black and white.

Rob doesn't have any power to speak of. Will he get his vindication? Or will the system turn its back on him like it's always done for me?

A few days after Sanchez secured the transfer of Linda Maxwell to the Federal Correctional Institution in Hazelton, Justyne delivered the file of evidence on Harry Cogan to the FBI Director as she had promised.

Less than twenty-four hours later, Rob received an urgent call from a lawyer with the Department of Justice, stating that the Office of the Inspector General wished to discuss the new information with Rob during an informal hearing the following morning. The government lawyer suggested that Rob may want to bring legal counsel, but that it wasn't necessary.

Lara strongly advised Rob to give his lawyer a call, but he refused, saying he didn't have the money to cover the expensive billing hours. She offered to pay for it, but he wouldn't hear anything of it.

Ahead of her, Rob had come to a standstill in front of a closed oak panel door. Lara picked up her pace and joined him at the door. "Are you sure I should be here for this?" she asked, fidgeting with her navy jacket and skirt.

Rob's face was tense, and his hands balled into fists. Even with the dark look on his cleanshaven face, he was more handsome than usual with suit jacket, pants, and a tie. Lara was quite relieved that Rob had abandoned the untidy appearance he'd assumed since losing his job at the FBI.

"I don't see why not. They said I could bring legal counsel," Rob said, glancing down at her with watery, bloodshot eyes. "Plus, I don't really care. What more can they do to me?"

His breath reeked of whiskey.

Great, he's been drinking.

"Here goes nothing," Rob said, placing his hand on the door knob.

The door opened into a large paneled room with high ceilings and tall windows. To Lara, it looked a bit like a courtroom, only a bit less friendly. As if that were possible. At the front of the room stood a long wooden panel table slightly elevated from the rest of the room. There was an aisle down the center of the space with two tables at the front, presumably for opposing sides. Off to the side, a middle-aged woman waited patiently at a stenotype machine. Four stern faces stared down at them from the panel table, three men and one woman.

I thought this was an informal hearing.

The man in the middle cleared his throat. "Robert Martin, I presume."

"Yes, sir," Rob said, taking his place at one of the tables in the front.

Lara slid behind him to stand next to him, avoiding direct eye contact with the people at the front of the room.

"My name is Special Agent Owen Jacobs. I was the lead investigator on the case against you as a special agent with the FBI. I assume the woman next to you is your legal counsel?" he asked.

"No, sir. This is Lara Kingsley. She's my friend… I mean, my boss. Well actually, she's both." He smiled at her, a hint of a slur in his voice.

Lara wanted to give herself a face palm but remained motionless. *Hopefully they don't notice his condition.*

"Special Agent Martin, we do not permit guests in this courtroom. If Ms. Kingsley is not serving as your legal counsel, then she must leave the room immediately. We do not discuss sensitive matters of the Office of the Inspector General in front of private citizens."

Lara turned to leave the room, but Rob grabbed her hand, stopping her.

His posture stiffened and his brow furrowed. "Then with all due respect, I decline to have this meeting. I have no interest in hearing what you have to say," Rob said, enunciating every word. He squeezed Lara's hand. "If you want to discuss the new information with me, then she stays. If she goes, I go. It's your choice."

The silence in the room was deafening.

Agent Jacobs grunted. "Fine. She stays. But if any of this information leaks to the press, I will hold you personally responsible."

Rob nodded and gave Lara a stern look.

Agent Jacobs put on a pair of silver-rimmed glasses and shuffled through a stack of papers. "As you know, six months ago, the Department of Justice Office of the Inspector General initiated an investigation upon receipt of information from the FBI alleging investigative misconduct for an unauthorized surveillance operation, criminal misconduct for buying black market encryption technology, and ethical misconduct for bribing D.C. officials."

Rob appeared to wince at the reminder of the charges that had been brought against him. Lara couldn't imagine how humiliating this must be, to relive his firing all over again.

Agent Jacobs flipped through some more papers and then continued: "You may recall that the Office of the Inspector General found you in violation of FBI policy and guilty of criminal behavior in the case of your dealings with the black market and bribery. Consequently, we recommended that the FBI move for your immediate dismissal and pursue criminal charges against you. The Office of the Inspector General completed its investigation and provided its report to the FBI for appropriate action."

Criminal charges?

Lara's jaw dropped, her face losing a shade of color. *Rob never told me about that.* She glanced over at him, but he refused to look at her. He just stared straight ahead at the panel of agents, stone-faced and without moving a muscle.

Agent Jacobs continued: "For some inexplicable reason, the FBI chose not to proceed with the criminal charges recommendation, even though the panel presented a preponderance of circumstantial evidence. I was so perplexed by it that I made a direct inquiry. That's when I learned the FBI Director himself had disagreed with our assessment and declined to pursue charges in the absence of direct evidence of your culpability." He paused for a moment. "Of course, that brings us to the new information that has come to light about the activities of FBI Supervisory Special Agent Harry Cogan."

Lara wrinkled her nose. *The FBI Director disagreed with the finding? Did he suspect something?*

Rob stood up a bit straighter at the mention of Harry's name. Lara leaned forward slightly as if to hear better.

Agent Jacobs looked directly at Rob, saying, "After reviewing the evidence gathered against Harry Cogan, the panel finds you innocent of all allegations of criminal and ethical misconduct. In light of this new evidence, the FBI has decided to rescind your dismissal. You may resume your position as Special Agent, pick up your badge and gun, and report for duty next week."

He got his job back!

Lara's stomach did a flip-flop and she suppressed a smile. Rob exhaled sharply, the corners of his mouth turning upward.

"However," Agent Jacobs continued, "the panel maintains that you are still guilty of investigative misconduct for the illegal surveillance operation. Even though your supervisor authorized the operation, under FBI policy it was your duty to report the violation to FBI leadership. For this reason, the Office of the Inspector General upholds your previous suspension without pay." He paused to peer over the rims of his glasses, a glint in his eye. "Special Agent Martin, do you have any questions about any of this?

"No, sir," Rob said, apparently trying hard to keep his face from breaking out into a huge grin.

"Good. Then you may go now," Agent Jacobs said, closing the file in front of him.

Rob grabbed Lara's hand again, pulling her out of the room with him as quickly as possible. As soon as the door closed behind them, he gave her a bear hug, lifting her off of her feet. When he pulled away, Lara saw tears in his eyes. He reached out and touched her cheek, sending a tingle down her spine.

"I don't know how I would have made it through all of this without you," Rob said, his eyes gleaming. "You're the best friend I've ever had, you know…"

At a loss for words, Lara felt warmth well within her chest. Tears filled her eyes. Rob pulled her closer into another tight embrace. Lara leaned into him, resting the side of her face against his chest.

Vindication at last.

FORTY-FOUR

Mensa

November 9, 2028

LARA STRAIGHTENED the edges of her stretchy black dress and scanned the swanky cocktail reception for Vik, Rob, and Sanchez. Her shoulders sagged at the lack of familiar faces. The luxurious furnishings at the Ritz-Carlton in Georgetown and the who's who of the District's high society made her skin itch. Across the room, Lara spotted Mayor Wanda Peters conversing animatedly with the Speaker of the House. Hoping not to be recognized, Lara ducked out of sight and found refuge at an empty high-top table.

Leaning against the table, her thoughts drifted to the successful conclusion of Rob's case. The evidence in the folder was sufficient to put Harry away for life. If they could find him. So far, authorities hadn't picked up a trace.

In the end, Mr. Langston had come through for her, giving her just the help she needed to set up Harry and get Rob's job back. She had tried her best to get over the fact that the billionaire had nearly gotten her killed in China. And committed several crimes in the process. She was having a hard time swallowing the steep price of justice for Rob.

Another powerful man gets his way.

She hadn't attended any Mensa events since Sully died and felt like a fish out of water. Even as members of the elite high-IQ group, Maggie and Lara weren't usually allowed to invite non-members to exclusive events. Of course, the organizers made an exception for friends of their honored guests and Nobel Prize winners—Dr. Patrick Brown and Anne Blackburn, Maggie's famous parents.

Where are Rob and Vik already?

Maggie wanted the whole gang to meet her parents but had been on pins and needles all day. She'd called Lara at least three times with detailed instructions. She'd asked Lara to make sure they all knew what to do. And more importantly what not to do. The hoopla was mostly about introducing Sanchez to her parents as her boyfriend. Maggie had invited Lara and the others mostly as a buffer.

I'm supposed to make sure Vik, Rob, and Sanchez don't blow it all on the same night? I might as well play the lottery.

Spotting a waiter with a tray of beverages, Lara walked over and helped herself to a glass of sparkling water with lime. Though she stared longingly at the tall glass of beer on the tray, Maggie had forbidden everyone from drinking anything until after first impressions were made. It was probably a good idea after the mishap with Vik on the plane. And Rob and Sanchez were not slackers in the drinking department.

But what if I need one tiny, little drink to make a good first impression?

Lara wiped her sweaty palms on her dress and bit her lip.

Maggie's nerves are contagious.

"Oh, there you are. I've been looking everywhere for you."

Her heart jumping through her throat, Lara whirled around to see Maggie decked out in a gorgeous cobalt lace dress that made her auburn hair, freckled face, and light blue eyes pop even more than usual. Despite her undeniable radiance, she had a rather stern expression.

"Sorry, I just got here."

"Sanchez is running late. I told him to be here early." Maggie pouted, crossing her arms. The detective had broken one of her rules. One of like a hundred.

Uh oh.

"Have you seen Rob or Vik yet?" Maggie asked, giving her a disapproving glance.

Lara pressed her lips together and shook her head. It had been her job to get everyone to the reception on time. But there were some things beyond her control. "Traffic was terrible and parking next to impossible," she said, shrugging her shoulders. "I took a GoGo cab, but I think Rob is driving. He had to pick up Vik along the way. And you know I have no influence whatsoever on that detective boyfriend of yours. I'm sure they'll be here soon."

Maggie rubbed her forehead and tried to relax her stance. "How you doing, luv?"

Lara gave her a strange look. "Why are you asking?"

"You broke up with Finn a few days ago."

Another failed relationship… surprise, surprise.

"Oh that… yeah, I'm fine. I think I've known where we were headed since Vik's wedding. We hit the fateful three-month mark when, in my case, relationships either go bust or survive only to go bust a bit later."

"Don't worry, hon. You'll find Mr. Right someday."

Lara grunted. *There is no such thing as Mr. Right.*

Her mind drifted to the long embrace she and Rob shared at the Department of Justice. She shook her head at the thought.

"How did your doctor's visit go yesterday?" Maggie asked.

"Actually, not as bad as I thought," Lara said. "They didn't stick any needles in me this time."

Maggie rolled her eyes and sighed. "That's not what I meant. What did the doctor say about your condition and treatment plan?"

Lara grimaced. "My blood counts are good, so I didn't need another transfusion. For now. The doctor wants to start with some gene therapy. I have an appointment in two days for my first injection to start fixing the mutation in my DNA. No more mutant cells for me."

"I do hope she explained the risks," Maggie said, frowning. "The therapy may not take the first time. Your target cells divide rapidly. If the new gene does not get into most of them, the treated cells will be outnumbered."

Lara took a deep, satisfied breath. "Yep, I could also have an immune response to the nanoparticles the doctor uses to deliver the therapy. While we wait to see if it works, the doctor plans to give me anti-aging therapy to increase my production of the telomerase enzyme. She told me it creates telomeric DNA repeats and pastes them onto the ends of my chromosomes. She said this will prevent further shortening of my telomeres and possibly even lengthen them. Who knows? Maybe I'll never age again." Lara grinned.

Maggie looked skeptical. "Huh. I didn't realize anti-aging therapeutics had already come so far with reversing cellular aging. Last year, I did some research, and scientists hadn't figured out how to get the telomerase enzyme to restore lost telomeric DNA repeats." She furrowed her brow. "Isn't this the stuff you said your father was working on before he died?"

"Yeah, it's weird. Even weirder… the anti-aging therapy was produced by none other than GenTech Industries, which bought my parents' company."

"Mr. Langston's company?" Maggie asked.

"It's kinda ironic, isn't it? He put my life at risk by luring me to China and now is indirectly responsible for saving it." Lara rubbed her chin. "Say, did you get a chance to sequence the DNA samples?"

Maggie nodded. "Oh yes, sorry. I forgot to tell you. No big surprises for your mum's sample. Your mother had the same gene mutation as you. And I was able to verify from the condition of her telomeres that the sample was taken at the time of her death. At least now I have an inkling of why I developed aplastic anemia," Lara said. "I sure wish I had the chance to grab my father's DNA as well. It would be like having a full health record again."

"Hon, I wasn't quite finished. I found something interesting in your sample."

Lara's eyes grew large. "What did you find?"

"Your DNA sample appears to be synthetic," Maggie said.

"Meaning…"

"Meaning it didn't come from you, but rather was synthesized in a lab from your genomic data," Maggie said.

Huh.

"Did you get a chance to examine the DNA profiles for the clones?" Lara asked, not wanting to dwell on the topic of her family. She hadn't told Maggie yet about her sister Mia.

"Oh yes… there are some significant changes to the genomes for each girl. As I suspected before, the Macrobians are running some sort of experiment to study epigenetics of different disorders. Sorry, I don't have anything more to report. I know you wanted to learn more about your parents."

Lara waved off the tinge of disappointment. "Thanks, Mags. It's better than nothing.

The sound of a man's throat clearing made them both turn around.

"I'm here," a gruff voice said from behind them. "Dr. Brown can stop freaking out now."

They turned to see a smiling Sanchez dressed in a black suit and red tie, more clean-shaven than normal, and looking quite dapper. In his hand, he held a half-empty glass of beer. He leaned in to kiss Maggie on the cheek, but she pulled away. Sanchez pretended not to notice.

He's in so much trouble.

"Uh, sorry I'm late. I had to… uh… shave again to make sure I'd meet certain expectations." He smirked at Lara.

Not helping.

Maggie narrowed her eyes at him, a flush appearing in her cheeks.

"What? I can't help it my beard grows in like fucking bamboo."

Maggie grimaced and stomped off.

"What did I say?" Sanchez flashed her an innocent look.

"Uh, you just swore. She told you none of that tonight."

"Did she tell you to watch your tongue, too?" Sanchez asked.

"Yep… but my potty mouth is not nearly as bad as yours."

"Damn straight," he smirked.

"Exactly."

Sanchez rubbed his chin. "By the way, I got some interesting news about Agent Carter's murder," he said.

"Are you working his case?" Lara asked.

"Nah, I haven't had time with my mother's funeral. But the lead detective has been sharing the details with me. Anyway, the DNA they found on Agent Carter's body…" He closed his mouth and studied her face for a moment, a twinkle in his brown eyes.

Lara glared at him. "You're killing me here."

Sanchez raised his eyebrows and grinned. "You like solving crimes after all, don't you? All that song and dance about not being able to handle the darkness of humanity was a complete load of crap."

Lara put her finger to her lips. "Shhh."

"Crap isn't a swear word," Sanchez said, his eyes twinkling.

"Yes, it is. Stop it. What if Maggie hears?"

Sanchez lifted his palms in the air. "So what? Then she'll just dump me again. I've always been on thin ice with her anyway. Who knows how long it will last this time?"

Why does he bother?

Lara exhaled with exasperation. "Are you going to tell me about Agent Carter or not?"

"Tell ya what we're gonna do… I'll tell you about Agent Carter when you agree to be on retainer for my new Future Crimes unit."

Lara grinned. "You got the promotion?"

"Hell yeah, I did. You can call me Captain Sanchez from now on."

"Sssst," Lara said.

He is on a roll tonight.

"Sorry. So?" He looked at her expectantly. "Are we gonna be partners or what?"

Lara didn't have to think about it for very long. Sanchez was right. Solving crimes was starting to grow on her. And she realized that not only did she have the stomach for it, she had quite the knack for it.

"Why the hell not?" Lara smiled mischievously but looked over her shoulder to make sure Maggie wasn't nearby. "But don't get any ideas about me calling you Captain, okay?"

Sanchez smiled. "Deal."

"Now you owe me the details," Lara said.

After she answered, relief crossed his face, followed by a look of satisfaction. "The DNA from Agent Carter's body doesn't belong to Harry."

What?

Lara's eyes widened. "Do you have a match in your database?"

"Nope. But our analyst said the DNA profile belongs to Harry's brother."

Harry has a brother?

"And I assume you have no idea who this brother is..." Lara said.

"Nada. Zilch. Zero. Never heard of him. You?"

"I had no idea Harry had a brother," Lara said. "Rob never mentioned one."

They stood in silence for a few moments. Lara contemplated the evidence on the case. *Harry's brother killed Agent Carter. Is his brother BlackDragon?* She shook her head at her own theory. *Why would they speak Chinese to each other?*

"How are Bucky and Ball doing, by the way?" she asked. On

their last case, he'd surprised her by adopting the Westlocks' two Boston Terriers after Olivia's arrest.

His brown eyes gleamed. "They're little rascals, but they're great. I can't imagine life without those two creating mayhem in my house."

"We should organize a playdate sometime," Lara said without thinking. Seconds later, a shockwave of embarrassment traveled through her body. *Did I just ask Sanchez to a social outing?* "Loki loves to play with other dogs, I mean," she added, feeling her face flush hot.

Sanchez wrinkled his forehead. "I'd say yes if I could be certain your dog wouldn't eat my pups for lunch."

He does have a point. At only seven months, Loki already weighed sixty pounds and was still growing fast. He was three times the weight of the Bostons.

"Loki is smart. He knows how to be gentle with smaller dogs."

"Yeah, I'd have to see it to believe it."

A strong hand touched the back of her shoulder, and Lara turned to see Rob and Vik standing behind her.

"You guys finally made it. Maggie is not happy with you all." Sanchez shrugged.

"We got held up by the motorcade," Vik exclaimed excitedly.

"Did you get to see the President?" Lara asked.

"We got to see his tinted windows," Vik said, grinning. "I'm going to go find something to drink."

"Whatever you do, stay away from the Champagne, okay?" Lara said, giving him a knowing look.

"Don't worry, I learned my lesson."

Lara smirked at the memory of Vik stumbling about the private jet and then complaining of his hangover during the break-and-enter op. It felt like a million years ago.

Maggie marched over to them, grabbed Sanchez by the arm, and dragged him over to a tight circle of people. Lara's eyes landed on an attractive couple in their sixties.

All eyes focused on a white-haired man with a thick white

beard and glasses at the center of the crowd. He wore a dark blue suit, a pinstriped shirt, and even a matching pocket square. Holding a glass of sparkling wine in one hand, he moved his other hand through the air and spoke as if he were giving a speech in a large lecture hall. His thick Australian accent tickled Lara's ears.

He told a story about his youth, regaling his adventures of pipetting in the lab after hours to impress a young woman. He gazed lovingly at the distinguished woman standing next to him.

They must be Maggie's parents.

Maggie's mother wore a green dress that complimented her freckled face and gray-streaked, auburn hair. She smiled at Maggie's father as he spoke, nodded occasionally, and offered snarky comments, at which the crowd laughed heartily.

Despite their glossy appearance, Lara sensed some underlying tension between them. Maggie's father's jaw appeared tense, and her mother's hands were clenched.

Lara cringed as Maggie pushed Sanchez forward and introduced him. Their reproachful faces said everything Lara needed to know about them. The world-renowned scientists were snobs like the Martin family and looked down upon Sanchez for his job and education. Hopefully not also for his race. Her stomach knotted up.

What will they think of me?

Rob motioned with his head and gave her a look. "Uh oh. I think we're next."

Lara grimaced. "You never told me how things went at the FBI when you picked up your gun and badge," Lara said.

I still can't believe Justyne came through for us.

Rob stared at the floor. "Yeah, about that..."

"What did your parents say when you told them you got your job back?" Lara asked.

Rob didn't reply.

"Don't tell me the FBI changed its mind and doesn't want you back after all this," Lara said.

"Oh, they want me back all right. Harry's former boss sat me down and offered me my old job back. With the promise of a promotion. They want my help tracking down Harry."

"Well, then what's wrong?"

"I declined the offer," Rob said, avoiding eye contact.

"You what?" Lara gaped at him, not believing her own ears. "After all the work we did to find evidence against Harry and vindicate you? But why?"

Rob's face turned red. "I know… I feel terrible about it. I wouldn't have put you all through that stuff… but I didn't know I'd decline the job until I was sitting there, listening to the Supervisory Special Agent say I could come back. And for some reason, I just didn't want to go back."

"But I thought working at the FBI was your dream," Lara said.

"It was. I'm not sure it is anymore. They say the door's open anytime I want to come back. I think they feel pretty guilty about the hell they put me through."

Lara blinked her eyes several times. "So, what now?"

Rob turned to her, his eyes pleading with her. "Would it be okay if I keep working for Kingsley Investigations?"

Lara took a step back. "You want to work for me? I don't under—"

"I really missed you and Vik while you were both in China. That's when I realized we're becoming a real team. And it's a team I want to be part of. At least for now." He looked down at her, his eyes moist. "Is that okay?"

Lara gulped, wondering about the real reason behind his decision. "Rob, of course that's okay. We're glad to have you on board."

Maggie cleared her throat behind her, and Lara turned around to come face to face with the famous parents.

"Mum and Dad, this is Lara Kingsley. She's the dear friend I've told you about. And this is her friend, Rob. Lara and Rob, meet Patrick and Anne."

Lara and Rob shook both of their hands.

"It's a pleasure to meet you," Lara said.

Patrick gave his wife a strange look. "Don't we know someone with the name Kingsley?" He put his finger to his mouth and stared at the ceiling, trying to recall the name.

"Dear, you're thinking about Ethan Kingsley," Anne said, "the geneticist we met at the biotechnology conference in Sydney. He made quite the impression. He was working on lengthening telomeres and looking for funding for his startup company. You remember that, don't you?"

Lara's eyes widened. "Ethan Kingsley is my father. When did you meet him?"

"I think it was at that genetics conference in Boston in 2003," Patrick said.

"No, we were in Sweden that year. It was definitely in 2004. The Green Biotechnology Conference in Sydney in March of that year. Remember, you were giving the paper on the prospects for gene editing tools and precision medicine."

He nodded.

The blood drained from Lara's face as she did the math. "No, that's not possible. It couldn't have been in 2004. My parents died in a car accident in July of 2003."

Patrick looked down at her. "My wife's right. It had to be 2004 when we met Ethan..." He stopped speaking and seemed distracted by something across the room. His body tense, he turned to Lara. "It was such a pleasure to meet you, but we have to go say hello to a few new arrivals." With that, Patrick and Anne rushed across the room to mingle with other guests.

They met my father in Sydney in 2004?

Vik returned to their circle with a half-empty glass of sparkling wine in his hand and nudged Lara, who was in a daze. "What did I miss?"

FORTY-FIVE

The Painting

November 10, 2028

LARA SAT on the metal chair surrounded by open boxes and stacks of books in her storage unit, the door hanging wide open. Parked in the alley, her shiny blue Harley Davidson Street 500 gleamed in the sun with its new sidecar.

Shivering, she breathed the crisp fall air. The morning sunlight trickled into the space, warming her ever so slightly. She snuggled into her jacket and rubbed her hands together. Despite the chill, she preferred to keep the door open for situational awareness.

After all, the storage unit was where she was hit over the head by Justyne and kidnapped by Fiddler, something she would never forget. Since then, she couldn't relax when she visited it and rarely came alone.

Hence, I brought a guard dog.

Loki lay at her feet, playing with his new rope toy, and worked hard to tear it apart string by string. A waft of something foul tickled her nose, and she waved her hands around frantically.

Ew, Loki!

She glared down at the pup and wondered how one living creature could produce such a powerful stench. For the past hour, soft toots erupted from the pup in regular intervals. The noise was inevitably followed by the release of a thick cloud of hydrogen sulfide. Sometimes, the farts were so strong it nearly knocked her off her chair.

When she'd decided to get a Doberman, she hadn't realized the breed was so gassy. She was too focused on the breed's intelligence and loyalty to notice the downsides. Since then, she'd looked it up online and read that the breed was well known for being particularly stinky.

Another reason to keep the door open.

Sensing her gaze, Loki took a break from his toy and looked up at her, yawning contently. Then he laid his head down and closed his eyes.

Lara turned her attention back to the task at hand. She'd been searching the unit from top to bottom for any new information about her parents. The startling revelation from Maggie's parents had her on edge since the previous night.

They can't be right. My father was dead in 2004.

Most likely, they'd just remembered it wrong and refused to admit it. The conference had taken place twenty-four years ago. Lara was surprised they could even remember meeting her father that long ago. It wasn't like they'd had ongoing dealings with him. Maybe they'd met someone else and gotten her father mixed up with another scientist.

So far, in her search of her parents' stuff, she'd come up completely dry. She didn't expect to find anything big, but she'd not yet gone through all of their things with a fine-toothed comb.

Leaning against the wall in the corner, her father's painting caught her attention. The back of the paper packaging was ripped and crinkled from getting peed on by Loki.

Huh, that got moved.

Frowning, Lara got up and walked over to inspect it. Then

she remembered how Rob had cleaned up after Loki's mess. *He must have moved it over here.*

Reaching down, she pulled the painting out of the remaining packaging and took a closer look. As she studied the scene of people bathing in the fountain, a sinister feeling stirred inside her.

Closing her eyes, Lara recalled seeing the massive reproduction at the Macrobian Institute. She knew now that her father had been obsessed with telomeres and finding a way to extend human life, to achieve immortality through science.

The Macrobians had the same painting. Why did my father leave this to me?

She examined the brush strokes and realized the quality of the reproduction was quite poor. It probably wasn't even worth a penny. Her shoulders sagging, she turned the painting over in her hands and inspected the dust cover on the back. In the bottom right corner, there was a small marking. She gave it a closer look. It was an infinity symbol with the letter *h* and a plus sign.

I've seen that marking before. Lara rubbed her chin, trying to recall where she'd see it. *It was on the fountain at the Macrobian Institute.*

Lara took a picture of the marking and spoke into her smartphone.

"Watson," she said.

Her screen sprang to life.

"Yes, Ms. Kingsley."

"Please look at my most recent picture and identify the symbol."

"Of course. Right away." A few moments later, Watson said, "The symbol in your picture is a well-known symbol for transhumanists. It has been used by people espousing transhumanist beliefs since about 2002."

"Thank you, Watson," Lara said.

"My pleasure."

Lara thought for a moment. Lance mentioned her father was

a founding member of the group, something that had bothered her since she learned about it. Especially since her father's transhumanist lover tried to dump her into a tank of blue goo. She had so many unanswered questions about her parents, their health, and why they joined the Macrobians, and it was driving her crazy.

He left this painting for me for a reason. Does X mark the spot?

Without further hesitation, Lara tore open the dust cover at the bottom right corner. She stuck her hand into the opening, expecting to feel the back of the canvas. Instead she touched an envelope pinned to the canvas. She groped around, pulling out the tiny pins one by one, and pulled the envelope through the gap. Turning it over in her hands, she saw her name written by hand.

Her hands trembling, she opened the envelope and found a letter. It was dated a few days before her parents died, and it was signed by her father. Her head throbbing, she started at the beginning.

June 16, 2003

MY DEAREST LARA,

If you are reading this letter, then something terrible has happened. I am sorry we left you alone in this world. It tears me up inside knowing that the choices your mother and I made have caused you such pain. That was never our intention.

Your mother and I joined a group called the Macrobians. We agreed with their determination and commitment to use science to better humanity and eagerly joined their cause. It wasn't long, however, before we discovered that many Macrobians were willing to turn a blind eye to ethics in their experimentation on humans in the name of science. We tried to express our concerns, but our questions were met with aggression. At some point, we realized we were in danger of being eliminated. No one leaves the Macrobians through life, only death. Your mother and I are very sorry to have put you in danger. We are doing whatever we can to neutralize the threat. If you're reading this, we have failed. Whatever you do, stay far away from the Macrobians.

You may be wondering why I am writing you this letter on my own and not with your mother. That is because I have to make a difficult confession to you alone, my daughter. All I can say is that marriage is hard, and your father is human. I met a young woman during my time at Stanford. Her name was Yingyue. You met her a few times as a child. She understood me in a way your mother did not. I made a terrible mistake and betrayed the love I had for your mother. Yingyue became pregnant and had a baby girl named Mei Xing. I called her Mia. She is your sister. It is my dearest hope that you will come to know her and love her as I do.

My darling daughter, I wish things could have been different. Unfortunately, you will learn that we cannot turn back the clock. There are some decisions that set things in motion that we cannot possibly understand. Until it is too late. My dear, you are the sweetest part of life I've ever known. I am so sorry if we have put you in danger. Please know that even in death, I am with you. Be strong, Lara.

Love,
Dad

TEARS WELLING IN HER EYES, Lara's hands shook as she folded up the letter and put it back in the envelope.

___

Loki's ears pricked up, and he lifted his head.

"What did you hear, buddy?" Lara asked, her ears strained and her eyes darting back and forth, looking for any shadow near the entrance of the unit. Her heart pounded hard in her chest, and she put her hand on her pistol.

Loki growled at the door and got onto his hind legs.

She smelled him first, the telltale smoke wrapping itself around the edge of the door in familiar rings. She wondered how long he had been standing there, lurking and listening. A few seconds later, Hickerson appeared in the doorway of the storage unit, wearing a trench coat and puffing on a cigarette.

How did he find me?

"What are you doing here?" she asked, fully aware she would not get a straight answer.

"I was in the neighborhood and thought—"

"Bullshit. Why don't you tell me the truth for once?"

"You called me about Mia. I tracked you by your smartphone."

Lara's eyes widened. Then she glared at the wearable smartphone on her wrist and sighed.

They should really call these things tracking devices.

"Thank you for your honesty," Lara said, giving him a fake smile.

"He looks like a sweetheart," Hickerson said, pointing to Loki.

"More like sweetfart. He's been farting all morning. Hopefully, you didn't think it was me stinking up this place."

"No, no, of course not." Hickerson laughed for a moment, then glanced at her motorcycle and gave her a strange look. "You actually drove over here in that thing?"

"Yep," Lara said, unwilling to make friendly with him.

"He didn't try to jump out?"

"Why are you here?" Lara asked again, not in the mood for small talk.

Hickerson's face became serious. "Mia is fine."

"She wasn't burned?"

"Yingyue doesn't suspect she's working for the CIA. She knows Mia let you escape but doesn't think she had anything to do with it. She just thinks Mia has a soft spot for you, being her new sister and all."

"Well, that's a relief."

"Yeah, for me as well. We invested a great deal of time and effort to have her reinserted into the Macrobian Institute. If she'd been burned for good, I would have had to start over from the beginning."

Lara narrowed her eyes.

Mia is just an asset to him. He's using her too.

Hickerson read her mind. "Don't get all thin-skinned on me now. You were more than pleased to assist me when it suited your own interests. Don't fool yourself, Lara. You're shrewd to the core. If someone can help you achieve your own ends, you use them just the same way I do."

"She's my sister," Lara said, a protective urge rising within her.

"She's a vital asset to the U.S. Government." Hickerson looked her directly in the face. "And to you."

Lara shrank back. "How so?"

"Between your mission to China to get Molly and Mia's undercover work at the Institute, we've been able to piece together a more detailed picture of the Macrobian network and their various ties. In the past week, Mia has discovered a few things that would be of great interest to you. If it were up to me, you'd stay comfortably in the dark. But Mia requested that I relay them for your safety." He flashed her a toothy grin. "I like to keep my assets happy whenever I can."

"What sort of things?"

"Well… you asked about BlackDragon. I think it's time you know who she is."

Now he's telling me?

"Yingyue uses BlackDragon as her pseudonym on the Dark Web. Recently, she's had Mia run some transactions for her using the same name. That's how we know for sure."

Suddenly, Lara remembered the photo from the file of evidence against Harry, the one with Mr. Zhang and Hai Xu. Lara now knew the woman in the background was Yingyue and considered the implications.

Yingyue knew Mr. Zhang somehow. Or is she connected with the PLA?

"So, Harry Cogan was communicating with Yingyue over the Dark Web under that pseudonym," Lara said. "I thought she was a customer of his black market operation. Is Yingyue more than that? Is she his boss or something?"

Was Harry following me for Yingyue?

Hickerson shook his head. "No, you were right the first time. Yingyue is one of many international customers served by Harry's global illicit trading ring. He sold her the advanced technology you saw at the institute—the exoskeletons and the invisibility cloak. Trading stolen technology is how they first got to know each other many years ago. At least that's what we think thus far."

Lara put her hand to her forehead. "That's how they first got to know each other? What are you saying?"

"It seems that their relationship has deepened. When you

turned up the heat on Harry's operation here and threatened to expose him at the FBI, he put an escape plan into action…"

"And that involves Yingyue somehow?"

"As far as we can tell from the wire and Mia's information, Yingyue formed some sort of partnership with Harry. She's agreed to shelter him at her institute for the time being. In exchange, he appears to be working for her now. Mia and I are trying to figure out why Yingyue would help him in the first place, but we still don't have many ideas."

"Did you find out for sure if Yingyue is connected to the PLA?" Lara asked. "That might have something to do with it."

Hickerson shrugged. "We're still trying to get Mia to find hard evidence, but we do know a few things. Based on analysis of their Dark Web communications, Yingyue made a deal with Harry for gaining access to certain technologies including the exoskeletons and invisibility formula."

Which he delivered on…

"Was there something else?" Lara asked, her head swaying slightly.

"Mia uncovered Harry's real name," Hickerson said.

Harry is a fake name?

Lara stared at him, her eyes bulging.

"He's gone by Harry Cogan since he immigrated to the United States from Russia when he was thirty years old. His real name is Nikolai Kaganovitch."

"Did you know Harry has a brother?" Lara asked.

Hickerson's mouth fell open slightly, a rare show of his inner thoughts.

Lara shot him a triumphant smile. For once, she had more information than the spook. "The D.C. Police found DNA on Agent Carter's body. Initially, they thought it must belong to Harry. It was a match for Harry's brother."

Hickerson rubbed his chin. "That's very interesting."

"Did you find anything more on Harry?"

Hickerson nodded. "I asked the Russia team at the CIA to do some digging. He's the son of a former Soviet nuclear weapons scientist turned diplomat. Harry got a PhD in nuclear engineering before coming to the United States."

Harry has a PhD in nuclear engineering?

"But his English is perfect... how did the FBI miss all this?" Lara asked.

"Harry came to this country without any family members and developed an impressive cover to hide his true ancestry."

Lara sat still for several moments as she absorbed everything Hickerson had told her. Then a lightbulb went off in her head.

Is he the real Dr. K?

Want More From Lara and Her Friends?

Get Volume One of the Kingsley Files when you sign up for Lara's VIP Reader Club (www.natashabajema.com/kingsley-files-one). You'll get to go behind the scenes for exclusive clues to the series, release notifications, and regular updates via email. You'll also get the opportunity to join the Facebook Group where you'll provide input on character names, settings, storyline, and cool technologies.

Acknowledgments

Sometimes, it's a bit hard to believe that I've finished a third novel in the Lara Kingsley Series—especially since this year, I moved across the country from Washington D.C. to my new home in Rockport, Texas. I didn't expect the characters to grow on me so much, but when I'm not writing them, I miss having them in my life—so never fear, another Lara Kingsley novel is in the works for the future. I'm grateful to my devoted readers who feel the same way.

As I've done with previous books in this series, I often turned to my friends and family as well as the Lara Kingsley Facebook Group for their ideas on naming various things in the novel. Thank you to Darren Cogan, Becca Erin, Min Kim, Garon Whited, and many others for brainstorming ideas and becoming part of my novel and my story as an author.

This novel benefited from the insights and skills of amazing editors. I would like to thank Brianna Boes for finessing the manuscript with her brilliant line edits and polishes as well as catching some important plot issues. Thank you to Christie Hartman who helped catch any loose errors and typos.

Special thanks to my National Defense University colleague, Dr. Diane DiEuliis for reading my book and providing feedback.

I'm also extremely grateful to Dr. Sterling Sawaya, Founder and CEO of GeneInfoSec, for providing expert insights on technical issues. Any inaccuracy in the novel is my own and should not reflect on them in any way. Moreover, the views expressed in this novel are those of the author and do not reflect the official policy or position of the National Defense University, the Department of Defense, or the U.S. Government.

Many thanks to cover designer Karen at Magic Design Co. for perfectly capturing the mood and essence of Genomic Data and being such a joy to work with.

I am dedicating this book to my parents, John and Maria Bajema. They have always encouraged me to pursue my creativity through art and writing stories, but wisely counseled me in my youth against the life of a starving artist. Without my first career in national security, I wouldn't have found my muse or the financial freedom to invest in a writing career. Now that I've embarked on becoming a full-time creative entrepreneur, my continue to root for me, and I couldn't be more grateful. Of course, I never anticipated that my parents would actually like reading my fiction. And so, you have my mom to thank for even less swear words than before.

About the Author

NATASHA BAJEMA lives in Rockport, Texas with her two dogs, Malachi and Charlie, and works as an independent consultant on national security. She has been an expert on national security issues for over 20 years, specializing in weapons of mass destruction (WMD), nuclear proliferation, terrorism, and emerging technologies. For ten years, Natasha worked for the National Defense University where she taught an elective course to senior military officers on WMD and film and led a research project on the impact of emerging technologies on national security. Natasha holds a Ph.D. in international relations from the Fletcher School of Law and Diplomacy at Tufts University.

For more information:
www.natashabajema.com